May Agnes Fleming

Lost for a Woman

A novel

May Agnes Fleming

Lost for a Woman
A novel

ISBN/EAN: 9783337027384

Printed in Europe, USA, Canada, Australia, Japan

Cover: Foto ©Andreas Hilbeck / pixelio.de

More available books at **www.hansebooks.com**

LOST FOR A WOMAN.

A Novel.

BY

MAY AGNES FLEMING,

AUTHOR OF

SILENT AND TRUE," "A MAD MARRIAGE," "A TERRIBLE SECRET,"
"GUY EARLSCOURT'S WIFE," "A WONDERFUL WOMAN,"
" ONE NIGHT'S MYSTERY," ETC., ETC.

—— "That I might all forget the human race,
And, hating no one, love but only her !"
Byron—Childe Harold.

NEW YORK:
Copyright, 1880, by
G. W. Carleton & Co., Publishers,
LONDON: S. LOW & CO.
MDCCCLXXXIV.

Stereotyped by
SAMUEL STODDER,
ELECTROTYPER & STEREOTYPER,
90 ANN STREET, N. Y.

TROW
PRINTING AND BOOK-BINDING CO.
N. Y.

CONTENTS.

PART I.

PART II.

[v]

PART III.

PART IV.

LOST FOR A WOMAN.

PART I.

"In mine eyes she is the sweetest lady that I ever looked on."
Much Ado About Nothing.

CHAPTER I.

WHICH PRESENTS JEMIMA ANN.

T is a dreary prospect. All day long it has rained ; as the short afternoon wears apace, it pours. Mrs. Hopkins' niece, laying down the novel, over which for the past hour she has been absorbed, regards the weather through the grated kitchen window with a gentle melancholy upon her, begotten of its gloom, and returns despondently to her novel. A soft step stealing down the back stairs, a soft, deprecating voice, breaks in upon the narrative and her solitude.

"If you please, Miss Jim ?"

"Oh !" says Jemima Ann, "is that you ? Come in, Mr. Doolittle. Dreadful nasty evening, now, ain't it ?"

"Well, it *ain't* nice," says Mr. Doolittle, apologetically ; "and I guess I won't muss your clean floor by coming in. What I've looked in for, Miss Jim, is a pair o' rubbers. Mrs. Hopkins she don't like gum shoes left

[7]

clutterin' about the bedrooms, so she says, and totes 'em all down here. Number nines, Miss Jemima, and with a hole in one of the heels. Thanky; them's them."

Jemima Ann produces the rubbers, and Mr. Doolittle meekly departs. He is a soft-spoken little man, with weak eyes, a bald spot, a henpecked and depressed manner. Jemima Ann wishes all the boarders were like him—thankful for small mercies, and never finding fault with the victuals, or swearing at her down the back stairs. The boarders do swear at Jemima Ann sometimes, curses both loud and deep, and hurl boots, and brushes, and maledictions down the area, when, absorbed in the æsthetic woes of her heroine, she forgets the gross material needs of these sinful young men. But long habit, seven years of boarding-house drudgery, has inured her to all this; and imprecations and bootjacks alike rain unheeded on her frowzy head. A sensible head, too, in the main, and with an ugly, good-humored face looking out of it, and at boarding-house life in general, through two round, bright black eyes.

It is a rainy evening in early October, the dismal twilight of a wet and dismal day. Mrs. Hopkins' basement kitchen is lit by four greenish panes of mud-bespattered glass, six inches higher than the pavement. Through these six inches of green crystal Jemima Ann sees all she ever sees of the outdoor world on its winding way. Hundreds of ankles, male and female, thick and thin, clean and dirty, according to the state of the atmosphere, pass these four squares of dull light every day, and all day long, far into the night, too; for Mrs. Hopkins' boarding-house is in a popular street, handy for the workingmen—artisans in iron, mostly, who frequent it. A great foundry is near, where stoves and ranges, and heaters and grates are manufactured, with noise and grime, and clanking of great hammers, and clouds of blackest coal-smoke, until that way madness lies; and the "hands" emerge in scores, black as demons, and go home to wash and dine at Mrs. Hopkins' boarding-house. Limitless is the demand for water, great and mighty the cry for yellow soap, of these horny-handed Vulcans, who, like lobsters, go into these steaming caldrons very black and come out very red. For seven long years Jemima Ann has waited on these children of the forge, and been anathematized in the strongest vernacular for slowness and "muddle-headedness," and got dinners and teas, and washed dishes, and swept bedrooms, and made beds, and went errands, and read novels and story-papers, and watched the never-ending stream of boot-heels passing and repassing the dingy panes of glass, and waxed, from a country lass of seventeen, to a strong-armed, sallow-faced young woman of twenty-four ; and all the romance of life that ever came near her, to brighten the dull drab of every day, was contained in the "awful" nice stories devoured in every spare moment, left her in the busy caravansera of her aunt Samantha Hopkins.

The rain patters against the glass; the twilight deepens. Jemima Ann has to strain her eyes to catch the last entrancing sentences of chapter five. The ankles that scurry past are muddy, the skirts bedraggled. Jemima Ann wishes they were fewer; they come between her and the last bleak rays of light. A melancholy autumnal wind rises, and blows some whirling dead leaves down the area ; the gutter just outside swells to a miniature torrent, and has quite the romantic roar of a small river. Jemima Ann pensively thinks. Even she can read no more. She lays down her tattered book with a deep sigh of regret, props her elbows on her knees, sinks her chin in her palms, and gazes sentimentally upward at the greenish casement. It is nearly time to go and light the gas in the front hall and dining-room, she opines. The men will be here directly, all shouting out together for warm water and more soap, and another towel, and— be dashed to you ! Then there is cold corned-beef to be

1*

cut up for supper, and bread cut in great slices from four huge home-made loaves, and the stewed apples to be got out, and the tea put to draw, and after that to be poured, and after *that*, and far into the weary watches of the night, dishes to be washed, and the table reset for to-morrow's breakfast.

Jemima Ann sighs again, and this time it is not for the patrician sorrows of the lovely Duchess Isoline. In a general way she has not much time for melancholy musings. The life of Mrs. Hopkins' "help" does not hold many gaps for reflection. It is a breathless, dizzying round and rush—one long "demnition grind," from week's end to week's end. And perhaps it is best it should be so, else even Jemima Ann, patient, plodding, strong of arm, stout of heart, sweet of temper, willing of mind, might go slowly melancholy mad.

"It would be awful pleasant to be like they are in stories," muses Jemima Ann, still blinking upward at the gray squares of blurred light, "and have azure eyes, and golden tresses, and wear white Swiss and sweeping silks all the year round, and have lovely guardsmen and dukes and things, to gaze at a person passionately, and lift a person's hand to their lips." Jemima Ann lifts one of her own, a red right hand, at this point, and surveys it. It is not particularly clean ; it has no nails to speak of ; it is nearly as large, and altogether as hard, as that of any of the foundry " hands ;" and she sighs a third sigh, deepest and dolefullest of all. There are hands and hands ; the impossibility of any mortal man, in his senses, ever wanting to lift *this* hand to his lips, comes well home to her in this hour. The favorite "gulf" of her novels lies between her and such airy, fairy beings as the Duchess Isoline. And yet Jemima Ann fairly revels in the British aristocracy. Nothing less than a baronet can content her. No heroine under the rank of " my lady " can greatly interest her. Pictures of ordinary every-day life, of ordinary every-day

people, pall upon the highly-seasoned palate of Jemima
Ann. Her own life is so utterly unlovely, so grinding
in its sordid ugliness, that she will have no reflection of
it in her favorite literature. Dickens fails to interest
her. His men and women talk and act, and are but as
shadowy reflections of those she meets every day.

"Nothing Dickens ever wrote," says Jemima Ann,
with conviction, "is to be named in the same day with
the 'Doom of the Duchess,' or 'The Belle of Belgravia.'"

The darkness deepens, the rain falls, the wind of the
autumn night sighs outside. Through the gusty gloaming a shrieking whistle suddenly pierces, and Jemima
Ann springs to her feet, as if shot. The six o'clock
whistle! The moments for dreaming are at an end.
Life, at its ugliest, grimiest, most practical, is here. The
men will be home for supper in five minutes.

"Jim!" cries a breathless voice. It is a woman's
voice, sharp, thin, eager. There is a swish of woman's
petticoats down the dark stairs, a bounce into the kitchen,
then an angry exclamation : "You Jim ! are you here ?
What are you foolin' at *now*, and it blind man's holiday
all over the house !"

"I'm a lightin' up, Aunt Samanthy," responds Jemima
Ann, placidly; "you know you don't like the gas a
flarin' a minute before it's wanted, and the whistle's only
just blowed."

"I'm blowed myself," says Aunt Samantha—not meaning to be funny, merely stating a fact ; "and clean out o'
breath. I've run every step of the way here from——
Jemimy Ann, what d'ye think ? They want me to take
in a woman !"

"Do they ?" says Jemima Ann. The gas is lit by this
time, and flares out over the untidy kitchen and the two
women. "I wouldn't, if I was you. Who is she ?"

"Rogers has her," says Mrs. Hopkins, vaguely.
"She's with the rest at the hotel ; but there ain't no room
for her there. Rogers is full himself, and he wants me

to take her; says she ain't no bother; says she ain't that
sort; says she's a lady. That's what he says; but don't
tell me! Drat sich ladies! She's one of that circus lot."

"Oh!" says Jemima Ann, in a tone of suppressed rapture; "a circus actress! . Lor! you don't say so!"

"And she's got a little girl," goes on Mrs. Hopkins,
in an irritated tone, as if that were the last straw, and
rubbing her nose in a vexed way, "she's a *Miss* Mimi—
Something, and she's got a little girl! Think o' that!
Rogers says it's all right. Rogers says all them sort does
that way; marries and raises families, you know, and
stays miss right along. This one's a widow, he says.
And he wants me to take her in; says he knows I've got
a spare room, and would like to oblige a charming young
lady and a dear little child—not to speak of an old neighbor like him. Yar! I'll see 'em all furder first—the
whole bilin!"

"Oh, Aunt Samanthy, do let her come!" says Jemima
Ann. "I should love to know a circus lady. Next to a
duchess, an actress or a nun is the most romantic people
in any story."

"No, I sha'n't," Mrs. Hopkins snappishly responds;
"not if I know myself and my own sex when I see 'em.
When first I started in the boardin' line I took in females
—*ladies* they called themselves, too, and table boarded
'em—dressmakers, workin' girls, and that—and I know
all about it. One woman was more trouble in a day
than six foundry hands in a week. Always a hot iron
wanted please, and a little bilin' water to rinse out a
handkerchief or a pair of stockings in a basin, and cups
o' tea promiscuous, and finding fault continual with the
strength of the butter and the weakness of the coffee.
So I soon sent that lot packing, and made up my mind
to sink or swim with the foundry hands. Give a man a
latch-key, lots of soap and water, put his boots and hair
oil where he can lay his hand on 'em, let him have beef-
steak and onions, and plenty of 'em, for his breakfast,

and though he may grumble about the victuals, he don't go mussin' with his linen at all sorts of improper hours. I won't have the circus woman, and that's all about it.

"Did you tell Mr. Rogers so?" asks Jemima Ann, rather disappointed.

"Mr. Rogers is a yidyit; he wouldn't take no for an answer. 'I'll step round this evenin',' said the grinning old fool, 'and bring the lady with me, Mrs. Hopkins. You won't be able do say no to *her*—no one ever is. I know the supper and six-and-twenty foundry hands is lyin' heavy on your mind at the present moment,' says he, 'and your nat'rel sweetness of disposition,' he says, 'is a trifle cruddled by 'em.' Yas! I never see sich an old rattle-tongue. But he'll see! Let him fetch his— Lord's sake, Jemima Ann! there's them men, and not so much as a drop of tea put to dror! Run like mad, and light the gas!"

Jemima Ann literally obeys. She flies up stairs like a whirlwind, sets a match to the hall gas, and has it blazing as the front door is flung wide, and the foundry hands, black, hungry, noisy, muddy, troop in, and up stairs, or out back to the general "wash'us."

There is no more time for talking, for thinking, hardly for breathing—such a multiplicity of things are to be done, and all, it seems, to be done at once. Hot water, soap, towels—the tocsin of war rings loudly up stairs and down, and in their various chambers. Gas is lit, the long table set, knives rubbed, bread cut, meat sliced, chairs placed—all is confusion, Babel condensed.

Jemima Ann waits. Coarse jokes rain about her, a dozen voices call on her at once, demanding a dozen diferent things, and she is—somethinged—at intervals, for lacking as many hands as Briareus. But mostly it all falls harmless and half-unheard. She is regretting vaguely that lost circus lady. Since she may never be a duchess, nor even, in all human probability, a "my lady," it strikes Mrs. Hopkins' niece the next best thing

would be to turn circus rider, or become a gipsy and tell
fortunes.   To wear a scarlet cloak, to wander about the
" merry green wood," to tell fortunes at fairs, to sleep
under a cart or a hedge, in "the hotel of the beautiful
stars"—*this* would be bliss.   Not that scarlet is in the
least becoming to her, and to sleep under a hedge—say,
on a night like this—would not be quite unadulterated
bliss—might even be conducive to premature rheumat-
ism.   But to go jumping along one's life path through
paper hoops, on flying Arab steeds, in gauze and spangles—oh! that *would* be a little ahead of perpetual tea-
pouring, bread-cutting, bed-making for six-and-twenty
loud-voiced, rough-looking foundry men.

She has been to a circus just once, she remembers,
and saw some lovely creatures, in *very* short petticoats,
galloping round a sawdust ring in dizzying circles, on
the bare backs of five Arab steeds at once, leaping over
banners and through fiery hoops, and kissing finger-tips,
and throwing radiant smiles to the audience.

Jemima Ann feels she could never reach such a pitch
of perfection as that.   Her legs (if these members may
be thus lightly spoken of) are not of that sylph-like sort
a sculptor would pine to immortalize in marble.   She
wears a wide number **seven,** and her instep has *not* the
Andalusian arch, under which water may flow.   In point
of fact, Jemima is flat-footed.   In no way does the symmetry of her body correspond with that of her mind.
Still, it would have been something to have had this lady
rider come.   If not the rose herself, she would at least
for a little have lived near that peerless flower ; but the
gods have spoken—or Aunt Samantha has, which is much
the same—and it may never be.

Supper is over, the men hurry out, on pleasure and
pipes bent, not to return until ten o'clock brings back
the first straggler with virtuous thoughts of bed.

Mrs. Hopkins and her niece sit wearily down amid
the ruins of the feast, and brew themselves a fresh jorum

of tea. A plate of hot, buttered toast is made, some ham is cooked, "which," says Mrs. Hopkins, "a bit of br'iled ham is a tasty thing for tea, and, next to a pickled eyester, a relish I'm uncommon partial to, I do assure you."

And both draw a long breath of great relief as they take their first sip of the cup that cheers.

"I'm that dead beat, Jim," observes the lady of the house, "that I don't know whether I'm a sittin' on my head or my heels, as true as you're born!"

As Mrs. Hopkins in a general way sits on neither, this observation is difficult to answer lucidly, so Jemima Ann takes a thoughtful bite out of her toast, with her head plaintively on one side, and answers nothing.

Mrs. Hopkins is a tall, thin, worried-looking woman, with more of her bony construction visible than is consistent with personal beauty, and with more knowledge of her internal mechanism than is in any way comfortable, either for herself or Jemima Ann.

Mrs. Hopkins is on terms of ghastly familiarity with her own liver, and lungs, and spine, and stomach, and takes dismal views of these organs, and inflicts the dreadful diagnosis on her long-suffering niece.

"Aunt Hopkins," says Jemima Ann, "I'm most awful sorry you didn't take in that lady from Mr. Rogers'. I should love to a knowed her."

"Ah! I dare say, so's you could spend your time gaddin' up to her room, and losin' your morals, and ruinin' your shoes. No, you don't. She'd worrit my very life out, not to speak of my legs and temper, in two days. And a child, too—a play-actin' child! What would we do with a child in this house, I want to know, among twenty-six foundry hands, and not time in it to say 'Jack Robinson'—no, nor room either?"

Jemima Ann opens her lips to admit the point of her knife, laden with crumb and gravy, and to remark that she doesn't want to say "Jack Robinson," when the door-bell sharply and loudly rings.

"There!" cries Mrs. Hopkins, exasperated. "I knowed it! It's her and him! Doose take the man, he sticks like a burr! Show 'em to the front room, Jim," says her aunt, wrathfully, adjusting her back hair, "and tell 'em I'll be there. But I ain't agoin' to stir neither," adds Mrs. Hopkins to herself, resuming her toast, "until I've staid my stomach."

Jemima Ann springs up breathless and radiant, and hastens to the door.

And so, like one of her cherished heroines, hastens, without knowing it, to her "fate." For with the opening of the street door on this eventful evening of her most uneventful life, there opens for poor, hard-worked Jemima Ann the one romance of her existence, never quite to close again till that life's end.

CHAPTER II.

IN WHICH WE MEET TWO PROFESSIONAL LADIES.

A GUST of October wind, a dash of October rain, a black, October sky, the smiling face of a stout little man, waiting on the threshold—these greet Jemima Ann as she opens the door. A carriage stands just outside, its twin lamps beaming redly in the blackness.

"Ah, Miss Jemima, good evening," says this smiling apparition, "although it is anything *but* a good evening. A most uncommon bad evening, I should say, instead. How are you, and how is Aunt Hopkins, now that the supper and the six-and-twenty are off her mind? And

is she in? But of course she's in," says Mr. Rogers, waiting for no answers. "Who would be out that could be
in such a night? Just tell her I'm here, Jemima Ann—
come by appointment, you know; and there's a lady in
the hack at the door, *and* a little girl. You go and tell
Mrs. Hopkins, Jim, my dear, and I'll fetch the lady along ,
to the parlor. One pair front, isn't it? Thanks! Don't
mind me ; I know the way."

Evidently he does, and stands not on the order of his
going.

"Run along, Jemimy," he says, pleasantly, "and call
the aunty. I'll fetch the lady up stairs. Now, then,
mademoiselle," he calls, going to the door of the carriage ; "and if you'll be kind enough to step in out of
the rain, I'll carry Petite here. Up stairs, please. Wait
a minute. Now, then, this way."

All this time Jemima Ann stands, eyes and mouth
ajar, looking, listening with breathless interest.

Mr. Rogers, gentlemanly proprietor of the Stars and
Stripes Hotel, further down the street, assists a lady out
of the chariot at the door, says "Come along, little 'un,"
lifts a child in his arms, and leads the way jauntily up to
the "one pair front."

"This is the place, Mademoiselle Mimi," he says,
somewhat suddenly, "Mrs. Hopkins' select boarding-
house for single gentlemen."

"Faugh!" says Mademoiselle Mimi, curling dis-
gustedly an extremely pretty nose ; "it smells of corned
beef and cabbage, and all the three hundred and sixty-
five nasty dinners cooked in it the past year."

And indeed a most ancient and cabbage-like odor
does pervade the halls and passages of the Hotel Hopkins. It is one of those unhappy houses in which smells
(like prayers) ascend, and the lodgers in the attic can
always tell to a little what is going on in the kitchen.

"Mrs. Hopkins can get up a nice little dinner, for all
that," says Mr. Rogers. "She's done it for me before

now, when the cook has left me in the lurch. She'll do
it for you, Mam'selle Mimi. You won't be served with
boiled beef and cabbage while you're here, let me tell
you. And she's as clean as silver. This is the parlor;
take a chair. And *this* is Jemima Ann, Mrs. Hopkins'
niece, and the idol of six-and-twenty stalwart young men.
Jemimy, my love, let me present you—Mademoiselle
Mimi Trillon, the famous bare-back rider and trapeze
performer, of whom all the world has heard, and La
Petite Mademoiselle Trillon, the younger."

Mr. Rogers waves his hand with the grace of a court
chamberlain and the smile of an angel, and Mademoiselle
Mimi Trillon laughs and bows. It is a musical, merry
little laugh, and the lady, Jemima Ann thinks, in a
bewildered way, is the most brilliant and beautiful her
eyes have ever looked on. The Duchess Isoline herself
was less fair! She feels quite dazzled and dizzy for a
moment, anything beautiful or bright is so far outside
her pathetically ugly life. She is conscious of a face,
small, rather pale just now, looking out of a coquettish
little bonnet; of profuse rippling hair of flaxen fairness
waving low on a low forehead; of a dress of dark silk,
that emits perfume as she moves; of a seal jacket, of
two large blue-bell eyes, laughing out of the loveliness of
that "flower face."

"Oh!" she says, under her breath, and stands and
stares.

Mlle. Mimi laughs again. Her teeth are as nearly
like "pearls" as it is in the nature of little white teeth
to be. She can afford to laugh, and knows it.

"Now, then, Jemimy!" cries the brisk voice of Mr.
Rogers. "I know you are lost in a trance of admiration.
We all are, bless you, when we first meet Mam'selle
Mimi. Nevertheless, my dear girl, business before
pleasure, and business has brought us here to-night.
Call your aunt, and let us get it over."

"Here is Aunt Samanthy" responds Jemima: and

at that moment enters unto them Mrs. Hopkins, her "stomach staid," and considerably humanized by the mellowing influence of sundry cups of tea, and quantities of hot toast and broiled ham.

Mr. Rogers rises, receives her with effusion, presents to her the Mesdemoiselles Trillon, mother and daughter, and Mam'selle Mimi holds out one gray-gloved hand, with a charming smile, and says some charming words of first greeting.

Jemima Ann watches in an agony of suspense. She hopes—oh! she *hopes* Aunt Samantha will not steel her heart, and bolt her front door against this radiant vision of golden hair, and silk, and seal.

But Aunt Samantha is not impressionable. Long years of foundry hands, of struggles with her liver and other organs, of much taxes and many butcher bills, have turned to bitterness her natural milk of human kindness, and she casts a cold and disapproving glance on the blonde Mimi, and bobs a stiff little courtesy, and sits down severely on the extreme edge of a chair.

"*So* sorry to intrude," says the sweet voice of Mlle. Mimi, in coaxing accents, "*dear* Mrs. Hopkins, at this abnormal hour. It is really *quite* too dreadful of me, I admit. But what was I to do? Mr. Rogers' hotel is quite full, and even if it were not, there are reasons"— a pause, a sigh, the blue-bell eyes cast a pathetic glance, first at her child, then appealingly at Mr. Rogers, then more appealingly at frigid Mrs. Hopkins—"there is a *person* at the hotel with whom I cannot possibly associate. I am a mother, my dear Mrs. Hopkins; that dear child is my only treasure. In my absence there would be no one at the hotel to look after her. I can *not* leave her to the tender mercies of the ladies of our company. So I am here. You will take compassion upon us, I am sure "—clasping the gray-gloved hands—"and afford us hospitality during our brief stay in this town. Snow·

ball, come here. Go directly to this nice lady, and say,
'How do you do?'"

"Won't!" says Mlle. Trillon, the younger—she is a
young person of some three or four years—in the
promptest way; "her's not a nice lady. Her's a narsy,
narsy lady!"

The child is almost prettier than the mother, if prettier were possible. She is a duplicate in little rose and
lily skin, flaxen curls, blue-bell eyes, sweet little mouth,
that to look at is to long to kiss.

A wild impulse is on Jemima Ann to snatch her up
and smother her with kisses, but something in the blue-
bell eyes warned her such liberties would not be safe.

"For shame, you bad Snowball!" says Mlle. Mimi,
shocked, while Mr. Rogers chuckles in appreciation of
the joke, and Jemima Ann holds out a timid hand of
conciliation, and smiles her most winning smile. The
turquois eyes turn slowly, and scan her with the slow,
steadfast, terrible look of childhood, from head to foot.
Evidently the result is unsatisfactory.' She, too, is a
"narsy lady." The disdainful sprite turns away with a
little *moue* of disdain, and stands slim and silent at Mr.
Rogers' knee. For Jemima Ann, she had fallen in love
at first sight, and from that hour until the last of her life
is Mlle. Snowball's abject slave.

"Now, don't you think you can manage it, Mrs. Hopkins," says, suavely, Mr. Rogers; "there's such a lot of
them at my place, and it may be only for a week; and,
as Mlle. Mimi says, it is for the child's sake. It won't
do to have her running about wild, while mamma is
away at the circus, you know—eh, little Snowball? And
here's our Jemima can keep an eye to her just as well as
not, while the other's on the dinner. Not a mite of
trouble, are you, Snowball? Quite a grown-up young
lady in everything but feet and inches. Come, Mrs.
Hopkins, say Yes."

"And I will *not* stay in the same house with Madame

Olympe!" exclaims, suddenly, Mlle. Mimi, her blue eyes emitting one quick, sharp, lurid flash. And here, at last, as it dawns on Mrs. Hopkins, is the "cat out of the bag;" the true reason of this late visit and petition. In the circus company are two leading ladies—Madame Olympe and Mlle. Mimi—and war to the knife has naturally, from first to last, been their motto. They are rivals in everything; they disagree in everything. They hate each other with a heartiness and vim that borders, at times, on frenzy! All that there is of the most blonde and sprightly is Mlle. Mimi; a brunette of brunettes, dashing, dark, and dangerous, is Madame Olympe. Mimi professes to be French, and was "raised" in the back slums of New York. Olympe *is* French—a *soi-disant* grisette of Mabille.. Paris is written on her face. And two tomcats on the tiles, at dead of night, never fought for mastery with tongue and claws as do the lovely Mimi, the superb Olympe.

"Ladies! ladies!" the long suffering manager is wont to remonstrate, on the verge of bursting into tears, "*how* can you, you know? Your little hands were never made to tear each other's eyes! Upon my soul I wonder at you—French and everything as you are. And I've always heard the French beat the d—l for politeness. But it ain't polite to call each other liars and hussies, and heave hairbrushes at each other. Now, I'm blest if it is!"

All this time Mrs. Hopkins sits, upright, grim, rigid, virtuous, on the slippery edge of her horse-hair chair; "No," written in capital letters in her eye of stone, on her brow of adamant, when suddenly, and most unexpectedly, the child with the odd name comes to the rescue. Snowball fixes her azure eyes on the frozen visage; some fascination is for her there surely, for out ripples all at once the sweet tinkle of a child's merry laugh; she toddles over to her side, and slips her rose-leaf hand into the hard old palm.

"Not a narsy lady. 'Noball likes you. 'Nobal seepy. Her wants to go to bed."

"Bless your pretty little heart!" exclaims Mrs. Hopkins, involuntarily. Even Achilles, it will be remembered, had a vulnerable spot in his heel. Whether Aunt Samantha's is in her heels or in her heart, Snowball has found it. But then to find people's hearts and keep them is a trick of Snowball's all her life-long.

"Seepy, seepy," reiterates Snowball with pretty imperiousness. "Put 'Noball to bed. Mamma, make her put 'Noball to bed."

"You *must* put us up, you see," says mamma. "Come, my dear madam, it will be inhuman to refuse."

It will. Mrs. Hopkins feels she cannot say "No;" and Mrs. Hopkins also feels she will repent in wrath and bitterness, saying "Yes." She casts one scathing glance at serene Mr. Rogers, and says, "Well, yes, then," with the very worst grace in the world.

"Oh, I'm *awful* glad!" cries out Jemima Ann in the fullness of her heart. "Oh, you little darling, come to me, and let *me* get you ready for bed!"

"Go to the nice, nice girl, Snowball," says Mlle. Mimi, "and tell her you will have some bread and milk and your hair brushed before you go to sleep. Ever so many thanks, Mrs. Hopkins, though that *yes* had rather an uncordial tone. Rogers"—she uses no prefix—"the trunks are coming by express; you will find a valise and satchel in the cab. Send them up. I won't trouble you for supper to-night, Mrs. Hopkins; we had a snack at the hotel. But get my room ready as soon as you can. There's a good soul. We've been on the go all day, and I am dead tired."

A swift and subtle change has come over Mlle. Mimi. Her pleading lady-like manner drops from her as a garment: her present tone has an easy ring of command, a touch of vulgarity, that Mrs. Hopkins is quick to feel and resent, but cannot define.

"Make up a bed for Snowball on a sofa or lounge near mine," she says to Jemima Ann, "and don't let her have too much milk. She is a perfect little pig for country milk, and I don't want her to get fat. I hate flat by children. And I'll lie on this couch while you're getting my room ready, I really and truly am fit to drop. Goodnight, Rogers; tell Olympe, with my compliments, I hope she means to go to bed sober this first night."

Her musical laugh follows Mr. Rogers down-stairs. Then she glides out of her seal-skin like a beautiful little serpent slipping its skin, throws off the coquettish bonnet, stretches herself on the sofa, and before her hostess or niece are fairly out of the room, is fast asleep.

"Well, I never !" says Mrs. Hopkins, drawing a long breath. "Upon my word and honor, Jemima Ann, I do assure you I *never !*"

"'Noball sceepy, 'Noball hundry, want her bed and milk, want go to bed," pipes plaintively the child.

Jemima gathers her up in her arms, and ventures to kiss the satin smooth cheek.

"You dear little pet," she says, "you shall have your bread and milk, and go to bed in two minutes. Oh, you pretty little love ! I never saw anything half so lovely as you in my life !"

"Land's sake, Jemimy Ann, don't spile the young one!" says, irritably, her aunt. · "Handsome is as handsome does, is a true motto the world over, and if her or her mar does handsome, I'm a Dutchman. 'Goodnight, Rogers, and tell Alimp to go to bed sober this *first* night ;' pretty sort o' talk that for a temperance boardin'-house. There! get that sleepy baby somethin' and put her to bed. I'll go and fix Miss Flyaway's room, before the men come in, and find her sleepin' here and make fools of themselves."

And so, still wrathful and grumbling, but in for it now, Mrs. Hopkins goes to put her best bedroom in order. Jemima carries Snowball down to the dining-room. The flaxen head lies against her shoulder, the drowsy lids sway over the sweet blue eyes, the very lips are apart and dewy. Oh! how lovely she is, how lovely, how lovely, thinks Jemima Ann, in a sort of rapture. Oh! if she could but keep this beautiful baby with her forever and ever!

At sight of the bread and milk, Snowball wakes up enough to partake of that refreshment. But she sleepily declines conversation, and the pretty head sways as the long light curls are being braided, and her clothes taken off, and she is sound again, when Jemima bears her tenderly up to the little extempore bed Aunt Samantha has prepared. She stands and gazes at her in a rapture as she sleeps.

"She looks like a duchess's daughter! She looks like an angel, Aunt Samanthy!" she says, under her breath.

"Yas!" cries Aunt Samantha, in bitter scorn. "I never see an angel—no more did you. And if you did, I don't believe they'd a rid at a circus. Now go down and shake up t'other angel in the parlor, and tell her she can tumble into bed as soon as she likes. And mark my words, Jemima Ann," concludes Mrs. Hopkins, solemnly prophetic, "that woman will give us trouble, such as we ain't had in many a long day, afore we're rid of her!"

CHAPTER III.

IN WHICH WE GO TO THE CIRCUS.

T is the evening of another day; crisp, clear, cool. The town-hall has tolled seven, and all the town, in its Sunday best, is trooping gayly to the great common on the outskirts, where the huge circus tent is erected, where flags fly, and drums beat, and brass instruments blare, and great doings will be done to-night.

A great rope stretches from the center of the common to the top of the tent, quite a giddy height, and the celebrated tight-rope dancer, Mlle. Mimi, is to walk up this before the performance, giving a gratis taste of her, qualities to an admiring world.

Other outward and visible signs of the inward and to-be-paid-for graces going on within, are there as well. Every dead wall, every fence all over the town, is placarded with huge posters, announcing in lofty letters of gorgeous colors, the wonderful doings to be beheld for the small sum of fifty cents, children half price, clergymen free!

Pictures of all the animals whose ancestors came over in the Ark with Noah and family, together with portraits of the unparalleled Daughter of the Desert, Madame Olympe, on her fiery steed Whirlwind, of the daring and fearless trapezist and tight-rope dancer, Mlle. Mimi, direct from Paris, of the little Fairy Queen, Snowball, who is to be borne aloft in one hand by the Bounding Brothers of Bohemia, in the thrilling one-act drama of the "Peruvian Princess."

The portraits of the rival stars attract much admiration and comment—in rather a coarse and highly-colored state of art, it must be admitted, but sweetly pretty and simpering all the same, displaying a great redundancy of salmon-colored bust and arms, and pronounced by those who have seen the fair originals, speaking likenesses.

And now all the town is to see them, the chariot races, the Bounding Brothers, the Fairy Queen, the Daughter of the Desert, the clown, and the rest of the menagerie.

It is a crisp, cool, fresh, yellow twilight; the world looks clean and well washed, after last night's rain. The sky is turquois blue, there is a comfortable little new

2

moon smiling down, as if it, too, had come out expressly to go to the circus.

Everybody is in fine spirits, there is much laughter and good-humored chaffing, there are troops and troops of children—children of a larger growth, too, who affect to treat the whole affair with off-hand, good-natured contempt—only come to look after the young ones, you know—old boys and girls, who in their secret souls are as keen for the sport as any nine-year-old of them all.

An immense throng is gathered on the common, watching with beating hearts and bated breath, for their first taste of rapture, the free sight of Mlle. Mimi walking up the rope. And amid this throng, in her Sunday "things" quite "of a tremble" with joyous expectancy stands Jemima Ann, waiting with the deepest interest of all for the first glimpse in her public capacity of the fair performer she has the honor of knowing in private life.

The band stands at ease giving the public tantalizing little tastes of its quality, working up the suspense of small boys to an agonizing pitch, laughing and talking to another, as if this magical sort of thing were quite every-day life to them, when suddenly everybody is galvanized, every neck is strained, an indescribable murmur and rush goes through the crowd: "Oh, hush! Here she is! Oh, ma! isn't she lovely? Oh-h-h!" It is a long-drawn, rapturous breath.

A vision has appeared—a vision all gold and glitter, all gauze and spangles, all rosy floating skirts, a little flag in each hand, bare white arms, streaming yellow curls, twinkling pink feet, rosy, smiling face! The band strikes up a spirited strain, and up, and up, and up floats the fairy in rose and spangles.

Every throat stretches, every eye follows, every breath seems suspended, every mouth is agape. Profound stillness reigns. And up, and up, and up still floats the rose-pink vision; and now she stands on the dizzy top, a pink star against the blue sky, waving her flags, and kissing hands to the breathless crowd below! Now, she descends slowly, slowly, and slowly plays the band, and the tension is painful to all these good, simple souls.

A sort of involuntary gasp goes through them as with a light buoyant bound she is on *terra firma*, bowing right and left, and vanishing into the tent like the fairy she is.

"Oh-h-h! wasn't it lovely! Oh, ma, she is just too sweet for anything! Oh, pa! do let us hurry in and get a good seat. Was it Olympe? No, it wasn't, it was the other one, Mamzel Mimi. Oh! I'm being scrooged to death! Pa, *do* let us hurry in—don't you see everybody is going?"

Jemima Ann goes with the rest. It is the rarest of rare things for her to be off duty, but Aunt Samantha has relented for once, and her niece is here, fairly palpitating with expectant rapture.

All the boarders, washed and shining with good humor, much friction, and yellow soap, in brave array muster strong, and kindly little Mr. Doolittle has meekly presented "Miss Jim" with a ticket. So she is swept onward and inward, with the crowd into the great canvas arena, and presently finds herself perched on an exquisitely uncomfortable shelf, her knees on a level with her chin, gazing with awe at the vast sawdust ring and the red curtain beyond, whence it is whispered the performers will presently emerge.

Then she glances about her—yes, there are the boarders, there is Mr. Rogers, there is the butcher and his family, there is the undertaker and his wife, there is the family grocer and his seven sons and daughters, there are quite numbers of ladies and gentlemen she knows. And all over the place there are swarms of children, children beyond any possibility of computation. A smell of sawdust and orange-peel, a pervading sense of hilarity and peanuts is in the atmosphere, the band plays as if it

would burst itself with enthusiasm, and the evening performance triumphantly begins.

Long after this festive night, Jemima Ann tries to
recall, dispassionately, all she has seen in this her first
glimpse of wonder-land, but it is all so splendid, so rapid,
so bewildering, to a mind used only to underground
kitchens, and the society of black beetles, and blacker
foundry hands, that her dazzled brain fails to grasp it
with any coherence. There are horses—good gracious!
such horses as one could hardly imagine existed out of
the Arabian Nights; horses that dance polkas and jigs,
that put the kettle on, that listen to the clown, and understood every word he said, horses that laughed, horses
that made courtesies to the audience, horses that stood
on their hind legs, that knelt down, that jumped through
hoops, and over banners. Jemima Ann would not have
been surprised to see a peg turned in their side, and
behold them spread their wings and soar to the ceiling.
Only they didn't. And then the clown, with his startling,
curious, and white visage, his huge, grinning mouth, and
amazing nose, his funny dress, and funnier retorts to the
exasperated ring-master—Jemima Ann nearly died of
laughing at *him*. Only to hear his jovial " Here we are
again !" was worth the whole fifty cents; so said the
good people about her, laughing till they cried, and so,
with all her heart, said Jemima Ann.

But this was only a little of it. When Mlle. Mimi
appeared, more gauzy, more spangly, more lovely even
than outside, careening round and round, on four fiery
bare-backed steeds, in that breathless manner that your
head swam, and your respiration came in gasps, *then* the
enthusiasm rose to fever heat, if you like ! They shouted,
they stamped, they applauded the very knobs off their
walking-sticks, and Jemima Ann, faint with bliss, shuts
her eyes for a moment, and feels she is in the mad vor-
tex of high life at last, feels that she is living a chapter out
of one of her own weekly "dreadfuls." How beautiful

Mimi looks, as she sweeps by, smiling, painted, radiant!
And now—it is a moment never to be forgotten—Mimi
sees her, smiles at her—yes, in full tilt pauses to smile at
her and throw her a kiss from her finger tips! All heads
turn, all eyes fix wonderingly, enviously on the crimson
visage of Jemima Ann.

"Do you know her?" asks in a tone of awe those
nearest, and Jemima Ann glows and responds:

" Yes."

It is a proud moment; it is a case of "greatness
thrust." People scan her as she sits, and wonder if per-
chance she too is not a professional lady taking her fifty
cents' worth here for a change, among the common herd.

Madame Olympe comes as the Daughter of the Desert, a big, handsome, bold brunette, with flashing eyes
and raven locks. These same raven locks, together with
the brief allowance of cloth of gold, and bullion fringe,
and a pair of tinkling anklets, comprise nearly all she
has about her in the way of costume. She is distinctly
indecent; the virtuous maids and matrons blush in their
secret souls, and feel that this is worse, very much worse,
than the pink gauze. And though the Daughter of the
Desert seems to fly through the air, and does some wonderful things, she is coldly received, and the audience
break into a laugh when a forward small boy suggests
that before she does any more she'd better go in and put
something on, else maybe she'll ketch a cold in her
head! It is felt as a relief when she does go, and the
Bounding Brothers take her place. One, in the dress of
an Indian chief, all feathers, beads, and scarlet cloth,
makes a raid in the territory of another, the Prince of
Peru, captures the child of that potentate, and rides at
break-neck speed with her held aloft in one hand in triumph. And Jemima Ann gasps painfully, for it is little
Snowball, all in white, her long fair curls floating, her
rosebud lips smiling, the tiny creature stands erect, and is
whirled round and round by the Indian chief. She

kisses her baby hand, she smiles her sweet baby smile, her dauntless blue eyes wander over the house. If she should fall! Jemima Ann shuts her eyes, sick with the thought, and does not look again, until after a free fight, and a great deal of shooting with bows and arrows, the princess is recaptured, and the Bounding Brothers bound out of sight.

Mlle. Mimi on the trapeze winds up the performance. Her agility, her strength, her daring, here, are something to marvel at. Her springs from one swinging bar to another, look perilous in the extreme. It is wonderful where, in that slight, graceful frame, these delicate hands and wrists, all that steel-like strength of muscle can lie. This also Jemima feels to be more painful than pleasant —it is a relief when it is over, and though it had been an evening of much bliss and great excitement, it is something of a relief to rise and stretch one's cramped limbs, and breathe the cool fresh night air, and see the sparkling frosty stars. Too much pleasure palls, Jemima Ann's head swims with so much merry-go-round—she will be glad to get back to the cool attic and flock mattress and think over at her leisure how happy she has been.

"I wonder what time Mlle. Mimi and that dear little Snowball will get home?" she muses; "the dear little love ought to be fit to drop with tiredness. No wonder her ma wanted some supper, I wish Aunt Samanthy hadn't been so cross."

A vivid remembrance of the scene of that afternoon flashes through her mind, as she trudges home through the quiet streets. Mlle. Mimi just back from rehearsal, she and Aunt Samantha busy in the kitchen, Snowball tripping about, asking pretty baby questions—a swish of silk, a waft of strong perfume, and Mimi, bright in silk and velvet, lace and jewelry, presents herself.

"How nice and hot it is here," she says, coming in, with a shiver; "the rest of the house is as cold as a barn. Why don't you have a fire in your parlor this October

weather, Mrs. Hopkins? And how good you smell!"
sniffing the warm air, and seating herself in front of the
glowing stove. "What are you cooking, Jemima Ann?"

"Johnny-cake and gingerbread for the men's teas,"
responds, modestly, Jemima Ann ; "a pan of each. The
men like 'em."

"Do they?" says Mimi, laughing. "What nice, innocent sort of men yours must be, my dear, judging by
their food ! *I* should not like gingerbread and the other
thing. Apropos, though (no, Snowball, I don't want
you ; run away), I should like a hot supper when I come
back to-night. I am always tired, and hungry as a
hunter. I always have a hot supper ; cold things make
me dyspeptic. Will you see to it, Jemima Ann?"

Jemima Ann glances apprehensively at Aunt Samantha. Aunt Samantha draws up her mouth like the mouth
of a purse, and stands ominously silent.

"What time would you like it?" timidly ventures
Jemima Ann.

'Oh, about eleven ; I shall not be later than that.
Nothing very elaborate, you know—just a fowl, a chicken
or duck, mashed potatoes, one sweet and one savory.
Coffee, of course, as strong as you like, and cream if it is
to be had for love or money. Something simple like
that ! And I shall need some boiling water for pun—
well, I shall need it. I may bring a friend home to supper. I hate eating alone, so lay covers for two. Don't
serve it in that big, dismal place you call the dining-
room ; let us have it cozily in the parlor. And *do* light
a fire ; your black grate is enough to send a chill to the
marrow of one's bones. Snowball will not sit up, of
course. You will put her to bed as soon as she comes
home. You will not forget anything, will you, Jemima
Ann?"

Jemima Ann is too paralyzed to answer ; Mrs. Hopkins is literally petrified with indignation. Only for a
moment, though ; then she faces the audacious Mimi,

her eyes flashing, her face peony red, her hands on her hips, war and defiance in every snorting word.

"So! this is all, 'm, is it? Jest somethin' simple and easy, like that! And at eleven o'clock at night! Wouldn't you like a soup, and fish, and oysters, ma'am, and a side-dish and Charley Roose, and ice-cream, and strawberries to top the lot! Why, hang your impidence!" cries Mrs. Hopkins, waxing suddenly from the bitterly sardonic to the furiously wrathful—"what do you think we are? You come here and fairly force yourself on a respectable house, and try to begin your scandalous goin's on before you're twenty-four hours in it! But I'll see you furder first, 'm, and Rogers, too, I do assure you! No friends is let in this house," says Mrs. Hopkins, with vindictive emphasis, "after ten o'clock at night—no, not for Queen Victorious, if she begged it on her bended knees!"

Mlle. Mimi, toasting her little high-heeled French shoes before the fire, turns coolly, and listens, first in surprise, then in amusement, to this tirade.

"My good soul," she says, calmly, "don't lose your temper. You'll have a fit of some kind, and go off like a shot, if you go on like that. And what do you mean by scandalous proceedings? You really ought to be careful in your talk—people get taken up sometimes for actionable language. It is not scandalous to eat a late supper, is it? I am a very proper person, my dear Mrs. Hopkins, and never scandalize anybody. If I can't have supper here, I will have it elsewhere—it is much the same to me. You will give me a latch-key, I suppose— or do you allow such a demoralizing thing to your art- less black lambkins? Or would you prefer sitting up for me? I like to be obliging, and I will be back by one."

"Miss Mimi," begins Mrs. Hopkins, "if that's your name,"—Mimi laughs—"this house ain't no place for the likes of, you." Miss Mimi glances disdainfully about, and shrugs her shoulders. " It's a homely place, and we're homely people." Mimi laughs again, and glances amusedly from the hot and angry face of the aunt, to the flushed and distressed face of the niece—a glance that says, " I agree with you." " Your ways ain't our ways "—(" No, thank Heaven !" says Mimi, *sotto voce*) —" and so the sooner we part, the better, I do assure you. You'll jest be good enough, ma'am, to take yourself, and your traps, and your little girl, out of this as soon as you like—and the sooner the better, I do assure you."

Mimi looks at her. There is a laugh still on her rose-red mouth ; there is a laughing light in her blue eyes ; but there is a laughing devil in them, too.

" My good creature," she says, slowly, " you labor under a mistake. I will not go, and you shall not make me. You agreed to take me in the presence of witnesses. I have paid you a week's board in advance, and no power on earth will move me out of this hospitable mansion until it suits me to go. And I will keep what hours I please. And I will invite what friends I like. I shall return at once, and you shall shut your doors on me at your peril. And I will see you—no ! don't cry out before you are hurt—*inconvenienced* is the word I will use," she breaks off, laughing aloud in genuine amusement at the horror in the face of her hostess, and rises gracefully. " Now, Jemima Ann, the sooner you bring me up some tea the better, *I do assure you*," mimicking perfectly Mrs. Hopkins' nasal tones ; " and if your gingercake is *very* good, you may bring me some of that, too. Come, Snowball, and let me curl your hair."

It is the first time in all her seven years' experience that Jemima Ann has seen her intrepid chieftainess taken down. She is almost afraid to look at her ; but when she does, she finds her gazing after her enemy with a blank and stony stare, and rigid lips and eyeballs, alarmingly suggestive of fits ! No fit ensues, however. There

2*

is a gasping breath, a stifled, "Well, this *does* cap the globe!" and then silence. Aunt Samantha has been routed with slaughter, and in her secret soul Jemima Ann rejoices.

She goes home now, through the crisp, starlit night, and finds her stormy kinswoman waiting up with a tongue and temper soured and sharpened by long hours of solitude and stocking-darning. She is first, but the boarders follow close, noisy, hungry, and enthusiastic in their loud praises of the charming Mimi. Olympe is a fine woman, no doubt, and not stingy of herself, but Mimi's the girl for their money. And thus they have a proud feeling of proprietorship in Mimi. She is one of the family, so to speak. They feel that her beauty and success reflect glory on the house of Hopkins. Aunt Samantha listens to it all with grim scorn; declines snappishly to be entertained with the brilliant doings of the night; declines more snappishly to go to bed, and leave her, Jemima Ann, to wait up for Mlle. Mimi.

"I'll see it out, if I sit here till I take root," is her grim ultimatum. "I'll see that she brings no trollopin' characters into this house; so, hold your jaw, Jemima Ann Hopkins."

The door-bell rings as she speaks. Is it Mimi, so soon? No, it is a man from the circus with little Snowball, sleepy and tired. Jemima Ann takes her tenderly, kisses and pets her, undresses and puts her to bed. It is midnight, and still Mimi is not here. Grimmer and grimmer grows the rigid face of Aunt Samantha, colder and colder grows the night, drearier and drearier looks the kitchen, quieter and more quiet seem the lonesome midnight streets. *One.* Half-past—with her arms on the table, her face lying on them, sleep as a garment drops on Jemima, when, once more, sharp, loud, startling the door-bell rings.

"It's her!" cries Jemima Ann, and springs up, "for which, 'Oh! be joyful!'"

She runs up-stairs, Aunt Samantha follows. Outside there are voices, one the voice of a man, and loud laughter. The key is turned, the door is opened, Mimi stands before them. She comes in laughing—aunt and niece fall back. What is the matter? Her fair face is flushed, her blue eyes glassy, there is a smell, strong subtle, spirituous. In horror the truth dawns upon them —she is—(it is the phrase of Jemima Ann)—she is *tight!*

They fall back. Even Aunt Samantha, prepared for the worst, is not prepared for *this*. She is absolutely dumb! Mlle. Mimi laughs in their faces—a tipsy laugh.

"Car' lamp up-stairs, 'Mimy Ann," she says, indistinctly, "sor' to keep you up, Miss Hopkins. Goo' night."

In dead silence Mrs. Hopkins falls back, in dead silence Jemima Ann obeys—words fail them both. She precedes Mimi to her room, where sweet little Snowball sleeps, pure and peaceful, sets the lamp in a place of safety, sees their boarder fling off hat and jacket, and throw herself, dressed as she is, on the bed, too far gone even to undress!

CHAPTER IV.

WHICH RECORDS THE DARK DOINGS OF MLLE. MIMI.

"COLD chicking," says Jemima Ann—"that's one, buttered short-cake—that's two, cranberry sass—that's three, and frizzled beef—that's four. Yes, four. I've got 'em all. And tea—that's five. There ain't nothin' the matter with her appetite, whatever there may be with her morals."

The antecedent of this personal pronoun is, of course, Mlle. Mimi, and Jemima Ann is busily engaged arranging her supper on a tray. Up in the parlor, in a pale-blue *negligée*, and looking more or less like an angel, with her floating, untidy, fair hair, Mimi is yawning over a fashion-magazine, and listening to the prattle of her small daughter.

"Enter, Jemima Ann !" she cries, gayly, springing up, "laden with the fruits of the earth. Snowball and I were beginning to think you had forgotten us. And where is the precious auntie, my Jemima, and is she still as far gone as ever, in blackest sulks ?"

It is the afternoon succeeding *that* night, and no thundercloud ever gloomed more darkly than does the countenance of Mrs. Hopkins whenever it turns upon her audacious boarder.

"She is feeling dreadful bad, Miss Mimi," responds Mrs. Hopkins' niece, gravely, "and no wonder. You really hadn't ought to done it."

Mimi laughs, with genuine, unaffected amusement, and pinches Jemima Ann's hard, red cheek, in passing.

" I really hadn't ought to done it ! Dew tell ! Here, Snowball, come on—here's a lovely bit of chicken for you. Well, now, Jemima Ann, I admit I *did* imbibe a little too freely last night ; but what will you ? I was dead beat, I was warm and aching with fatigue, and Lacy's Clicquot was the very best, and iced to perfection. Did you ever drink iced champagne, my poor Jemima ? Ah ! the wine of life is not for such as you. If I had to exchange places with you, and grub down in that abominable kitchen among pots and pans, and wait on dirty, oily foundrymen, and be girded at by that virago, your aunt ; I would simply cut my throat in a week, and of two evils think it the least."

"Aunt ain't a bad sort. Please don't abuse her," returned Jemima, still gravely, "her bark is worse than her bite. Who is Lacy, Miss Mimi ?"

The first shyness of new acquaintance is over. Mimi is a free-and-easy, touch-and-go sort of person, easy to grow familiar with, and Miss Hopkins has her full share of feminine curiosity.

"Is he that aristocratic-looking gent, with the raven black mustache and diamond studs, a stoppin' at the Washington House?" asks Jemima, in considerable awe, as she assists Snowball to milk and short-cake.

"Dyed, Jemima—dyed, my dear," laughs Mimi; "that mustache gets mangy sometimes and purple. But the studs are real, and he is rich enough to wear a whole diamond shirt front, if he chose. Yes, my Jemima, 'tis he! the gent at the Washington; and a very swell young man he is! And he is dead in love with me; but this is a secret, mind," and Mimi laughs again at the simple, puzzled face of Miss Hopkins. "He is down here from New York, wasting his sweetness on Clangville air, for me and for me alone. I might be Mrs. Lacy to-morrow, my Jemima, if I chose."

"And you don't choose?"

"No, I don't. I have had enough of men and matrimony. They're a mistake, Jemima. The game isn't worth the candle. No!" her face sets and darkens suddenly, "at the very best, it's not worth it."

"Are—are you a widow?" Jemima Ann ventures, timidly.

There is no reply; Mimi is carving her chicken with a certain vicious energy, and all the laughing light has vanished from her insouciant face.

"A widow," she says, impatiently. "Oh, yes, of course I'm a widow—Rogers told you that, didn't he? Snowball, don't choke yourself with that chicken wing, you little gourmand. Take her away from the table, Jemima Ann; she's had enough."

"Wasn't had 'nuff," cries out Snowball, lustily, clinging to her plate with both hands; "s'ant go. 'Noball wants more sort-cake, 'Mimy Ann."

"Oh, let her have some more," says Jemima. "The dear little pet is hungry."

"The dear little pet will be as fat as a dear little pig, directly, under your injudicious indulgence, Miss Hopkins. No, Snowball, not another morsel, and no more milk. Leave the table this moment; you ought to know by now that what mamma says she means."

She rises and bears Snowball bodily from the victuals. And straightway Snowball opens her mouth, and there rises to heaven such a shriek, as it is to be hoped few children have the lungs and temper to emit.

"There!" says Mimi, composedly, "that is the sort of angelic disposition your dear little pet is blessed with, Jemima. Please open the window if she doesn't stop this instant, and throw her out!"

Jemima Ann declines to act on this summary hint. She soothes the enraged child, instead, and surreptitiously conveys to her a contraband wedge of short-cake.

"What an odd name you have given her," she remarks, clearing away the things; "she never was christened Snowball, was she? That's not a Christian name."

"She never was christened anything, my good Jemima," responds her mother, with a shrug. "What is the use of christening? She was a little white, roly-poly baby; white hair, white skin, white clothes—so her father used to toss her up and call her his snowbird, his snowflake, his snowball, and all sorts of silly, snowy names. As she had to be called something, Snowball it finally came to be, and Snowball I suppose it always will be now. It suits the little white monkey as well as anything else. Pearl or Lily would be more sentimental, but I don't profess to be a sentimental person myself. I leave that for you, O romance-reading Jemima Snow!"

The door opens as she speaks.

"Samantha," says a pleasant voice, "are you here?"

The pleasant voice belongs to a pleasant face, and both are the property of a pretty matron all in drab, like a Quaker, who opens the door, and stands gazing inquiringly around.

"Why, Mrs. Tinker!" exclaims Jemima Ann, "*is* it
you? When did you come? Aunt Samanthy's jest gone
out marketin'. Do come in and wait. I know she's been
wantin' to see you, and a talkin' of going to the cottage
all week."

"How do you do, Jemima Ann?" is the smiling response of the drab matron. "Well, perhaps I had better——"

She stops suddenly. Her eyes have fallen on Snowball, then on Mimi, and the words die on her lips.

A startled look comes into her eyes, a startled pallor
falls on her face, her lips part breathlessly, she stands
and stares like one who has received a shock.

"Oh!" says Jemima Ann, remembering her manners,
"this is Mrs. Tinker, Miss Mimi. Mrs. Tinker, this is
Mamzel Mimi, a lady that boards here, and her little
girl."

Mimi smiles easily, shows her small white teeth, and
nods.

Mrs. Tinker tries to bow, but some sudden, and
strange, and great dread and surprise have fallen upon
her—she retreats backward in a sort of panic, without a
word. Mimi lifts her eyebrows and laughs.

"Upon my word!" she exclaims, "is that nice motherly old party cracked, Jemima Ann?"

Jemima Ann hurries out without reply. The elderly
lady stands in the passage, still pale as whitewash, her
hands pressed over her heart.

"Goodness me, Mrs. Tinker!" she cries. "Whatever
is it?"

"Oh, my dear," says Mrs. Tinker. "I've had a turn,
I've had a turn, my dear. *Who* is that lady in the parlor?"

"Mamzel Mimi, Mrs. Tinker. Surely *you* don't know
her?"

"Oh, my dear, I'm afeared I do—I'm sore afeared I
do. *What* is she, Jemima Ann? An actress?"

"A tight-rope dancer — a circus performer. Lor! Mrs. Tinker, you ain't a-going to faint?"

For Mrs. Tinker, breathing in gasps, lays sudden and violent hold of Jemima, as if an immediate swoon were indeed her intention. And Mrs. Tinker weighs ten stone, and Jemima Ann feels that with the best wishes in the world, she is not equal to bearing her to the nearest cold-water tap. Mrs. Tinker thinks better of it, however, and does not swoon.

"No," she says, weakly. "No, Jemima, my dear, I shall not faint. Oh, me! oh, me! to think it should come at last. I've always feared it, my dear, always feared it. Sooner or later, I said, she will find us, and she will come. Oh, me, my dear mistress! How will she bear this?"

"Do you mean Madam Valentine?" says Jemima Ann, looking sympathetic, and deeply puzzled. "Does *she* know Mamzel Mimi? Good gracious me, Mrs. Tinker, you can never mean that?"

"Don't ask me any questions, Jemima Ann; you will hear it all soon enough. Come down-stairs, I feel fit to drop, and answer me a few questions. Tell me when this—this person came, and all about her."

They descend to Mrs. Hopkins' own particular sitting-room, and Mrs. Tinker, still in a weak and collapsed state, is provided with a fan and a glass of water, which stimulants bring her slowly round to calmness and coherence. Jemima Ann unfolds all she knows of Mlle. Mimi, which is not very much, but which is listened to with profound and painful intensity of interest.

"It's the same, it's the same," says Mrs. Tinker, mournfully. "I know it's the same, I never heard the name afore, but I knew the face at once. It is many and many a weary day ago, but she hasn't changed. Oh, me! oh, me! to think of her coming at this late day, and all the harm she's done! It's wicked, my dear, but I hoped she was dead—I did, indeed. And the child, too. Oh ! *what* will Madam Valentine say ?"

"Mrs. Tinker," begins Jemima, literally devoured by curiosity—but Mrs. Tinker rises, a distressed look on her face, and motions for silence with her hand.

"No, my dear," she says, in the same mournful tone, "I can't tell you. I can't tell any one. I can't stay and see Samantha. I don't feel fit to talk or anything. I've had a blow, Jemima Ann, a blow. I'll go home, my dear, and read a chapter in my Bible, and try to compose my mind."

Jemima Ann escorts her to the door, more mystified than she has ever been before in her life, and watches her out of sight, walking slowly and heavily as if burdened with painful thoughts. Then she returns upstairs and into the parlor, where Mimi lies indolently on the sofa, her little feet crossed in an attitude more suggestive of laziness and ease than lady-like grace.

"Well, Jemima, has that flustered old person departed? And what was the matter with her? Is she generally knocked over in that uncomfortable manner by the sight of a stranger? And is she on her way back to the highly respectable lunatic asylum whence she escaped ?"

"Miss Mimi, are you sure? Do you mean to say you never saw her before?"

"Never, to the best of my belief. Why? Does she seem to say that she knows *me ?*"

Jemima Ann is silent. There is a mystery here, and she feels that discretion may be judicious.

"Who is the venerable party anyhow? She is a nice kindly-looking body, too, the sort of motherly soul one would like for a nurse or that."

"She is Mrs. Tinker—Mrs. Susan Tinker."

"Susan Tinker. Euphonious cognomen !" laughs Mimi. "What else is she, oh, reticent Jemima Ann ?"

"Well, she is housekeeper for Madam Valentine.

She has been her housekeeper for more than twenty years."

Jemima is just about lifting the tray to go, but Mlle Mimi springs erect so suddenly, utters an exclamation so sharply that she drops her load.

"Land above!" she exclaims, in terror, "what is the matter with *you?*"

"*Who* did you say?" Mimi cries out, breathlessly;, "housekeeper for whom?"

"Madam Valentine—old Madam Valentine of the Cottage. So then you do know something of the secret after all?"

Mlle. Mimi is standing up. A flush sweeps over the pearly fairness of her face—then it fades and leaves her very pale. She turns abruptly away, walks to a window, and stands with her back to curious Jemima Ann. She stands for fully five minutes staring out; but she sees nothing of the dull, darkening street, the leaden October sky, the few passers-by, the ugly shops over the way. The blue eyes gleam with a light not good to see.

"Don't go," she says at last, turning round as she sees Jemima Ann gathering up the tray, "I want to ask you a question. Who is Madam Valentine?"

"Who is she? Why, she is Madam Valentine, though why madam any more than other folks I don't know, except that she is very rich—immensely rich and aristocratic. Oh, my goodness!" says Jemima Ann, despairing of conveying any idea of the pinnacle of patrician loftiness and wealth, which Madam Valentine has attained.

"Rich and aristocratic! What in the world, then," asks Mimi, with a gesture of infinite contempt out of the window, "does she do here?"

"It ain't such a bad place, Clangville ain't," retorts Jemima, rather hurt; "but she don't live here. She don't live nowhere, Mrs. Tinker says, for good; she just goes about. She has houses and places everywhere, in

cities and in the country. She came here three or four
years ago, and took a fancy to a place out of town, and
thought the air agreed with her. So she bought the cottage, and comes for a month or two every fall since.
And her nephew likes it for the shooting—pa'tridges,
and that. She is going away next week, and won't come
again till next September."

"Her nephew?" Mimi repeats quickly. "Who is her
nephew?"

"Mr. Vane Valentine, a young English gentleman,
and her heir. You oughter see *him* a ridin' through the
town, mounted on a big black horse, as tall and straight
as anything, and looking as if everybody he met was
dirt under his feet!" cries Jemima Ann, in a burst of enthusiastic admiration.

"Indeed! Mr. Vane Valentine puts on airs, does he?
So he is the heir! I knew there was a British cousin,
and an heir to the title. Do you know that high-stepping
young gentleman will be a baronet one day, Jemima
Ann?"

"Yes," says Jemima Ann; "Mrs. Tinker told me.
But how do you come to know? You ain't acquainted
with him, are you?"

"I have not that pleasure—at present. I may have,
possibly, before long. No — don't ask questions; all
you have to do is to answer them. There are only the
old lady and this patrician nephew?"

"That's all. Mr. Valentine is dead."

"Yes. But used there not be some one else—a son?"

Jemima Ann looks at her with ever-growing curiosity.
But her back is to the waning light, and there is nothing
to be seen.

"It's odd," she says, "that you should know about
that; not many people do. Even Mrs. Tinker hates to
talk of it. But, yes—there was a son."

"What became of him?"

"Well, he went wild, and ran away, and made a low

marriage, and was cut off, and drowned. I don't know nothin' more—I don't, indeed. I only found that out by chance. And now I must go," says, nervously, Jemima Ann, "for its nearly six, and aunt will be back, and the hands' supper is to get."

Mimi makes no effort to detain her; but when she is alone she stands for a very long time quite still, the dark look deepening and ever deepening in her face. She hears the house door open, and the shrill, vinegar voice of Mrs. Hopkins—hears the sweet, shrill singing of her baby daughter, chanting with much spirit and "go," the ballad of the "Ten Little Injun Boys"—hears the ear-splitting workmen's whistle—and still stands rapt and motionless, though the night has long since fallen, and all the room and all the street is dark.

But Mlle. Mimi belongs to the public, and a couple of hours later, flashes before it in all the wonted bravery of tinsel and glitter, and even eclipses herself in the matter of hazardous flying leaps on the trapeze, and daring doings on the dizzy slack-wire. All trace of that darkly-brooding cloud of thought has vanished from her *riante* face, and at the after-circus supper she outsparkles her sparkling self, and returns home after one, flushed and excited, as usual, with the amber vintages of France, as furnished by the Hotel Washington, and paid for by Mr. Lacy.

For Mrs. Hopkins, keeper of the most respectable temperance boarding-house in the good New England town of Clangville, it is the bitterest trial of her life. And she is powerless to help herself; the sting lies there. Mrs. Hopkins is total abstinence or she is nothing, the most daring foundry hand never returns muddled more than once. "There is the door," says Mrs. Hopkins, with flashing eyes, "and here is you. You git!" There is something in this Spartan brevity that takes down the biggest and blackest hand of them all. But Mlle. Mimi absolutely laughs in her face. "My good soul," she says, "don't put yourself in a passion. I intend to go when my week is up, not an hour sooner, I require stimulants, prescribed by my medical attendant, I assure you. The life I lead is frightfully exhausting. I am not going to change my habits and injure my health to accommodate your old-fashioned prejudices, my very dear Madam Hopkins."

There is nothing for it but to suffer and be strong. Aunt Samantha knocks under to the inevitable, and counts every hour until the blessed one of her happy release.

.   .   .   .

"Land o' hope!" cries out, despairingly, Mrs. Hopkins. "Jemima Ann, *will* you look at this! Of all the shameful creeters,"—a hollow groan finishes the sentence —words are weak to express her sense of reprobation.

Jemima Ann looks. She is not so easily scandalized as Aunt Samantha, and in her heart of hearts, rather envies Mimi her "right good time," but even she is startled at what she beholds. An open, double-seated carriage, bright with varnish, is flashing past; and perched high on the driver's seat, beside the renowned Mr. Lacy, holding the reins, and "hi-ing" to four spirited horses, is Mlle. Mimi. An expert whip she evidently is, and remarkably jaunty and audacious she looks, a pretty hat set coquettishly on the gilded hair, a cigarette between her rosy lips, she smokes with gusto while she drives. Behind sits one of the Bounding Brothers and his young woman, also with cigarettes alight, and loud laughter ringing forth, and as they fly past, the whole deeply shocked town of Clangville seems to rush to their doors and windows, to catch a glimpse of the demoralizing vision.

"I knew she smoked," Jemima Ann remarks, in a subdued voice; "she does in her own room sometimes of an afternoon."

Mrs. Hopkins sinks into a chair, faint with despair. *What* will this reckless creature do next?

"She'll give the house a bad name," she says, weakly, "and there don't seem nothin' I can do to prevent it. To sit up there, drivin' two team of rarin', prancin' horses, smokin' cigars, and likely 's not half tight. I'll go over to Rogers this very minute and give *him* a piece of my mind anyhow."

The landau, with its four laughing, smoking occupants flashes out of town, leaving the coal smoke, the noise, and black grime of foundries and manufactories far behind, and whirls along a pleasant country road, trees on every hand, brilliant with the crimson and orange glories of bright October.

"Does anybody happen to know a place called The Cottage?" asks Mimi, "the residence, I believe, of one Mrs. or Madam Valentine?"

"I do," replies Mr. Lacy. "I've met young Valentine; dused stiff young prig; puts on airs of British nobility—'aw, don't you know, my deah fellah'—that sort of thing. Felt like kicking him on the only occasion we met. Sour-looking, black-looking beggar! But he lives right out here, with his grandmother, or fairy godmother, or something."

"His aunt, my friend; be definite. There is a painful lack of lucidity in your remarks, Lacy," says Mimi "Well, I want to stop at The Cottage. I am going to make a call. Don t ask questions; it is my whim; that is enough for *you*. Madam Valentine is a real *grande dame*, so they tell me, and I've never had the pleasure of meeting one of the breed. So I am going to call, and see for myself. I may never have another chance."

"You have the audacity of the devil," says Mr. Lacy, with artless admiration. "By George! I should like to see the old lady's face when you announce yourself. Judging from what I hear, and from the look of that black-visaged nephew, she is more like a venerable empress run to seed than an every-day, rich old woman. Shall we all call, or will you go it alone?"

Mimi responds that she will go it alone. Her cigarette is smoked out. Mr. Lacy lights her another, as she pulls the four prancing bays up at the gates of The Cottage.

Her pretty face is slightly paler than usual; her lips are set in a tight line; a somber light, that bodes no good to the lady she proposes to visit, is in her blue eyes. She sits a moment, and scans the house and grounds."

"Not much of a place," remarks Mr. Lacy, slightingly; "only a shootin'-box for the black boy—I mean the nephew. Lots of space, though; could be made a tip-top country-seat if they liked. Want to get down?"

Mimi waves his hand aside, and leaps lightly to the ground.

"Wait for me here," she says, and out of her voice all the snap and *timbre* have gone—"or no; drive on, and come back in half an hour. I will be ready for you then."

"Wish we had an old shoe to throw after you for luck, Mimi," calls out the Bounding Brother. "Don't let the Ogress of the Castle eat you alive if you can help it."

"And don't fall in love with the high-toned nephew," says the young person by his side.

"Or, what is the more likely, don't let the high-toned nephew fall in love with you," adds Mr. Lacy. "Sure to do it once he sets eyes on you. Ta, ta, Mimi! Speak up prettily to the old lady. Don't be ashamed of yourself."

She waves her cigarette, opens the iron gates, and enters. The carriage and four-in-hand whirl on—vanish.

With the yellow afternoon sun sifting down on her through the lofty maples and larches, Mimi, with head defiantly erect, and blue eyes dangerously alight, walks up to the front door of The Cottage.

CHAPTER V.

IN WHICH WE VISIT MADAM VALENTINE.

T is an unpretentious building, as its name im-
plies, a low, white frame structure, with a
"stoop," or veranda, running the whole length
of its front; set in wide, wild grounds, and
nothing anywhere to betoken that the lady, who is mistress there, is a lady of great wealth, and still greater
dignity and social distinction. There are great beds of
gorgeous, flaunting dáhlias, Mimi notices, and other beds
of brilliant geraniums: no other flowers. Two great
dogs start up at her approach, and bark loudly; otherwise it is all still, in its afternoon hush, as the Castle of
the Sleeping Beauty. But human life is there, too, and
not asleep. A lady, slowly pacing up and down the
long stoop in the warm sunshine, pauses, turns, stands,
looks, and waits for the visitor to approach.

It is Madam Valentine herself. Mimi knows it at a
glance, though she has never seen her before. But she
has seen her picture, and heard her described, ah! many
times. She is a tall, spare old lady, with silvery hair,
combed high over a roll, *à la* Pompadour, silvery, severe
face, made vivid by a pair of piercing dark eyes. She
wears a dress of soundless, lusterless black silk, that
sweeps the boards behind her. She looks like one born
to rich, soundless silks, and priceless laces, and diamond
rings. Many of these sparkle on the slender white
hands, folded on the gold knob of her ebony cane, as
she stands and waits. A lofty, stately figure, her trained
robe trailing, her jewels gleaming; but her majesty of
bearing is altogether lost on her daring and dauntless
visitor. With her fair head well up and back, her blue
eyes alight smiling defiance in every feature, and still

smoking, straight up and on marches Mimi, until the two women stand face to face.

The dogs, at a sign from their mistress, have ceased barking, and crouch, growling, near. The cottage rests in its afternoon hush, the long shadows of the western sun fall on and gild the two faces—one so fair, so youthful, so bold, so reckless; the other so stern, so old, so set, so proud. Madam Valentine breaks the silence first.

"To whom have I the pleasure of speaking?" she asks, her voice as hard as her face, deep and strong almost as a man's.

"You don't know me," Mimi says, airily; "well, that is your fault. *I* never was proud. Still, you might recognize me, I think. Look hard, Madam Valentine; look again, and as long as you like. I am used to it; it's in my line of business, you know; and tell me did you never see any one at all like me?"

She removes her cigarette, knocks off the ash daintily with her little finger-tip, and holds it poised, as she stands at ease, a smile on her face, and stares straight into Madam Valentine's eyes.

"I do not know you," that lady answers in accents of chill disgust. "I have no wish to know you. If you have any business, state it, and go."

"Hospitable!" Mimi laughs, "and polite. So, you do not know me, and have no desire to know me? Well, I can believe *that.* No, you do not know me. You never met me before, but I have every reason to believe you have heard a great deal of me. I think your elderly housekeeper knows who I am; she looked as if she did yesterday afternoon."

Madam Valentine takes a step back, a sudden change passes over her face—a sudden wild fear comes into her eyes. And it has chanced to few people ever to see Madam Valentine look afraid.

"My God!" she says, under her breath, "is it—is it——"

3

"George's wife.   Yes, my dear mother-in-law.   You
behold your daughter !   I am Mary Valentine—known
to the circus-going world as Mimi Trillon.   For professional reasons a French name has hitherto suited me
best, but my reputation is made now as a dashing trapezist, and tight-rope dancer, and I am tired of sailing
under false colors.   I propose from this day forth assum-
ing my own name.   'Mrs. George Valentine' will look
well on the bills, I think, and sounds solid and respectable.   Unless—*unless*,"—she pauses, and the blue eyes
flash out upon the black ones with a look of spite and
hatred not good to see.   "I owe you something these last
eight years, Madam Valentine, and I have vowed a vow
to pay my debt.   But I am willing, after all, to forget
and forgive—on one condition.   Do you know I have a
child ?"

There is no reply.   Abhorrence, hatred, disgust, look
at her out of Madam Valentine's dark, glowing eyes.

"A little girl of three years and three months—
George's daughter—your only grandchild, madam ; the
heiress, if right is done, of every farthing you possess.
I love my child ; provide for her, provide for me ; you
count your wealth by millions ; I drudge like a galley
slave.   Buy me off ; I don't use fine phrases, you see,
and I have my price.   Buy me off from the circus.   It is
not half a bad life for me, but for my little girl's sake,
and for the honor of the highly respectable family I have
married into, I will quit it.   But at a fair price—a carriage, servants, diamonds, a fixed and sufficient annuity
—all that.   And you may take your granddaughter and
place her at school ; I shall not object, mothers must
sacrifice their own feelings for the good of their children.
Do all this, and I promise to forget the past, and trouble
you no more."

She pauses.   Madam Valentine still stands, but more
erect, if possible, her hands resting one over the other on
the top of her cane, her face as set as steel.

"If you have finished," is her icy answer, "go !"
A flush of rage crimsons Mimi's face. She plants
her little feet, and comes a step closer to her foe.
"I have not finished !" she cries, fiercely ; "this is one
side of the medal—let me show you the reverse. Refuse
—treat me with scorn and insult, as you have hitherto
done, and by this light I swear I'll make you repent it !
I ll placard your name—the name you are all so proud
of—on every dead wall, and every fence, in every newspaper, the length and breadth of the land ! I'll proclaim
from the house-tops whose daughter-in-law I have the
honor to be, whose wife I have been, whose widow I am !
For you know, I suppose, that your son is dead?"

The haughty, inflexible old face changes for a moment, there is a brief quiver of the thin, set lips—then
perfect repose again.

"Yes, he is dead," goes on Mimi, "killed by your
hardness and cruelty. He was your only son, but you
killed him with your pride. It must be a consoling
thought that, in your childless old age ! But you have
your nephew—I forgot—he is to have poor George's
birthright. *He* perished in misery and want, Madam
Valentine, and his last thought was for you. It will
comfort you on your own death-bed, one of these days,
to remember it. Now choose—will you provide for my
future and for my child's, or shall I proclaim to the
world who I am, and what manner of woman are you?"

"Will you go?" repeats Madam Valentine, in the
same voice of icy contempt, "or must I set my dogs on
you to drive you out?"

"If you dare !" cries Mimi, her face ablaze. "I defy
you and your dogs ! I shall remain in Clangville until
Saturday—this is Thursday—I give you until Saturday
to decide. If I do not hear from you before I leave this
place, look to the consequences ! The whole country
shall know my story ; the world shall judge between us.
My story shall be told in every way in which it is pos-

sible to tell it, the story of the wronged wife, and the
mother who murdered her only son! You are warned!
I wish you good-day, and a very good appetite for your
dinner, Madam' Valentine!"

She takes her skirts after the stately old fashion, and
sweeps a profound and mocking courtesy. Then singing as she goes a snatch of a drinking song, and walking
with an exaggerated swagger, she marches back to re-
join her friends, by this time waiting at the gate.

Madam Valentine stands and looks after her, a lofty,
lonely, dark-draped figure, in the yellow waning light.
So still she stands, her hands folded on the top of her
gold and black cane, that it is nearly half an hour before
she wakes from her trance.

The lengthy afternoon shadows are at their longest,
the October wind sighs fitfully through the trees, the
air grows sharp and frosty, but she feels no chill, sees no
change. The dead seems to have arisen, her drowned
son has come from his grave and spoken to her through
this woman's lips—this low-born, low-bred, violent creature, this jumper of horizontal bars, this rough rider of
horses! This is the wife he has wedded, the daughter he
has given her, the mother of the last daughter of the
house of Valentine! If vindictive little Mimi, laughing,
jesting, smoking, driving four-in-hand, loudly and reck-
lessly all the way back, could but read the heart she has
left behind, even *her* vengeance would ask no more!

CHAPTER VI.

WHICH INTRODUCES MR. VANE VALENTINE.

HE rouses herself at last, and goes in, shivering in the first consciousness she has yet felt of the rising wind. It is dusk already in the hall, but the sitting-room she enters is lit by a bright wood fire. The last pale primrose glitter of the western sky shows through the muslin curtains of the one bay-window—a window with no womanly litter of bird-cages and flower-pots, or fancy-work. And yet it is a cozy room, and sufficiently home-like, with an abundance of books and magazines strewn everywhere, many pictures on the papered walls, and half a dozen chairs of the order *pouf.*

She pulls the bell-rope in crossing to her own particular seat, and sinks wearily into its downy depths, in front of the fire. She still rests upon her cane, and droops a little forward, but the stern old face keeps its hard frigidity of look, and shows little more trace of suffering than a face cut in gray stone.

"Jane," she says, quietly, to the woman who appears, "send Mrs. Tinker to me."

Jane says "Yes'm," and goes. The dark, resolute eyes turn to the fire and gaze into its ruddy depths, until the door reopens, and the housekeeper, fluttered and nervous, enters. She has caught a glimpse of the visitor, and stands almost like a culprit before her mistress.

Madam Valentine eyes her for a moment as she stands smoothing down her black silk apron with two restless old hands.

"Susan," she says, in the same quiet tone, "I have had a caller. You may have seen her—you may even have heard her, she spoke loudly enough. She men

tioned you incidentally in something she said—spoke of
your recognizing her, or something of the kind. Do you
know who I mean ?"

" Mistress, I am afeard I do."

" You have seen this—this person, then—where ?"

"She lodges with my cousin in the town, ma'am—
leastways she was poor, dear Tinker's cousin, afore he
departed ; she keeps a boardin'-house, which her name it
is Samantha Hopkins——"

Madam Valentine waves her hand impatiently—a
hand that flashes in the fire-light. Samantha Hopkins
is something less than nothing to her.

"She lodges in Clangville, and you have seen her.
Have you spoken to her?"

" Oh, no, ma'am, no—not for the world ! And—and
I didn't know she knew *me*."

"How did you know her?"

" Mistress," in a low tone, "I used to see— I often
saw—her picture with—with Master——"

Again the white, ringed hand flashes in the fire-light,
quickly—angrily, this time.

"Stop ! I want to hear no names. Do you know who
she claims to be ?"

" Mistress, yes," still very low.

" Do you believe it ?" the voice this time sharp with
angry pain.

" Oh, my dear mistress, I am afeard—I am afeard—I
do !"

A pause.   The fire leaps and sparkles, and gilds the
pictures on the walls, and brings out in its vivid glow
the faces of the two women, mistress and servant.   The
last gray light of the waning day lingers on these two
gray old faces—one so agitated, so tear-wet, so stricken
with sorrow and shame—one in its chill, pale pride,
showing nothing of the agony within.

"You recognized her at first sight," says Madam Valentine, mastering her voice with an effort—*it* is hardly as

well trained as her face—"without a word—from the photographs you used to see?"

"I did, ma'am."

"Then I suppose there can be no mistake. I would not have believed that—that person's word. You know there is a child?"

"I saw her, madam. Oh, my dear mistress, I saw her! —Master George's own little child! Oh! my heart! my heart!"

She breaks down suddenly, and covering her old face with her old hands, sobs as if her heart would break. Madam Valentine's face changes, works, and turns quite ghastly as she listens and looks.

"Oh, forgive me!" Mrs. Tinker sobs, "my own dear mistress. I have no right to cry and distress you in your sore trouble, but I loved him so! And to see her—that pretty, pretty little one, and to know that he was dead, my bright, bonny boy, and that *she* was his child—oh! my mistress, it goes near to break my heart. Don't 'ee be angry wi' me, I am only an old woman, and I held him in my arms many and many a time, and my own flesh and blood could never be dearer than my dearest Master George!"

"You may go, Susan."

She speaks with measured quiet, but not coldly nor impatiently.

"And you are not angry wi' me? Oh! mistress, don't 'ee be angry—don't 'ee, now! Indeed, and in very deed, I——"

"I am not angry. You are a good soul, Tinker. I have a great respect for you. When Mr. Vane comes in send him to me at once."

"He is here now, ma'am. I hear his steps in the 'all."

A slow, rather heavy step, is indeed audible, and a man's voice calls through the utter dusk for somebody to show a light.

"Yes," says madam, listening, "tell him to come in here, before he goes to his room to dress for dinner."

"Shall I send in lamps, ma'am ?"

"No—not until I ring. The twilight is enough."

Mrs. Tinker, wiping her eyes, departs, and her mistress turns her brooding gaze once again upon the fire. A very somber gaze.

All her life of fifty years and more, this woman has been trained to self-repression, and in this supreme hour she is true to her training and traditions.

He would be a keen observer, who, at this moment, could read what she is enduring in her still face. And yet she has been a mother, a passionately loving mother, and all the martyrdom of maternity is rending her heart in this hour. But of all the men in the world, the man who enters now, is the very last to whom she will show it.

He is Vane Valentine, a young Englishman, a nephew of her late husband, and the last male of the Valentine race, heir-at-law to a baronetcy, and heir presumptive of Catherine Valentine's millions, *vice* George Hamilton Valentine, cashiered and deceased.

He is a slim, dark young man, not much over twenty, with a sallow, thin face, a thin aquiline nose, a thin, rather womanish mouth, a thin, black mustache, and thin black hair, parted down the middle.

Thinness and blackness, indeed, at the present stage of his existence, are the most salient points about him, if you except a certain expression of obstinacy about the whole face, and an air of hauteur, amounting almost to insolence in everything he says and does.

The pride of these Valentines, for that matter, is quite out of proportion to their purse, if not to their pedigree, madam being the only member of the family out of the absolute reach of poverty—but pride and poverty run in harness together often enough.

He comes in quickly, surprised at Mrs. Tinker's mes

sage, for madam, in a general way, is not over fond of him, does not greatly affect his society, and *never* sends for him.

" You are not ill, aunt?" he inquires.

He speaks with something of a drawl, but not an affected one. He never has much to say for himself, so perhaps is wise to make the most of the little he has.

"Ill? No," she answers, contemptuously. "I am never ill. You should know that. I have sent for you to discuss a very serious matter. I consider you have a right to know, and perhaps—to decide. You may be my heir ; the honor of the Valentine name is in your keeping, and she threatens—Vane!" abruptly, "you know the story of—my son?"

"Unfortunately, yes. A very sad and shocking story," he answers, gravely.

He is standing by the mantel, leaning his elbow on it, facing her. She, too, steadfastly regards him.

"You were told as a matter of course when you first came. Not many people know it—it is a disgrace that has been well hidden. But it is a disgrace that all the world may soon know. That woman is here."

"Aunt !" he cries. "You do not mean to say—*not* the woman he——"

"Married. Yes. Once his wife, now his widow. And her little girl—his child."

"Good Heaven !" exclaims Vane Valentine.

Then there is silence. They look at one another across the red light of the fire, two proud, dark faces, confronting, with the same fear and pain in both.

"She is a circus performer—bare-back rider—trapezist—so she tells me. She dances on a tight-rope. She is everything that is brazen and bad, and vulgar and horrible. And she is extremely pretty. She is here with the circus in the town. She called at this house not more than two hours ago. And she threatens to proclaim to the whole country—in posters, in papers, in

3*

every way, that she is—has been—George Valentine's wife."

"Good Heaven!" says Mr. Vane Valentine.

It seems the only thing left him to say. He stands absolutely stunned by the tremendousness of the catastrophe. He stares at his aunt with dilating eyes, from which a very real horror looks.

"She calls herself Mimi Trillon at present. She lodges with Mrs. Tinker's cousin, in Clangville, and will remain until Saturday. After Saturday the whole world is to know who she is."

"Good Heaven!" repeats, blankly, Mr. Vane Valentine. It has been said his command of language is not great. "Can—can nothing be done, you know?" he asks in blankest accents. "I—I wouldn't for anything, by Jove!"

"She offers one alternative. I mentioned the child— a little girl. She may be bought off. Her price is the adoption, education, care of the child, and an annuity— a tolerably large one, I fancy, for herself. She is tired of her present life—so she says; she will leave it, give up the little girl, retain her incognito, and live on the annuity—if it is provided. Otherwise, she will proclaim her wrongs and her identity to all who choose to listen. That is her offer."

"By Jove!" says, still more blankly, Mr. Vane Valentine, "she is a cool hand. Mlle. Mimi Trillon—yes, I saw her name blazing all over the town, and her picture, too, by Jove! All bare neck and arms, like a grisette of Mabille. And *that* is George's widow? Good Heaven!"

"You have made that remark a number of times already," says, disdainfully, his aunt. "There is no use in standing there and saying, 'Good Heaven!' I fancy Heaven has very little to do with Mlle. Mimi Trillon. But she is the person she claims to be; there is no doubt of that. Tinker recognized her in a moment from the

photograph she used to see. She has been good enough
to give me until Saturday to come to a decision. I waive
my right to decide, and place the matter in your hands.
You have your full share of the Valentine pride, and you
are the last of the name. You will bear it—with honor,
I trust—when I am dead. Decide—do we agree or
refuse?"

Mr. Vane Valentine is not a fool; very far from it
where a point of family honor is concerned. He decides
with a promptitude his somewhat weak-looking mouth
would not seem to promise.

"We agree, of course. We *must* agree. Good Heaven!
there is no other course. If she is the person she professes to be, and has a right to the name—good God!
only to think of that—a circus rider! She must be
bought off at any price. Think of the publicity! think
of your feelings! think of *mine!* of my sister's—of
Camilla's—of—of everybody's—of Sir Rupert's! Good
Heaven! it's awful, don't you know. She *must* be bought
off at any price, and at once—at once!"

"Very well," responds the chilly voice of the lady.
"Do not excite yourself; there is no haste. We have
until Saturday, remember—two days. Do nothing to-
night; sleep upon it. At the same time, I may say, I
think with you. Money is nothing in a case like this.
She must be bought off; and at her own price."

"Of course," says, promptly, Vane Valentine; "but
I will make the best terms I can. The best will be bad,
no doubt. She must be a dused sharper all through!
It is well she will give up the child. A little girl, you
say? Aw, that is best, certainly," says Mr. Valentine,
stroking his thin, black mustache, and reflecting it might
have been "dused unpleasant and that" if George's
child had been a son. Inconceivable ass, George Valentine—doing the all for love and the world well lost business in the nineteenth century, when passions and emotions, and—aw—that sort of thing, are extinct."

But the ill-wind has blown him (Vane) into a prospective fortune and title, so he is not disposed to quarrel with the shade of his late idiotic cousin, nor even with his rascally relict, if he can buy that lady off at a fair price.

"I'll go to the circus this evening," he says, after that ruminative pause, "and take a look at her. Pretty, is she, you say? But of course ; that was the reason—confound her!—that she fooled your—*him!* Yes, it is well she will resign the child. She, of course, is not a proper person to bring up a little girl, and, aw, a relative of ours. Good Heaven! to think of it! I will see her, and settle this, aw, dused unpleasant business, you know, for good and all."

"Very well," madam says, wearily; "and I think, if you will excuse me, I will not dine this evening. I will have a cup of tea here, and retire early. I over-fatigued myself this afternoon, I fancy."

It is a tired and aching heart that weighs down Madam Valentine, not her afternoon constitutional in the sunshine, up and down the stoop. Perhaps Vane Valentine guesses—he has more penetration than he looks to have. He murmurs a few appropriate words of regret, and, a little later, goes to the dining-room, and eats his dinner in solitary state, somewhat gloomy and preoccupied, but with a very good appetite. Then, as the starry October night falls mistily over the world, puts on his light overcoat, and sets out at a brisk walk for the town, the circus, and his first sight of Mlle. Mimi Trillon.

CHAPTER VII.

WHICH TREATS OF LOVE'S YOUNG DREAM.

HE moon is shining brightly as he quits the cottage, a frosty moon, and the sky is all alight with stars. Mr. Vane Valentine glances approvingly upward as he lights a cigar, and opines he will have a pleasant night for his return walk. His step rings like steel on the hard ground, and reaches the ear of madam, sitting alone and lonely before the fire. She glances after him—a tall, slender figure—and in that look, for one instant, there flashes out something strangely akin to aversion. For he stands in the stead of her son, her only son, her bright, brave, handsome, joyous George, the latchet of. whose shoes, at his worst, this stiff young prig is unworthy to loose. Yet the aversion is unjust; it is no fault of Vane Valentine's that he is here, he has neither sought for, nor forced himself into the position, rather his kinship has been thrust upon him, and Katherine Valentine knows it well. But her spirit is sore to-night, she is a very desolate woman, with all her pride, and pedigree, and wealth, an old, a lonely, a widowed, a childless woman. The cruel words of that other—George's wife—George's wife! how strange the thought—nay, George's widow—the woman he has loved, has married, the mother of his child, ring in her ears, and will not be exorcised.

"You murdered him! You left him to perish in want! You killed him with your pride!" Oh! God, is it true? George in want—suffering—dying! A low, moaning cry, strange, and dreary, and terrible to hear, breaks from her lips, she covers her face with her hands there as she sits alone. Here, with no eye to see, no ear to hear, her pride may drop from her for a little, and love and memory awake. Firelight and moonlight meet and mingle in the room, a fitting spectral light for ghosts to rise out of their graves and keep her company. The house is very still, the servants, with Mrs. Tinker, are at supper. Vane Valentine is on his way to the circus, excited and stimulated by the thought of beholding the adventuress who erstwhile fooled his infatuated Cousin George. Here, alone, she is free to break her heart in silence, after the fashion of some strong women. To-morrow she will be cold and hard, no trace of weakness or tears will betray her—to-night she is at liberty, and tears as bitter, as burning as ever childish mother shed, wet the pale cheeks as she sits and thinks.

It is not such a long story, this tragedy, to think over —the tragedies of life are mostly briefly told. To Katherine Valentine it is but as yesterday since she last kissed her son—in reality it is eight years since he gave up father, mother, home, friends, name, a fortune—all that men hold best worth the keeping, for sake of the pink and white face, the bold, blue eyes, and flaxen hair she saw a few hours ago.

Let me tell you the story she thinks out, sitting here, a bowed and forsaken figure, that Vane Valentine ruminates over, with contemptuous wonder on his way to the circus—the old story of a " young man married, a young man married."

Some forty years before this starry October night, another Valentine—Austin Mordred Valentine—said good-by to old England, to Valentine Manor, to his elder brother, Sir Rupert, and sailed for the new world to seek his fortune. Literally to seek his fortune, and fully resolved to find it. He was twenty years old, good-looking, well educated, fairly clever, possessed of plenty of British pluck and " go," and backbone ; not afraid of plodding, of waiting, of hard work, absolutely determined to succeed.

That sort of man does succeed. Austin Valentine

succeeded beyond even his most sanguine expectations, and like all men of ability believed implicitly in himself. He took to trade, the first of the name of Valentine who had ever so demeaned himself. They had been free-booters, raiders, hard fighters, hard hunters, hard spend-thrifts; had been soldiers, sailors, rectors, lived hard, died hard, distinguished themselves in many ways, but tradesmen none of them had been, until young Austin threw off the traditions and shackles of centuries, eman-cipated himself, took this new departure, demeaned him-self, and made his fortune.

It was time, too, for the Valentine guineas had come to a very low ebb. Riotous living is apt to empty al-ready depleted coffers. Sir Rupert, with every inch of land mortgaged, the manor rented, wandering about the Continent, striving drearily to make the most of nothing, was perhaps a greater object of compassion than Austin in the shipping business and fur trade, with wealth roll-ing in like a golden river, a millionaire already at thirty years. But Sir Rupert did not think so.

From the heights of his untarnished position, as one of the oldest baronets of the baronetage, he looked in honor from the first, on his only brother's decadence, spoke of him always as "poor Austin," and to do him justice declined to avail himself in any way of such ill-gotten gain. Austin laughed; he was philosophical as well as shrewd, went on the even tenor of his wealthy way, and finally at three-and-thirty looked about him for a wife.

He found one there in Toronto ready to his hand, a *rara avis*, possessing in herself every quality he most desired in a wife—beauty, family, high-breeding, an ancient name. Her father was Colonel Hamilton, she was the eldest of a family of daughters, scantily provided for. Like the Valentines, the Hamiltons were uncomfortably poor and proud.

The young lady had many suitors, was a belle and a

"toast" in the rather exclusive circle in which she moved, but from the first Austin Valentine stood to win. Nothing succeeds like success. His name, his family, his good looks, his riches, all were in his favor.

Colonel Hamilton moved with the world, and had no patrician's scruples in regard to the shipping interest and vast fur trade with Indians and trappers, whatever the stately Katherine may have had.

But she was a prudent young lady, too; not so very young either, seven-and-twenty perhaps, and there were all the younger ones, and life was rather a dingy affair in the crowded household, and, besides, she was not sentimental at all; but she really—well—had a very sincere regard and—and esteem (it is difficult to find the correct word) for Mr. Austin Valentine.

She said yes when he proposed, and looked quite regal in her white satin and point laces and pearls, every one said, on her wedding-day.

They went abroad for a year, met Sir Rupert still drearily economizing on the Continent, and the bridegroom received his forgiveness and blessing and two lean fingers to shake. He even promised to come over and visit them "some time," an indefinite period that never arrived.

They visited Manor Valentine, which fine ancestral old place Mrs. Austin resented seeing in the possession of aliens, much more than either of the brothers.

"I'll pay off these confounded mortages, and come and live here one day," said Mr. Austin, coolly.

"And I shall be Lady Valentine," thought his bride.

For all the world knew Sir Rupert never meant to marry—did not care for that sort of thing—was a confirmed invalid, hypochondriac rather, absorbed in himself and his many ailments.

But "creaking doors hang long"—confirmed invalids are mostly tenacious of life, and Mrs. Austin never became my Lady Valentine

On this October night Austin Valentine has lain for years under the turf, while the hypochondriacal elder brother is still on it, and likely indefinitely there to remain.

They returned to Toronto and set up house-keeping on a princely scale.

Katherine Valentine amply renumerated herself for the dingy years of her maiden life. She spent money lavishly, extravagantly, on every whim and caprice, until even generous Austin winced. But he signed the big checks and laughed.

Let it go—she did honor to him, to his name, to their position as leaders of society—her tastes were æsthetic, and æsthetic tastes are mostly expensive.

Everything turned to gold in his hands, he was a modern Midas without the ass' ears. Let her spend as she might the coffers would still be full.

And then after ten years a son was born.

When a prince of the blood is born, cannons boom, bells ring, and the world throws up its hat and hoorays. None of these things were done when Katherine Valentine's son came into the world, but it was an event for all that.

Toronto talked, there was feasting below stairs, there were congratulations from very august quarters, a governor-general and an earl's daughter were his sponsors, the christening presents were something exquisite. Sir Rupert wrote a very correct letter from Spa—a weak little pean of rejoicing, but very warmly welcomed. He looked on the boy as his successor, hoped he would grow up to be an honor to the name of Valentine—had no doubt of it with such a mother, trusted he inherited some of her beauty, must be excused from sending anything more substantial than good wishes, the distance, etc.

They named the baby George, after his paternal grandfather—George Hamilton Valentine it stood on the record, and the happiness of Austin and Katherine Valentine was complete. Surely if ever a child came into the world with the traditional silver spoon in its mouth, it was this one. He *did* inherit his mother's statuesque beauty—he was an uncommonly handsome child, healthy, merry—a boy to gladden any mother's heart.

Years passed—there was no other child. It can be imagined, perhaps, the life this "golden youth" led, it can hardly be described. And yet he was not spoiled. Idolizing his mother might be, but judicious she was also, and very firm—firmness was a salient point of her character. But she loved him, he was the one creature on earth she ever *had* absolutely loved—she loved him with all her heart and strength, and mind and soul, as saints ove God, as He above should be loved. No human heart can make a human idol, and not pay the penalty even here below, in heart-break and despair. And Madam Valentine was no exception. She would not have him sent abroad to school. His uncle, Sir Rupert, wished him to go to Eton and Oxford, as an English lad, and a future baronet, should, but neither father nor mother could bear their darling out of their sight. The boy himself wished it ; he was a bold, bright, fearless little fellow at ten, with big, black, laughing eyes, a curly crop of black brown hair, the whitest teeth, the most genial laugh in the world. Even if he had not been a prince by right divine of his birth and heirship, he would still have been charming with that frank bonny face, and winsome smile and glance. He was born a prince by right of that kingly brow, and handsome face—he won all hearts—even as a beggar he would still have been born a conqueror. As heir to fabulous wealth, to a title, it is again more easy to imagine than describe *what* he was in the provincial city of Toronto.

He grew and prospered ; he had masters for every language, every science, every ology under the sun. He had his horse and his dogs, and he drove, and he rode, and he studied, or let it alone, and made glad the hearts of a doting man and woman. But mostly he studied, he was fairly industrious, he had his own notions of *noblesse oblige*, and what it became a prince to know ere he came into his kingdom. He had a resident tutor, besides these masters, he had a pretty taste for music, played the piano and sang, until his mother thought him a modern Mozart, did himself credit on 'the violin, painted a little, sketched a great deal, wrote Latin verses with fluency, spoke French and German. With it all he grew and grew ; shot up like Jack's beanstalk, indeed, and at eighteen stood five-feet-eleven, in his very much embroidered velvet slippers.

As a matter of course he broke hearts, though eighteen is full young for a gentleman to go energetically into that business. But the truth is, he could not help it. He looked and—played the mischief ! Those dark bright eyes that laughed so frankly on all the world, wrought sad havoc with sixteen-year-old hearts—indeed, with hearts old enough to know better.

He waltzed—" oh ! like an angel !" cried out a chorus of young soprano voices. He sang *deliciously*. He was past master of the art of croquet, of flirtation, of billiards, boating, archery, base-ball ; what was there he did *not* do to perfection? At eighteen and a half, his mother was not the only lady in the Canadian universe who thought the sun arose with *his* rising, and set when his bewildering presence disappeared.

And just here, when Eden was at its fairest, sunniest, sweetest, the serpent came, and after him—the deluge !

" Mother," said George Hamilton Valentine, one day at breakfast, " I think I shall take a run over the border, and spend a week or two in New York. Parker can come, too, if you think the wicked Gothamites will gobble your only one up alive. Too prolonged a course of Toronto is apt to pall on a frivolous mind."

Of course, she said Yes. He did pretty much as he pleased in eve.ything by this time. Even her gentle,

silken chain was felt as a fetter, and rebelled against.
He took the discreet resident tutor, Mr. Parker, and a
drawing-room car for New York.   But he did not return
in a week, nor in two, nor in three ; and at the end of
five, Mr. Parker wrote a letter, that fell like a bursting
bomb into the palatial. mansion at home, and caused a
message to flash over the wires with electric swiftness,
summoning the wanderers back.

They came back. Nothing was said. A glance of
intelligence passed between madam and the tutor ; then
she looked furtively, anxiously at her son. He was precisely the same as ever, in high health, fine spirits, and
full of his recent flying trip. The mother drew a deep
breath of relief. There was no change that she could
see. Only Mrs. Tinker, who had washed Master Georgie's
face at five years old, and combed his hair, and kissed
him to the point of extinction, saw a change. She did
more ; she saw *her* photograph. A confidant George
must have ; and after a hundred extorted vows of secrecy,
reducing Mrs. Tinker almost to the verge of tears with
protestations of eternal silence he forced from her, he
showed her the photographs. And Mrs. Tinker looked
at them, and shrieked a shriek, and covered her shocked
old eyes with her virtuous old hands. For—the hussy
had no clothes on, or next to none, or what Mrs. Tinker
considered none—never having seen the Black Crook, or
a ballet, or anything enlightened or Parisian, in her
stupid old life.

"Oh! Master George, my dear, how can you ! The
wicked, improper young—young person !" cried Mrs.
T nker, in strong reprobation ; "take them away, Master
Georgie, my dear—do'ee, now. I wonder at you for
showing me such things ! I do, indeed !"

"Oh, come, I say !" cries George, but being only a boy,
and nearly as innocent as Mrs. Tinker herself, he blushes
a fire red too. "Look here, you dear old goose ! Don't
you see she is in tights? How could she perform on the

trapeze with petticoats flapping about her heels? Here is one. Now, look at this; she has a dress on her—well, a costume; they're all in costume. Bother your modesty! You're old enough to know better! Look here, I say; did you ever in all your life see any one half so lovely?"

"I never saw any one half so indecent! Do you call that a dress—*that* thing! Why, it don't cover her nasty knees! Oh, my dear, my dear, take 'em away, and put 'em in the fire! She must be a little trollop to be took in that—that scandalous costoom, if that's its name. What would your blessed mamma say, Master George, if she saw them sinful pictures?"

"I say, look here," says Master George, rather alarmed, "don't you go and say anything to the mater about this. You're as good as sworn, you know. And I'll thank you not to call names, Mrs. Tinker. She's no more a trollop than—'than you are,'" is on the point of George's tongue, but having a general respect for old age, and a very particular respect for Mrs. Tinker, he suppresses it, and stands looking rather sulky.

"Bless the dear boy!" cries Mrs. Tinker, mollified at sight of her darling in dudgeon; "I won't, then, only, if she's a friend of yours, Master Georgie, do beg of her to put on her clothes next time! Do 'ee now, like a lovey!"

George laughs; it is not in his sunny, boyish nature to be irate for more than a minute at a time.

"I'll tell her," he says, gleefully; "she'll enjoy the joke. Tinker, she's just the jolliest, prettiest, sweetest little soul the sun shines on to-day! And she's the dearest friend I have in the world."

"Ah!" says Tinker, with a deep groan. "What's her name, Master George?"

"Mimi; isn't it a pretty name? It seems to suit her somehow. Mimi Trillon."

He pauses a dreamy rapturous look comes into his

eyes; a flush passes over his face. "Mimi! Mimi!" he repeats, softly, to himself.

Mrs Tinker knows the symptoms. At an early period of her career the fatal disease attacked herself. Tinker was the object, and she attained Tinker. He is dead and gone now, and it is thirty years ago, but Mrs. Tinker remembers, and a vague, and sudden, and great dread for her boy stirs within her.

"*What* is she, Master George?" she asks next.

"Well, she's—she's a professional lady," answers George.

The reply does not come fluently. He looks tenderly down at the picture he holds, as if he would like to kiss it while he speaks.

"She is not rich, she—she works for her living. She's—a sort of actress. But she's the dearest, prettiest little love in all the world."

"She looks like a jumping Jack!" cries out Mrs. Tinker, in the bitterness of her feeling, "and a misbehaved jumping Jack, at that!"

With which she goes, and George goes, too, laughing. She feels that duty bids her tell all this to Madam Valentine, but loyalty to Master George forbids; she cannot bring herself to tell tales of her boy. So she says nothing, but fears much, and trusts to time to set crooked things straight, and to absence to make this youthful swain forget.

But he does not forget; neither does the professional lady he met in New York, doing the flying trapeze. For, one day, some two months later, in pulling out his handkerchief, he pulls a letter out of his pocket, and quits the room without noticing it. It is his mother who chances to pick it up. The peaky, school-girlish looking scrawl surprises her.

"Dear old Georgie," it begins, and the signature is "Your ever-loving little 'Jumping Jack.'"

Madam Valentine, inexpressibly horrified, reads it

through, her face flashing with haughty amaze and disgust. Then another feeling—fear—comes, and turns her white to the very lips. Illy spelt, illy written, vulgar in every word, it is yet a love-letter—a love-letter in which a promised marriage is spoken of. The signature puzzles her. George has told his beloved Mrs. Tinker's fancy name for her, and it has tickled the erratic humor of the vivacious Mimi. She has adopted it.

"Some horrible pet name, no doubt," the lady thinks. "Gracious Heaven! what a strange infatuation for George!"

Nothing is said. Mr. Valentine is consulted, is shocked, is enraged, is panic-stricken, but his wife is convinced it is not yet too late. She will take him away, and at once—at once! They will go to Europe; he shall make the tour of the world, if necessary, with Sir Rupert; he shall *never* return to Toronto. What a mercy —what a direct interposition of Providence—that this letter fell into her hands when it did!

George is told the wish of his heart shall be gratified. He shall throw up study, and travel for the next three years. Uncle Rupert wishes it so much! She will go with him to Spa, where Sir Rupert at present is, will spend the winter in Italy, and return home in the spring. Is not George delighted?

George does not look delighted. Six months ago he would have done so, but we change in six months. He looks reflective, and a good deal put out, and goes up to his room and writes rather a long letter, and takes it to the post himself. Then he waits.

Preparations begin, go on rapidly; in a week they will be ready to start. But just two days before the week ends the terrible blow falls. He goes up to his room one night and—is seen no more! He makes a moonlight flitting, with a knapsack and a well-filled pocket-book. He is "o'er the border and awa' wi'"—

Mimi Trillon, the trapezist, the tight-rope dancer, the "fair girl graduate with golden hair" from the back slums of New York!

CHAPTER VIII.

LOST FOR A WOMAN.

E is gone! They do not hear from him for two weeks, and long days before that the marriage is an accomplished fact. He sends a copy of the *Herald* containing the marriage notice heavily inked, and a lengthy letter petitioning forgiveness—a long pean of praise of his beauteous bride. He calls her an actress—he wants to let them down gently, and come to the circus and the trapeze by degrees. It matters not—were she a queen of tragedy—as stainless as some queens of tragedy have been, it would still matter not. Utter ruin he's befallen, disgrace so deep that no condoning can be possible. He might have died in these gallant and golden days of his youth, and their hearts might have broken, but still broken proudly, and his memory been cherished as the one beautiful and perfect thing of earth—too perfect to last. That radiant memory would have consoled. Now there can be nothing of this. Blank ruin, utter misery, deepest shame, covers them as a garment—it is in their hearts to curse him in the first frenzy of woe. He is worse than dead, a thousand times worse. They burn his portrait, they erase his name from the family Bible, they hang from sight and existence everything that ever belonged to him, they tear his letters to atoms—they would cover their heads with ashes, and wear sackcloth if it could help them to forget. Their hearts go in sackcloth and

ashes, all the rest of their lives. The world of Toronto
is stirred to its deepest depths; it is more than a nine-
days' wonder—it is whispered with bated breath, and
awe-stricken faces, in very patrician families indeed, for
many and many a day.

And so George Valentine gives the world for love,
and his place knows him no more.

His father and mother live, and bear their misery and
shame, and after the first blow, show a brave front to the
world. It is in their nature. They hold themselves
more defiantly erect if possible, but he would be a brave
man who would venture to name their son to either of
them. And years go by, and richer and still richer
Austin Valentine grows, and Sir Rupert writes from
Nice in a despondent strain, that he is breaking fast, and
that the actress stands a chance of writing herself Lady
Valentine all too soon. Lady Valentine she may be—
curse her! Austin Valentine mutters, for he, too, is a
broken man, but never heir to his millions. He bethinks
him all at once of a youthful cousin, also a Valentine,
half forgotten until now, very poor, and living in a remote part of Cornwall, and sends for him at once, with
the assurance that if he pleases him he shall be his heir.

Vane Valentine comes, wondering, and hardly able
to realize his fairy future. He has been brought up in
poverty and obscurity—has never expected anything else.
Three lives stand between him and the baronetcy, Sir
Rupert, Austin, George—what chance has he? Take
away these three lives and give him the title—what is
there for him to keep it up on? No, Vane Valentine
has hoped for nothing, and Fate thrusts fortune in a moment into his hands.

He comes—a slim, dark youth of twenty, with good
manners, and not much to say for himself. A little stiff
and formal, his uncle (so he is told to term Mr. Austin
Valentine) finds him—a contrast in all ways to the heir
who is lost. All the better for that, perhaps; no chance

trick of resemblance will ever make their hearts bleed. It is a young man this, who will never do a foolish or a generous, or a reckless, or an unselfish thing; who will weigh well the name and status of the lady he marries; whose heart will never run away with his head.

"The heart of a cucumber fried in snow," quotes, contemptuously, Madam Valentine. "We need not be afraid of *him*. What a pompous young prig the little fool is!"

But Vane Valentine never dreams of the estimate these rich relations of his hold him in. He thinks exceedingly well of himself, and infers, with the complacent simplicity of extreme conceit, that all the world does the same. The Valentine blue blood runs in his calm veins, his manners and morals are of the best, his temper well under control, his taste in dress verging on perfection, his health good without being vulgarly robust, his education leaves nothing to be desired—what more will you?

He accepts with complacent ease the golden showers Fortune rains upon him, does not oppress his benefactress with words of gratitude, feels that Destiny has come to a sense of her duty, and that the "king has got his own again."

He writes long letters to Cornwall to his sister Dorothea, who has trained him since the death of his parents in early boyhood, and to a certain Cousin Camilla, of whom he is very fond, and whose picture he wears in a locket.

And Austin and Katherine Valentine accept him for what he is, and make the most of him; and all the time the aching void is there in their hearts, and aches and aches wearily the long year round.

Mr. Valentine visibly droops, breaks, retires from business, and begins that other business in whose performance we must all one day engage—the business of dying.

The name of the lost idol is never spoken between

this father and mother. If the waters of Lethe were no fable, they would drink of it greedily, and so forget. But they remember only the more, perhaps, for this unbroken silence.

Six months after the arrival of Vane Valentine his twentieth birthday occurs, and for the first time since the thunderbolt had riven their hearts, a party is given at Valentine House, in honor of the occasion. It is a dinner party, to which, in addition to the young people invited to meet the heir, many very great personages are bidden and come. It is a dinner party that Mrs. Tinker, for one, never forgets. Something occurs that night that is marked with a white stone forever after in her life.

No one has mourned the lost heir more deeply, more despairingly than she. Hers is gentler grief than that of the parents, it is unmixed with anger or bitterness—her tears flow at first in ceaseless streams.

She has loved her boy almost as dearly as his own mother, only with a love that has in it no pride, no baser alloy with its pure metal. She has loved and she has lost.

She is a stout, unromantic-looking old woman, but to love and lose is as bitter to her faithful heart, it may be, as though she were a slim, sentimental maid of sixteen.

Her handsome Master George, her bonny boy, the apple of her eye and the pride of her life—what was the world without him!

And on this night of the birthday *fête* some bitter drops rain from the royal old eyes at the thought of the days and the heir forever gone.

She has resented the coming of this young usurper from the first, but she has resented in silence, of course—she has never liked him, she would feel it as treason to her lost darling to like him even if he were likeable.

But he is not, he is black-a-vised, he is 'aughty, he

has a nasty, stiff way with servants, he is stingy, he loves money.

Yes he loves money Mrs. Tinker decides with disgust, he has been brought up to count every penny he spends, and he counts them yet.   He will not let himself lack for anything, but he never gives away, he never throws a beggar a penny, nor a servant a tip.   He is profuse in his "Aw—thanks," but this politeness is the only thing about him he is lavish of.

So on this night of the dinner party, when Mr. Vane is twenty, and all the city is called upon to feast and rejoice, Mrs. Tinker sits in her own comfortable little room, and wipes her eyes and her glasses, and looks at the fire, and shakes her head, and is dismally retrospective.

It is a March night, and the wildest of its kind.   It is late in the month, and March is going out like a lion, roaring like Bottom, the weaver, "so that it would do any man's heart good to hear him."

It might, if the man were seated like Susan Tinker at a cheery coal fire, a cup of tea and a plate of buttered toast at her elbow, but if he were breasting the elemental war, as was the man who slowly made his way to a side entrance of the great house—it also might not.

A tall man, in a rough great-coat, and fur cap, striding along in the teeth of the wind and sleet, over the slippery city pavements, and who rang the bell of the side door, and shrunk back into the shadow as it was answered.

One of the men-servants opened it, and peered out into the wild blackness of the night.

"Well, my man," he said, espying the tall, dark shadow, "and what may you want, you know?"

"I want to see Mrs. Tinker.   She lives here, doesn't she?" the shadow replied.

"Well she do," the footman admits, leisurely; "but

whether she'll want to see you—what's your business my good fellar?"

"My business is with Mrs. Tinker. Just go and tell her I have a message for her I think she will be glad to hear—·my good fellar!" in excellent imitation of the pompous tone of Plush. "And look sharp, will you? It is not exactly a balmy evening in June."

"Well, it's *not*," says Plush, reflecting as if that fact strikes him now for the first time. "I'll tell her," and goes.

The shadow leans wearily against the door and waits. Dinner is over above stairs, and music, and coffee, and conversation are on. Some lines he has read, somewhere, long before, and forgotten until this moment, start up in his mind, as he stands and looks with tired, haggard eyes, up at these gleaming and lace-draped windows.

> " I note the flow of the weary years
>   Like the flow of this flowing river,
> But dead in my heart are its hopes and fears
>   Forever and forever !
> For never a light in the distance gleams,
>   No eye looks out for the rover,
> Oh ! sweet be your sleep, love, sweet be your dreams,
>   Under the blossoming clover,
> The sweet-scented, bee-haunted clover !"

A strange, sudden pang rends his heart.

"Oh, God !" he cries out, "am I indeed forgotten ! They feast and make merry, and I—well, I have earned it all. Even my mother—but mothers forget too, when their hearts are wrung and broken, and she had always more pride than love. And through both her love and pride, I stabbed her. Forgotten ! what other fate have I deserved than to be forgotten !"

"You wanted me, my friend?" says a gentle voice, a dear old voice he remembers well, and a sob rises in his throat as he hears it again after long years. He looks from under the visor of his fur cap, and sees Mrs. Tinker.

She is alone, the tall, plush young man has been sum·
moned to upper spheres. No one is near. He takes a
step forward.

"Hush!" he says; "do not be alarmed — do not
scream. Look at me—have *you*, too, forgotten me, Mrs.
Tinker?"

He lifts his fur cap ; the gas-flare falls upon his face.
Forgotten him! Oh! never, never, never! She clasps
her hands, there is a wordless, sobbing sound, not
scream. She stands with dilated eyes, and joy—joy unutterable, making the old face beautiful.

"Dear old friend, yes, I see you remember. It is
your scapegrace—your runaway 'Master Georgie' come
back."

"Oh, my dear, my dear, my dear!" is all Mrs. Tinker
can say. And now down the wrinkled cheeks tears roll
—tears of joy beyond all words. "Oh! my own boy! my
own boy—my own dear, dear, dearest Master George!"

He takes the old hand, wrinkled, toil-worn, and
kisses it.

"Always my friend—my true, good, loyal old friend!
Thank God! some one remembers me. It is more than
I deserve though—more than I ever expected."

"Oh, my own love! my own dear, brave, bright
beautiful boy! don't'ee talk like that! Don't'ee, now—
it do nigh break my heart. Oh, Master George! Master
George! I'm fit to die wi' joy. I know'd you'd come
back to see the mother some day—I always said so.
Thanks and praise be! But come in, come in. It's your
own house, and I'm keepin' you here."

"*My* own house, Mrs. Tinker!" he says, with a dreary
laugh. "My good soul, I have not a garret in the world
I can call my own."

But he lets her lead him in, and shivers as he passes
out of the bleak, sleety night.

"Oh, my dear, how wet you are! and how pale, and
thin, and fagged like, now that I see you in the light!

My dear, my dear, my own Master George ! how changed you are !"

" Changed !" he says. " Good Heavens, yes ! If you knew the life I have led—— But we cannot stand talking here—some of the servants will be passing, and I must not be seen. Take me somewhere where we can talk undisturbed, and where I may get warm ; I am chilled to the bone."

Her eyes are running over again. The change in him ! Oh, the change in him !—so worn, so jaded, so hollow-eyed, so poorly-clad, so utterly fallen from his high estate !

She leads the way to her little sitting-room, and he sinks wearily into the easy-chair she places for him before the fire, and places his hand over his eyes, as if the leaping, cheery light dazzled and blinded him.

" Sit thee there, Master George, and don't'ee talk for a bit. ˙Rest and get warm, and I'll go and fetch summat to eat."

He is well disposed to obey ; he is worn out in body and mind. He has been recently ill, he has eaten scarcely anything all day, he has hardly a penny in his pocket, and "the world is all before him, where to choose."

He sits, and half sleeps, so utterly weary is he, so sweet to him are the rest, and the warmth of the fire. But he wakes up as Mrs. Tinker returns laden with hot coffee, chicken, meats, bread and wine. His eyes light with the gladness of hard, grinding hunger.

" Thanks, my dear old woman ! you have not forgotten my tastes. By Jove ! I am glad you brought me something, for I am uncommonly sharp-set."

She watches him eating and drinking, with the keen delight women feel in ministering to the bodily wants of men they love. He pushes the things away at last, and laughs at her rapt look.

" I wonder if Ne'er-do-well ever had such a loving old heart to cling to him before," he says : " the world is

a better place, Mrs. Tinker, for having such women as
you in it. I wonder if I might smoke in this matronly
bower without desecration now?"

It is an anti-climax, but it does Mrs. Tinker's heart
good. Smoke! Yes, from now until sunrise if he likes.

"Well, not quite so long as that. By sunrise I expect that I and the *Belle O'Brien* will be well on our
way to ——, but never mind where—if you don't know
you can't tell. I've a berth as foremast hand, being a
friend—after a fashion—of the captain's, and am going
to work my passage out to—never mind where again,
Mrs. Tinker. If I live and prosper, and redeem the past
out there, I'll come back and see you one day, and make
a clean breast of it. If not—and it is more than likely
not—I will have seen you to-night at least. But I'm off
in an hour or two, and that is why I am here—to
take away with me a last look of ·your good, plump,
motherly old face—bless it! Because, you see, in the
words of the song, 'it may be for years, and it may be
forever.' And very likely it will be forever, for I'm an
unlucky beggar, and like Mrs. Gummidge, 'thinks go
contrary with me!'"

He laughs; it is almost like the mellow laugh of old,
but it makes faithful Susan Tinker's heart ache.

"Oh, my dear! my dear! You a sailor? You in want
of anything, and him—that there young hupstart——"

"Ah! I know about that," George says, quickly, "I
heard down yonder in the town. It is his birthday, and
there are highjinks in consequence up-stairs. What's he
like—this successor of mine?"

"He's black and stiff, and that high-stomached, and
proud of himself that I can't abide the sight of him!
He's not fit to black your shoes, that he ain't, Master ·
George. Oh! my dear, it's not too late to come back
and do well. Let me go up and tell my mistress——"

But he stops her with a motion of his hand.

"No, Tinker, you shall tell no one. I have not re-

turned to whine and beg. Not that I would not go down
on my knees, mind you, to crave their pardon for the
heart-break I have caused them if that were all. But it
would not be all—it would be misunderstood. I might
be repulsed, and—and I know myself—*that* might awake
the devil within me. I would be thought to have returned for the money—a comfortable home—I could not
stand that. I wrote again and again that first year to ask
their forgiveness—I never asked, nor meant to ask for
anything besides, and they never answered me. A man
can't go on doing that sort of thing forever. Some day
—months from this—you will tell them if you like, and
if you think they would care to hear. Tell my mother I
ask her pardon with all my soul ; tell her I love her with
all my heart. Tell her I would give my life—ay, twice
over, to undo the past. But tell her nothing to-night.
I was homesick, Mrs. Tinker ; I wanted to see you—I
really think I wanted to see you most of all. Think of
that—a fellow being in love with you, and you—fifty-five,
isn't it ?"

He laughs again, but the dark bright eyes that look
at the fire see it dimly, as if through water. In the
pause comes the sound of singing from up-stairs—a
man's voice—a tenor, tolerably strong and tuneful, but
Mrs. Tinker listens with a look of much distaste, and
makes a face, as though she were tasting something very
nasty indeed.

"It's him !" she says, in explanation, and George
smiles ; he knows she means Vane Valentine.

"'*Le roi est mort—vive le roi*,' is evidently not your
motto, you foolish old person," he remarks ; "don't you
know a live dog is better than a dead lion ? Be wise in
your advancing years, my dear old nurse, and cultivate
Mr. Vane Valentine. He is to be a baronet, and a millionaire, and a very great personage one day, let me tell
you."

He rises, puts his pipe in his pocket, and stretches

4*

out his hand for his hat. She rises, too, with a sort of
cry.

"Not going! Not like this! Oh, Master George,
dear Master George, not like this!"

"Like this, my friend. See! I am weak as water already—don't unman me altogether—don't make it harder
for me than you can help. It must be. I have seen you,
and I am satisfied. Tell them by and by——"

He stops, for she is crying as if her very heart would
break.

"Ah, me! ah, me!" she sobs, how shall I bear it?
How can I ever let him go? Master George, Master
George! Oh, my boy, that I have rocked in these arms
many and many a time—that has gone to sleep on my
breast, that I love like my own flesh and blood! Oh, my
heart, how will I let him go?"

She cries so dreadfully that he puts down his hat and
takes her in his arms, and tries to soothe her. His own
eyes are wet. She cries as if indeed her old heart were
breaking.

"I *must* go," he says, at last, almost wildly. "My
dear, dear nurse, have a little mercy! Stop crying, for
Heaven's sake! I can't stand this."

There is such desperate trouble in his tone, in his
face, that it pierces through all her sorrow, and checks
its flow for a moment. In that moment he snatches up
his hat.

"Good-by, good-by!" he exclaims. "God bless you,
faithful, loving old friend. I'll come back to see *you* if
I never come to see any one else."

And then he is gone. There comes floating down the
stairs the last melodious words of Vane Valentine's
hunting song, as the door opens.

> "For the fences run strong in the Leicestershire vale,
> And there's bellows to mend, and a lengthening tail,
> With a ' Forward! Away!' in the morning."

But there mingles with it a quick step running down

the stairs, and the opening and shutting of a street door. And then she is alone, and outside the sleet is beating against the glass, and the wind is shrieking through the black streets, and up-stairs there is the sound of faint applause, and a soft murmur of pleasant voices. And George Valentine has been, and is gone.

The dinner party goes off well, and so does the new heir. People admire his repose of manner and modest good breeding, and consider him a credit to his sister's training.

Mrs. Tinker is indisposed next day, and keeps her bed. Her eyes are very red, her face very pale and troubled, her mistress observes, when she visits her. Being questioned as to these symptoms, Mrs. Tinker turns her face to the wall, and her tears silently flow again. If she only knew !

The storm continues all night, all next day ; there are many disasters and wrecks along the coast chronicled in the papers for days after. And among them there is narrated the total wreck of the bark *Belle O'Brien*, and the loss of every soul on board.

This item of shipping news is read aloud below stairs by the butler, and that magnate is electrified by a shriek from one of the women, who drops in a dead faint. It is Mrs. Tinker, to the surprise of every one ; and Mrs. Tinker is laid on the floor, and sprinkled with water, and slapped on the palms, and brought to with infinite difficulty. And when she *is* brought to, she "goes on" like a mad woman, beating the air with her hands, screaming hysterical screams, calling out for her mistress, and misconducting herself generally in a way perfectly frenzied.

Her mistress comes ; every one else is turned out of the room, and then·—Susan Tinker never knows how— the terrible truth is told. George Valentine is one of the "hands" who has gone down to his death in the ill-fated *Belle O'Brien*.

Blood tells, pride tells, training tells. Madam listens,

with blanched cheeks and wide, horror-stricken eyes, but *she* neither faints nor screams. She is deadly still, deadly cold; but almost the calmness of death, too, is in her face. She makes no comment whatever; she listens to the end—to the narrative of the visit and all that passed —and rises and seeks out her husband.

He comes in horror to the old servant's bedside, his hands trembling, his mouth twitching, far more agitated, in seeming, than his wife, and listens to the story sobbed out again between ever-flowing tears.

"You—you did not ask him anything about—about *her ?*" the father says, tremulously.

"No; I forgot. There wasn't time to ask him any-thing. And I was so took up with him," Mrs. Tinker sobs.

She understands Mr. Valentine refers to the wife.

"Oh, my dear master, you are not angry with me, are you ?"

"You should have spoken sooner—that night," he says, still tremulously ; "all—all might have been well." Then he breaks down for a moment, and lays his head on the table, and Susan Tinker is silent before a grief greater and more sacred than her own. "But I am not angry," he adds, rising slowly. "You did as he told you. I am not angry with you, Mrs. Tinker," he says, with strange pathos and gentleness for that stern, proud man. "George loved you !"

It is the first time that name has passed his lips for years. As he speaks it he turns and hurries out of the room.

He goes to the little sea-coast village where the bones of the luckless bark rest, and the crew—such of them as have been washed ashore, lie buried. One or two of the bodies have been identified and claimed ; others were cast up by the sea with every trace of humanity beaten out by the ruthless waves. The clothes and other relics are preserved. Among them is a jacket, and on the lining, which is black, there is marked in small, distinct red letters, a name, " G. H. Valentine." The body on which this garment, tightly buttoned, was found, was that of a tall young man with dark hair and a mustache; a fine-looking, muscular young fellow, so far as could be discovered, after some days in the water. He is buried yonder. The father goes and kneels by the little mound of snow-covered sod, and what passes in his heart is known only to Heaven and himself.

Five months after that, Austin Valentine, the merchant prince, dies. He has never held up his head again ; the sight of his heir becomes insupportable to him. That young gentleman is sent on his travels, and the funeral is over before he returns.

For Madam Valentine—well, she goes on with the burden of life somehow. It is an old story. "The heart may break, yet brokenly live on." The world does not see much difference. Only the Toronto home is broken up forever ; life there all at once grows hateful, and she becomes a wanderer. She will have no fixed place of abode, a singular restlessness possesses her—she resides here, there, everywhere, as the fancy seizes her. Vane Valentine waits dutifully on every whim. " What comfort he must be to you ; such a good young man," everybody says, and she agrees, and tries to think it is so—but he *is* a comfort to her. She has a cold sort of liking for him, a respect for his judgment and good sense, but love —Ah ! well, she has loved once, and once suffices. And so existence goes on for still three years more. Mrs. Tinker accompanies her always ; she clings to this old servant. she is a link that binds her to the past—the only one. She comes with Vane Valentine to the cottage in the suburbs of this dull little New England town of Clangville, because it is a pleasant place for a few autumn weeks, and one place is much the same as another.

Life goes on—almost stagnant in its quiet ; she grows

old gracefully; she is a woman of fine presence and commanding mien still, her health is unbroken, only—she has almost forgotten to smile.

Her face is set like a flint to all the world; she is chill and hard, self-repressed and self-centered, a woman sufficient unto herself.

And here—where peace and a sort of forgetfulness seem to have found her, the widow of her dead son appears, the miserable, low-born cause of her life's woe and loss, and destroys it all.

Comes with her fair mocking face, her fresh, insolent young beauty, her bold, evil blue eyes, her coarse, defiant taunts, and threatens to tear bare her half-healed heart, and show it bleeding to all the gaping world.

And this is the danger Vane Valentine has gone tonight to avert, this is the wretched story of passion and pain, and loss, and death, and shame, she thinks out, as she sits with clasped hands gazing at the cold, white October moonlight—all wrought by this one woman's hand !

——————◆——————

CHAPTER IX.

WHICH RECORDS A TRAGEDY.

"EMIMA ANN!" says Mlle. Mimi. She is lying in her customary afternoon lounging attitude upon the parlor sofa, occupied in her usual afternoon fashion in smoking cigarettes, and teaching her little girl a new ballet step, "Jemima Ann, are you happy ?"

"Lor !" says Jemima Ann.

"Yes, I know—that is your favorite expletive. You say it when you step on and scrunch a black beetle; you would say it if the whole six-and-twenty were blown up in their boiler shop, foundry-shop —whatever it is, to-morrow. I swear myself sometimes when things go wrong, but not in such mild fashion. 'Lor' is no answer, Jemima Ann, are—you—happy!"

"Well—railly"—begins Miss Hopkins, modestly, but Mimi waves her white hand, and cuts her short.

"Oh, if it requires reflection, say no more, you're not. Neither am I, Jemima—I never was. No, never," says Mimi, biting her cigarette through with her little sharp, white teeth, "not even when I was first married, and I suppose most girls who marry for love are happy then—for a month or so, at least! *Did* I marry for love, I wonder—did I ever care for him, or any one else, really—really, in my whole life?"

Mimi is evidently retrospective. She rolls a fresh cigarette between her deft fingers, and looks with somber blue eyes at the graceful capers of Mademoiselle Snow-ball.

"I like Petite, there—she amuses me; but so would the gambols of a little white kitten. She is pretty, and I like to dress her prettily, but I would tie ribbons round the kitten's neck, and trick *her* out, just the same. Is that love? If she died I would be sorry—I expect her to be a comfort and companion to me by and by. I quarrel with most people—I have no friends, and I am lonely sometimes, Jemima Ann. But—is that love? And her father——"

The darkest, most vindictive look Jemima Ann has ever seen there, sweeps like a cloud over the blonde face.

"I hated her father," she says between her teeth. "I hate him still."

"Do tell!" exclaims shocked Jemima Ann.

Mimi laughs—her transitions are like lightning, her volatile nature flashes to and fro, as a comet. Miss Hopkins' round-eyed simplicity amuses her always.

"Listen here, Jim," she says, "your aunt calls you 'Jim' sometimes, doesn't she? What would you say of

a poor girl, a grisette of New York, born in poverty, bred
in poverty, in vice, in ignorance, with only her face for
her fortune, what would you say of such a one when a
gentleman, young, handsome as one of the heroes of
your novels—tall, dark-eyed, finely educated, and the
heir of millions, falls in love with her ; runs away from
home and friends for her ; marries her. What would
you say ?"

"That she was the very luckiest and happiest creeter
on airth," responds, promptly, Jemima Ann. "But was
the love all on his side? Didn't she love him too?"

"Ah!" says Mimi, "that is what I have never been
able to find out. I—don't—know. She didn't act as if
she did ; it was more like hate sometimes, but she never
could bear him to look at any one else. She drove him
to his death, anyway. The love-story ended in a tragedy.
Snowball, you have got that *pas* all wrong. Look here
little dunce !"

She rises lazily, draws her skirts up a little to display
two trim feet, and executes the step to which Snowball
aspires, makes her little daughter repeat the performance
until she has it quite correctly. Then she flings herself
again on the lounge. Jemima Ann looks on in perplexity—this erratically acting and talking Mimi has been her
puzzle from the first—puzzles her more than ever to-
day ; in one breath talking of the tragical death of the
young husband, who left all for her, and with the words
still on her lips, absorbed in teaching Snowball a ballet
step ! The simple soul of Jemima Ann is upset.

"No," says Mimi, going back to the starting point,
"no one is happy. Even animals are wretched. Look
at a horse—beaten, loaded, worn out—look at a cow—
what melancholy meditation meets you in her big, pathetic eyes. A pig is the only contented-looking beast
I know of ; a pig wallowing in mud, surrounded by ten
or so dirty little piglings, is a picture of perfect earthly
felicity ! If, in the transmigration of souls—if that is

the correct big word—mine is permitted to return and
have its choice of a future dwelling, I think we will be
a fat little white porker and be happy! Oh! here is
Lacy, and I am not dressed. Take away Snowball, Jemima, like a good girl. I'm due at a dinner to-day—
Mr. Lacy gives it at the hotel, and here he comes after
me."

She springs to her feet and runs up-stairs.

"Tell him to wait, Jim," she calls; "I will be ready in
half an hour."

Miss Hopkins delivers the message, and bears Snowball to the regions below.

Mr. Lacy takes a seat at the parlor window, calling
familiarly to Mlle. Trillon, up-stairs to tittivate and be
quick about it, for the rest are waiting and the banquet
is ordered for five, sharp.

.   .   .   .

It is late when Vane Valentine reaches the circus.
He has dined leisurely and well, as it is in his nature to
do all things, and the brass band is banging away inside
the monster tent when he reaches it, and the first of the
performance is over. Still he is not the only late arrival
—a few others are still straggling in, and one man leans
with his back against a dead wall, his hands in his coat
pockets, waiting at his ease for his turn. Something
familiar in the look of this man, even in the dim light,
arrests Vane Valentine's attention; he looks again, looks
still again, comes forward, with a sudden lifting of his
dark face, and lays his hand on the man's shoulder.

"Farrar!" he exclaims. "My dear fellow, is it you
or your wraith?"

The man looks up, regards the speaker a moment,
after a cool fashion, and holds out his hand.

"How are you, Valentine? Yes, it is I. You wouldn't
have thought it, would you? But the world is not such
a big place as we are apt to think it, and Fayal, though
some distance off, is not absolutely out of the universe."

"Well, I'm uncommonly glad to see you, old boy," says Vane Valentine, and really looks it. "Have you come all the way from the Azores to go to the circus?"

"What would you say if I should say yes?"

"Regret to find you falling into your second child-hood at five-and-twenty, but no end glad to see you again, all the same."

"I should think, after a very few weeks of this place, you might be no end glad to see almost any one," says Mr. Farrar. "Fayal may be dull, but at least it has beauty to recommend it. But *this* beast of a town——"

"It *is* a beastly place," assents Vane Valentine, "but I am not staying in the town itself. We live in the suburbs, my aunt and I—not a bad spot in the month of September. We go to Philadelphia next week. Madam Valentine has a house there that she likes rather, and where she stays until she goes south for the winter."

"She is well, I trust?"

"She is always well. She is a wonderful old lady in that way—no headaches or hysterics, or feminine non-sense of any kind about her. But are you really going to the circus, you know?" inquires Mr. Valentine, smiling.

"Most undoubtedly. Behold the open sesame," show-ing his ticket. "And you—it is about the last place of all places I should expect to find the fastidious Vane Valentine."

Vane Valentine shrugs his shoulders, but looks rather ashamed of himself, too.

"I don't come to see the thing, don't you know; I come on—business. I want particularly to see one of the performers."

"Ah!" remarks, in deep bass, Mr. Farrar.

"Pshaw! my dear fellow, nothing of the sort. You might know me better. I have never set eyes on one of these women yet."

"Austere young aristocrat, I ask pardon! If we are

going to see anything of ˜it at all, we had better not linger longer here, for the raree-show is half over by ˋ this time."

"Where are you stopping?" young Valentine asks, as they turn to go in.

"They put me up at the Washington—not a bad sort of hostelry. Have I ever spoken to you of my friend, Dr. Macdonald, of Isle Perdrix? I am on my way to give him a week or two of my delectable society."

"Somewhere in Canada, among·the French, isn't it? Yes, I remember. Stay over to-morrow, though, won't you, and come and dine with me? I haven't seen a soul to speak to for three weeks! A civilized face is a god-send here among the sooty aborigines of Clangville."

"You *are* a supercilious lot, upon my word, Valentine," observes Mr. Farrar. "You always were. Here we are at last, in the thick of the tumblers and merry-go-rounds. ι feel like a boy again. I have not been inside a circus tent for fifteen years. They were the joy of my existence *then*."

They take their seats, and become for the space of five seconds the focus of several hundred pairs of examining eyes. Madame Olympe is cavorting round the ring on four bare-backed chargers at once, "hi-ing," leaping, jumping through lighted hoops, startling the nervous systems of everybody, and the several hundred eyes return to the sawdust circle. The two new-comers look sufficiently unlike the generality of the crowd around them, to attract considerable attention, if it could be spared from the performance.

Vane Valentine, dressed to perfection, with just a suspicion of dandyism, very erect, very stiff, and contemptuous of manner, glancing, with a sneer he takes no trouble to conceal, at the simple souls around him, all agape at the amazing doings of the magnificent Olympe. Mr. Farrar, tall, broad-shouldered, with a look of great latent strength, that lends a grace of its own to his well-knit figure, a silky brown-black beard and moustache, hair close-cropped and still darker, straight heavy eyebrows, and a pair of brilliant brown eyes. He is a man of commanding presence, looking far more thoroughbred than his companion, distinctly a handsome man—a man at whom most women look twice, and look with interest. He laughs, and strokes his brown beard, as he watches the astonishing evolutions of Olympe.

"Is it *she?*" he says; "if you want to take lessons in rough-riding you could hardly have a more accomplished teacher. A handsome animal too."

"Which?" asks Vane Valentine, "the woman or the horse?"

"Both. How does she call herself? Ah, Olympe, the Daughter of the Desert. *Which* desert?—this is vague. Whew—that was a leap—what superb muscles the creature must have. Now she has gone. What have we next?"

" Mlle. Mimi on the tight-rope," reads Vane Valentine. "Astonishing feats on the wire—sixty feet in the air! Oh, nere she is!"

He looks up with vivid interest, and levels his glass. Far above, a shining small figure is seen, all white gauze, spangles, gilded hair, balancing pole. A shout of applause greets her. Mimi has become a favorite with the circus-going public, in the last two or three days. Vane Valentine looks long and intently—his glass is powerful, and brings out every feature distinctly. He lowers it at last, and draws a deep breath.

"Take a look," he says to his companion, "and tell me what you think of her."

Mr. Farrar obeys. He, too, looks long and steadily at the fair Mimi, balancing far up in that dizzy line— going through a performance that makes more than one nervous head swim to look at. He also drops the glass after that prolonged stare, in silence.

"Do you think her pretty?" Valentine asks.

"There can be no two opinions about that, I should think. She is exceedingly pretty."

Vane Valentine shrugs his shoulders.

"Who knows? These people owe so much to paint and powder, and padding and wigs, and so on. In this case, too, distance lends enchantment to the view. I dare say nearer, with her face washed, and half these blonde tresses on her dressing-table, we should find our fair one a blowsy beauty, with a greasy skin and a pasty complexion. She does her tight-rope business well, though. By Jove, it looks dangerous!"

"It *is* dangerous," the other answers, "and—I may be mistaken—but there is something the matter. She nearly lost her balance a moment ago. Good! good! there! she nearly lost it again!"

The words have scarcely passed his lips when a hoarse, terrible cry arises simultaneously from a hundred throats. There is a sudden upheaval of the whole multitude to their feet. Over all, piercing, frightful, never to be forgotten, a woman's shriek rings—then a silence, a pause so awful that every heart stands still. *Then*—a dull, dreadful, sickening thud, something white and glittering has whirled like a leaf through the air, and lies now, crushed, bleeding, broken, senseless—a tumbled heap of gauze, and ribbons, and tinsel, and shining hair, and shattered flesh and blood.

And now there rises a chorus of screams, a stampede of feet, confusion, uproar, chaos. Above it sounds the voice of the manager, imploring them to be orderly, to be silent, to disperse. Mlle. Mimi is seriously hurt. Her only chance is for the audience to go, and leave her to the care of her friends. Hers, in any case, was to have been the close of the performance.

The audience are sorry and horrified, and obey, but slowly, and with much talk and confusion. They pour out into the bright, chilly night, and that crushed and bleeding heap is lifted somehow, and laid on a stretcher,

and the company crowd around. Some one has already
gone for a doctor, when Vane Valentine, who, with Mr.
Farrar, has already pushed his way into their midst,
speaks :

"This gentleman, although not a practicing physician, has studied medicine, and is skillful. Farrar, look
at the poor creature, and see if anything can be done."

. Mr. Farrar is already bending over her, and Vane
Valentine, who has a horror of the sight of blood and
wounds, turns away, feeling quite sick and giddy. But
it is his stomach that is tender, not his heart. In this
moment his first thought is, "If she is dead, what a lot of
trouble, and what a pot of money it will save, to be
sure !"

There is profound silence ; even Olympe looks pale
and panic-stricken in this first moment, in the face of
this direful tragedy. Mr. Farrar is quite pale with the
pity of it, when he looks up at last. A moment ago, so
fair, so full of life and youth ; now, this mangled, dully
moaning mass. For *it* moans feebly at times, and the
sound thrills through every heart.

"She is insensible, in spite of that," he says; "she is
terribly, frightfully injured. It is utterly impossible for
her to recover. With all these compound fractures, there
is concussion of the brain. She will probably never recover consciousness, even for a moment. She will die."

He pronounces the dread *fiat*, pale and grave. He
stands with folded arms, and looks down at the motionless form on the stretcher. Olympe—a judge of a fine
man—glances at him, even in this tragic moment, with an
approving eye. Time and opportunity favoring, she
would like to cultivate *Monsieur le Medicin's* acquaintance,
she thinks.

"Can she be moved?" the manager asks. "Poor little Mimi ! poor little soul ! I'm sorry for this. I've
known her for years, and in spite of her little failings, I
always liked her. Poor little soul !"

The manager is a personage of very few words. He rarely commits himself to a speech as long as this. He looks sorry as he says it.

"Poor little Mimi!" he repeats ; "poor little woman! poor little soul!"

"Where does she live?" Mr. Farrar asks. "Yes, she can be removed—she feels nothing ; and it had better be done at once. I will go with you until the doctor comes, but neither of us will be of any use. I will remain if there is anything that *can* be done," he says to the manager, "as long as you like."

"Thank you! I shall take it as a favor. You see, I have known her so long ; and, poor little thing, hers might have been such a different fate if she had chose. It has been a strange life and death. Poor, poor little Mimi!"

"How long do you give her to hold out, you know?" Vane Valentine asks his friend, in a subdued tone, as he too turns to follow.

Something in his voice, a latent eagerness, a sort of hope, makes Farrar look at him suddenly. The brown eyes are keen and quick to catch and read.

"She will hardly live—hold out, as you call it—until morning," he answers, coldly. "Why?"

"Nothing, except that I too would like to wait for— the end. It is all very sudden and shocking."

Mr. Farrar says nothing. The sympathy sounds forced and unmeant.

Vane Valentine is neither sorry nor shocked ; he thinks, indeed, it is a very fit and natural ending for such a life, altogether to have been expected. And what an easy solution of the problem of the day ! No fear of exposure or blackmail *now.*

"Will she ever speak again?" he asks, thinking his own thoughts, as they slowly follow the sad cortege that bears poor Mimi home.

"Have I not said she would not? She will never recover consciousness. She will lie moaning like that for a little, and then life will go out."

There is silence. It has chanced to Mr. Farrar to see a good deal of death and the darker sides of life, but habit has not hardened him. There is that in his face which tells Vane Valentine he is in no mood to answer idle questions. So he discreetly holds his tongue, and follows through the starry darkness to Mrs. Hopkins' home.

Jemima Ann snd Aunt Samantha are waiting up as usual, sewing in silence, a kerosene lamp between them.

Snowball has not been taken to the circus this evening, but as she has a profound disbelief, in her small way, of the early-to-bed system, she is still up, singing gleefully, and playing with a couple of kittens in front of the stove. Her song, sung at the full pitch of her powerful little lungs, is her favorite ballad of the " Ten Little Injun Boys."

The door-bell is rung by the messenger, who runs on ahead ; the direful news is broken, and in a moment all is confusion.

Mrs. Hopkins is acid of temper, but pitiful of heart. A great remorse and compassion seizes her. She has spent the evening in wordy abuse of her boarder—her smoking, her drinking, her flirting, her generally shameful goings on ; and now—a bleeding and mangled creature is borne in to die in her house.

" I wouldn't a said a word if I'd a thought," she says, crying, to Jemima Ann. " I kinder feel as if she'd oughter haunt me for all the things I've up and said of her. Poor little creetur ! she was only young and flighty, and knowed no better, likely, when all is said and done."

Jemima is crying too, very sincere tears. She has learned to like, has always liked, the light, *insouciant*, devil-may-care little trapezist. But then Jemima Ann would have cried for any one in pain or trouble as freely as she weeps over her heroines in weekly installments.

She prepares the bed, and sees Mimi laid upon it, still faintly moaning, and assists in removing as much as can be removed of the flimsy, tinseled drapery. The beautiful fair hair, all clotted and sticky with blood, is gathered up in a great knot. The face seems the only part of her uninjured—it is drawn into a strange, dreadful expression of fear and pain—the look that froze upon it in the instant of her fall. The features are not marred, but the face is ghastly—the blue eyes seem half open, a little stream of blood and foam trickles from the lips. Jemima Ann wipes it, and her own tears, away, as she stands looking down.

Down in the parlor is Mr. Lacy, like a man distraught. He has been in love with Mimi, off and on, since he saw her first ; he has followed her about from place to place like her shadow ; he has offered her marriage again and again—and he is rich. That she has not married him has surprised everybody ; but Mlle. Trillon has always been erratic, has liked her freedom and her wandering life, has persistently laughed at him, and taken his presents with two greedy little hands, and eaten his dinners, and drank his wines, and smoked his cigarettes, and driven behind his high-steppers, and said *No.*

"I've had enough of marriage, Lacy," she has said, in her reckless fashion ; " it's no end of a humbug. I wouldn't marry the Prince of Wales if he came over and asked me."

"Which it would be bigamy if you did," says Mr. Lacy ; "but you might marry me, Mimi—*I've* not got a Princess Alexandra at home. You could leave off the flying trapeze, and have a good time as Mrs. Augustus Lacy."

" I have a better time as Mlle. Mimi Trillon. Thanks, old fellow, very much, but not any !" laughs Mimi.

And she has adhered to it. No later than this very day, after dinner, a-flush with champagne and turkey,

5

Mr. Lacy has renewed his honorable proposals, and for the twenty-fifth time been refused. Mimi, too, is elate with the fizzing beverage, which she is but too fond of, and it is this thought that adds the sting of poignant self-reproach to Mr. Lacy's grief. She had taken too much wine, she was in no condition to mount that fatal wire when she left his hotel, and he should have told the manager so. But how could he tell?—and she would never have forgiven him if he had, and now—— He lays his head on the table, and cries, in the deepest depths of misery, and remorse, and despair. So Mr. Farrar finds him later, and stands looking at him, with that grave, thoughtful face of his, in silent wonder.

"I was so fond of her," the poor young man says, wiping his eyes; "I was awfully fond of her always. I would have married her if she'd have had me. But she wouldn't. And now to think of her lying up there, all crushed and disfigured. It's too horrid. And it's dused hard on *me*, by George! Ain't there no hope, doctor? You *are* the doctor, ain't you?"

"I am not a doctor," Mr. Farrar answers, "but the doctor is with her. No—there is no hope."

He does not look contemptuous by these womanish tears, and this foolish little speech. A sort of compassion is in the glance that rests so gravely on poor love-stricken, grief-stricken Mr. Lacy.

"How—how long will she——"

Mr. Lacy applies his handkerchief to his eyes, and walks away abruptly to one of the windows.

"She may last the night out. She will not know you or any one—she is past all that. She will never speak again."

He pauses.

A little child comes in, a fairy in a blue dress the color of its eyes, with fluffy, flaxen hair, falling to its waist, and a lovely rosebud face.

"Seben 'lttle Injuns nebba heard ob hebben," sings

the fairy, looking about her with wide open, fearless eyes.·

She espies Mr. Lacy, and peers up at him curiously. "What you cryin' for, Lacy?" she asks. "Want your supper?"

Mr. Lacy is too far gone to reply.

"Want go to bed?" persists inquisitive Snowball, the two sole wants *she* is ever conscious of uppermost in her mind.

"Oh! Snowball, Snowball!" says poor Mr. Lacy. "Little Snowball, if you only knew!"

"Where Mimy Ann?" Snowball demands, unmoved by this apostrophe. "'Noball wants her Mimy Ann. Want go to bed."

"It is *her* child," Mr. Lacy explains to the silent Farrar. "She was a widow, you know. I haven't an idea what will become of this little mite now. And she is very like *her*. It's dused hard, by George!"

He is overcome again.

Mr. Farrar holds out his hand to the child.

"Come here, little Snowball," he says.

She looks at him after her fashion for a moment, then still quite fearlessly goes over, climbs upon his knee, and kisses his bearded lips.

"You is a pritty man," she says. "'Noball likes pritty men. Does *you* know where is my Mimy Ann?"

"She will be here presently. She is busy up-stairs."

He puts the flaxen hair back from the baby face, and gazes long and earnestly.

"Yes, you are like her," he says, "you are very like her, my poor little Snowball."

Snowball is sleepy, and says as much; she cuddles closer, lays her fair baby head confidingly against his breast closes the blue eyes, and instantly drops asleep. He sits and holds her, lifting lightly the long pretty hair, until Jemima, coming down in search of her, bears her off to her cot.

It is a night never to be forgotten in the Hotel Hopkins. No one goes to bed. Even the six-and-twenty
hands stray afield until abnormal hours, and meander
in and out, unrebuked.

Mrs. Hopkins retires, it is true, to freshen herself for
the labors of the dawning new day, which promises to be
one of the busiest of her busy life. Jemima Ann retires
not. She is up-stairs, and down-stairs, and on her feet the
weary night through. Mr. Lacy cannot tear himself
away. Mr. Vane Valentine sends a message to the cottage, and he, too, lingers to see how the poor creature
fares, and wins golden opinions from hero-worshiping
Miss Hopkins. So much goodness of heart, so much
condescension in so great a personage, she wouldn't a
thought it, railly. She falls partly in love with him indeed, in the brief intervals she has for that soft emotion,
during her rapid skirmishing up and down stairs—would
do so wholly but that her admiration is about equally
divided between him and his friend Mr. Farrar.

This latter gentleman remains without offering any
particular reasons, but in a general way, in case he can
be of any further assistance.

For Mimi, she lies prone, not opening her eyes, not
stirring, only still moaning feebly at intervals. Up in
her cot, in Jemima's room, little Snowball sleeps, her
pretty cheeks flushed, her pretty hair tossed, and dreams
not that the fair frail young mother is drifting out further
and further from this world, with each of those dark, sad,
early hours.

The night-light burns low, the sick-room is very still,
the street outside is dead quiet; Jemima Ann sits on one
side of the bed, her numberless errands over for the
present, dozing in the stillness, spent with fatigue; Mr.
Farrar paces the corridor without, coming to the bed at
intervals to feel the flickering pulse, and see if life yet
lingers. Mr. Lacy slumbers in a chair in the parlor, and
Mr. Valentine has stretched his slender limbs on the

sofa, where poor Mimi was wont in after-dinner mood to recline, and smoke, and chaff Jemima. The belated six-and-twenty have clambered up to their cots at last ; only the black beetles, the mice, and Mr. Paul Farrar are thoroughly awake in the whole crowded household.

Four strikes with a metallic clang from the big wooden clock in the hall, and is taken up by a time-piece of feebler tone, far down in the underground kitchen. He pauses in his restless walk, enters the sick-room, glances at the quiet figure on the bed, walks to one of the windows, draws the curtain and looks out. The moon has set, the morning is very dark, a wild wind shudders down the deserted street with a whistling sound, inexpressibly dreary.

He remembers suddenly it is the first of November, the eve of All Souls' Day ; the moaning of the sweeping blast sounds to him like the wordless cry of some of these disembodied souls, wandering up and down for-lornly, the places that knew them once. Another soul will go to join that "silent majority" before the new day dawns. The thought makes him drop the curtain, and sends him back to the bedside.

The change has come. A gray shadow, not there a moment since, lies on the white face, a clammy dew wets it, the fluttering of the heart can hardly be detected now, as he bends his ear to listen.

Jemima Ann, waking from some uncomfortable dream, starts up.

He lifts one warning hand, and still bends his ear downward, his fingers on the flickering pulse.

"Oh ! what is it?" Jemima says, in a terrified whis-per ; "is she worse?"

"Hush—she is dying. No !" he cries out. "She is dead !"

The shock of sudden emotion is in his tone. He drops the wrist and stands quite white, looking down upon the marble face. A shudder has passed through the shattered limbs, through the crushed, frail, pretty little body; then, with a faint, fluttering sigh, she is gone.

"Dead!" says Jemima Ann.

She drops on her knees with a sobbing cry, and looks piteously at the rigid face.

"Oh, dear! oh, dear! oh, dear!" she sobs, under her breath; "dead! and only this afternoon, only this very afternoon, she lay on the sofa down-stairs talkin' to me, and laughin', so full of life, and health, and strength, and everything; so pretty, so pretty, so young! Oh, dear! oh, dear! and now she is dead—and such a death! She was talkin' of years ago, and of her husband—poor, poor thing!" says Jemima Ann, rocking to and fro, through her raining tears, "tellin' me how handsome he was, and how he loved her, and how he run away with her from his home, and riches, and all. And now, and now, she is there—and dead—and never, never, never, will I hear her pretty voice again!"

Mr. Farrar lifts his eyes from the dead woman, and looks across at the homely, tear-wet, honest countenance of Mrs. Hopkins' niece, and thinks that beauty is not the only thing that makes a woman's face lovely.

"You are a good girl," he says. "You are sorry for this poor creature. You do well. Yours will be the only tears shed over her—poor unfortunate little soul!"

"Did you know her, sir?" asks Jemima.

"I know of her. Hers has been a pathetic life and death—the saddest that can be conceived. Poor pretty little Mimi! And she talked to you of her early life—and her husband? What of him?"

"Oh, he is dead—drounded—so she said. But I guess he treated her bad—at least I think it was that, I ain't sure. Mr. Lacy wanted to marry her, but she wouldn't. Ah! poor little dear. She'd had a dose already, I reckon. What's to be done next, sir?"

There is so much to be done next, it seems, that Je-

mima Ann is forced to call up her aunt. Monsieurs
Lacy and Valentine, aroused from their matutinal nap,
are informed, and start up to hear the details.

"Gone, is she?" says Mr. Lacy, the first sharp edge
of his affliction a trifle blunted by slumber. "It's—it's
dused hard on me, by George! I'll never be so fond of
any one again as long as I live."

"Did she speak at all?" inquires Valentine, with interest.

"No, she has not spoken."

Mr. Farrar turns abruptly away as he answers, but
looks over his shoulder to speak again as he goes.

"I see no reason why *you* should linger longer," he
says, roughly, to the heir of many Valentines. "She is
dead. There is nothing you can do."

"Are you sure—nothing?"

"Nothing. You had better go. I suppose they will
lay her out in this room. She will be buried, I infer, from
this house."

Mr. Vane Valentine is not used to being thus summarily dismissed, but he wants to go, and does not resent
it. But why Mr. Paul Farrar should speak and act as
one having authority is not so clear, except that his mas-
terful character is rather apt to assert itself wherever he
goes.

"And you," he says; "I must see you again, Farrar
you know, before you leave."

"I shall not leave for a day or two, I shall wait until
after the funeral. I am in no particular hurry."

"At the Washington you put up? Very well, I will
go now, and look in on you later. You ought to turn
in for an hour or two—you look quite fagged with your
night's watch. Good-morning."

Through the bleak chill darkness of the dawning
day, Vane Valentine hurries home, full of his news. It
is a *very* bleak and nipping morning, it tweaks Mr. Valentine's thin aquiline nose rosy red, and powders his

weak young mustache with white rime. The blast he faces seems to cut him in two, a sleety rain begins to pelt frequently, and he has no umbrella. He cannot but think that it is rather hard he should have to undergo all this, for a trapeze performer, and the consummate foolery of his cousin George seven long years ago. But he has slept well, and is a good pedestrian, and gets over the ground with rapid strides, not willing to admit even to himself how thoroughly well satisfied he is with the way in which fate has cut for him his Gordian knot. It has all been very shocking and tragical, and of course it is all very sad, poor creature, but then—but then, on the whole, perhaps it is as well, and it simplifies matters exceedingly. Here is the child, of course, but the child will be easily disposed of. With Mimi has died probably all trace of that one blot on the spotless Valentine shield. Yes, on the whole it is as well.

He lies down for an hour when he gets home; then rises, has his bath, his morning coffee and chop, and then sends word to his aunt that he will like to see her at her earliest convenience. Her earliest convenience is close upon noon, for she is not an early riser.

He finds her in the sitting-room of last evening, seated in front of the fire, wrapped in a fluffy white shawl, and with the remains of a breakfast of chocolate and dry toast at her side.

She glances indifferently up at him, murmurs a slight greeting, and returns to the fire.

"Good-morning, my dear aunt!" Mr. Vane Valentine says, with unusual briskness of manner.

He looks altogether brighter and crispier than is his high-bred wont.

"I trust you slept well. I hope the—aw—unpleasant little rencontre of yesterday, did not disturb you at all?"

"You have something to say to me," she responds, abruptly. "Have you seen that woman?"

"I have seen her. That woman will never trouble you or me any more."

She looks up at him again, quickly. Something in his look and tone tell her a surprise is coming.

"What do you mean?" sharply and imperiously; "speak out!"

"She is dead!"

There is a pause. Even Madam Valentine, cold, impenetrable, hard, is dumb for a moment. Dead! and only yesterday so full of strong, young, insolent life! She catches her breath, and looks at him with eyes that dilate.

"Dead!" she repeats, incredulously.

"Dead; and after a very sudden and dreadful manner; and yet, after a manner that might easily have been expected."

And then he begins, and in his slow, formal way, but with a quickened interest he cannot wholly suppress, tells the story of the tragedy at the circus.

"And so it ends," he concludes; "and with it all trouble for us as well."

And so it ends! Ay, as troubles of life and the glory thereof shall one day end, even for you, Mr. Vane Valentine—for us all, O my brothers—in the solemn wonder of the winding-sheet.

In the warmth and glow of the fire he sees his aunt shiver, and draw her white fleecy shawl close.

And so it ends—in another tragedy! George lying beneath the bleak, sandy hillocks, in his wind-swept, sea-side grave—his wife lying with life mangled and beaten out of her, about to be laid by strangers, far from him, in death as in life. So it ends, the pretty love idyl, as so many other love idyls of a summer day have ended—in ruin, and disaster, and death.

"It is very sad—it is terrible," she says, a sudden huskiness in her voice—all the womanhood in her astir. "Poor creature—she had a beautiful face."

5*

There is pity, very real, very womanly, in her tone.

"And George loved her," she thinks. "Oh! my son! my son!"

"Yes, it is sad," breaks in the hard metallic tones of Mr. Vane Valentine; "but not surprising. She will be buried from the house where she was boarding—a wretched place filled with grimy working men. My friend Farrar was with her at the last."

She looks up once more. It is so very unusual to hear the young man apply the term friend to any human being, but a faint, angry, incredulous smile crosses her face.

"Who is your friend Farrar?"

"Oh! no one you know. Man I met in Fayal last year—manager of an immense place there, very good sort of fellow, a Bohemian rather, but a thorough gentleman. Stopping here for a couple of days on his way to Canada. Capital company, Farrar—no end a fine fellow, but not distinguished in any way."

"Except by the notice of Vane Valentine. And the child," after a pause, "what of *it?*"

"Oh—aw—the child. Exactly. What I was about to ask. But need we trouble?" hesitatingly. "No one knows anything—aw—at least, I infer not."

Her eyes blaze out on him for a moment, a flash of black lightning.

"She is my son's child—my grandchild. Do you wish her sent to the workhouse, Mr. Vane Valentine?"

"My dear aunt——"

The flash is but momentary. She sinks back wearily in her chair, and draws her shawl still closer around her.

"It is a very cold morning, I think—I cannot get warm. Throw on another log, Vane. Something must be done about the child—she must be provided for."

Vane Valentine turns pale under his swarthy skin.

He bends over the fire and arranges it with some precipitation.

"What do you wish?" he asks, and in his voice there is ever so slight a touch of sullenness.

"Nothing that can affect you—do not fear it," she retorts, scornfully. "I have no desire that the world should know that this child of an unfortunate tight-rope dancer, is anything to me—has any claim upon the name of Valentine. At the same time she must be provided for. I do not ask how, or where, but you must see that she is suitably cared for, and educated, and wants for nothing. Have you tact enough to manage this, without exciting suspicion?"

"I hope so," Mr. Valentine responds, rather stiffly. "It seems a simple matter enough. You are a rich lady; as an act of pure benevolence you compassionate the forlorn condition—aw—of this little child, and offer to provide for her in that—aw—state of life in which it has pleased Providence to place her. No one else has any claim that I hear of. I will go and see about it at once."

"Whom will you see?"

Mr. Valentine strokes his youthful mustache, and looks thoughtful.

"The manager, I infer; it doesn't seem quite clear to whom the little one belongs now. I can find out, however. Farrar will help me. He is a wonderfully shrewd fellow and that."

"Very well, go."

Mr. Vane Valentine goes, and tries his hand at diplomacy.

Mr. Farrar looks a little surprised when his young friend's mission is made known to him, but is ready with any assistance that may be needed.

They see the manager, and find that that gentleman has no claim on the little Trillon, nor, so far as he knows, has any one else.

"The little one is totally unprovided for," he says,

"I know that. If nothing better offered I would keep her myself for her poor mother's sake, and get one of our women to take charge of her. But this is better. Ours is but a vagabond life for a child. It is very good of your aunt, sir. She's a pretty little thing, this Snowball, and will grow up a charming girl. Is it Madam Valentine's intention to adopt her, or anything of that sort, Mr. Valentine?"

"If my aunt takes her she will be suitably provided for," says, in his stiff way, Mr. Vane Valentine.

"No doubt, sir. Well, I see no reason why your aunt shouldn't. Little un's father is dead; her mother had no relatives that I ever heard of; she is as much alone in the world, poor little thing, as any waif and stray can well be. Still she should never have wanted. But this is better. Best leave her where she is until after the funeral, the girl at that boarding-house is good to her, and then take her away."

"When is the funeral?"

"To-morrow. No time for delay. We are off Monday morning. I look after the burying myself; all expenses, and so on. She got her death in my service. Hope you will attend the funeral, gentlemen, both."

They promise, and go, both very thoughtful and rather silent.

Mr. Farrar is the first to speak.

"This is very good of your aunt," he says; "it speaks well for her kindness and gentleness of heart."

"Well," Vane Valentine replies, dryly, "kindness and gentleness, in a general way, are not Madam Valentine's chief characteristics, but as you say, *this* is good of her—the more so as she is not fond of children—or poodles, or cats, or birds, or things of that kind. She is what is called strong-minded. The little one has fallen on her feet, though, all the same. Best thing that could have happened to her; that trapeze woman was not fit to bring up a child."

"Don't agree with you," says Mr. Farrar, shortly.
"It is never best for a child to lose its mother, unless she
is a monster. There are exceptional cases, I grant you,
but I don't call this one. I hope the poor baby will be
happy, whatever comes."

"Come home and dine with me," says Vane Valentine, who is in good spirits. He does not much fear the
child, and a large sum of money has been saved. "You
will not see my aunt, very likely, but I shall be dusedly
glad of your company—and that. After the first flush of
partridge shooting, it's confoundedly slow down here, let
me tell you."

"So I should infer. But you must excuse me to-day,
and to-morrow you must dine with me instead, at the
hotel."

"But why? You don't pretend to say you have such
a thing as an engagement in Clangville," incredulously.

"No. Still you will be good enough to excuse me.
You will think it queer, I suppose, and squeamish, but
the death-bed scene of this morning has upset me. It
would be unfair to you to inflict myself upon you. So
good-day, my dear boy—here is Mrs. Hopkins'. I shall
drop in for a moment. Will you come?"

"Not for the world," says young Valentine, with a
glance of strong repulsion. "It upsets *me* to look at
dead people, and—that sort of thing. Until to-morrow,
then, *au revoir.*"

The two men part, and unconscious little Snowball's
fate is thus summarily settled, and Vane Valentine goes
home through the melancholy autumn afternoon to tell
his aunt.

CHAPTER X.

IN WHICH SNOWBALL IS DISPOSED OF.

HERE is a funeral next day from the Hotel Hopkins, such a funeral as the quiet little town of Clangville has rarely turned out to see. The Six-and-Twenty attend to a man ; the circus people are all there ; there, too, are Mr. Farrar and Mr. Vane Valentine.

It is a gusty November day—the stripped brown trees rattle in the bleak blast, an overnight fall of snow lies on the ground, and whitens the black gulf down which they lower the coffin. It looks a desolate resting place, cold, wet, forlorn—Vane Valentine turns away with a shudder—death, graves, all things mortuary are horrible to him.

Perhaps they remind him too forcibly that his turn too must come ; that all the wealth of all the Valentines will not be able to avert it one hour. Mr. Farrar stands grave and pale—an impressive figure in the scene ; standing with folded arms—dark and tall, looking down at the wet sods, rattling rapidly on the coffin lid. Poor little Mimi ! Poor little frail, reckless butterfly ! What a hollow sound the frozen clay has as it tumbles heavily down on the shining plate. What a tragic ending of a shallow, selfish—perhaps sinful life !

It is over.

As the dusk of the short November afternoon shuts down, the two young men—friends, as Vane Valentine terms it, though, perhaps, it is hardly the correct term— find themselves back in Mrs. Hopkins' parlor, with that severe lady, still moist and tearful after the funeral, and Jemima Ann, with eyes quite red and swollen from much sympathetic weeping. Little Snowball is present, too, and it is little Snowball, and her future they are there to discuss.

The child has on a black frock and black shoes—things she has never worn before, and she eyes both with much disapprobation.

"Narsy, narsy," she remarks, with some asperity. "Narsy brack dress; narsy brack shoes. 'Noball not like 'em. Take 'em off, Mimy Ann."

"No, deary," says Jemima Ann, wiping her red eyes. "Snowball must wear the poor little black dress. It is for mamma, Snowball knows."

"W.iere my mamma gone? When her tum back?"

This inquiry causes Jemima's tears to flow afresh. Snowball eyes them with considerable disgust.

"What you cwyin for? What you *always* cwyin for? 'Noball tired you cwyin. Want see 'Noball dance?"

Forthwith Snowball flirts out her somber skirts and cuts an infantile pigeon wing—that last ballet step poor Mimi taught her bantling. If anything can comfort Jemima Ann, and stem the torrent of her tears, Snowball is convinced this must.

"Look at that child," says Vane Valentine, much amused. "Blood tells, doesn't it? Do what you please with her, that fairy changeling will grow up like her mother before her—a thorough Bohemian."

Mr. Farrar is looking, and thoughtfully enough, at Snowball's performance. She dances wonderfully well for such a baby, every motion is instinct with lithe, fairy-like, inborn grace. The cloud of pale flaxen hair floats over her shoulders like a banner, the black dress brings out the pearly tints of the milk-white skin, the sweet baby face is like a star set in jet.

"She is a lovely little creature," Mr. Farrar says. "She bids fair to become a beautiful woman."

"Ten to one she grows up blowsy or freckled," replies Vane Valentine, in a bold cheap voice; "these very blonde girls often do. But yes—she is pretty at present.

Let us hope judicious training may eradicate somewhat the wild vagrant strain that flows in her veins, and turn her out a civilized young woman."

Mr. Farrar looks at him—a look half amused, half sardonic. "You abominable young prig!" is his thought. "Let us hope so," he says, aloud, dryly. "To whom do you propose confiding that herculean task? Does Madam Valentine intend taking her in hand herself?"

"My aunt? My dear fellow, you never saw my aunt, did you? She would as soon take in hand the training of a young gorilla. I told you she detests pets—poodles and little girls included. No; whatever is done with the waif, it will not be that."

"And yet, I should have thought, after her offer to provide for her—adopt her, after a fashion—she would like, at least, to see her. We mostly are interested in that for which we provide. But perhaps I have misunderstood. It is your intention to take her home with you to-night?"

"My good Farrar," retorts Vane Valentine, with a very marked touch of impatience, "no! My aunt has expressed no wish, none whatever, to see this little girl. How could it be possible for her—her—to be interested in the child of a strolling acrobat—a vagrant by profession?"

"Mlle. Mimi is dead, Mr. Vane Valentine," says Mr. Farrar, with a sudden dark flash leaping angrily from his eyes. "Your patrician feelings are rather carrying you away!"

"Beg pardon. I speak warmly—the idea is so preposterous. It was bad form all the same."

Mr. Valentine turns away, at his stiffest, but decidedly discomposed. He speaks warmly, because, although it is true in the letter, that Madam Valentine has expressed no distinct desire to see Snowball Trillon—to have George's daughter brought home—he is perfectly conscious that she *does* desire it, that she desires it strongly,

that it is only her pride that prevents her putting the
desire in words. And Vane Valentine is horribly afraid
of any such consummation. Who knows what may follow? This small girl—as George's daughter, and owned
as such—has a claim on the Valentine millions far, and
away, better than his own. And she is so perilously
pretty—so winning—so charming—with all her infantile
sweetness and grace, that—oh! that is out of the question—quite out of the question to let Madam Valentine
set eyes on her at all. She is not in the least like the
family, that is something, the Valentines are all dark and
dour, as the Scotch say—this child is fair as a lily.

"It is the dickens own puzzle to know *what* to do
with her," he says, gnawing the end of his callow mustache, "she cannot stay in here, I suppose, and she can't
come to the cottage, that is clear. She might go to a
boarding-school, or a nunnery, or—or that," helplessly.
"What would *you* do, Farrar? You're a man of resources."

"It's rather like having a white elephant on your
hands, isn't it? Poor little elephant—that a man could
take up between his finger and thumb—to be such a dead
weight, such an Old Man of the Sea, on any one's shoulders! Are you really serious in that question, Valentine? I know what you *could* do, but will you do it? It
would be a capital thing for the child too."

"My dear fellow, speak out. I will do anything—
the little thing's good, of course, being paramount."

"Of course," dryly. "Well, you might give her to
me."

" What ?"

"Not to adopt—not to bring back to Fayal—only to
take off your hands for the present. I will make a handsome sacrifice on the altar of friendship, my boy, put
your small white elephant in my overcoat pocket, and
take her ' over the hills and far away.' "

Vane Valentine stands and stares at him, half in anger at his ill-timed jesting—half in doubt whether it be jesting."

Farrar is a queer fellow, full of whims and oddities, but, also, as he has said, full of resources.

"Don't stand there looking as if you thought I had gone idiotic!" exclaims Farrar, impatiently. "Have I not said I don't want the little one for myself? Look here, Valentine, I am going to my friends, the Macdonalds. Dr. Macdonald lives on an island in Bay Chalette, if you ever heard of such a place. Isle Perdrix is the name. He is an old Scotchman, his wife is a young French Canadian lady, and the sweetest woman that ever drew breath. That is saying a good deal, isn't it?

"They have two sons, little chaps of six and nine. There is no girl, and the desire of Madam Macdonald's heart is a little girl.

"She will take this one, and bring her up in the very choicest French fashion; if there is any possibility of changing and improving that Bohemian's nature, you so deeply deplore, she is the lady to do it.

"As they are by no means wealthy, you will make compensation, of course. The flourishing township of St. Gildas is over the river from the island, and there is an excellent convent school, when she attains the age for it. I start to-morrow morning; if you think well of this, Petite shall be my traveling companion. There is my offer."

"My dear fellow!" cries Mr. Vane Valentine—"my dear Farrar!"

He is not generally effusive, it is not "form;" but he grasps his friend's hand now, or tries to do so—for Mr. Farrar stands with his hands in his pockets, and is slow to take them out.

"I accept with delight; take her, by all means; nothing could be better. You say you will start to-morrow. Sorry to lose you, of course. These good women will see that the child is ready. The question of ample, of liberal compensation, we will arrange later.   Nothing in the world could be better than what you propose."

"Madam Valentine will be satisfied?"

"Perfectly satisfied.   She will amply provide for the child."

"Had you not better put it to her? as it is she who is virtually Snowball's guardian now, should you not?"

"My dear Farrar, I can answer for her.   It is not necessary at all.   I have full power to act for her in this matter.   She does not want to see the little one, or be annoyed with questions about her."

"It would annoy her, would it?   That makes a difference, of course.   Come here, little white elephant—such a poor little helpless elephant! and tell me if you will leave your Minny Ann, and come with me?"

He lifts the fairy to his knee, with infinite tenderness, and puts back with gentle fingers the falling, flaxen hair.

"Will you come with me, little Snowball?   I want to take you to the kindest lady in the world—a pretty new mamma, who will love little Snowball with all her good heart."

The child puts up her two snow-flake hands and strokes the cheeks of her big friend.

"'Noball like you," she says.   "You is a pritty, pritty man.   'Noball will give you a kiss."

Which she does, an emphatic little smack right on the bearded lips.

"Flattering, upon my word," says Vane Valentine. 'Don't you like me, too, Snowball?"

"No," says Snowball, curling her mite of a nose. "You is not a pritty genpyman.   You is very narsy."

"By Jove!" says Mr. Valentine, and stands discomfited.

Mr. Farrar laughs.

"And you will come with me, Snowball?"

"Yes," nods Snowball. "'Noball tum wiz you. May my Mimy Ann tum, too?"

"Well—no—not unless you wish it very much, Miss Trillon. And your Mimy Ann, I take it, cannot be spared."

"You will want some one," suggests Valentine. "You cannot travel with that child alone, Farrar; think of the dressing and undressing, the feeding and sleeping, and all that. You couldn't manage it. You must have a woman."

"Not if I know it. There are always ladies traveling—nice matronly ladies, ready to interest themselves in helpless manhood and childhood. They will attend to Mademoiselle Snowball's infantine wants and wardrobe. St. Gildas is only two days off. I am willing to risk it. No woman, Valentine, my boy, an' thou lovest me."

"Wretched misogynist," laughs Mr. Valentine. "Some one must have used you shamefully in days gone by, Farrar. I wonder why—you are a tall and proper fellow enough. You must have been jilted in cold blood. Well, as you like it, only I would rather it were you traveling two days and nights with a girl-baby in charge than myself."

Thus it is settled, and life opens on a new page for little Snowball. The circus, with its lights and its leaps, its riding, its dancing, its danger, and its wanderings, its flavor of vagabondism, is to be left behind forever, and seclusion, and respectability, and training in the way she should go *à la Française*, begins for the motherless waif, afloat like a lost straw on life's great tide.

All is speedily settled. Mr. Farrar is eminently a man of promptitude and dispatch. Vane Valentine is only too anxious to get it all over and have the child out of the town. His aunt will shut up the cottage, and depart in a day or two. Money matters are arranged, and are liberal as young Valentine has promised. He shakes hands with his friend late that evening, full of self-congratulation that a knotty point has been so well and easily gotten over.

"If she had seen the young one," he says to himself, thinking of his aunt, "no one knows what might have happened. Shut out of the world on this far-away island, she will speedily forget, I trust, all about her. It shall be the business of my life to compel her to forget. Until the fortune is actually mine, I am daily in danger of losing it, unless she forgets her son's daughter."

Early the next morning the first train bears away among its passengers Mr. Paul Farrar and Miss Snowball Trillon. Jemima Ann weeps copiously at the parting. A glimpse of romance has come to brighten the dull drab of her existence, and it goes with the going of Snowball.

"Good-by, good-by," she sobs. "Don't, oh! don't forget poor Mimi Ann, little Snowball!"

"What you cwyin' for *now?*" demands Snowball, touching a tear with one minute finger, and an expression of much distaste. "'Noball don't like cwyin'. You is always cwyin'. What you want for cwy some more?"

Snowball cries not. Her small black cloak is fastened, her little black bonnet tied under one delicious dimple, she is kissed, and departs in high glee, and even the memory of good Jemima Ann waxes pale and dim before the first hour has passed.

Mr. Farrar has been right. All the way, ladies take a profound interest in pretty Snowball. Her deep mourning, her exquisite face, her feathery, floating hair, her blue, fearless eyes, her enchanting baby smile, her piquant little remarks, captivate all whom she meets.

"Isn't she sweet?"

"Oh, what a pet!"

Mr. Farrar hears the changes rung on these two feminine remarks the whole way. Snowball fraternizes with every one—she does not know what bashfulness means; she flits about like a bird the whole day long. Perhaps,

too, some of these good ladies are a trifle interested in
the tall, silent, bearded, handsome gentleman, who has
her in charge, and who is not her father, brother, uncle,
anything to her, so far as they can find out fro.n the
small demoiselle herself, whose name she does not even
know. She comes back to him once from her pere-
grniations, replete with cake and questions, perches
herself on his knee, gives one bronzed cheek a preliminary peck with her rosy lips, and puts this leading
question :

" Is you my papa ?"

" No, Snowball, I don't think I am."

" Is you my untle ?"

" Nor your uncle."

" Is you my broder ?"

" Not even you brother."

" What is you, den ?   Tause de lady she ast 'Noball."

" The lady had better not ask too many questions.   A
thirst for knowledge, you may inform her, has been the
bane of her sex.   And Snowball must not distend herself like a small anaconda with confectionery.   The lady
means to be kind, but perhaps Snowball has heard of
people who were killed with kindness ?"

To which Snowball's reply is that she is sleepy.   And
then the flaxen head cuddles comfortably over the region
of Mr. Farrar's heart, and the blue eyes close, and the
dewy lips part, and Snowball is safely in the land of
dreams.

The close of the second day brings them to St. Gildas.
Cold weather awaits them, in this Canadian seaport.
The snow lies deep, winds blow keenly.   Snowball shivers under her wraps in Mr. Farrar's arms.   They spend
the night at a hotel, and after breakfast next morning, cross the St. Gildas river to Isle Perdrix.   There
an amazed and joyful welcome awaits them.   Snowball's
reception is all Mr. Farrar has predicted, both from the
elderly Scotch doctor and the youthful French wife.

They accept the charge with delight, the two boys of the household alone eying the intruder with dubious eyes, as it is in the nature of boys under nine to regard small girls. But nature is sometimes outgrown.

Mr. Farrar remains ten days—ten days of transport to the two Macdonald lads, who worship him, or thereabouts, ten days of gladness to their parents, ten days of much caressing and infantile love-making on the part of Snowball, ten happy, peaceful days. Then he goes back to Fayal, out there in the Azores, and to the monotonous life of the manager of a large estate, in that duilest of fair tropical islands. And Snowball remaina and life on its new page, a breezy and charming and hea thful life on the sea-girt isle, begins.

PART II.

Don Carlos.—" All things that live have some means of defense."
Lucas.—" Ay, all—save only lovely helpless woman."
Don Carlos.—" Nay, woman has her tongue armed to the teeth '·

CHAPTER XI.

ISLE PERDRIX.

AR away from grimy New England manufac-
turing towns, from coal smoke, and roaring
furnaces, and brisk Yankee trade and bustle,
from circuses and flying trapeze, there rests,
rock-bound, and bare, and bleak, a green dot in a blue
waste of waters—Isle Perdrix. Lonely and barren, it
rears its craggy headland, crowned with stunted spruce
and dwarf-cedars, and runs out its sandy spits and
tongues, like an ugly, sprawling spider, into the chilly
waters of Bay Chalette. Through the brief Canadian
summer, through the long snow-bound Canadian winter, with the fierce August suns beating and blistering it,
with dank sea-fogs mapping it, with whirling snow-
storms shrouding it, Isle Perdrix rests placid, unchanged,
almost unchangeable, the high tides of Bay Chalette
threatening sometimes to rise in their might and sweep
it away, altogether, into the stormy Atlantic beyond.

Long ago, when all this Canadian land was French,
and the beautiful language the only one spoken, it had
been christened Isle Perdrix. Later, with Irish, and
English, and Scotch immigration, to confound all names,

it became Dree Island; otherwise it is unaltered, since
fifty, sixty, more years ago. Its headland light burns as
of yore, a beacon in dark and dangerous Bay Chalette—
its resident physician is still résident, as when in that
far-off time it was a quarantine station, and men and
women died in the long sheds, erected in the sands, of
"ship fever," faster than hands could bury them. It is
an island undermined with graves, haunted by ghostly
memories. The world moves, but it moves languidly
about Dree Island. It is a quarantine station still, but
its hospitals have stood empty for the past decade of
years; emigrant ships come rarely now to dull St. Gildas, and Dr. Macdonald finds his office pretty well a
sinecure. He lives there still though, a sort of family
Robinson Crusoe, in his cottage, practices as he gets it
over in St. Gildas, and brings up his two boys in their
breezy home, and would not change his secluded, peaceful, plodding life to be made viceroy of all Her Majesty's
dominions.

Dr. Macdonald's island castle is a cottage—a long,
white cottage, only one story and an attic high. But
though low, it is lengthy, and contains some nine or ten
pretty rooms, and always a spare chamber for the pilgrim
and the stranger within its gates. They come sometimes
to sketch, and fish, and shoot—bronzed and bearded pil-
grims, artists from the States, officers from Ottawa and
Montreal, and go away charmed with the doctor, the
house, the cuisine, the sport, the sea. He would be difficult indeed whom Dr. Angus Macdonald's genial manners, and Madam Aloysia's cookery would fail to charm.
Most kindly of hosts, most gentle of gentlemen, is the
dreamy doctor, and in her way "Ma'am Weesy"—so the
children shorten her stately baptismal—is a *cordon bleu.*

The cottage sits comfortably in a garden, and the
garden is shut in on the north and east by craggy bluffs,
that break the force of the beetling Atlantic winds.
Behind is a vegetable garden, with currant and goose-

6

berry bushes, flourishing among the potatoes and cabbages; in front is a flower garden—such flowers as with infinite coaxing will consent to blossom in so bleak a spot. Hardy old-fashioned poppies and dahlias, London pride, queen of the meadow, bachelor buttons, and lilac trees—these with southern sunshine and western breezes, brighten the island-garden for three or four months out of the twelve. A great picturesque trail of hop-vine and scarlet runner drapes the porch, and twines in pretty festoons round the window of the doctor's study. Take it for all in all, the bearded artists, who carry away so many sketches of it in their portfolios, may be sincere enough in pronouncing it one of the most capital little hermitages the round world holds.

It is a July morning—forenoon rather—for eleven has struck by the doctor's clock. Peace reigns on Isle Perdrix, a peace that may almost be felt, a great calm of winds and sea. The summer sky is without a cloud; it is blue, blue, blue, and flecked with rolling billows of white wool—a languid zephyr, with the saline freshness of the ocean, just stirs the hop-vines, but faintly, as if it too were a-weary in the unusual heat. Little baby wavelets lap with murmurous motion upon the gray sands—the gulls that whirl and circle round the island do not even shriek.

Peace reigns too within the cottage, the doctor is from home, the boys are at St. Gildas, and the other disturbing element of the household is—well, Ma'am Weesy does not exactly know where, but where she will remain she devoutly hopes for another hour or two. Vain hope —as the thought crosses the old woman's mind, there comes the sound of shrill, sweet singing, a quick rush and patter of small feet, a shout, and there whirls into the cottage kitchen a girl of twelve, out of breath, flushed with running, but singing her chorus still—

> " Here's to the wind that blows,
> And the ship that goes,
> And the lass that loves a sailor."

"Oh, Ma'am Weesy !" cries this breathless apparition, "*where* is Johnny?"

She stands in the doorway directly in the stream of yellow morning sunshine, her sailor hat on the back of her head—a charming head "sunning over with curls," and looks with two eyes as blue and bright as the July sky itself, into the old woman's face.

She is a charming vision altogether, a tall, slim girl, in a blue print dress made sailor-fashion, and trimmed with white braid, a strap of crimson leather belting it about the slender waist. Long ringlets of flaxen fairness fall until they touch this belt. The face is bewitching, so fair, so spirited, so full of life and eagerness, and joyous healthful youth. It matches the blonde hair and sky-blue eyes—it is all rose-pink and pearl-white.

Ma'am Weesy pauses in her work with a sort of groan. She is peeling potatoes for dinner, and throwing them into a tin pan of cold water beside her. The sunny kitchen is a gem of cleanliness and comfort; Ma'am Weesy herself is a little brown old person of fifty, as active and agile as a young girl, and housekeeper for fifteen years in the doctor's cottage. She is monarch of all she surveys at present, for Madame Macdonald is dead. and an autocratic ruler. That kitchen "interior" is a picture; everything it contains glows and gleams again with friction, tinware takes on the brilliance of silver, the rows of dishes sparkle in the sunshine. In the place of honor, in a gilt frame, hangs her patron, that handsome Saint Aloysius Gonzaga, to whom in all her difficulties, culinary as well as conscientious, she is accustomed to promptly, not to say peremptorily, appeal.

She casts an imploring glance at him now, for this youthful person is the one of all the family, who rasps and exasperates her most, but Aloysius continues to regard them with his grave smile, and responds not.

" Where is Johnny?" repeats impatiently the vision in flaxen curls and sailor suit; " is he up-stairs? I can't find him. He isn't anywhere, and he said—you heard him yourself last night, Ma'am Weesy "—in shrill indignation—" you heard him say he would take me out in the Boule-de-neige this forenoon. And now it is past eleven o'clock, and I can't find him. Johnny! John-ne-ee!" the shrill tones rise to an ear-splitting shriek.

"Ah, *Mon Dieu!*" cries out old Weesy, and covers her ears with her hands. "Mademoiselle, leave the kitchen —leave directly, I say! I will not be deafened like this. You must not come screaming at me like a sea-gull, it is not to be borne; your voice is worse than the steam-whistle down at the Point in a fog. Master Jean is not here—is not here, I tell you. He went to St. Gildas right after breakfast, and has not yet returned."

"To St. Gildas?" repeats the young person in blue, and an expression of blank despair crosses the sunny face.

Then she looks at Ma'am Weesy and brightens a bit.

"I don't believe it," she says, promptly.

"It is true, nevertheless, ma'amselle. I wanted coffee and sugar, and he offered to go. But he must be back by now—it is hours since he went. Go down to the Point and call. M'sieur Rene, at least, is sure to be there."

"I don't want M'sieur Rene," says mademoiselle, in an aggressive tone. "I want Johnny. I think it is horrid of you, Ma'am Weesy, to go sending him for sugar and things, when you might know *I'd* want him. You might have sent old Tim. And now it is fourteen minutes past eleven, and the best of the day gone. You wait until you want me to shell peas for you, or rake clams, and you'll see."

With which dark threat this young person crushes her sailor hat with some asperity down on her pale gold curls, and turns despondently to go.

Ma'am Weesy looks after her with a chuckle; it is not always she can get rid of her thus easily, and a gad-fly about the kitchen would be less of a torment over her work than mademoiselle.

Mademoiselle, meantime, recovers her spirits with great rapidity, the moment she is out of the house, and starts off at racing speed, despite the blazing sun, to the Point. It is a lofty peak, at the extreme outer edge of a projecting tongue of land, overlooking the bay and the town, across the river, and all boats passing up or down. If the missing Johnny is on sea or shore, mademoiselle is determined he shall know she awaits him and hastens his lagging steps. So standing erect on her lofty perch, overlooking the vasty deep, she uplifts her strong young voice, and

"Johnny! Johnny-y! Johnny-y-y!" pierces the circumambient air. Even the sea-gulls pause in consternation as they listen.

"Good Heaven!" cries a voice, at last. "Stop that awful row, Snowball. Your shrieks are enough to wake the dead."

The speaker is a youth of sixteen or so, stretched in the shadow of the great rock on which the girl stands, his hat pulled over his eyes, trying to read. Vain effort, with those maddening cries for Johnny rending the summer silence.

Snowball glances down at him, and her only answer is a still more ear-splitting and distracted appeal for the lost and longed-for "Johnny."

"They may wake the dead if they like," she says, disdainfully, "but they needn't wake *you*. I don't want you. I want Johnny."

"Yes, I hear you do," retorts the reader. "You always *do* want Johnny, don't you? You want Johnny a good deal more than Johnny ever wants *you*."

It is an uncivil speech, and, it may be remarked just here, that the amenities of life, as passing between M. Rene Macdonald and Mlle. Snowball Trillon, are mostly of an acid and acrid character. Open rupture indeed is often imminent, and is only avoided by the fact that the young lady is constitutionally unable to retain indignation for over five minutes at any one time. Her reply to this particularly ungallant speech, is one of her very sweetest smiles—a smile that dances in the blue eyes, and flashes out two rows of small pearl-white teeth.

"Look here, Rene," she says, "I wish you would come, too. You'll make yourself as blind as a bat, if you keep on over books forever and ever. I think I see Johnny and the batteau coming across, and we're going to Chapeau Dieu for raspberries. Do—do put that stupid book in your pocket," impatiently, "and come."

"It isn't a stupid book," says Rene Macdonald, "and berrying is much too hard work this scorcher of a day. You'll inveigle Johnny into a sunstroke if you don't take care."

"Look here!" repeats Snowball, and comes dashing down the steep side of the cliff like a young chamois. The last five feet she takes with a flying leap, and lands like a tornado at the lad's side. "Just look here!"

Sne produces from a hiding-place a basket—a market-basket of noble proportions, whips off the cover, and displays the contents.

"Sandwiches," she says, with unction, "made of minced veal and ham, lovely and thin—cold chicken pie, pound cake—all stolen from Ma'am Weesy, Rene!—biscuits, and a blueberry tart! The basket is full—*full*—I packed it myself. It's for our lunch. And the raspberries are thick—thick, Rene, over on the Banens. Johnny was there yesterday, and says so. And Weesy is going to make jam, and says we can have raspberry shortcake every evening for a week. For a week—think of that!"

She is fairly dancing with eagerness as she speaks, her great blue eyes flash like stars, her whole piquant, spirited face aglow and flushed. Even Rene—Rene the phlegmatic—catches a little of her enthusiasm. Raspberry shortcake every day for a week—and raspberry jam for ever after ! His resolution staggers—he hesitates—he is lost !

"*Do* ccme !" reiterates Snowball, and eyes and lips, and clasped hands repeat the prayer. She looks lovely as she stands in that beseeching attitude, but it is not her beauty, nor her entreating tone that moves the obdurate Rene—it is the sweet prospect of shortcake and jam.

"Well," he says, condescendingly, "I don't care if I do. It's always easier yielding than rowing with *you*, and papa told me to keep you and Jack out of mischief whenever I got a chance."

He is a slender, dark-skinned, dark-eyed, French-looking boy, very like his dead Canadian mother—not exactly handsome, and yet sufficiently attractive, with that broad, pale forehead, and those dark, luminous eyes. All sort of misty, dreamy ideas float behind that thought-ful-looking brow; he is quite a prodigy of industry and talent, head boy of St. Francis College, over at St. Gildas, where he and his brother are students.

"There's Johnny, now !" cries Snowball, in accents of exquisite delight. She drops the basket and bounds away fleet as a fawn. "Johnny! Johnny!" she calls, "I've been looking for you everywhere, and calling until I am hoarse. How could you be so awfully horrid as to go to St. Gildas and never tell *me* ?"

"Hadn't time," responds Master Johnny, resting on the gunwale of his boat, the "*Boule-de-neige.*" "Weesy wanted her groceries in no end of a hurry. I'm here now, though ; what do you want ?"

John Macdonald is fourteen years old, and is at this moment, perhaps, the handsomest boy in Canada. His face is simply beautiful. He is handsomer even, in his boyish fashion, than the pretty girl who stands beside him. He is not in the least like his brother ; he is taller at fourteen than Rene at sixteen—he is fair, like his Scottish forefathers, with sea-gray eyes, and a face per-fect enough, in form and color, for an ideal god. His hair light brown, profuse and curling, his skin is tanned by much exposure to sea and sun and wind, and a certain simplicity and unconsciousness of his own good looks lends a last charm to a face that wins all hearts at sight.

"What do I want?" repeats Snowball, fixing two reproachful eyes on the placid countenance before her; "*that's* a question for you to sit there and ask without a blush, isn't it?"

"Don't see anything to blush about," retorts Johnny, with a grim; "it's too hot to go to Chapeau Dieu, if that's what's the matter. The sun is a blazer on the water, let me tell you."

"Oh, Johnny," in blankest disappointment, "*dearest* Johnny, don't say so. And after all the trouble I've had, too—fixing the loveliest lunch—chicken-pie, tarts and everything! Oh, Johnny, *don't* back out at the last minute."

Tears spring into the blue, beseeching eyes, the hands clasp again, she stands a picture of heart-broken supplication before him.

"Oh, all right," says Johnny, who hates tears. "I wouldn't cry about it if I were you. Where's Rene? Shinning up the tree of knowledge, as usual, I suppose."

"He's coming too. Johnny, you're a darling!" cries Snowball, in a rapture; "don't let us lose a minute; the lunch basket is here. It is half-past eleven—we ought to have been off two hours ago."

"I must go up to the house with the things," says Johnny, unmoved by all this adulation. "You and Rene can pile in and wait. I won't be a minute."

"Don't tell Weesy where we're going," calls Snowball after him; "she hates me to go berrying, because I tear my clothes and stain my stockings. And, for goodness sake, hurry up. It will be two o'clock now before we get there, do your best."

"Which I'm not going to do it, in the present state of

the thermometer," responds Johnny, leisurely taking up his parcels, and leisurely departing. He is never in hurry, this boy, and is thereby a striking contrast to Snowball, who always is. Extremes meet indeed, in their case, for they are as utterly unlike in most ways, as boy and girl can well be. In all conflict of opinion between them, it may be added, mademoiselle invariably comes off victorious. It is always easier, as Rene has said, and as Johnny knows, where she is concerned, to yield than to do battle. Not that Rene ever yields—he and Snowball fight it out to the bitter end, and Rene *will* be minded, or know the reason why.

The batteau is large for that sort of boat, carries a small sail, is a beauty in her way, and the idol of young John Macdonald's heart.

" She walks the water like a thing of life," he is fond of quoting, gazing at her with glistening eyes, and it is the only poetry he is ever guilty of quoting. She is painted virgin white, is as clean and dry as old Weesy's kitchen, and carries her name in gilt letters on her stern, " Boule-de-neige." The original Boule-de-neige, with Rene, "piles in " according to the skipper's orders, and with the precious basket stowed away, sit and wait his return. Snowball taps impatiently with one slim, sandaled foot.

Rene impassively reads.

" What tiresome book have you got *now ?*" demands Snowball, in a resentful tone. " I do think, Rene, you are the stupidest boy that ever lived, and read the stupidest books that ever were printed."

" Thanks !—I mean for self and books," retorts Rene, "you, who never open a book, are a judge, of course."

" What is that ?"

" Shakespeare's tragedies, mademoiselle."

"There will be another tragedy in this boat, in five minutes if you don't put it in your pocket. Look at that sky, look at this sea, feel this velvety wind freshening;

6*

and see yourself, a great hobbledehoy, who can sit and read dull old English murders in the face of it all! I suppose you are at Macbeth; I think Lady Macbeth would have been a splendid wife for you, Rene."

Rene grunts, assent or dissent, as she likes to take it, and reads on.

"Stern, and sulky, and horrid. Oh, Rene—be good-natured for *once*—only for once—by way of a change, and shut up that book, and talk like a Christian—do!"

"Like a noodle, if I talk to you. It is polite to adapt one's conversation to one's company. And I would rather not. It is *triste* to talk rubbish. Speech is silver, silence is gold."

"Here is Johnny," cries Snowball, joyfully; "now we will have a little rational conversation—for which, *Dieu merci!* I sometimes wonder *what* I should do without Johnny. If I had to live here—if I had to live on this island alone with you, Rene, do you know what would happen?"

"That you would drive me to jump over Headland Point to escape your everlasting chatter, I dare say," says Rene.

"That you would drive *me* into melancholy madness with your silence, and your dismal books. Fancy yourself stalking about like your favorite Hamlet, in a black velvet dressing-gown, and me, like a gloomy Ophelia, with a wreath of sun-flowers and sea-weed in my hair, trailing after, singing tail-ends of songs out of tune."

Something in this picture tickles the not too easily aroused sense of humor latent in Dr. Macdonald's elder son.

Rather to the surprise of Snowball, who does not mean to be funny, he throws back his dark head, and laughs outright. And Rene Macdonald has a wonderfully pleasant and mellow laugh.

"What's the joke?" asks Johnny, bearing down upon

them rapidly. "Got the basket, Snowball? Yes, I see Bear a hand, Rene, old boy. Hooray, off she goes!"

The boat slips easily off the shelving beach, and out into the shining waters of Bay Chalette. A fresh breeze has sprung up, and tempers the fierce heat of the noonday sun. The sail is set, and away the pretty Boule-de- . neige flies in the teeth of the brisk breeze.

Johnny is past-master of the art of handling a boat; he and his batteau are known everywhere, for miles along the coast. He has been a toiler of the sea ever since he was seven years old.

"You didn't tell Weesy, did you?" asks Snowball, as they fly along at a spanking rate.

"She didn't ask me," answers Johnny. "I told her we were all going out for a sail, and wouldn't be back until dark. She cast a grateful look at St. Aloysius, over the chimney, and murmured a prayer of thanksgiving. Have you brought tin pails for the berries?— yes, I see—all right."

They fly along. And presently Snowball, lying idly over the side, her sailor hat well back on her head, defiant alike of sun and wind, breaks into a song, and presently Johnny joins in the chorus. It is a sailor's song—a monotonous chant the French sailors sing along the wharves of St. Gildas, as they coil down ropes, and the two fresh young voices blend sweetly, and float over the summer waters. And still a little later Rene pockets his book, and his clear tenor adds force to the refrain as they rapidly increase the distance between themselves and Isle Perdrix.

"Where are you going to land, Johnny?" he asks, at length. "At Sugar Scoop beach, I suppose?"

"No, don't, Johnny," cuts in Snowball, who is nothing if not contradictory, "land at Needle's Point, like a good fellow."

"Sha'n't," returns Johnny. "I don't want to stove a hole in the bottom of the batteau. Needle's Point, in-

deed ! the worst bit of beach all along Chapeau Dieu.
Catch me !"

"But I say you shall !" cries Snowball, sitting up,
and violently excited all in a moment. "You *must*.
Never mind the batteau—at least she won't get a hole in
her. If you land at Sugar Scoop we will have two full
miles to walk to Raspberry Plains—two—full—miles,"
says mademoiselle, gesticulating wildly, "in this blazing
hot sun. Whereas, if you land at Needle's Point——"

"The Boule-de-neige is ruined for life," interposes
Rene. "Don't you mind her, Johnny; she's always a little
cracked."

"You *must* mind me, Johnny ! If you land at Sugar
Scoop I—I'll sit right here !" cries Snowball, vindictively.
"I'll never stir. And I'll keep the lunch basket—it's
mine, anyhow—I put it up. And I'll eat everything ! I
won't walk two miles. It's nearly two o'clock now ; it
would be four when we got there. We would just have
time for one look at the berries, and then march back
again ! You shall land at Needle's Point, or you needn't
land at all. There !"

Johnny shrugs his shoulders resignedly. When the
torrent of Snowball's angry eloquence floods him after
this fashion, Johnny always gives up. Anything for a
quiet life, is his peaceful motto. But the belligerent fire
awakes within the less-yielding Rene.

"Johnny," he says, in an ominously quiet tone, "let
us put *her* ashore,'' indicating mademoiselle by a scornful gesture, "at her beloved Needle's Point, and you and
I will take the boat round to Sugar Scoop beach. It
will be madness to run the batteau up on those rocks."

Snowball starts to her feet, defiance flashing in the
azure eyes, flushing the rose-pink cheeks to angry crimson.

"Yes, Johnny," she cries out, "put me ashore at
Needle's Point ; put me ashore here, anywhere ; but
mind"—wildest wrath flaming upon Rene—"I keep the

basket. No matter what you do, or where you put me, I keep the lunch basket."

"Oh, stow all that!" says the badgered but pacific Johnny. "Sit down, Snowball; do you want to upset yourself and your precious lunch basket into the bay? Let her alone, Rene; it's never any use fighting with *her;* you know she'll have her way, if she dies for it. I'll land you at Needle's Point or on top of Chapeau Dieu, if you like, Snowball, only, for goodness' sake, don't make such an awful row."

"Very well," says Rene; "it is you who will repent, not I. The batteau is yours. If you like to scuttle her——"

His shoulders go up for a moment expressively; then he pulls out his book, and relapses into dignity—and Shakespeare.

"I guess it won't be so bad as that. It will be high tide when we get there, and I'll manage to run her up." Thus hopefully, Johnny, and thus, in silence, the rest of the voyage is performed.

Chapeau Dieu—so called from its fancied resemblance to a cardinal's hat—is a mountain of ponderous proportions, as to circumference, though nothing remarkable as to height. Its base is the terror of all mariners and coasters —rock-bound, beetling, undermined with sunken reefs; a spot marked dangerous on all charts; a place to be given the widest possible berth on a dark night or a foggy day. Many, many good ships have lain their bones to rest forever in the seething reefs that encircle Chapeau Dieu. But the mountain is famous, the country round, as a place for picnics, berrying parties, and the like, though anxious parents tremble a little, even in the sunniest weather, at thought of their young people there. For sudden squalls have been known to rise, and gay pleasure-boats, with their merry crews, have gone down in one dreadful minute, to be seen no more. There is but one safe landing-place—Sugar Scoop beach—but

Snowball will none of it ; so, perforce, they must try the more dangerous Needle's Point.

They reach it—a black jagged ledge, the stately cliff rising sheer above, hundreds of feet—a black, perpendicular wall of rock. It is an anxious moment, as Johnny steers the *Boule-de-neige* between two sheets of white churning foam, its bottom grating on the rocks as it goes. But there is no surf, and the lad is an expert, and the pretty little boat slips in like a white snake, and is safe inside the churning foam.

"You've done it," says Rene, "but you're a fool to have risked it, old boy, and a sweet time you are likely to have getting her off with the ebb tide. However, it is your lookout. Make her fast, as far out as you can. We will have a wade for it, and *she* will be wet to the elbows —that is some comfort."

This last brotherly remark Snowball does not hear, being busy with her tin pails and basket. But she over· takes him at this point.

"Now then ! hasn't he done it ?" she exclaims, tri- umphantly, "anybody could do it. *I* could do it—even you could do it, though you can't do much. Hurry up, Johnny—you must be famished, I am sure," with exag- gerated sympathy and affection. "You've had the whole work of bringing us here, and deserve your luncheon."

Which is unjust to Rene, who has helped manfully. A contemptuous glance, however, is his only retort—he, too, is hungry, and silence is safest, until appetite is ap- peased. Snowball is queen regnant of the lunch basket.

" All right," says Johnny, " go ahead. I'll be there. Set out the prog, Snowball—I *am* uncommonly sharp- set."

"Now you see," continues Snowball to Rene, "how much better it was to land here than at the other place. But that is all over—there is nothing more hateful than a person always trying to have his own way. Sugar Scoop is two miles from everywhere. I do hope you'll not be so obstinate another time, Rene, but let people judge for you who know best !"

Snowball is one of that exasperating class who never can let well enough alone ; who say, "I told you so " on every occasion, with a superior look that makes you long to commit murder. Rene could throw her over the cliff at the present moment, with the utmost pleasure, but still she holds the basket, and still he holds his tongue.

" Hand us those pails," he says, gruffly, and rather snatches them than otherwise. But there is no time Snowball feels for rebuke ; Johnny is bounding up the cliff in agile leaps.

"Here is a place," says the small vixen, "perhaps you'll stop being sulky, M'sieur Rene, and help me to lay the things."

Rene obeys in dignified silence, the twain work with a will, and spread chicken pie, and pound cake, and sand-wiches in a tempting way. Here is a twinkling tin cup to drink out of, and a spring of ice-cold water bubbles near, so theirs is a feast for the gods.

They fall to, with appetites naturally healthful, and set painfully on edge by two hours and a half of salt sea air.

Luncheon has the soothing effect of clearing the moral atmosphere—they eat and drink, and laugh and talk, in highest good humor. Indeed, lest you should think too badly of Mademoiselle Snowball—that we have got hold of a youthful virago in fact, it may be said, that she only quarrels with Rene on principle, and for his good. She feels he needs putting down, and she puts him down accordingly. It is rather a motherly—a grandmotherly if you like—sort of thing. And she never (hardly ever) quarrels with any one else. And her wildest outburst of indignation never lasts, as has been stated, more than five minutes at any one time. It is a constitutional impossibility for Snowball to retain anger. For Johnny—she loves him and bullies him—is his chum

and comrade, would die for him, or box his ears with
equal readiness. She is never altogether happy away from
him, while Master Jean in a general way sees her go
with a sense of profound relief, and never wholly dare
call his soul his own in her whirlwind presence. At the
present stage of his existence he feels her overpowering
affection a little too much for him, and could cheerfully
dispense with—say two-thirds of it, with all the pleasure
in life.

"Now, I call this splendid," says Snowball, gathering
up the fragments of the feast. "Rene, you have a watch,
what's the time?"

"Quarter past three," answers Rene, lazily, looking
at his gold repeater, a last birthday-gift from his father.
"If you intend to get any raspberries to-day, it strikes
me it is time you and Johnny were at it!"

"Me and Johnny!" cries Snowball, shrilly, "and you,
for example—what of you, my friend?"

"I," says Rene, pulling out the obnoxious Shakespeare, "will lie here and look at you, and improve my
mind with 'Richard the Third.'"

Snowball makes one flying leap, pounces upon
Shakespeare, and hugs him to her breast.

"Never!" she cries, "never, while life beats in this
bosom! Johnny, you help me. Will you come and
pick, sir, or will you not?"

"Not," says Rene, "much rather not. Give me back
my book, Snowball!" in quick alarm. "Stop!"

She stands on the dizzy edge of the cliff, and Shakespeare is poised high—perilously high—above her head.

"Promise," she exclaims, "promise to pick, else here
I vow over the cliff Shakespeare goes, full fifty fathoms
under Bay Chalette. Promise, or never see him more."

"Snowball, you would not dare!" in angry alarm ;
for he knows she *would* dare—has dared more daring
deeds than this. And Johnny stands and grins approval.

"Chuck it over, Snowball," he says, "or make him help us—I'll back you up."

"One !—two !——" cries Snowball, eyes and cheeks aglow with wicked delight. "If I say three, over it goes. One !—two !—— Do you promise, or——"

"Oh, confound you ! yes, I promise. Give me my book !" says enraged Rene. "I would like to throw you over instead—I will, some day, if you exasperate me too far."

"The spirit is willing, but the flesh is weak. You daren't, Rene, dearest," laughs Snowball. She hands him the book as she speaks, knowing well he will not break his word.

> " ' Come on, my merry men all,
> We will to the greenwood hie !' "

she sings, gleefully, and snatches up one of the tin pails and bounds away.

Rene consigns his cherished volume to his pocket, picks up a tin pail, and prepares to follow, when a cry from Johnny—a low, hoarse, agonized cry—makes him stop. He looks. His brother stands, every trace of color fading from his face, his gray eyes wide with dismay, one flickering finger pointing seaward. Rene follows the finger, and gazes, and sees—yards away, floating out with the turning tide, farther and farther every second—the *Boule-de-neige !*

"*Mon Dieu !*" he cries, and stands stunned.

It is a moment before he can take in the full magnitude of the disaster. The boat is gone, past all recall, and they are here, lost on Chapeau Dieu.

"Good Heaven !" Rene exclaims, under his breath ; "Johnny, how is this ?"

"I did not make her fast," Johnny answers, huskily. "I thought I did, but it was a hard place, and Snowball was calling. I did not make her secure—and now she is gone, my *Boule-de-neige*, and I may never see her again !"

There is agony, real agony, in his voice. Not for himself, in this first moment, does he care—not for the misfortune that has come upon them, that may end in darkost disaster—but for his darling, his treasure, the joy of his heart, his white idol, *Boule-de-neige.*

Rene says nothing ; he feels for his brother's bereavement too deeply, and consternation is in his soul. So they stand and gaze, and farther, and farther, and farther away, with the swelling tide, floats the faithless *Boule-de-neige !*

CHAPTER XII.

CHAPEAU DIEU.

"AND it is all Snowball's fault !"

It is Rene who speaks the words, passionate anger in his voice—the first words that break the long silence. Far off, the battcau is but a white drifting speck, after which they strain their eyes until they are half blind. Johnny's eyes arc dim.

"It is all Snowball's fault !" passionately repeats Rene. Far away and faint, her sweet singing reaches them, broken now and then, as the fruit she picks finds its way between her rosy lips, instead of into the shining pail. The sound is to his wrath as "vinegar upon niter."

"It is all her fault. She *would* come to Chapeau Dieu, she *would* land here and nowhere else. Johnny, it serves you right ! You yield to her in everything. You should *not* have let her force you to land here."

Johnny says nothing. "His heart is with his eyes, and that is far away"—far away, to where *Boule-de-neige*, beautiful, traitorous *Boule-de-neige*, floats out to the open sea.

"She is a tyrant. Every one spoils her—you all do—papa, Weesy, and you, Johnny, worst of all. You let her have her way in everything, and no good ever can come of it. Now, we are here, and here we may remain. And it is all her doing from first to last."

"It's no use talking now," says Johnny, huskily, "the batteau's gone—gone !"

"Yes, I see it's gone," bitterly, "and I hear her singing over yonder still ! You had better go and tell her, and see if she will not change her tune !"

Johnny turns away—not to tell Snowball, however. The boat is quite out of sight now, gone forever it may be, and Johnny feels that his voice is not to be trusted, with this great lump rising and falling in his throat !

There is a pause. Rene stands, a statue of angry grief and despair, and still strains his eyes over the blue shining sea. No boats are to be seen ; far off on the horizon there are sails, but none of these sails will ever come near. All craft steer wide of fatal Chapeau Dieu.

"What *are* we to do ?" he bursts out at length ; "look here, Johnny, it's no time to sit down and cry."

"I'm not crying !" retorts Johnny, angrily, looking up, but his eyes look red as he says it, and his voice breaks short.

"The batteau's gone," pursues the relentless Rene, "and we are here. Now how are we to get off ?"

"Wait until something comes along and takes us off, I suppose."

"And how long may that be ? Nothing ever comes this way—no one in their senses ever lands at Needle's Point. You know that. Unless a storm drives a fishing boat or a coaster out of their course, nothing will ever come within miles of us. Then what are we to do ?"

"They will miss us, and search for us," says Johnny, waking up somewhat to a sense of personal danger.

"Will they? No one knows where we are. More of Snowball's doing—she wouldn't let you tell Ma'am Weesy. Weesy will not miss us until bedtime—then who is to search? She and old Tim are alone on the island, and he can't leave the Light. If he feels in the humor, he may perhaps go to St. Gildas to-morrow, and give the alarm. Then, by noon, some one may be ready to start in the search, but where are they to look? You and Snowball go everywhere, up and down the coast for twenty miles—a wide circuit to search over—and no one will think of Chapeau Dieu until every other place has been given up. That may not be for days, and in three days papa will be back home. How do you suppose *he* will feel?"

"By George !" says Johnny, blankly.

"I suppose we will not starve," goes on Rene, still bitterly ; "there are the berries we came for, and here is a spring. And it won't hurt us to sleep on the ground. We can rough it. But our father—it will about kill him."

"And Snowball," says Johnny, pitifully, "poor little Snowball. She can't rough it. What will become of Snowball ?"

"Nothing she does not richly deserve. Let us hope it will be a lesson to her—if she—we—any of us leave this mountain alive. It is her doing from first to last. Let her take the consequences ! I, for one, don't pity her."

"Poor little Snowball," repeats Johnny, softly. He never argues, but he is not easily convinced. Even the loss of *Boule-de-neige* is forgotten, in this new state of things. "I'm awfully sorry for Snowball."

"You are an idiot, Johnny !" savagely ; "think of yourself."

"Well—I do. I can't help thinking of her, though,

too. Poor little thing, how is she to sleep on the turf? And she is not strong. And she never meant any harm. Don't be so hard, old fellow."

The gentle sea-gray eyes look wistfully up—the brown, bright, angry eyes look down. "Have a little pity," the gray eyes say. And "You're a good fellow, Johnny," the brown eyes answer. They soften as they turn away. "It's an awful fix, though!" he mutters, and looks seaward again, and begins to whistle.

There is a stifled sob behind, but neither hear it. Then, like a guilty thing, Snowball creeps away. It is not her wont to advance unheard—she can make noise enough at any time for a dozen—but the turf has muffled her steps, and raspberries have stopped her mouth. And she has come upon them, unfelt, unseen, and overheard all. All! Rene's scathing words, Johnny's regretful pleading. An awful panic of remorse falls upon her. The whole situation as exposed by Rene opens before her, and it is all her doing—hers—her willfulness, obstinacy, selfishness, from first to last! They may perish here. And Dr. Macdonald will break his heart. And she is the cause of it all! She *would* come, she would land at Needle's Point, where no boat could be safely moored; she would call to Johnny to hurry! Rene is right—it is all her fault, from beginning to end.

She flings herself on the ground, and buries her wicked face in the grass. All the misdeeds of her life— neither few nor far between—rise up before her in remorseful array, but pale into insignificance before this crowning crime. She lies prone, bedewing the dry ferns with her despairing tears, and so, half an hour after, when he quits his brother, Johnny finds her. He looks at her ruefully and uncomfortably—even at fourteen he has a genuine masculine horror of crying—and touches her up gently with the toe of his shoe.

"I say," he says, with an attempt at gruffness, "stop that, will you!"

Two lovely, blue, shining eyes look up at him, pathetic with heart-broken despair.

"Oh, Johnny!" she cries out in anguished tones.

Johnny has nothing to say to this; indeed, the situation quite goes without saying. He stands gnawing a raspberry branch, and looking still more uncomfortable. But Snowball must talk—if death were the penalty Snowball would talk; talking is her forte, and she has been silent now for over an hour. So she sits up, wipes her eyes, sobs a last sob, and looks at him solemnly.

"Johnny!"

"Yes."

"This is awful, isn't it?"

"Pretty awful," dismally; "the batteau's gone."

"Never mind; *she* won't go far—somebody will pick her up. Every one knows the *Boule-de-neige.* She's all right. Johnny!"

"Yes."

"Rene feels awfully, don't he?"

"Pretty awfully. So do I."

"But it isn't so bad as he makes out. If there is any chance of seeing the blackest side of things"—the innate spirit of contrariety rising at the bare mention of Rene's name—"he is sure to see it. It isn't half so bad."

"I hope not, I'm sure," still dismally; "it's bad enough, I reckon. We've got to stay here all night. What do you call that?"

"Oh!—one night—that makes nothing!" loftily. "And we will be taken off to-morrow. I am sure of it."

"I wish I was, by George! I ain't, though. And papa will be home in a day or two. That is what Rene —both of us—feel bad about."

"And don't you think *I* do?" indignantly—"would, I mean, only I am certain we will be safe home long before he comes. Now look here. Ma'am Weesy will miss us, won't she, and be so scared she won't be able to sleep a wink all night!"

"I dare say."

"Then to-morrow morning, the first thing, she will rout out old Tim, and make him row her over to St. Gildas. Do you know who will be the first person she will go to see there?"

"No, I don't."

"You might, then, if you ever thought at all. She will go to Père Louis. She goes to him first in every worry she has. And you know what *he* is. Old Tim may take it easy, and let the grass grow under his feet, but Père Louis won't. He'll never rest until we're found."

"By George!" says Johnny, brightening.

"He'll move heaven and earth to find us," pursues Snowball, more and more excited, "and there isn't a man in St. Gildas isn't ready to fly, if Père Louis but holds up his finger. You know that. And besides——"

"Well?"

"I told Innocente Desereaux only yesterday we were coming to Chapeau Dieu for raspberries this week. I wanted her to come, but she couldn't, Rene says. It shows all he knows about it!" resentfully. "They'll never think of Chapeau Dieu! Don't you suppose Inno will hear of our being missing, and will tell what I said? And then won't they come straight here and take us off? Rene indeed! he thinks he knows everything! He isn't so much wiser than other people, after all, in spite of his big books!"

"You had better go and tell him so," says Johnny, with a grimace of delight.

He has quite come over to Snowball's view of the question, and his spirits rise proportionately.

"I would in a minute," retorts Snowball, with fine defiance.

She does not, however; she glances over at him, and her courage, like Bob Acres', oozes out at the palms of her hands. Truth to tell, he does look rather unapproachable, standing slim, and straight, and dark, with folded arms, his back against a rock, his pale, rather stern face set seaward.

"How will you stow yourself for the night?" asks Johnny, after a pause.

"Oh, anywhere—it doesn't matter. I will lie under those bushes on the moss—it is soft and dry. Besides, I don't expect to sleep. Johnny, if Rene wasn't so grumpy, I would enjoy this."

"Would you, by George?"

"And you," says Snowball, with some resentment, "if I've heard you say once I've heard you ten hundred thousand times say you envied Robinson Crusoe—that you would fairly love to be wrecked on a desert island. And now—isn't this as good as any desert island, only we'll get taken off sooner, and you don't look pleased one bit! You look as sulky as sulky."

"It's not half as good as Crusoe's island," says Johnny; "we have nothing to eat but raspberries, and a fellow gets tired of raspberries as a steady diet. He had goats, and grapes, and Friday——"

"He didn't eat Friday. I," smiling radiantly, "will be your Friday, Johnny."

"And savages——"

"Rene will do for the savages. And talking of eating"—briskly—"we have enough left in the basket for supper. Suppose we have supper, Johnny? It must be six o'clock, and eating will be better than doing nothing."

"All right," responds Johnny, who is always open to anything in this line; "fix things, and I'll go and tell Rene."

He tells Rene all Snowball has told him, ending with a fraternal invitation as sent by that young person to come to supper.

"Tell her to eat it herself," says Rene, shortly, "I don't want any of her supper. And you had better not take much either, Johnny; pick berries if you are hungry. Snowball may be glad of the leavings of her luncheon before we get off yet."

"Why? Don't you believe what she says!"

"I believe she believes it. I have not much faith in Snowball's rosy predictions."

"But it seems likely enough," says the perplexed Johnny. Père Louis *will* search for us high and low, and——"

"Ay, if Père Louis is at home. Half the time, as you know, he is away on missions in the outlying parishes. And July and August are his mission months. I am positive he is not in town."

Johnny stands blankly, his new-born hopes knocked from under him at one fell blow. To Père Louis all things are possible—wanting him, Ma'am Weesy and old Tim, the light-house keeper, are but rickety reeds.

"For which reason," continues Rene, the relentless, "you had better tell Snowball to keep the contents of the basket for herself. *I* want none of it, at least."

The dusk face, fine as a cameo, looks at this moment as if cut in adamant. Snowball glancing across, thinks she has never before seen Rene look so hatefully cross.

There is a long pause; the brothers stand and gaze far and vainly over the sea, Johnny with the old patient, wistful light in his most beautiful eyes, Rene with knitted brows, and dark, stern, resolute gaze.

"It's an awful go!" says Johnny, at last, under his breath. "I wish you wouldn't be so tremendously hard on Snowball, though. She couldn't help it. It isn't fair, by George! You make the poor little thing feel miserable, Rene. She was crying her eyes out a little while ago."

"Let her cry!" savagely.

"She heard every word you said."

"Let her hear! Too much of her own way will be the ruin of that girl. She is spoiled by over-indulgence. You all pet her—I shall not."

7

"No," says Johnny, turning away, "you will never spoil anybody in that way, I think. What a fellow you are, Rene—as hard as nails."

With which he goes back, with lagging steps, his newly-lit hopes ruthlessly snuffed out. He feels himself a sort of shuttlecock between these two belligerent battledoors, and would lose his temper if he knew how. Fortunately, John Macdonald out of temper is a sight no mortal eye has ever yet seen—so he only looks a trifle blank and rueful, as he returns to Snowball now.

"Well," that small maiden demands, imperiously, "he wouldn't come?"

"No," slowly, "he wouldn't come."

"Of course he wouldn't!" in a rising key; "it's exactly like him. I think if Rene ever does a good-natured thing the novelty will be the death of him. Now, why wouldn't he come?"

"Oh—he says he's not hungry. He says to eat it yourself. Now, Snowball, *don't* nag—I've had enough of it—let a fellow have some peace, can't you. *I* haven't done anything."

"What else does he say?" with pursed-up lips and brightening eyes.

"He says that Pere Louis is away on missions, and may not be home when Weesy gets there. He says you'll be hungry enough to want that cake you're crumbling all to pieces, maybe, before you get another."

"Have one, Johnny?" says Snowball, politely, tendering one of those confections.

But Johnny shakes his head gloomily, and declines.

"Keep it for yourself. He won't touch anything but berries, he says—no more will I. Eat it yourself—or better still, keep it for your breakfast to-morrow."

Without a word, mademoiselle puts back cakes, pie, sandwiches, etcetera, in the basket, covers these provisions with exaggerated care, then sits down a little way off, her sailor hat tilted well over her nose, her hands folded in her lap. So she sits for a long time, Johnny extended in a melancholy attitude on the grass near by. So long she sits indeed, that his suspicions are awakened ; he rises on his elbow and peers under the hat. Big, silent tears are raining down—big, clear, globular drops, chasing each other, and falling almost with a plash !—they look large enough—on the folded hands.

" Hallo !" cries Master John, taken aback, "you ain't at it again, are you. What is there to cry for now ?"

Silence—deeper sobs—bigger tears.

" Say—can't you," fretfully. "I wish you wouldn't. You never used to be a cry-baby, Snowball. Stop it, can't you. What's the matter *now* ?"

" Johnny !" a great sob. " Jo-ohn-ny !" another.

" Yes," says Johnny, " all right. What ?"

" Jo-ohnny I—I *hate* Rene !"

The vindictive emphasis with which this is brought out, staggers pacific Johnny. There is a pause.

"Oh ! I say. You mustn't, you know. Not that there is any love lost," *sotto voce.*

" I—I," increase of sobbing, "I always *did* hate him. I always shall. I would like to get a boat, and go away, and leave him here forever, and ever, and ever !"

" By George !" And then, all at once, Johnny throws himself back on the furze, and laughs long and loudly.

" So," he gasps, " it is crying with rage you are, after all. Wasn't it Dr. Johnson who liked a good hater ? He ought to have known Snowball Macdonald."

" My name isn't Macdonald ; I wouldn't have a name he "—ferociously pointing—" has ! If ever I get off this horrid, abominable place, Johnny, do you know what I mean to do ?"

" Not at present," returns Johnny, who is immensely amused. "Something tremendous, I guess. What ?"

" I mean to write to Mr. Farrar, Monsieur Paul, to come and take me away. I belong to him—he brought me here. I wish he hadn't now. Anywhere would be better than where *he* is. And I'll go away, and I'll *never*, NEVER, NEVER speak to Rene again !"

All this is, as the reader must know, long anterior to the days of "Pinafore," else Johnny might have asked just here, with his customary grin, "What, *never?*" And Snowball, with a relenting inflection, might have safely responded, "Well, hardly ever," and so truthfully expressed her feelings; for, having reached this powerful climax, and gotten to the very tip-top of the mountain of her indignation, she proceeds, with great rapidity and compunction, to come down.

"Not that I wouldn't be dreadfully sorry to leave papa, and you, Johnny, and even old Weesy and Tim— and Père Louis, and Mère Maddelena, and Sœur Ignatia, and Innocente Desereaux, and——"

"Oh, hold on !" cries Johnny. "That list won't end until midnight if you name all the people you know. Besides, it will be all no use—you will only waste a sheet of paper and a stamp for nothing. Monsieur Paul will not take you."

"Why won't he?" But she asks it as if the assurance were rather a relief.

"Because you don't belong to him—not really, you know. In point of fact, old girl," says Johnny, smiling sweetly upon her, "you don't seem to belong to any one. I guess you sprung up one night somewhere, all by yourself, like a mushroom."

"I must belong to the people who pay for me," says Snowball, rather crestfallen, "whoever they are."

"Yes — whoever they are ! I should admire to know. So would you, I dare say. Papa doesn't—Mr. Farrar may, but he doesn't tell—only you don't belong to *him*, and he won't take you away. You're a fixture for life on Isle Perdrix, like old Tim and the light-house. When Weesy dies—she can't go on living for-ever—and I grow up and get rich, and am captain of a ship, I'll take you with me as cook. You ain't half a bad cook, Snowball—your apple-dumplings are 'things to dream of.' I wish I had a few now."

"Are you hungry, Johnny?" eagerly. "If you are——" Her hand is in the basket in a moment.

"I'm not hungry for anything you have there. No, thanks, I won't take it. You will keep all that for yourself, as Rene says."

"Johnny,"—in a drooping voice—"please don't mention Rene. I can't bear the sound of his name. Oh, dear me!"—a deep, deep, deep sigh—"I don't see why some people ever were born!"

> "What shall I be at fifty,
>   Should nature keep me alive,
> If I find the world so weary
>   When I am but twenty-five?"

chants Johnny, and laughs. It is a physical impossibility for this boy to remain despondent. After a fashion, he is trying to enjoy being shipwrecked on the top of this big, bare mountain. Rene glances round in wonder at the singing and laughing.

"Would anything make these two serious for five minutes?" he thinks, with a contemptuous shrug. "Singing! and they may never leave this hideous desert alive."

"Let us sing some more," says Snowball, waking up promptly to badness. "Rene looks as if he didn't like it. Let us sing—let us sing the evening hymn."

"Pious thought—let us," laughs Johnny. And so to aggravate further the dark and silent M. Rene, these two uplift their fresh young voices, and send them in unison over the darkening waters.

> "*Ave Sanctissima!*
> We lift our souls to thee,
>   *Ora pro nobis,*
> 'Tis nightfall on the sea!
>   Watch us while shadows lie
> Far o'er the water spread;
>   Hear the heart's lonely sigh—
> Thine, too, hath bled."

Snowball glances at her foe. He stands and makes no sign, and his dark thoughtful face is turned away. A little pang of remorse begins to shoot through her, but she finishes her hymn.

> " *Ora, pro nobis,*
> The waves must rock our sleep ;
> *Ora, Mater, ora,*
> Star of the deep !"

"'Tis nightfall on the sea." It is indeed nightfall now. The sun has dipped long since into the waters of Bay Chalette, and gone down—the long, star-lit northern twilight is paling to dull drab. The evening wind comes to them with all the chill of the wide Atlantic in its salt breath.

"And you have no wrap," says Johnny, compassionately. Snowball has shivered involuntarily in her thin dress, and he sees it. He is in blue flanel himself, and is the best provided of the three, Rene being clad in white linen, which he greatly affects in summer time.

"It doesn't matter," Snowball answers. "Never mind me."

But her voice sounds weary, and she leans spiritlessly enough against the rough bole of a big tamarack.

"Suppose you lie down, and take a nap," suggests Johnny, "it will rest you, and it's of no use sitting up. We're in for it to-night, anyhow—better luck to-morrow. I'll fix you a bed before it gets any darker."

But there is nothing much to "fix," as he finds. There is only the dry, rough furze, and long marsh grass and hard penitential branches of spruce and cedar. With these he does the best he can ; he piles up the furze, strews it with the long tough grass, twists the little spruce branches into a sort of arbor, and the best he can do is done.

"There you are," he says, "there's a bed and board for you. Rosamond's Bower—Boffin's Bower—not to be named in the same day. Turn in, and don't open your peepers till to-morrow morning. Let us hope it will be your last, as well as your first night, camping out. I'll go and shake up Rene, before he is transmogrified into the rock against which he has leaned so long. Good-night, young 'un !"

"Good-night, Johnny," responds Snowball falter-ingly.

She is afraid, but she would die rather than say so. Afraid of snakes, of bears, of ghosts, of the wind in the tree-tops, the sound of the sea, the awful silence, and loneliness, and majesty of night.

She creeps into her bower, but sits peering out—such a pale, anxious, pretty little face, in the dim starlight.

She can see the boys standing together, and still ever gazing over the bay.

"Will Rene ever stir?" she thinks. "He looks as if he could stand there forever. And how cross he did look. I—wish—I—hadn't made Rene mad !"

The admission comes reluctantly—even in her own mind, but having made it, she is disposed to descend to still deeper depths of the valley of humiliation.

"It is all my fault—Rene is right—it is always my fault ! I must be horrid. I wonder everybody don't hate me as well as him. Maybe they do, only they don't like to show it. Yes, I always *do* want my own way, and make a time if I don't get it. I give Johnny no peace of his life. I fight with Rene from morning till night. And I don't belong to anybody—I suppose I am too hate-ful even for that ! I wonder why I ever was born—I wonder if I will always be horrid as long as I live ! I wonder," draggingly, "if—Rene—would forgive me, if —I begged his pardon, and promised never to do it any more ?"'

The "it" is rather vague, but in Snowball's penitent mind, it stands for all the enormities of her life, too many to be particularized, so she "lumps" them ! The brothers meantime stand, with that seaward gaze, that takes in the blue black world of waters.

The night wind sighs around them, the surf laps, with a hoarse, ceaseless moan and wash, over the sunken surf, far below. Rene is very pale in the light of the stars.

"You look used up already, old chap," Johnny says; "take a snooze, why don't you, and forget it. It's no use fretting. Sorrow may abide for a night, but joy cometh with the morning! Something like that was Père Louis' text last Sunday. It fits in now, I think—make a meditation on it, old man, and cheer up!"

"If we get off before our father comes home I shall not care," returns Rene, moodily; "it is that that worries me, Johnny!"

"Oh! we will—never fear. We are sure to get off to-morrow—something tells me so. Don't cross your bridges before you come to them. Turn in like a good fellow, and let us try to forget it. I'm as sleepy as the duse!"

A great yawn indorses the statement. Rene glances behind him.

"What have you done with Snowball?"

"Rigged her up as well as I was able. Twisted some boughs to break the wind, and gathered moss and grass for a bed. It's the best I could do."

"Has she had anything to eat?"

"Wouldn't eat anything when you wouldn't," says Johnny, maliciously; "nearly cried her eyes out into the bargain. Feels pretty badly, let me tell you, about the way you take it. Now *don't* say again serves her right! It doesn't."

"I am not going to say it. She must not be foolish, however; if she wants to be friends with me she must eat what there is left to-morrow morning. We boys are responsible for her. We must take care of her to—to the last."

"That means until we are taken off! Of course we

will," says hopeful Johnny; "now let us turn in and go to sleep."

"Turn in—where?"

"Oh, anywhere. You pays your money, and you takes your choice.. All the beds in the '*hôtel de la belle étoile*' are at our service. Here is mine. *A demain;* good-night."

"Good-night," responds Rene, and looks at his brother almost in envy.

Johnny has thrown himself down just where he stood, and in less than a minute seems to be sound asleep. But it is a long time before Rene follows; he sits there beside his big rock, his face still faithfully turned seaward, his head resting against its mossy side, his eyes closed.

The night is far advanced; it is long past midnight, indeed, and he is half asleep, half awake, when a light chill touch falls on his hand, and awakes him with a great nervous start. A slim figure, with loosely blowing hair, pale, pleading face and pathetic eyes stands by his side.

"Rene!"—a pause—"Rene!" tremulously. "*Dear* Rene! forgive me."

"Snowball! You! I thought you were asleep hours ago."

"I could not sleep, Rene! I am sorry!"—a suppressed sob. "I know I'm horrid. I don't wonder you hate me. It *does* serve me right. Nothing is too bad to happen to me! It's all my fault. I—I—I'm *awfully* sorry, Rene!"

"Snowball——"

"I want you to forgive me," in a sobbing whisper, "Oh! Rene, don't be mad! I—I—can't help being hateful, but I'll try. Oh! I mean to try ever so hard after this. I'll never contradict you again! I'll do everything you say! Only I can't bear you to be angry with me" (great sobbing here, sternly repressed, for slumbering Johnny's sake). "Oh! Rene, forgive me!"

7*

"Snowball! you dear little soul!"

And all in a moment, obdurate Rene melts, and puts his arms around her, and gives her a hearty, forgiving, fraternal smack—the first kiss he had ever favored her with, in his life. Perhaps the hour, the scene, the loneliness, have something to do with it. It opens the full floodgates of Snowball's tears; she puts her arms around his neck, and cries on his shoulder, until that portion of his raiment is quite damp through. Conducts herself generally, in short, for the space of five minutes, like a juvenile Niobe. Then she recovers. Rene has had enough of it, and rather lifts his lovely burden off his neck.

"There, now, Snowball, don't cry any more; it's all right; I'm not angry. I don't know that it was your fault, much, after all. Go back, and try to sleep. You'll be fit for nothing to-morrow, if you spend the night crying like this."

And thus in the "dead waste and middle of the night," peace is proclaimed, and next morning, to his great amazement, Johnny finds the twain he has left mortal foes the night before, excellent friends in the morning. He is puzzled, but thankful, and accepts the fact without too many questions. Only Snowball nearly has a relapse when she finds neither of the boys will touch the hoarded remains of the basket, and propose to sustain existence on berries.

"Then the things may go uneaten!" she is beginning vehemently, "*I* shan't touch them!"

Rene looks at her.

"Is this your promise of last night?" the severe young eyes demand. And mademoiselle's head droops, and her hand goes into the basket, and she swallows a lump in her throat, and—the last of the sandwiches.

The morning is fine—promises to equal yesterday in sunshine and warmth, and keeps its promise. But it is a long day—a long, long, weary day. They lie about listlessly, pick berries, talk in a perfunctory fashion ; even Snowball's fine flow of tittle-tattle flags. Rene reads ; Johnny tries to rig a fishing-line and catch something, but fails. He reclines at Snowball's feet mostly, and lets her tell him stories—sea stories, if she knows any. All her life she has been an omnivorous reader devouring everything that has come in her way. Her repertoire, therefore, is considerable. She sings to him, too. Johnny always likes to hear her sing. She feels it a point of honor to keep her boys' spirits up. It is all her fault, but they are here ; that fact keeps well uppermost in her mind, and she does her poor little best. It is easy enough with Johnny, who is cheery and sanguine by nature ; but Rene looks so pale, so troubled, sits so silent, so grave, it is depressing only to look at him.

The long day wears on. Afternoon comes, and evening, and night, and still no boat, no rescue. Still nothing but the hollow, monotonous moan of the sea, the whistling of the wind, the whispering of the branches, the white flash of a sea-gull's wing, the circling swoop of a fish-hawk—and far off, far, far off, white sails, that never draw near.

The stars shine out, a little, slim new moon cuts sharply and cleanly the blue waste of sky, and a second night finds these castaway mariners high and dry on top of Chapeau Dieu.

CHAPTER XIII.

FOUR DAYS.

NOTHER night, another dawn, another day—night, a third time, and still the lost ones are lost in the wild mountain side !

With the breaking of the third day, there breaks, also, the fine weather that up to this time has

served them.   This third day dawns with a coppery sky,
a lurid, angry-looking sun rises redly over the water, a
dead calm holds land and sea locked in an ominous hush.
The heat is intolerable.   A sultry cloud rises slowly, and
gathers and enlarges, grows and advances, and slowly,
surely, the whole red sky glooms over.   The surf breaks
down below, in a dull, threatening whisper, there are fitful soughs of wind, from every quarter of the compass,
it seems, at once.   Sea-birds whirl and scream, white
sails, hull down on the horizon, furl and vanish, the sky
lowers, until its dark pall seems to rest on the mountain
top.   All nature is gathering her forces to hurl out, and
meet the coming storm.

These three weary days have brought little change
that can be written down, to the hapless trio left stranded.
They have dawned and darkened, and between morning
and night nothing more exciting than raspberry picking
and reading Shakespeare have gone on.   Nothing *can*
possibly happen here ; no boats approach, there are no
wild animals, no reptiles more deadly than garter snakes
and grasshoppers, no savages, no anything !   And they
dare not leave where they are ; it is the one spot accessible
on all the mountain ; the rest is a howling, untrodden,
inaccessible wilderness.

The most important event has been the improvement
and enlargement of Snowball's bower.   From that inex-
haustible receptacle, a boy's pocket, Johnny has exhumed
a ball of string and half a dozen nails.   With these he
and Rene have widened and tightened the bower, twisted
more supple branches, until the little shelter is comparatively strong, and prepared to keep out bleak night
blasts, and even withstand a tolerably strong gale.   It
stands with its back to a great bowlder, the north wind
thus cut off, and the branches closely enough locked to
exclude at all times the rays of the fierce sea-side sun.
Here Snowball has already learned to sleep on her turfy
bed as deeply and soundly as ever in the little white cot

at home. There is room enough in the bower for her to
lie at full length, but decidedly none for superfluous
turning round, or standing up. She crawls in on her
hands and knees, and backs out—as people do from the
presence of royalty—but always on all fours. Here, too,
the boys, who remain alternately on the lookout at night,
take turns during the day, to woo balmy slumber. And
there is nothing else to be done. No fishing, snaring,
shooting—nothing but to pick the everlasting raspberry,
of which their souls long since wearied, and lie on the
furze, and gaze with longing, haggard eyes over the pitiless sea. Sails come and go, but always afar off. They
have hoisted their handkerchiefs on trees, they light fires
during the day on the hill-side—all in vain. They dare
not burn beacons at night, lest vessels should mistake
the signal for Dree Island Light, and so be lured on the
fatal reefs. And it is the afternoon of this third day, and
rescue cometh not.

They rest in different positions on the grass, all silent
and sad, and watch, with vague fear, the rising storm.
It promises to be a very violent one—a tempest of thunder and lightning—a tornado of wind and rain—a swift
summer cyclone, dealing death and destruction upon
land and sea.

"And Snowball is so afraid of lightning and thunder,"
thinks Rene, "and the bower, that we have tried so hard
to rig up for her—will it stand five minutes in the teeth
of this rising gale?"

His languid gaze turns to where Snowball lies, prone,
and listless, and mute, and pale, with closed eyes, her
fair head pillowed on one wasted arm. Yes, wasted, although the remains of the luncheon and the chief share
of the raspberries have been hers. She has passionately
protested and appealed for an equal division, but Rene,
the inflexible, has not yielded a jot.

"You will take what we give you ; do as I tell you,
or we will never be friends again !" he says, in his most

obstinate voice, and she has sobbed and succumbed. But he is very good to her in all else, very gentle, surprisingly tender, amazingly yielding—altogether unlike the self-willed, domineering Rene she has hitherto known. No other quarrel has followed that memorable reconciliation ; she may be fretful and irritable at times —she is indeed—but his patience with her never flags. Johnny himself is not sweeter of temper, in these disastrous days. But it is an unnatural state of goodness on both sides, not in the least likely to last, if they only get off with life, but Rene has made up his mind it shall last during their stay on Chapeau Dieu, and Rene's resolutions are as those of the Mede and the Persian. His Shakespeare is as a diamond mine to them all. The volume contains four of the tragedies, and Rene, a fine reader, both of English and French, reads aloud to them, and never tires. He dips, too, into the depths of his memory and brings forth such store of anecdote, story, fable, poetry—Victor Hugo's and Beranger's, mostly— that his two hearers can only listen in gratitude and admiration, and wonder if this most entertaining companion can be the silent and somewhat grim Rene they have hitherto had the honor of knowing.

"I never would have thought you had it in you," Snowball says to him, with that charming candor, which is a distinguishing character of their intimacy. " No one would. You always seemed to me about as silent and stupid as a white owl. Didn't he to you, Johnny? I dare say he may grow up to be quite a credit to us yet— mightn't he, Johnny?"

"He won't grow up much if he has to spend three more days on Chapeau Dieu," responds Johnny, languidly. "He doesn't look good for over twenty-four more hours of it. You don't eat enough, Rene, old boy. You keep all you pick for Sn—I mean you are slowly starving. Let me go and gather you a cupful of berries."

He makes a weary motion to rise—truth to tell, he—
they all—are almost too weak to stir. The raspberries
are not so very plentiful, and an utter distaste for their
insipid sweetness has seized them all. Rene looks decidedly the worst. His dark, thin face, pale at all times,
is blanched to a dull, clayey hue—its outline against the
darkening sky has the shrunk, pinched look that only
starving gives. He is worn with anxiety; he hardly
sleeps ; he gives, as Johnny says, the lion's share of all
the fruit he gathers to Snowball, and compels her to take
it. His great dark eyes look hollow, and twice their
natural size—they shine with a dry, feverish glitter not
well to see. But the light that looks out of them now,
on his brother, is very sweet.

" Never mind me, *mon ami*, I am all right. I haven't
much flesh to lose, you know, and we black people show
this sort of thing soonest. Look out for yourself. If I
can take you and Snowball back in tolerable condition,
nothing else matters."

Then there is silence again ; they are too weak, too
spent, too thoroughly worn out and spiritless in mind
and body to care for talking. And Rene's voice is past
reading. It is husky and broken, and pretty well gone.
With a tired sigh Johnny relapses on his hillock, his
brown, curly head clasped in his laced fingers, his blue,
gentle eyes wandering aimlessly over the bay.

He never complains, never is cross, never wishes,
audibly, even for rescue. His face has a dull, slow, patient look of pain and waiting. He is consumed with
grinding hunger and filled with dire forebodings. For
raspberries are giving out, and, after another day or two,
if help does not come——

He never gets further. A fellow can die but once,
he says to himself, with forlorn philosophy. Only this
is such slow dying. And then there is papa—always
there is papa—back by now, and frantic with fear and

grief. At this point Johnny's face goes down on the turf, and he lies very still for a long time.

"Johnny is sleeping," Snowball will say to herself, in a loud whisper, and keep very close to her boy, and ward off gnats and bees, with a cedar branch.

For her, surprising to relate, she keeps up the best of the three, is cross and fractious at times, and full of loud complaints—on the hardship of things in general, and the stupidity of old Tim, and Ma'am Weesy, and all St. Gildas, in particular.

Perhaps this natural mental vent has something to do with her superior physical endurance ; but then she is a girl, and needs less, and the slender frame is wonderfully vigorous and healthful.

Still more, she has double rations of berries, although she does not know it. She eats what she picks herself, and, as has been said, the larger share of Rene's. If she refuses, Rene's great, dark, lustrous, solemn, severe eyes, transfix her.

"You promised," he says, and the resolute young lips set.

And then Snowball knows she has found her master, and meekly yields.

"But if ever I get off this horrid place," she says, in protest to Johnny, "this sort of thing will come to an end, let me tell you. Rene may think he is going to tyrannize over me like this all his life ! Just you wait until we are back home and you will see."

"I will," groans Johnny ; "I wish I was back to see now. I sometimes think, Snowball——"

"Well ?"

"That "—in a low tone—"we will never go back !"

"Oh, Johnny !"

"This is the afternoon of the third day. Papa must have come back yesterday. Snowball, think of papa !"

"Oh, Johnny ! dear, old Johnny !" a great sob, "l do."

"A storm is rising—look at that sky. We have not had a storm for over two weeks—it will be all the worse when it comes. You know what storms are on this coast. It may last for days."

"Yes," sobs Snowball, in despair.

"No boat can put off to come to us while it lasts, even if they knew where we were. No boat could land even at Sugar Scoop, except in calm weather. The surf all along the base of Chapeau Dieu is something that requires to be seen to be believed in."

Snowball is sobbing, with her face in her lap.

The sound arouses Rene, who is lying in a sort of torpor, but is neither sleeping nor waking, and he looks angry at his brother.

"I wish you wouldn't," he says; "why do you make her cry? What are you telling her?"

"Nothing much," says Johnny, surprised at his own performance. "I didn't mean to make her cry; I was saying a storm is rising—a bad one—and no boat can come until it is over. I say, Snowball, hold up."

But Snowball, weak, frightened, hungry, sobs on.

"You need not tell her such things—time enough for trouble when it comes, Snowball!" Rene cries out, and his voice is sharp with nervous pain, "don't. It *hurts* me to hear you. Oh, my God!" he says, under his breath, "help us—help *her!* Do not leave us here to die!"

Then, with the prayer still on his lips, he sinks back, too weary even to sit upright, and seems to sleep. Rene is in a very bad way—indeed, is the worst case of the three, and somehow the knowledge comes home to Snowball, and stills her tears.

She looks at him—if Rene, their mainstay, fails, what is to become of them. As she looks, a smile crosses his worn, pallid face—Rene has a very sweet smile, the more sweet for being rare.

"Give it to her," he says; "we don't want it, Johnny. For me, I will have coffee, I think."

"Oh, hear him!" Snowball says, her ready tears streaming again. "He is dreaming of home and something to eat. And look at his face—like death. He is starving, Johnny. Oh, Johnny, it breaks my heart."

Johnny says nothing, he has nothing to say. He turns away, that he may not see his brother's face, and watches the rapidly rising storm.

"Here it is!" he cries out.

A great drop of rain falls from the sullen sky and flashes in his upturned face, then another, and another. There is a profound hush, nature seems to hold her breath for a second, then in its might the swift.summer tempest is upon them. The lightning leaps out like a fiery sword, a terrific clap of thunder shakes the sky and sea. The bay *wrinkles* for a moment in an awful way; it crouches before the fury of the wind; and then the hurricane sweeps down upon them like a giant let loose. Flash after flash cuts the sky asunder, peal after peal shakes the mighty mountain to its base, the blast roars down from the summit with hoarse bellowing; the sea answers back with deep and hollow echo. Spruce and cedar saplings are torn up with one fierce rush, and whirled out to sea. The bower went hurling at the first stroke of the tornado, torn wildly into shreds.

Rene grasps his rock, his hat blown into space in the first gust, and clings for his life, his thin clothes drenched through in a moment.

Johnny and Snowball are together; Snowball, with a shriek, has flung her arms about him at the first flash of lightning, and so clings, her face hidden on his shoulder, her long, light hair streaming in the gale.

Johnny holds her hand; he can feel her quiver from head to foot at each flash, at each clap—except for that she is still.

So they crouch, beaten down, soaked through, breathless atoms, in the mad hurly-burly of wind, and lightning, and rain. Darkness has fallen, too, swift, dense—

they can hardly see each other's faces, though but a few yards apart.

It lasts for nearly an hour—a lifetime it seems to them. Then slowly, as if with reluctance, to see the evil it has wrought, the dark clouds light, the sky brightens, the thunder rumbles off into space, the wind lulls, the rain ceases. Only the sea, like some sullen monster, slow to wrath, is slow also to forgive, keeps up its dull bellowing, and breaks, and beetles, and thunders in huge great breakers over the sunken reefs, and up against the granite sides of Chapeau Dieu.

But they can breathe once more, and Snowball lifts her head, with all its dripping flaxen hair; and three white young faces—blue eyes, gray eyes, brown eyes—look into each other, in awful hush. There is nothing to be said, nothing to be done; they are wet to the skin; the breath is nearly beaten out of their bodies; the surf may roll heavily for days around the mountain ; no help can come now—and the last of the raspberries have been beaten off the bushes and washed into pulp by the fury of the storm. It is the crowning disaster of all.

"So be it !" Rene says at last, aloud, as if in answer to their thought—"we can but die !"

"It was death before," Johnny responds, "and no fellow can die more than once."

"Snowball," the elder boy says, and rises slowly, and sits beside her, "you are not afraid, are you ? Dear little Snowball. I am sorry for *you !*"

She makes no reply. She is only conscious of being very tired—very, very tired. She is not conscious of being afraid, but Rene sees that nervous quiver strike through her again.

"Are you cold ?" he asks, in his weak voice.

"No ; only tired. Let me rest—so—Rene, dear."

He holds her, and so they sit ; and so night finds them, when it falls. It falls soft and star-lit, but very chill ; the clouds sweep away before the bright wind,

and the moon looks down on these three forlorn lost
children sitting helpless here, waiting for the end. For
hope has died out, and it is death now, they know—slow,
dragging death, far from friends and home. There is
nothing more that can be done, or said, or planned for—
no need of further bowers — no strength left to make
them. They only want to keep close together, and so let
death find them when its slow mercy comes.

Johnny lies on his face on the soaked grass. Rene
and Snowball rest against the great, mossy bowlder, her
head on his shoulder, in stupor, or sleep. Strange, that
in this supreme hour, with the end so near, it is to Rene
she clings—her last hold on earth as life slips away.
Such a feeble hold! the weak little arms have scarcely
strength enough left to clasp his neck.

So the night wears. The breeze blows; they are
chilled to the marrow of their bones. All through the
cold, bright, pale hours, the surf thunders below—their
lullaby—and life wanes weaker with the deathly chill
coming of the new day. But when the night has passed,
and the stars paled and waned, and another sun has risen,
they are still alive. Alive—and but little more. It is
with a labored, painful effort that Johnny gathers himself together and stands on his feet.

"Try it, Snowball," he says, huskily. "See if you
can stand. Let us go and look for—for berries."

She does as she is told, but in a dazed sort of way.
Yes, she can stand, can walk, but not easily, over the
sodden furze.

"Will *you* come, Rene?" she says. "We are going—
to look for—berries."

Each word comes with pain, her throat and lips are
swollen and dry. But starvation is stronger than weakness, even with Rene, most spent of the three, and he,
too, gets on his feet in a blind and giddy fashion.

"Come," he says, and holds out his hand.

She takes it, and they totter on a few steps. Johnny

recovers first and most, and manages to walk tolerably well after a moment ; but it is hard work for the other two.

" There is something—the matter—with the ground," Rene gasps, giddily. " It is—going—up and down, Snowball !"

He utters a cry. Earth and sky go up, and come down, and seem to strike him with a crash on the back of his head. With that cry he reels forward, and falls at her feet like the dead.

CHAPTER XIV.

MONSIEUR PAUL.

N' this is the sixth day, an' if the Lord hasn't said it, it's dead they are ! It's maybe at the bottom av the say they are. I say I'm sayin' it's at the bottom av the say they are !"

The speaker is old Tim, light-house-keeper of Dree Island, and his audience are a group of men, gathered in the bar-room of the St. Gildas Hotel. They listen with anxious faces, in silence, while old Tim tells his tale. Old Tim is a short man, of sixty or more, with an ugly, surly, honest, weather-beaten face, crimson with much Irish whisky and Canadian sunshine—something of an oddity in his way. Old Tim never, by any chance, listens to what is said to him by anybody, if he can help it, so, judging others subject to the same infirmity, he has a habit of raising his voice, as he goes on, asserting and repeating himself, and so drowning all ill-bred interruption.

" It's that slip av a gerrel. The byes is well enough. I'm not sayin' a word agen the byes. It's that gerrel. I say it's that gerrel. The divil himself wudn't be up to her for divilment. She'd drowned thim in a minute for pure divarsion. It's that gerrel. I say I'm sayin' it's that slip av a gerrel!"

"The *Boule-de-neige* was picked up yesterday adrift off Point Tormentine," says one of the listeners. "This is a bad business, Tim. Couldn't you have given the alarm sooner? Six days ago!" the speaker whistles with up-lifted eyebrows.

"Is it give the alarrum sooner? Sorra haporth I've done for the last four days but give alarrums. Arrah! me very heart's bruk with the alarrums I've been givin', an' sorra a sowl's been alarrumed about it, barrin' ould Wasy herself, bad scran to her! I say me heart's bruk wid the alarrums I'm givin'. Faix, it's hardly a minute I've left to attind to the light. Alarrums *inagh!* Wisha! 'tis wishin' thim well I am for alarrums!"

"And Dr. Macdonald away from home, too," another says, and looks blankly about him. "What are we to do?"

"Faix he is," responds old Tim; "an', more betoken, some others is away that's wanted at home. Father Looey is away among the Injuns and the Frinch, bad cess to thim! As if craters like *thim* wanted the praste! I say Father Louis is away preachin' a station to thim nagers av Injuns. Av he was to the fore it's not the likes o' *ye* I'd be thrubblin' wid alarrums. Sure he'd do more in a minute thin the lot av ye in a week. I say I'm say-in'——"

"Oh! confound you, Tim; you needn't repeat your impertinence. We will do what we can, no matter where Père Louis is."

"I say it's not to the likes o' ye," repeats old Tim, raising his voice, and ignoring the interruption, "I'd be talkin' if Father Louis was to the fore. And now here's the *Bowld-naige* picked up adrift. Isn't that what ye're sayin', ye beyant there? An' where's them that wint in her?—tell me that."

They look at one another, and are silent. Dr. Macdonald is well known, and better liked, by every man of them. They know the boys too, and the pretty blonde girl with the waving fair hair.

" It's a bad lookout."

" Six days missing! Mon Dieu! it is terrible!"

" Old Tim ought to be shot!"

" Who will tell the doctor this?"

" After the storms of Thursday too. Even if they *did* make land somewhere——"

" Ma foi! was not the *Boule-de-neige* found, keel up, three miles the other side of Tormentine? Make land! The first land they made, my friend, was the bottom."

" Poor children! Two fine lads; handsome and manly, and the prettiest little girl you could see! It is a great pity."

" What is to be done?"

" Yes," says old Tim, chiming in like a Greek chorus, " I'm sayin' what's to be done? It's not standin' here like sticks o' salin' wax that'll resky thim av they're anywhere. I'm sayin' it's not standin' here——"

He breaks off. There has entered quietly among them a stranger, so different in appearance from most of the men around him, as to be conspicuous at a glance A tall, dark-bearded, brown, traveled-looking man, with a stamp that is not of St. Gildas upon him, handsome beyond question, and having, perhaps, thirty or more years.

Old Tim's jaw drops; he gazes, and still the wonder grows, his mouth agape, his small eyes opening wide Then his wonder suddenly bursts into vehement speech.

" It's him!" cries old Tim. " Oh, that I may niver, av it isn't him! Munsheer Paul!" he bustles aside all who interpose, and grasps the new-comer's hand. " Misther Farrar, darlin', don't ye know me?"

"Tim, old boy! Yes, I know your jolly old figure-head, of course," returns the stranger, laughing, and slapping him on the shoulder. "Dear old chap, how are you? And what is all this I——"

"An' it's back for good an' all ye are, I hope, from thim parts I'd not be namin'? Musha, but the ould docther will be as glad as if somebody had left him a ligacy. I'm not sayin' they didn't agree wid ye, though, thim parts," peering up at him admiringly ; "it's fine, an' big, an' brown ye are, this minute. I'm sayin' it's fine, and sthrong, and good-lukin' ye are, Misther Farrar. An' ye're back ! Well, well ! faix, they do be sayin' at home bad shillins iver an' always come back !"

"Think you, Tim. But the children——"

"It's the wonderful rowlin' stone ye are, if all tales about ye bees thrue. An' ye've been livin' out there in thim parts all this time? Sure there niver come a batch o' letters to the ould docther that I didn't go up an' ax for ye. 'I've a bit av a letther, Tim,' sez he, 'from thim ve know.' 'Arrah, have ye ?' sez I ; 'how is he at all ?' 'Well, Tim, glory be to God, an' he does be sayin' he'll be wid us soon.' But, oh ! wirra, sure I knowed betther thin to b'lave that. An' here ye are ! I say, I'm sayin', here ye——"

"But these children, Tim? For Heaven's sake, never mind me ! What of the doctor's boys, and my girl ?"

"An' your gerrel ! 'Pon me conscience thin but she's a han'ful av a gerrel ? It's all her doin's from——"

"Yes, yes, yes, Tim ! but what has she done ? What talk is this of wreck and storm, and a boat accident ? Don't you know I'm all at sea ?"

"Yis, faith, an' there's more like ye. That's where they are, or may be at the bottom. I say, that's where they are av the Lord hasn't a han' in thim. It's six blissid days since an eye was clapt on thim, and the *Bowld-naige*, starn up, off the wildest point on the coast."

The stranger groans, and turns an appealing glance

along the row of faces. Evidently he knows better than to try longer to stem the flow of Tim's talk.

"Tell me, some of you," he says, "the girl is mine."

"We are sorry, m'sieur," a small, brown-faced man, with gold ear-rings, says, touching his cap; "it is all ver bad. It is now six days since they have went away. They went in the boy's boat—a batteau—since yesterday found adrift many miles down the bay. And," with quick compassion, "it is suppose they must be lost. M'sieur will be good enough to remind himself of the storm of two days since."

But, yes; monsieur remembers, and grows very pale.

"And Dr. Macdonald is away!" he exclaims.

"Ah, m'sieur! how that is unfortunate. If he had been home they would have been discover since long time. But thees Tim," a shrug, "he say he give the alarm many time, but my faith! no one have hear until to-day. Ha! how that is droll!"

"I heard some rumor yesterday," another adds, "but I paid no great attention. They are often out in the little boat, and—well, I paid no attention. I suppose others felt as I did—that they would turn up all right."

"It is ver great peety," says the Frenchman; "we will do all our possib, but what will you? Six days! Mon Dieu!"

It is, indeed, a blank prospect. They stand for a little, silent, deep concern in every face.

"Have you no idea—has no one any idea," the new-comer, Mr. Farrar, asks, "of which direction they took? They must have had some distinct idea of going somewhere, when they put off. Does Ma'am Weesy not know?"

"Here she is for ye, let her spake for hersilf," says Tim. "Wasy, woman, I'm sayin', come here a minute. It's wanted, ye are—I say it's wanted ye are, and by thim as maybe ye thought was far away."

Ma'am Weesy, her brown face one pucker of anxious

8

wr.nkles, all wild with alarm, and vague with ejacula-
tions, bustles in among the men.

"Look at him now," says Tim, "there he is forninst
ye; an' it's many a long day ye'll luk among thim beg-
garly spalpeens av Frinchmin afore ye see he's like!"

But this last old Tim is polite enough to add under
his breath, as he points one stubby index finger at the
last arrival.

Ma'am Weesy does look, in puzzled wonder and incredulity, perplexity, recognition, doubt in her mahogany
face. He holds out his hand.

"It is I, Ma'am Weesy, your troublesome boarder of
nine years ago, and back in a very disastrous time, I
fear."

"M. Paul!" the old woman cries out, joyfully. "Ah,
how this is well. Oh, m'sieu, I rejoice to welcome you
back, if one may rejoice in anything at such a time. You
have hear?"

"Yes, I have heard. It is a terrible thing; but perhaps you can help us, if indeed it is not too late for all
help. Surely you know something of where they intended
to go?"

"No, m'sieu," with a sob, "I do not. Ah, *grande ceil!*
they went so often, look you—and I fear not. What was
there to fear, with Master Jean in the boat, that has been
in a boat since he could walk alone? They went all the
days—I never thought of asking. I rejoice to see them
go—me, wicked that I am—they so disarrange me at my
work. And that day I was glad—glad they go, for I
have great deal to do, and mademoiselle, she tease me
much. Helas! no, M. Paul, I know not where the dear
little ones may be. Only the good God, He know."

"Where were they most in the habit of going?"

"Everywhere, m'sieu. Up and down, here and there,
all places. They go sometime to the Indian villages for
moccasin, and basket, and bead-bag, even. Everywhere
they go—all places."

"And they said nothing, nothing at all? Tax your memory, Ma'am Weesy, the least hint may be of importance now."

Ma'am Weesy knits her brown brows, puckers her mouth, makes an effort, and shakes her head.

"It is of no use, M. Paul, they said nothing. Only they talk of raspberries the day before, perhaps, who know, they go for raspberry?"

"And where is the most likely place for raspberries? They would naturally go where they were most plentiful. Oh, my dear old woman, *how* could you leave this matter for six long days?"

"I did my best," Ma'am Weesy says, weeping. "I did tell Teem; I come to St. Gildas two, three, five time; I tell all I know. But what will you, M. Paul? Père Louis he is gone, M. le doctor he is gone, and for the rest—bah! what they care? They are beesy, it will be all right, they say, and go their way; no one can handle a boat better than Master Jean. And now they say to me la *Boule-de-neige* is found, and not my children. And to-morrow M. le doctor will be home, and me, how am I to face him? I promise him I care for them, and see how I keep my word."

As she sobs out the last words there is a bustle at the door, and a man enters hurriedly and looks around.

"Have you heard, Desereaux?" some one asks. "What is to be done?"

"Heard? yes," the new-comer says, excitedly. "I know where they are! Where they started to go to, at least. Is the doctor here? Is he back?"

"*I* am here; I am concerned in this matter. You remember me, perhaps, M. Desereaux? I am Paul Farrar."

"My dear M. Paul!" Desereaux grasps his hand, "welcome back to St. Gildas. You have come at a most opportune time. We must set off in search of these lost ones at once. They are safe and well still, I hope, in spite of the batteau's having slipped her moorings. *Mes amis*, they are at Chapeau Dieu !"

A murmur of surprise, consternation, relief, goes through the group. "Chapeau Dieu !" all exclaim. "They are found, and on Chapeau Dieu !"

"The way I know is this," M. Desereaux goes on. "Mademoiselle Snowball told my daughter Innocente, at the convent, the other day, that she and the boys proposed going to Chapeau Dieu for raspberries, and invited her to accompany them. Inno could not, she was going on a visit out of town with me, and went. We only returned to-day; that is why she did not hear and speak sooner. My idea is, they went up the mountain, moored the boat, and while they were in search of berries that the batteau floated out on the ebb tide. They might remain there a month, and no one chance upon them, unless they went on purpose. The question at present is, how to reach them. It will be a most difficult matter to effect a landing at the foot of the mountain, after the recent storm. Still we must try."

"We must, most certainly," says Mr. Farrar, "and without a moment's delay. Landing is always possible, even in the heaviest surf, at Sugar Scoop Beach. Men ! who of you will come ? Quick !"

There are half a dozen volunteers in a moment. The group disperses ; they hurry to the shore, and in ten minutes a large boat is launched and flying through the white caps to the rescue.

Ma'am Weesy, full of hope and fear, hastens home, across the river, to prepare food, and comforts of all sorts, for the little lost ones. Old Tim rows her over, and it is perhaps the first time in all their many years of intercourse that they do not quarrel by the way.

M. Desereaux accompanies Paul Farrar in his anxious quest. The two men talk little ; the thought of the children absorbs them, but Mr. Farrar informs him that this is merely one of his flying visits to his old friend,

preparatory to a still more prolonged absence abroad
He is going yet further afield—to Russia—he has received an appointment to St. Petersburg, through the
good offices of an influential friend, and will depart for
that far-off land in a very few weeks. He is tired of
Fayal, and his monotonous existence there.

"I am, as old Tim tells me, a rolling stone, that will
never gather much moss," he says; "but at least I need
not vegetate forever in one place."

"How fast it grows dark!" M. Desereaux exclaims,
scanning the horizon. "I wish we could have daylight
to effect a landing. At least we will have a full moon."

"It is rising now," Farrar says. "Surely we must be
within a mile or so of Sugar Scoop."

"We may search until morning before finding them,
even if they are on the mountain. It is a wide circuit,
my friend, and altogether impassable in places. And
this recent storm must have used them up badly."

"Do you think," Farrar says, with a hard breath,
"that there is really hope? Six days on that barren hill-
side without shelter or food——" He breaks off.

"Without shelter, perhaps, certainly not without food.
Raspberries abound — not very satisfactory diet, but
equal to sustaining life for a few days. And no doubt
they brought a luncheon basket with them—all do, who
are picnicing or berrying there. Hope for the best, *mon
ami.* It is true, we may find them in pitiable plight, but
also, I feel sure, we shall find them alive."

"Heaven grant it! If we can but get them home before the dear old doctor returns——"

He interrupts himself again, too anxious to put his
thoughts into words. The daylight is rapidly fading
out, and a brilliant night is beginning, moonlit, star-
lit, calm. The sea runs high; they can hear, long before
they approach, the thunder of the surf at the base of
Chateau Dieu; but the men who bend to the oars with
such right good will are men who will effect a landing,

if landing be within the limit of possibility. Sugar Scoop, too, when they reach it, seems fairly free of reefs and rollers. They steer with care; a great in-washing wave carries them with it, up and in on its crest. Two of them spring out, up to their waists in the water, and draw the big boat high and dry on the sands. The landing is effected.

"And no such troublesome matter after all," remarks M. Desereaux. "These fellows know their business—they are boatmen born. Now to find the children. Here is the path, M. Farrar—you have forgotten, doubtless, in all these years. Follow me."

"Make her fast, and come on, my friends," Mr. Farrar says. "We will disperse in different directions, and shout. If they are here, and alive, we will find them surely in an hour."

"Ah, m'sieur, Chapeau Dieu is a big place," one says. "We will do our best."

They secure the boat with à chain, and file up the steep path after their leaders. It is a path some two miles long, straggling and winding, in serpentine fashion, to a green plateau on the mountain side.

Here they pause for breath, Silence is about them, night is around them—silence and night, broken only by the dull booming of the surf. So still it is that the cedars and spruces stand up black and motionless, like sentinels guarding in grim array their rocky fortress over the sea. And then M. Desereaux uplifts his voice:

"Rene—Snowball—Jean! My children, answer. We are here."

But only the echo of his own shout comes back to him down the rocky slopes.

"Let us go farther up," suggests Mr. Farrar. "They may be near the summit. They may be on the other side."

"They will have landed at Sugar Scoop, surely," Desereaux responds; "there is no other safe landing.

But, of course, they went in search of berries, and would not remain near the landing. The raspberry thicket is over yonder, let us try it. Some of you, my men, take the other side."

So, they disperse, Farrar and Desereaux going toward the right, two men to the left, two more mounting toward the summit.

It is indescribably lonely, and even in the pallid moonlight, the wild sea sparkling in the white shimmer, the unutterable hush and solemnity of night overlying all.

They reach the raspberry thicket and pause.

"Shout with me," says M. Desereaux, "it is possible they may be somewhere near."

They shout, and shout, until they are hoarse, but only the melancholy echo of their shouts come back.

Far up they can hear the boatmen calling, too, and calling, also, in vain. A great fear falls upon them.

"Surely if they were in the mountain at all—and alive —they would hear," Mr. Farrar says; "let us try once more."

"Hush!" cries M. Desereaux, clutching his arm. "Listen! Do you hear nothing? Listen!"

They bend their ears, and—yes—faint, and far off, there comes to them a cry—a human cry.

"That is no night-hawk, no sea-bird!" Desereaux exclaims; "it is a voice responding to our shout. Thank God! Try it again."

Once more they raise their voices and shout with might and main.

"Rene! Snowball! Johnny! Where are you? Call!"

And once again, distinct though faint, that answering cry comes back.

"They are found! they are found!" Desereaux shouts exultingly. "This way, Farrar; this way, my men. We have them! *Dieu merci!* It is all right!"

He plunges in the direction of the feeble cry; it comes again, even as they go, and guides them.

"All right, my children!" he calls cheerily back, "we are coming. Keep up a good heart, poor little ones— we will be with you in a moment."

Once again the weak cry answers back—this time nearer yet—farther up the mountain side. And before it has quite died away—with a great, glad, terrified shout the two men are upon them, and have each seized one in his arms.

It is Johnny whom Mr. Farrar has caught; it is Snowball who is in the arms of M. Desereaux. And the two men are holding them close, hard, joyfully, and— Johnny blushes all the rest of his life to remember it, he is being absolutely *kissed* by the bearded lips of Paul Farrar.

"*Mon Dieu! Mon Dieu!*" cries the excitable Canadian, "how am I rejoiced! Snowball, *ma petite*—my angel—how is it with you?"

"Put me down," answers a weak—oh, such a poor, little, weak voice—but faintly imperious still. "Put me down, please, at once. I must—hold—Rene."

"Ah, Rene!—where is Rene? What—what—what—"

M. Desereaux pauses in consternation. She has slipped out of his arms, and down on the ground again, and lifted back into her lap the head of Rene. So she was sitting when they found her, so she had been sitting for hours, waiting for death—thus—Rene in her lap.

Mr. Farrar lets go Johnny, and is kneeling beside the prostrate boy. One glance only he gives to Snowball, reclining against a knoll, too far gone to support herself, Rene's dark head lying on her knees. She does not look at him; she seems past care, past hope, past help; she sits, her mournful eyes never leaving Rene's deathlike face.

"What is it?" Desereaux asks, "not——"

"No," with a quick breath, "I think not—I hope not —something terribly like it, though. He has swooned through exhaustion, I take it. He is very far gone. You will carry him to the boat, my good fellows—we will carry them all. None of these children can walk. Snowball, my little one, come to me—give us Rene. I will carry you. Come."

He gathers her in his arms—a light weight—a feather weight now. She makes no resistance ; she lets Rene go ; her head drops helplessly on his shoulder ; her eyes close. The men come after with the two boys, and Johnny, even in this supreme hour, is conscious of the indignity of being carried like a baby, and makes a feeble effort to assert himself, and his legs. It is of no use, however, he is unable to walk, and gives up, after a few yards, with the very worst possible grace. For Rene, he lies like one dead.

They reach the boat, get the young people in, and proceed to administer weak brandy and water. The stimulant acts well with Johnny, who sits up, after a swallow or two, and begins to fully comprehend what is taking place. They are being rescued—a fact that only clearly dawns upon him now.

Snowball, too, revives somewhat, but she will look at no one, care for nothing, save Rene.

"We will do," she whispers ; "give—something—to him. Make Rene—open—his eyes."

Easier said than done. All that is possible to do, Mr. Farrar does, the stimulant is placed between his locked teeth, his hands and face are bathed and chafed, but the rigid lips remain closed, the dark eyes remain shut, the hands and face icy cold—the ghastly hue of death leaves not.

"Can you talk, Johnny ? Don't try if it hurts you. How is it that we find Rene so much worse than you two ?" asks Paul Farrar.

Johnny tries to tell. " Rene starved himself to feed

8*

Snowball; never slept at all, hardly; was thinly clad, and so, and so——"

"Succumbed first—yes, I see. Brave boy—good Rene ! And he is not as strong as you, Johnny—never will be. But don't wear that frightened face, dear boy, we will bring him round yet. Once in Ma'am Weesy's kitchen, with warm blankets and hot grog, we will have Rene back, please Heaven, and able to talk to your father when he returns to-morrow, and tell him all about it."

Johnny utters a cry.

"Papa not home yet?"

"Not home yet, old boy—for which let us be duly thankful. Think what a story you will have to tell him to-morrow after dinner — *after dinner*, Johnny! You haven't dined lately, have you? What a story it will be for the rest of your life—six days and nights in Chapeau Dieu! Why, you will awake and find yourself famous— find greatness thrust upon you! For Snowball, here, she will be the most pronounced heroine of modern times."

But Snowball cares not, heeds not, hears not. Rene lies there, lifeless, and rescue or death—what are either now?

They talk no more; Johnny, with the best will in the world, finds the effort too painful, and he lies back and drops asleep. He is only wakened to find himself in some one's arms a second time, and being carried some-where, wakes for a moment, then is heavily off again. Presently he is lying on something soft and warm, and some one is crying over him and kissing him—Ma'am Weesy, he dimly thinks, and even in this state of coma, is sleepily conscious of feeling cross about it, and wish-ing she wouldn't. Then, something strong, and sweet, and delicious, is given him in a spoon, beef-tea, maybe; then sleep once more, sleep long, blessed, deep, life-giv-ing, and it is high noon of another day before he opens his eyes again on this world of woe.

CHAPTER XV.

SNOWBALL'S HERO.

IGH noon. A sunny, breezy, July day—hop vines and scarlet runners fluttering outside the muslin curtains of the open window, a sweet, salt, strong sea-wind coming in, and it is his own iron bed in which he lies, his own attic room in which he rests—it is Isle Perdrix—it is *home*—it is Weesy whose shrill tones he hears down-stairs, and it is—it is his father, whose face bends above him, as he awakes.

"Papa!" he cries out.

Two thin arms uplift, a great sob chokes him, then there is a long, long, long silence.

"My boy! my boy! my Johnny!" Dr. Macdonald says, and then there is silence again.

But Johnny recovers, and his first distinct thought is —that he is awfully hungry! His hollow, but always beautiful eyes, look at his father, then, around the room.

"Papa."

"My son."

"I want something to eat."

Dr. Macdonald laughs, but a trifle huskily. Instantly a china bowl and a silver spoon are in Johnny's hands.

"What is this, papa?"

"Weesy's very best, very strongest broth. Eat and fear not. A chicken is preparing, Johnny—such a fine, fat fellow—all for you! You shall have a breast and a liver wing in an hour. And a glass of such old port as you never tasted!"

Johnny rolls his eyes up in one rapturous glance, but pauses not for idle speech. There is no time. All at once he pauses.

"Oh-h! papa—Rene!"

"Is doing well, thanks to the good God and the un-
tiring care of my good Paul Farrar. I have but this
moment left his bedside. I am now going back. You
can spare me, my dear?"

"Oh, yes, papa," briskly re-attacking the bowl, "I can
spare you."

Silence again for a space—the bowl very near the
bottom by this time, and Dr. Macdonald, smiling down
on his son. Johnny looks up.

"And Snowball, papa?"

"Very well—*very* well, I am happy to say. My sweet
little Snowball! Johnny! Johnny! how can we ever be
thankful enough?"

No response from Johnny—the spoon and the bottom
of the bowl clinking by this time.

"Rene will not be ill?"

"We do not know—we hope not. He speaks little—
he is too far spent, but he takes what we give him, and
sleeps a great deal. In that, and in his youth, we hope.
If Heaven had not sent Paul Farrar, and my very good
friend, M. Desereaux, last night, Rene would never have
seen morning."

Dr. Macdonald's voice breaks—he turns and walks to
the window. He is a tall, stooping, gentle-looking old
man, with silvery hair, and beard, and face, and eyes soft,
gray, and wistful, exactly like Johnny's.

"Rene is a brick, papa," cries Johnny, warmly; "an
out-and-out trump! You would not think he had it in
him. He starved himself to look after Snowball; he
told us stories, he read to us while he could speak. Papa,
may I get up?"

"If you feel able, my son; but I would advise——"

"Oh! I feel all right—a giant refreshed. I can't lie
here, you know, like a mollycoddle, and have Ma'am
Weesy coming in and——" "Kissing me every minute,"
is his disgusted thought, but he restrains it. "Please

may I get up, papa, and go down? I'll be as careful of myself as if I were eggs."

His father smiles.

"Very well, my lad; dress and go down. Take your time about it, Johnny. M. Paul will come to you and amuse you."

"Papa, may I—I should like to see Snowball?"

"Presently, laddie, presently; let her sleep. She will be down, I think, before night."

"And Rene——"

"Ah! Rene—who knows? *he* will not be down. You may see him to-morrow. We shall have to take great care of Rene. I am going to him now."

Dr. Macdonald goes, and Johnny, very gingerly, and with many pauses, and a surprising sense of weakness, proceeds to dress himself and travel down-stairs.

It is rather more like a ghost of Johnny, than that brisk young gentleman himself, this wan lad, with the hollow eyes and pallid face.

Weesy shrieks with delight at sight of him, and makes a rush to clasp him precipitately to her breast, but Johnny jumps behind a table, with unexpected rapidity and alarm.

"No, you don't!" he says; "keep off! I've had enough of that. First, some brute with whiskers, last night, and then you, and now again—but you sha'n't if I die for it. Let a fellow alone, can't you, Weesy?"

And Weesy laughs, and cries, and yields. The misfortunes of her children have covered, for the time, their multitude of sins.

Johnny sits by the breezy window, and looks out over the little rocky garden, the rough path beyond, the beach below, the sea spreading away into the sky, and sighs a sigh of infinite content.

One might fancy he had had enough of the sea, but not so. John Macdonald will never have enough of the bright, watery world he loves. If only the *Boule-de-neige*

—but he must not think of *her*—there may be other bat-
teaux in time.

He is at home—they are all safe ; that is enough for
one day.   And presently comes Ma'am Weesy, with the
chicken and wine, and a book of sea-stories, and Johnny
slowly munches, and reads, and time passes, and at
last——

He starts up with a weak shout, for there is M. Paul
supporting Snowball, looking pallid and pathetic, but
otherwise not so much the worse for her week on the
barren furze of Chapeau Dieu.   Her blue eyes look like
azure moons, in her white small face.

"Oh, Johnny !" she solemnly says.

It is an adjuration with which Johnny is tolerably familiar, emotion of any sort evoking it some sixty times,
on an average, per day.   He laughs in response, and
looks shyly at her escort.

"Johnny, dear old chap," that gentleman says, and
gives his hand a cordial grasp, "don't stop.   Peg away
at the chicken, and give some to Snowball.   It does me
good to see you."

"How does Rene get on, sir ?"

"Ah, not so well ; Rene is hot and feverish, and a
trifle light-headed.   Fancy his giving in, while this little,
yellow-haired lassie holds out so well."

"It was my fault," says Snowball, in penitent tears.
"I know now he starved himself for me.   And he *made*
me mind him.   I didn't want to—now, did I, Johnny?"

"Rene is a young gentleman who will always make
people mind him.   There is nothing to cry for, Petite—
he is not going to die, not a bit of it.   Eat your chicken
and dry your eyes—he may have rather a hard bout of it
for a week or so, but he will come round like the hero
he is."

M. Paul Farrar proves a true prophet, only the
"bout" is rather harder than even he anticipates.   Rene
is quite delirious at times, and talks wildly of Chapeau

Dieu, and the storm, and the bower, and the berries, and gathers more in his heated imagination of that luscious fruit than he ever did in reality, and sings scraps of the evening hymn, and quotes Shakespeare, and conducts himself altogether in a noisy and objectionable manner. But at no time is there much real danger, and he is so faithfully nursed, so devotedly attended, that he must perforce turn the sharp corner of the fever, and come around, all cool and clear-headed, but deplorably weak and helpless, at the end of seven or eight days.

"And you and Johnny look as well as if it had never happened," he says, languidly, with a resentful sense of injury upon him " What a muff I must be !"

They do, indeed, look as well, as bright, as fresh, as plump, as though these six days on the desolate mountain side were but a dream. Johnny by this time is decidedly proud of his performance, though a trifle bored, too, by the questions with which he is plied whenever he appears at St. Gildas. The *Boule-de-neige* is safe at her moorings, none the worse for her playful little escapade ; Rene is all right, M. Paul is here, and Johnny is happy.

All these feverish and flighty days Snowball has devoted herself to the patient with a meekness, a docility, a sweetness almost alarming in its self-abnegation.

She reads to him, sings to him, brings him his beef-teas, and chicken broths, and toast, and water, and other nastiness, as Rene calls it, and watches him eat and drink, and recover, with the devotedness of a mother ! Rene submits to be petted, and cuddled, and made much of for a few days—she keeps Weesy out, and that is a great point—accepts her society, listens with languid graciousness to her gossip, lets her read him to sleep, lets her fan off the flies, and adorn his chamber with flowers, and then—all in a moment—turns round, and flatly declares he will have no more of it ! Strength and his normal state are returning, and this phase of supernatural goodness and calm comes as might be expected,

to a sudden and violent end. He isn't a baby—he won't
swallow gruel and disgusting beef-tea; he won't be
tucked in o' nights and have Snowball popping in and
out of his room like a Jack-in-a-box whenever she
pleases! Let her go with Johnny, as she used to, she
would rather, he knows—she needn't victimize herself
because he picked a few raspberries for her there on the
mountain! And she isn't much of a companion, anyway—he would far and away rather talk to M. Paul!
Which is ungrateful, to say the least, after the superhuman efforts she has been making to amuse him during
the past seven days. And Snowball, deeply hurt, but
relieved all the same, *does* give it up, does resume the
society of Johnny, and is prepared, the instant Rene is
strong enough for battle, to resume war to the knife as
of yore.

M. Paul is a prime favorite in the household. Dr.
Macdonald beams in his presence—he is the idol of
Ma'am Weesy's heart; the boys look upon him with
eyes of envy and admiration—a man who has been everywhere, and seen every thing, and place, and people.

Snowball falls in love with him, of course—that goes
without saying—and is never out of his presence a moment, when she can be in it. Even old Tim succumbs
to the spell of the charmer, yields to the fascination of M.
Paul's glance, and laugh, and voice, and old Tim's battered heart is not over susceptible. He has never, within
mortal ken, been known to invite a man into his domicile
to partake of a dhrop of dhrink before.

They sit together, one sleepy August afternoon, M.
Paul and Snowball, down on the sands, he reclining his
long length upon the rank reeds, and warm waving sea-
side grasses, his straw hat pulled half over his eyes. A
golden haze rests on the bay, sails come and go through
it as through a glory—fishing-boats take on a nimbus
around their brown rails. There is the faintest breeze—

little wavelets lap upon the white sand, the beautiful sea looks as though it could never be cruel.

By chance they are alone. Johnny has just left them. Old Tim is crooning to himself up in the light-house near, as he polishes his lamps. It is full three weeks since the rescue. Rene is himself again, and happy among his beloved books. Snowball sits on a rocky seat, her sailor hat well on the back of her head as usual, her face frankly and fearlessly exposed to sea-side sun and wind. Vanity is not one of this young person's many failings; freckles and blisters, and sunburn are matters of profoundest unconcern, at this period of her career. He has been telling her of some of his travels and adventures in far-off lands, thrilling enough and narrow enough some of them. No romance ever writ-ten, it seems to this small girl, as she listens, could be half so wonderful, no hero half so heroic.

But gradually silence has fallen, and M. Paul, from under his wide straw hat, looks with dark, dreaming eyes out over that yellow light on the sea.

Snowball steals a glance at him. Of what is he think-ing, she wonders. How *very* handsome he is! How brown, how strong, how big, how manly! Of what, of whom is he thinking, as he lies here, with that grave, steady glance? And what is he to her—he who brought her here, all those years ago? Why, in all this romance of wandering and strange adventures, has there never been a heroine? Or has there been one, and he will not tell the story to a little girl of twelve? There is something she longs to ask him—has often longed of late, but she is shy with him; somehow, in spite of his gentleness, he is formidable in her eyes. She makes one or two efforts—now is the time or never!—stops, blushes, and tries again.

" M. Paul !"

" Petite ?"

He wakes from his dream with a start, and then smiles

slowly to see the rosy tide mounting to her eye-brows.

"I—I want to ask you something. You will not mind?"

"Mind?" still smiling amusedly. "How? I don't understand."

"You will not be—mad?"

"Mad?" he laughs. "Offended with you, Petite? No; that could not be."

"M. Paul"—a pause. "You—you brought me here."

"Nine—more than nine, years ago. *Ma foi!* how time flies! Yes."

Another pause. Snowball pulls up the rank, flame-colored sedge-flowers waving in the wind, and finds going on hard work. The dark, amused eyes smile up at her, and intimidate her.

"I wish—I wish you would tell me something about myself. I don't know anything. I think sometimes it is not fair to me. I think a great deal, M. Paul, about it, and it makes me unhappy."

Her voice falters; she stops.

"Unhappy, Snowball? Ah! I am sorry for that."

"I am not like other girls—I feel it—they know it. They ask me questions over there at school that I can't answer. They whisper about it, and tell all the new girls—that I have no father or mother, or home of my own, or relations at all. And I think it is too bad. Every one is kind enough, but still it is hard. And I want to know who I am, M. Paul, please."

Silence.

The steady glance of M. Paul, out of which all amusement has died, turns from her and goes back once more to that amber glory of sea and sky. The grave, bronzed face looks as it looked before she spoke at all, thoughtful, and a little sad.

She has asked a harder question, it may be, than she

knows. He is silent so long that she breaks out again herself :

"Dr. Macdonald can tell me nothing—he would, if he could. Everybody is good to me, but—oh, M. Paul, tell me—tell me if you can !"

"Snowball, my dear little one, what shall I tell you?"

"Have I a name—a father—a mother? What is the reason I am hidden away here—as if the people who pay for me were ashamed of me? What have I done? They never write, they never send or come to see me. No one seems to know or care anything about me in all the whole world !"

A sob, but Snowball checks it by a great effort. She has thought this all out, and will not distress M. Paul by crying.

"Dear child, we all love you—you know that."

"Yes—here. You are all good. But there—who are they? Why do they cast me off and disown me? Oh, I cannot tell you all I feel, or ask questions as I ought, but won't you tell me all the same, please? I have no one in all the world to ask but you, and you are—going —away," another sudden break, "and—I may never see you again."

He reaches up, and takes her hand, and holds it in his large, warm clasp. He looks surprised. Who would have dreamed of so much thought and feeling under that child-like, gay, girl nature? He looks grieved, puzzled, at a loss.

"Little one," he says, slowly, "I hardly know how to answer. Some of your questions cannot be answered— now—some—what is it you want to know most?"

"Tell me my name. Snowball is no name. Mère Maddelena will not call me by it ; she says it is no name for a Christian child."

"It is no saint's name, certainly," he says, smiling. "I should fancy it would shock the good mother. She should give you another."

"She has; but what was I called before I came here?"

"Snowball—nothing but Snowball, that I ever heard. And you looked it, such a little, white, flaxen-haired girlie! It was the name your mother called you by."

"My mother—oh!" with a quick breath. "M. Paul, tell me of my mother."

He knits his brows abruptly, drops her hand, and stares straight before him, very hard, into space.

"Your mother?" a cold inflection of which he is quite unconscious, in his voice, "what is there to tell? When I saw her, just before I brought you here, she was on her death-bed. She met with an accident," very slowly; "she did not speak to me or any one. You and she were alone."

An older inquisitor than little Mlle. Snowball would have seen, it may be, something suspicious—a great deal held back, in this slow and careful selection of words. But Snowball takes the statement at the face of it.

"Then it was not my mother who asked you to take care of me?"

"It was not."

"M. Paul—what was she like?"

"Like you—very like you in all but expression. Eyes, hair, features, smile—almost the very same."

A pause. Snowball sits with fast-locked hands, an intense look upon her small pale face. M. Paul lies back in his former recumbent attitude, his hat again shading his eyes, and makes his responses in a rather reluctant sounding voice.

"You do not want to tell!" she cries out, after a little, in a faint tone. "You would not make me ask so many questions if you did. But I must know more. Some one pays for me here; Dr. Macdonald gets money every six months. Who is that?"

"Her name is Madam Valentine."

"Who is Madam Valentine? What am I to her?"

"Madam Valentine is an elderly lady, and very rich —richer, my Snowball, than you or I will ever be, our whole lives long. Her son married your mother—her only son. She is very proud as well as rich, and it was a low marriage. Do you know what a low marriage is, my little one? She cast him off—this proud lady. He was drowned, it appears, a few years after, in a storm, about the time you were born, I should think. That is the history, in brief, of Madam Valentine."

"Then my father is dead, too—drowned. My father drowned in a storm—my mother killed by an accident! Oh! M. Paul. And my grandmother casts me off—a little thing like that! She is a cruel, cruel woman, M. Paul!"

No reply.

"Where does she live?" resentfully, "this proud, hard Madam Valentine?"

"Everywhere; nowhere in particular. She is nearly always traveling about. She is of a restless temperament, it would seem."

"Does she wander about alone?"

"No," smiling at the scornful tone, "she is in keeping. Her nephew—also her heir—one Mr. Vane Valentine, accompanies her. It was from *him* I received you."

And then, still smiling at the angry, mystified face, he tells her, easily enough, his part. How, knowing Vane Valentine, and seeing him at a loss how to dispose of her, he had volunteered to bring her here, knowing Madam Macdonald would rejoice in her coming, and Mr. Valentine had at once closed with the offer.

"I knew you would grow up happy and healthful here, Petite, loved by all, and loving all. And I was not mistaken, was I? You *are* happy, in spite of this?"

"Happy?" she echoes. "Oh! yes, M. Paul, I am happy—happy as the day is long. Only sometimes—but I should *never* be happy with people like that—I should just hate them. I do now. I love everybody here——"

"Except Rene?" laughing. "You give Johnny his own share and Rene's too—eh, Petite? Although when we found you, that night, on Chapeau Dieu, it was Rene you were holding in your arms, not Johnny."

"Well," Snowball admits, "I *do* like Johnny best—no one could help that. It is not *my* fault if Rene is so stiff, and contrary, and so fond of his own way——"

"By no means," still laughing. "I will say for you, Snowball, you do your duty by Rene, and never miss a chance of snubbing him—for his good, of course—always for his good! It is very bad, very bad indeed, for big fellows, nearly seventeen, to have their own way—and you never spoil Rene in that manner, if you can help it. Well, Petite, is this all? Shall we drop this biographical subject here, and forever? It is not one I care to talk about, for reasons of my own. You are safe and happy, you love all here, and are beloved. What more can you want? All your life long, Mademoiselle Snowball, *you* will find it easy enough to win love—more than you may well know what to do with, one day. What more, I repeat, do you want?"

"Nothing more. Thank you, M. Paul, for telling me this much."

"And you are not sorry that, nine years ago, I brought you here? Rene is coming, with a big book under his arm, to call us to supper, I fancy. Answer, before we go."

He takes her hand again; his dark, kindly, but keen eyes search her face, her pretty, blonde, bright face—so like that other fair face laid under the turf in the distant New England town.

"Sorry! M. Paul, I owe all the happiness of my life to you! I thank you with my whole heart!"

She stoops, with a quick, childlike grace, and kisses the big, brown hand that clasps her own. This is the tableau that meets the gaze of Rene, and petrifies the gazer.

" *Sacr-r-re bleu !*" he exclaims. "Do these eyes deceive me? Snowball, trained in the way she should go (but doesn't) by Mère Maddelena, making love to M. Paul, here, all unprotected and alone. I *did* come to call you to supper, but——"

"But me no buts!" commands M. Paul, laughingly, springing to his legs; "and cease these jealous and censorious remarks. Has Weesy anything particularly good, do you know, Rene?"

"Any Greek or Latin roots *fricassee*, Rene?" impatiently puts in Snowball.

Side by side they turn their backs upon the amber glitter of sea and sky, and ascend to the cottage, and though M. Paul talks much as usual, Rene wonders what has come to loquacious Snowball, so silent, so thoughtful, so serious is she. For somehow, now that the long desired explanation is over, she feels dissatisfied still—things are not much clearer than before, and M. Paul has reasons of his own for never talking of this any more. He has said so. It is not until long after that she knows, and then the knowledge is fraught with keenest pain, of these secret reasons of M. Paul Farrar.

CHAPTER XVI.

VILLA DES ANGES.

HE summer days come, and the summer days go; twenty more are counted off, and it is the end of August, the close of the long vacation—a never-to-be-forgotten time, since M. Paul has passed it here. But with the going of this last week M. Paul goes too, and a strange blank is left in the doctor's home, and in these three youthful hearts.

"You and I, at least, will meet again before long," he says to Rene at parting; "remember when the time comes to call upon me—if I live I will not fail you."

For in the long and confidential hours of his convalescence, Rene, the reticent, has opened his whole heart to this sympathetic M. Paul, and told him of hopes, and dreams, and longings, and ambitions buried deep in his own heart up to this hour. He is a modest lad, and shy, and glances with dark, wistful eyes at the silent friend who sits beside him.

"Does it all sound very foolish and impossible to you, M. Paul?" he asks. "Sometimes it does to me. Sometimes I despair, buried here in this out-of-the-world place. And my father, you know, sir, wishes me to be a doctor. But that can never be, I am sure of it."

"Still you might study medicine," M. Farrar responds, thoughtfully; "it will please your father, and a knowledge of anatomy is absolutely essential, you know, if your aspirations are ever carried out. And they will be —you have it in you, Rene, lad. Foolish and impossible! Not at all; I always knew you had a spark of the divine fire of genius somewhere behind those level black brows of yours, only I did not know the particular direction in which it was bent. Wait, all things are possible to him who knows how to wait. Please your father for the present; keep your own counsel; I will send you books, and in every possible way in which I can further your condition, it shall be my great pleasure to do it. Abroad, you see, I may have opportunities. When the time comes, you shall go to Italy, to Rome, the city of dead and living art. I am proud of your confidence. I shall not fail you, believe me."

Rene's deep eyes glow, he is not expansive by nature, but he grasps the friendly hand held out to him in both hands, and his eloquent face speaks for him. His whole heart overflows with gratitude. Ah! *this* is friendship!

Indeed, the whole household, with Weesy and Tim, are in despair at this desertion. Snowball weeps her blue eyes all red and swollen, for days before, and will not be comforted.

"If I see Mr. Vane Valentine before I leave the country," he says to her, a mischievous gleam in his eyes, "your benefactor, you know, what shall I say to him from you ?"

"Say I hate him !" answers Mistress Snowball, viciously. "I always hated benefactors ! I owe it to you, not to him, that I am here. I never want to see him, or her, as long as I live."

The day comes, and Paul Farrar goes. Old Tim rows him over to St. Gildas, to take train from thence to the world without. Dr. Macdonald and Rene accompany him, in this first stage of his long journey ; Johnny, and Snowball, and Weesy stand on the island beach, and wave good-by. As the boat touches the St. Gildas shore he looks back. Johnny and Weesy have gone, but Snowball still stands where they left her, a slight, fluttering figure, her bright hair blowing, gazing after through tear-dimmed eyes still.

But life goes on, though dear ones depart. September comes, cool and breezy ; her convent school re-opens, and Snowball's freedom is at an end. No more long sails in the batteau, no more dangerous excursions to Chapeau Dieu, no more long rainy days of romance reading up in her attic chamber. The dull routine of lessons recommences, grammar and history, and Noel et Chapsel and fine needle-work, take the place of gypsy outdoor life, and the seventy-five boarders of Villa des Anges are her daily companions instead of the boys. Old Tim rows her over every morning, and back every afternoon. Life, as Johnny pathetically puts 't, is no longer "all beer and skittles ;" even he has to throw aside his beloved Captain Marryatt, and recommence mathematics and Latin, and Rene—but Rene dreams his own dreams

9

in these days with a steady aim and purpose in view, absorbs himself in his studies, writes long letters to M. Paul, and is mute to all the world beside.

Villa des Anges is a stately establishment, set in spacious grounds, on a breezy height overlooking town and bay. It is a boarding-school, and has within its vestal walls youthful angels from nearly every quarter of the globe. There are a dozen or more day-pupils, besides the *pensionnaires*—among these latter Snowball Trillon, although as a matter of fact there is no such name down on the school-roll. There is a Dolores Macdonald, and —Dolores of all names to Mère Maddelena, and her good sisters, Snowball is. This is how :

When the child first came to Isle Perdrix at three and a half, the doctor's wife took her training and education under her exclusive charge. For five years her two boys were hardly more to her than this little stray waif, dropped, as it seemed, from the skies. Then came a sad and sudden death. The good old doctor was almost in despair. The sight of the little girl in her black dress intensified his grief and remembrance so painfully, that Ma'am Weesy prevailed upon him to send her over for a year or two to Villa des Anges. So, at nine years old Snowball went, rebelliously and loudly protesting, a *pensionnaire* to the convent, full of direst anguish and wrath, at being thus forcibly wrenched from the society of her beloved Johnny. As a lamb to the shearers, she is led into the parlor by grim old Weesy, and there, in tears and trembling, awaits the coming of the dread Lady Abbess. But when there enters a tall and stately lady, whose pale, serene face the snowy coif becomes, with sweet, smiling eyes, and sweeter broken English, a great calm falls on the little damsel's perturbed spirit. She lays her flaxen head on Mère Maddelena's black serge shoulder, with a sigh of vast relief, and submits to be kissed on both tear-wet cheeks, and to be asked her name.

"Snowball Trillon, madame."

Now Mère Maddelena, having baptismals ot every sort and size in her villa, should not have been surprised at the odd sound of any cognomen, but she decidedly *is*, shocked even, at this. She gives a little cry of dismay, essays to repeat the name, and lamentably fails.

"But dat is not a nem," she says. "What you call it in French — *Boule-de-neige*? You hear, Sœur Ignatia? Dat is no nem. Was you christen dat, my chile?"

Snowball does not know—does not remember ever being christened. Has been called Snowball, nothing but Snowball, all her life.

Mère Maddelena listens in ever-growing dismay. Does not know if she has ever been christened! Has no father or mother! This must be seen to before she is admitted as pupil into Villa des Anges. Mère Maddelena does not want children of doubtful antecedents. Dr. Macdonald must be questioned about this.

"It is imposs dat chile shall keep de so foolish nem," she says, with some indignation, to the attendant Sister. "I am *shem* of it."

"I zink it is ze moze fonny nem I ever hear," replies, smiling, Sr. Ignatia; "it mek Père Louis ye so great laugh last time he come. We must baptize her anozzer— de nem of some saint."

Snowball is admitted on sufferance; Mère Maddelena calls her "dat chile," and utterly ignores the obnoxious "Snowball." The girls adopt it with glee, and "Snow-ball" and "Boule-de-neige" are shouted over the play-ground amid noisy laughter until its poor little owner is as much "shem of it" as the good mother herself. But the novelty wears off—Snowball sounds no longer oddly, and the little girl herself becomes a prime favorite with the pensionnaires.

Dr. Macdonald is sent for, and comes, and appears before the tribunal of Mère Maddelena, who there and then demands an unvarnished history of her new boarder.

The doctor has little to tell, he hardly realizes himself, how meager is the information Paul Farrar has given him, until called upon to retail it thus. The child is an orphan, her friends are wealthy and most respectable, but do not wish to have charge of her personally.

Snowball Trillon—which does not sound like a real name, he admits—is the only one he knows her by. Valentine is the name of her friends, he believes. As to whether she has ever been baptized or not—Dr. Macdonald shrugs his shoulders. What will the good mother? He knows nothing.

The good mother, with calm but inflexible resolution, wills that he finds out. Otherwise Snowball Trillon cannot be admitted as a *pensionnaire* into exclusive Villa des Anges. And if it is discovered that she is unbaptized, the omission must be at once set right—if she is to remain here. It is the rule. Meanwhile she can remain, and run about the play-ground with the rest.

Dr. Macdonald writes to M. Paul Farrar at Fayal. M. Paul Farrar writes to Mr. Vane Valentine, spending the winter in Florida with his aunt. Mr. Vane Valentine reads that letter, twirls it into a cigar-light, ignites his weed, and sets his heel on its ashes.

He scrawls a line in reply. He knows nothing about it, and cares less. They may call her what they please, or not call her at all, if they prefer it.

It is about as roughly insolent as scrawl can be; he hates the very thought of the trapeze woman's child. He does not lay the matter before Madam Valentine, as M. Farrar has suggested—the sooner Madam Valentine, obliterates from her memory the circus brat the better.

She seems to be doing so, she never asks any questions—he is not likely to revive her memory. In due course this reply reaches Fayal—M. Farrar forwards it in turn to Dr. Macdonald. If poor little Snowball were a princess incognito, there could hardly be more roundabout correspondence concerning her. The upshot is,

Mère Maddelena is at liberty to do as she pleases, and christen her what she likes, and as soon as she sees fit.

Mère Maddelena, full of vigor and zeal, sets to work at once. Next week is the feast of Our Lady of Dolors —could anything fall out more opportunely?—the child shall be baptized Marie Dolores. And so it is. The convent chapel, sparkling with wax-lights, fragrant with flowers, is thrown open; the ceremony has been announced, and quite a congregation of the ladies of St. Gildas, all the pupils, and the sisters attend. The pensionnaires, in their white dresses, the nuns in their black serge and great coifs, make a very effective picture. Père Louis is there to admit this stray lambkin into the fold. There is organ music, and chants, and litanies. And down at the baptismal font, in white Swiss, and a long tulle veil, and snowy wreath, like a fairy bride, wonderfully pretty, and exceedingly full of her own importance, stands Snowball, with her sponsors. Her boys are there in a corner; she glances at them complacently, and nearly has her gravity upset by an affectionate and sympathetic wink from Johnny. And then and there she becomes Marie Dolores for all time.

If Mère Maddelena had striven of set purpose, she could hardly have selected a seemingly more inappropriate name. Felicia, Letitia, Lucilla—anything meaning happiness, joy, light, would have seemed in keeping; but Dolores—*sorrowful*—for that radiant-looking little one! It strikes even the spectators—even Père Louis.

"Your new name does not seem to fit, Mademoiselle Dolores," he says, pulling her by one of her long curls. "Let us hope it never may. It seems a pity *notre mère* cannot reconcile herself to the other one—it suits you, I think."

But little girls can tolerate it, and decline to change it; thus while she is Dolores from thenceforth to the sisters, she remains Snowball to the boarders.

And the months slip by, and the seasons come and

go, and the years are counted off on the long bead roll of Old Time, and her twelfth birthday is a thing of the past. M. Paul has come and gone, and school, and German exercises, and piano practice, and drawing lessons, and Italian singing, all recommence, and the sharp edge of parting has worn off somehow before she knows it. She is busy and happy—a bright, joyous, fun-loving, mischief-making, truthful, loving, clever, and fairly studious girl—healthful, and handsome, and high-spirited—a granddaughter even haughty Madam Valentine might be proud of. Of the big, busy world outside St. Gildas she knows nothing, and cares very little; she has her own world here, her "boys" the center of her orbit, and hosts of friends whom she dearly loves. Wild wintry storms howl around Isle Perdrix, and the big waves rise in their majesty and might, and thunder all about them; white, whirling storms of snow fall for days, and even the little world of St. Gildas is shut out. *Those* are seasons of bliss never to be forgotten, when, with huge red fires in every room, they three sit and devour together the "thrilling" novel, the "delicious" poem. Like the little boy in the primer, Snowball's cry is, "Oh, that winter would last forever!"

Thirteen, fourteen, fifteen—the birthdays tread on each other's heels, it seems to her sometimes, so rapidly do the months slip round, and they surprise her, by coming again.

And now it is another September, and she is quite sixteen—a tall, slim, pale girl, with only a faint wild-rose tint in either cheek, but a tint that is ready to flutter into carnation, at a word, a look.

"Our Snowball wouldn't be half bad-looking," Johnny is wont to remark, altogether seriously, "if she wasn't so much on the hop-pole patterns. There is nothing of her but arms and legs, and a lot of light hair."

Johnny's taste leans to the dark, the plump, the rosy, as exemplified in Mlle. Innocente Desereaux.

It is her last year at Villa des Anges. Next commencement she will graduate, and after that——

Ah! after that life is not very clear. The boys are going away. Rene, indeed, has already gone to New York, as a preliminary step in the study of sculpture, which, it appears, is to be his vocation in life. He is over twenty now, and has made his final decision. It is a question she ponders over with knitted brows and anxious mind very often.

She will be qualified to go out as a governess, she supposes, or a teacher of music and languages, probably in Montreal.

Except for this perplexity, the girl's life is absolutely serene and free from care, and in after years—in the after years so full of strange bitterness and pain, she looks back to this peaceful time with an aching sense of wonder, that she could ever have wished it over, or thought it dull.

But changes are at hand, and suddenly, when change is expected least, it comes, and Isle Perdrix and St. Gildas, and Villa des Anges vanish out of her existence like the figures of a dream.

CHAPTER XVII.

LA VIVANDIERE.

WAY from wild and lonely Bay Chalette, with its gloomy fogs, its fierce Atlantic gales, its beetling surf breaking forever on its craggy shore, its blinding drifts of snow, its long, bleak winters, the sun is setting in rosy splendor over another sea, a fair, serene, southern sea. A low, white house stands with its face turned to this rose-light, its windows like glints of gold, and house and windows are half hidden behind a tangled, trailing wealth of cape jessamine and climbing roses. The house is built of stone, stuccoed and whitewashed, with a hanging balcony from the second story, and a veranda below. And in tropical luxuriance, the grounds are ablaze with flowers and shrubs, with the orange, the lemon, the banana, the fig, the stately date-palm. A soft wind, velvety and fragrant, floats up from the ocean. In the dim background, resting tranquil in an amber rain of mist, lies St. Augustine.

The long veranda, which runs the whole front of the house, is one glowing mass of color—one scented wealth of roses. Up and down this veranda a lady walks, drinking in the cool sea-breeze, and gazing at the rich glow of this southern sunset. An elderly lady, upright and stately, with white hair, puffed elaborately under a cap of finest point, a severe silvery face, piercing dark eyes that have lost at sixty-seven no whit of the fire of youth, a trained dress of dark silk, and some yellowish lace, of fabulous value, at the throat, held together by a cluster of brilliants. She supports herself on an ebony cane, mounted with gold, but carried more, it is evident, from habit, than through any real necessity. A handsome and haughty old lady, with broad, smooth brow, and thin mouth, set in a sort of hard and habitual disdain.

Up and down, up and down—it is her daily afternoon habit—thinking her thoughts alone. She is always alone, this woman; it seems to her sometimes, she has been alone all her life. She is worse than alone now, she is forced to endure uncongenial companionship.

Her walk takes her each time past two long lighted windows; she glances through the lace draperies sometimes, and the disdainful curve of the resolute mouth intensifies into absolute aversion. Two gentlemen sit in that lighted room, playing chess; it is at the elder of these two she looks with that half-veiled glance of dislike. The lady is Madam Valentine, the gentleman, Vane Valentine, her heir.

Sovereigns, it is said, have but little love for their successors. Perhaps this inborn instinct is the reason. The servants in the house will tell you the madam is afraid of him. And yet she does not look like a woman easily made afraid, easily cowed, easily brought into subjection to any will. Her own is very strong, and seemingly reigns paramount. But there is often a power behind the throne, which the throne fears in spite of itself. That power exists here. Mr. Vane Valentine, if not a man of powerful mind, is yet a man of profound obstinacy, whether in trifles or in matters of moment; there is a certain doggedness about him that does not know when it is beaten, and goes on, unabashed, until it has won the game. And he grows impatient, like all crown princes, to come into his kingdom. He has hopes and plans of his own, that depend for their fruition on this fortune, and the queen regnant is so long a dying! More, she looks as much like living as she did a score of years ago! He swears under his breath, sometimes over it, in the sanctuary of his chamber, but madam's vitality is a matter in which no amount of profanity, however heartfelt and sincere, can avail.

She lives, and is likely to live; she takes. excellent care of herself, and spends her money—*his* money rather, lavishly—with both hands, on every whim. For, close upon seventy, she still has whims. And she knows his feelings, and he knows she knows, and resents it bitterly, indignantly, silently. It seems to her basest treachery that he should wish to anticipate by one moment his succession. But then she knows nothing of those hidden plans—Vane Valentine is a secretive man by nature, even in trifles—knows nothing of the patiently waiting sister, Dorothea, who is to keep house for him at Manor

9*

Valentine when he is Sir Vane, and the American millions are his—nothing of Miss Camilla Rooth, a fair
cousin, who used to be younger, and who has spent her
youth, and dimmed her beauty, waiting, like Mariana in
the Moated Grange, for the coming of Cousin Vane,
baronet and millionaire.

Of these things she knows little—she only knows she
is growing to hate him, only knows that he is miserly
and mean, grasping and grudging, and longing for her
death, and sees in her, not his benefactress, but an ob-
stacle to his hopes and wishes, and her riches, by right,
already his own. There is never any open rupture, there
is cold civility and attention on one side, chill scorn and
indifference on the other, but she draws more and more
into herself, lives her own life, thinks her own thoughts.
What if she should disappoint him after all!—it is in
her power. There is a fierce sort of pleasure in the vindictive thought—she can leave her wealth as she pleases
—to endow hospitals, build churches, found libraries!
What if she does it! It would be justifiable reprisal!
And yet—to let it go out of the family—to disobey her
husband's dying wish! There is no one else—— Stay!
is there not? No one else? What of her son's daughter—her only son's only child? What of her? Nearer
in blood, her very own—George's little child!

The mere thought, put thus, softens her heart. What
if she should send for *her?* She breaks off—the idea
comprehends so much—it overwhelms her at first. But
she broods and broods upon it, until familiarity wears
off the first sharp repugnance of the thought. It is the
thin edge of the wedge—the "rift within the lute." Once
well in, for the rest to follow is but a matter of time.
From thinking to talking is a natural sequence—Mrs.
Tinker is her confidante; adroitly the topic is brought
round, one on which the old housekeeper is but too ready
to converse. All that she knows of the child and her

mother--of that last sad interview with **George,** is discussed over and over again.

It is wonderful how this going backward softens the
resolute old heart. George lives again, she hears his
voice, sees his smile, listens to his boyish, gladsome
laugh. Oh, George, George! how sharper than death is ·
the thought of her harshness now! But his child still
lives; it is in her power even yet to make compensation
through that child. Why should she fear Vane Valentine? why care for his displeasure? why not assert herself as of old, and claim her grandchild as her right?
She muses upon it until she is full of the thought; sleeping or waking, it is with her. It is of that she is thinking so intently now, as she paces up and down. It is
past her usual hour of lingering here; a moon is lifting
its shoulder over the tall date palms; the starlit southern night, full of sweetest odors of flower, and forest,
and sea, lies over the land. Still she keeps on, up and
down, up and down; still she thinks, and dreams, and
longs. Why not—why not—why not have George's
daughter—too long banished from this her rightful home
—here? why not now, at once? Thirteen years ago she
sent her from her—she is sixteen now, fair beyond
doubt; her mother was that, and her father—— Ah! was
there ever his like in all the world? So much bright,
brave beauty to lie under the merciless sea for thirteen
years! Tears—very rare tears—soften the hard brilliance of those deep, dark eyes. Seventeen years since
she cast him off, and only now thinking of reparation!
Surely there is little time to be lost here, if she means in
this life to do justice to his child!

"Is it not past your usual hour, aunt?" asks a bland
voice. Mr. Vane Valentine never leaves her too long at
once to melancholy retrospections. It is not good for
her—or for him either. He has dismissed his friend, and
appears by her side on the veranda. "Shall I assist
you in?"

He presents an arm, but she declines, with an impatient gesture.

"I thought you were absorbed in chess with young Payton," she says.

"Payton has gone. I beat him three games in succession," responds Mr. Valentine, complacently, twisting the ends of his mustache. It has grown in thirteen years, is long and drooping, and inky black. "It grew monotonous after that."

Thirteen years have not changed this gentleman much, except in the matter of mustache. Indeed, they have not changed him at all, have merely accented and emphasized all traits, personal and mental, existing then. He is still tall, still thin, still dark, still with scant allowance of hair, with black, restless eyes, and thin, obstinate mouth; still elaborate as to dress, fastidious in the minutest details about himself, from the glossy whiteness of his linen to the dainty-paring and purity of his nails. He looks like a man thoroughly well satisfied with himself—a man who could never, under any circumstances, imagine or own himself in the wrong.

"He walks beside her, and casts a complacent, self-satisfied, proprietor-like glance over the scene. There is the sea, bathed in a glory of moonlight; there is a mocking-bird, singing, whistling, twittering, like a whole aviary near; there is a whip-poor-will piping plaintively in the bracken; there are the roses, and the myrtle, and the orange trees, the passion-flowers, and the jessamine, scenting the night air; there is the Southern Cross, ablaze over their heads; there are warmth, and perfume, and beauty everywhere. It dawns upon Mr. Vane Valentine it is a fine night. He says so.

"Never saw such moonlight," he remarks, still complacently, as if the scene were gotten up especially for his delectation. "And that mocking-bird—listen to the fellow. As you say, aunt, it is much too fine to go in."

"I am not aware of having said so," shortly; "on

the contrary, I am going in almost immediately—Vane !" abruptly.

"Yes, aunt,"

"When did you hear from your friend—what is his name?—Farrar."

"Paul Farrar?" surprised. "Oh, not for ages. Not since that time, years ago, when he wrote to know——"

Mr. Vane Valentine pulls himself up short. "If that girl might be christened," is what he was going to say. But madam knows nothing of that, and it is one of the cases where ignorance is bliss.

"Well?" she says, sharply; "finish your sentence—since when?"

"Not for years. He is in Russia—got an appointment of some kind in St. Petersburg, and naturally—moving about as we always are," in a slight tone of grievance, for Mr. Valentine does not like a nomadic existence—"it is not likely we should keep up a very brisk correspondence. Besides, I hate letter-writing."

"Indeed !" sarcastically; "since when? I should never imagine it, seeing the voluminous epistles that go to England by every mail."

"I write to my sister Dorothea and my cousin Camilla, of course," rather stiffly.

A pause.

What is coming? Something out of the common, he sees, in the furtive glance he casts at her absorbed face. She breaks the pause abruptly.

"How often do you hear from that girl?"

"That girl?" bewildered. "Do you mean my cousin Camilla——"

"I mean," striking her stick sharply on the ground, and pausing in her walk, "I mean that girl you sent to Canada with the man Farrar, thirteen years ago."

"Oh!" Mr. Vane Valentine catches his breath. The bursting of a bomb at his feet could hardly have startled him more. "That girl ! Snowball Trillon."

"If that is what she is called. I mean," with icy distinctness, "my granddaughter."

Mr. Vane Valentine whitens under his lemon-hued skin—turns the livid hue of the moonlight on the whitewashed house-front.

"Your granddaughter!" with equal iciness. "Who is to tell if she is your granddaughter? The word of the woman who called herself her mother was not worth much, I fancy. The girl, Snowball Trillon, is in Canada still."

A frigid stare follows his answer, and Madam Valentine's "stony stares" are things not pleasant to meet. Then she laughs contemptuously.

"This is your latest *metier*, is it, to doubt her identity? Well, I am not disposed to doubt it, and that I take it is the main point. I mean Snowball Trillon, if you like. Where is she in Canada? Be more definite, my good Vane, if you please."

"The place is called St. Gildas. She lives, I believe, on an island near that town, in the family of one Dr. Macdonald."

He is recovering. The shock has been so utterly unexpected that he has been stunned for a moment, but his customary cold caution is returning. He draws a long breath, and his pulse quickens a little its methodical beat. What—what does this mean?

"Do you ever hear from her?"

"Never directly. The money you allotted for her maintenance is drawn semi-annually by Dr. Macdonald —was drawn two months ago, and she was then reported in the doctor's letter as alive and well. That is all I know."

"Alive and well," slowly, gladly, thoughtfully, "and sixteen years old, is she not? I wonder—I wonder," dreamily, "what she is like?"

"She is sixteen years old," coldly; "of her looks I know nothing—nor of her."

"It is my wish then," says madam, asserting herself

suddenly and heartily, "that you should know something. It is my own intention to know a great deal. I
have been culpably ignorant too long. Write to this Dr.
Macdonald," bringing down the ebony cane with an
authoritative bang—"ask him for all information regarding this young lady, my grandchild," loftily, and
looking him full in the face with her dark piercing eyes,
"her health, habits, education, and so on. Tell him to
inclose a photograph of her in his reply."

"Yes, madam. Anything else? Shall I write to-
night?"

"To-night or to-morrow, as you please. Tell him to
send the photograph without fail. I am curious to see
what she is like. Tell him to answer at once—*at once!*"

"You shall be obeyed. Now, what the devil," says
Mr. Vane Valentine to himself, "does this mean?"

It means no good to him—that at least is certain.
For a very long time, hour after hour, that night, he sits
smoking cigars at his open window, and gazing blankly
at the fair southern moon. He must obey; there is no
help for that. If balked in the slightest, this headstrong,
foolish, ridiculous old kinswoman of his is capable of
going in person, before another month is over her venerable head, straight to St. Gildas, and seeing for herself. The only wonder is, being curious on the subject
at all, that she has not done so already.

There is still one hope. The girl may not in any
way—supposing her even to be his daughter—resemble
the late George Valentine. Like mother like son, thinks
Mr. Valentine, savagely biting the top off a fresh cigar,
as if he thought it were madam's head—a precious pair
of fools both! In point of fact, he is certain, although
he has never seen George Valentine, nor even a picture
of him, that she does not resemble him. But if this old
lady—falling into her dotage, no doubt—should fancy a
resemblance, and be besotted enough to send for her, and
try to put her in *his* place—Mr. Valentine expresses his

feelings just here by a deep oath, ground out between fiercely closed teeth. When it comes to that—let them look to it! He is not to be whistled down the wind, after all these years, as his idiotic old relative shall find to her cost!

But he writes the letter—a slow and labored bit of composition; and as he writes, a cold, cruel, crafty smile dawns, in a diabolical fashion, around his hard, thin lips.

"If they answer this—if they send the photograph after this, then"—the smile intensifies as he folds and seals the epistle—"if that girl has the spirit of a worm, she will fling this letter into the fire, and send an answer, per return post, that will effectually cure madam of her folly!"

Now, Mistress Snowball Trillon, or Dolores Macdonald, as you please, has, as we know, the spirit of many worms—has a pride and a temper, alas! fully equal to Mr. Vane Valentine's own.

Dr. Macdonald, profoundly surprised, deeply hurt, and a little disgusted with the writer, puts the precious epistle, without a word, into her hands, and the blue eyes flash lightning fires of wrath as she reads.

"It is rather—rather offensive," the gentle old doctor says. "You need not send the photograph if you like, Snowball, my dear."

For a moment a storm seems imminent in the flushed cheeks and flashing eyes, then a wicked smile dawns on the rosy young mouth, a sparkle that forebodes badness to come creeps into the azure orbs, and quite quenches the fires of wrath.

"Oh! I don't mind," she says, cheerfully. "A little impertinence more or less, what does it signify? Beggars mustn't be choosers. I'll send it. Write the letter, and when it is ready I'll slip the photo in, and row myself over to St. Gildas this very afternoon and post it. By return mail, don't you see," he says.

"And I hope he'll like me when he sees me," thinks

Miss Trillon, going up to her maiden bower under the eaves; "but I am harassed by doubts."

She takes from a drawer a couple of photographs, tinted, and, as works of art, worthy of commendation They represent a young person in the striking, not to say startling, dress of a *vivandiere*—a short petticoat of brilliant dye, baggy trousers, a blue blouse, a red cap set rakishly on one side of the head, a little wine barrel slung over the shoulder, pistols in the belt, two little hands thrust there also, a smile of unutterable sauciness on the face. And the young person is Snowball! As a picture nothing can be more effective—as a portrait of a stately old lady's granddaughter, nothing could well be more reprehensible. Last winter some charades were acted at the house of Mlle. Innocente Desereaux ; Snowball appeared in one of them as a vivandiere, and the brother of Mlle. Innocente, a photograph artist, had been charmed, and insisted on immortalizing her in the dress next day. The photographs have since lain here, too *outre* to be shown; and it is one of these under which she pertly writes, "*a votre service, monsieur,*" and dispatches to Mr. Vane Valentine.

The interval between sending and receiving is about eight days, and eight more anxious and uncomfortable days Mr. Valentine never remembers to have spent. What is in madam's mind ?—what does she mean ?—why does she want the photograph ?—what change of dynasty does this forebode? Does she—*can* she—mean for one moment to throw him overboard for this upstart ? Does she dream he will permit it ? Is he a puppet, to be taken up and played with awhile, and then thrown aside, as the whim seizes her ? He will show her whether he is or not. Let her expose her hand, and then he will balk her new game.

Meantime there is nothing to be done but wait, and waiting is, he finds, the hardest work in the world.

She, too, is waiting. The subject is never resumed—

it is the "lull before the storm." Is it to be a drawn
battle between these two proud, unbending people from
thenceforth? It all depends on this girl—this *gauche*,
unformed girl of sixteen. If the photograph should by
any chance resemble ever so little that dead George—
well, if it does, and she takes the girl up, she shall see!

It comes—the letter with the Canadian postmark, and
something hard within.

His hand shakes as he opens it, and the *carte* drops
out.

It is a moment before he can summon resolution
enough to take it up, but he does at last, and then- —!

The letter is from Dr. Macdonald, it is brief, civil,
but cool. Mlle. Trillon is well, is quite happy, has
been well and carefully educated, and has no desire
whatever to change her home.

He incloses her photograph, by which Mr. Valentine
will see she is also extremely pretty; and he is his re-
spectfully, Angus Macdonald.

Madam Valentine is in her sitting-room. A storm of
wind and rain is sweeping over the fair landscape, and
blotting it out.

She sits watching it drearily, when Mr. Vane Valentine, with a more assured look and step than he has
used of late, comes into the room, an open letter in his
hand.

"It is the letter from Canada, and the picture," he
says.

He lays both in her lap.

His face is in good order, but there is an impercep-
tible thrill of triumph in his tone.

He does not go—he stands and waits.

A slight flush rises to her face, but she meets his look
with one of frigid reserve.

"Well?" she says, inquiringly.

"Will you be good enough to open the letter? The
photograph is inside."

"At my leisure. I will retain the picture. You need not take the trouble to wait!"

It is a curt dismissal; a flush of anger rises over his sallow face.

He has hoped to see her face when first she glances at the audacious photograph. He is destined to be disappointed. But he knows the look of angry surprise and disappointment that will follow, all the same. Without a word he goes.

Then, with fingers that shake with eagerness, she snatches the picture out, looks at it, drops it with an exclamation of anger, amaze, dismay.

What! another dancing girl! A juvenile copy of the bold, blue-eyed circus woman, who had confronted her that September afternoon, thirteen years ago.

And what outrageous costume is this? what defiant smile? what pert words written underneath?

Is this, indeed, her grandchild?—hers? Does the proud Valentine blood flow in the heart of such a frivolous creature as this?

What insolence to send it—it is a direct affront. And yet—what a pretty face! What a brightly pretty, piquant face. Not a bold one, either—only saucy, girlish, full of fun and healthful glee.

She looks at it again, reluctantly at first, relentingly after a little—then, long and earnestly.

No, there is no look of George—none whatever; it is a youthful repetition of that other face she remembers so well—only with the brazen recklessness left out.

She must be *very* pretty; she might, with proper training, become a lovely girl. What a wealth of rippling ringlets; what charming features; what an exquisite dimpled mouth! Only the dress—and yet—*that* might be only a girl's thoughtless joke.

The letter is all that can be desired, formal if you will—a trifle cold, but perfectly respectful. What if Vane Valentine has couched his request in impertinent

words—he is quite capable of it, and this defiant picture
is sent in reprisal? She hits the truth, and suspects that
she hits it; she guesses, quite accurately, what her heir
is feeling on this subject.

"I will disappoint him yet," she thinks, vindictively,
"in spite of the picture."

She meets him at dinner, some hours later, without a
trace of any emotion, except her usual severe reserve of
manner, and hands him back the letter.

"Well?" he asks, with rather a grim smile. "And the
picture—how do you find that?"

"I find it a trifle eccentric," she returns. "No, James
no soup. Taken in a fancy dress, I imagine. A pretty
girl, and very like her mother. Yes, James, the rock-
fish," to the man-servant. "If you please, my good Vane,
I will keep it."

No more is said. But the edge of the wedge is well
in, and, with a feeling akin to despair, Vane Valentine
realizes that his letter and fatal photograph are but the
beginning of the end.

CHAPTER XVIII.

A FLYING VISIT.

N April evening. Westward the sun is dipping
in Bay Chalette its very red face, and the
cool, greenish waters take on roseate hues in
consequence, that by no means belong to
them. A soft, pinkish, windless haze, indeed, encircles
as in a halo bay and town, Isle Perdrix, and the boats of
the Gaspereaux fishers, out in force, for is not this
"Gaspereaux Month," the silver harvest of these toilers
of the sea? "Ships, like lilies, lie tranquilly" at the

grimy in Gildas wharves ; the quaint hilly town itself rests all aflush in the bath of ruby sunlight, the sound of evening bells—the *Angelus* ringing out from Villa des Anges- floats sweetly over the hush, until listening, you imagine yourself for the moment in some far-off, old-world city of France.

Isle Perdrix rests, like the rocky emerald it is, in its lapis lazuli setting, its beacon already lit, and sending its golden stream of light far over the peaceful sea.

It is at this witching hour, of an April day, that a traveler stands on the St. Gildas shore, and waits for the ferry-boat to come and take him over to the island.

"You see, there ain't no regular ferry, as you may say, betwixt this and Dree Island," the landlady explains, at the little inn where he stops to make known his wishes ; "and there ain't no regular traffic. There's only the doctor's family and old Tim, that lives on the place for good like, and they rows over themselves when they come back and forrid, which is every day for that matter. We blows a horn when strangers come, and then old Tim, if he ain't too busy, comes across and takes 'em off. I'll blow the horn for you now, sir."

"I can call spirits from the vasty deep," quotes the gentleman, with a touch of humor. "'But will they come when we call them ?' It's a toss up then whether old Tim comes or not, madam ?"

"Jest so, sir. You takes your chance. But the light's lit I see, so he ain't like to be none so busy that he can't come. For he's that *near*—old Tim is, and that fond of turning a penny, that he never misses a fare if he can help it."

She lifts to her lips a sea-shell, and blows a blast that might wake old Charon himself and bring him across the Styx.

"You wait here a little, sir," she says. "Old Tim will hear that, if he's a mind to come. If you don't see him in fifteen minutes you won't see him at all."

"Humph!" says the traveler, "primitive customs obtain here upon my word! I wonder if the other aborigines are like these two?"

But he stands and waits. Many boats glide swiftly past, the red sunlight glinting on brown oar blades, or white sails. One boat in particular he notices; so pretty, so white, so dainty is it—a name in gilt letters on the stern; he cannot read it from where he stands. It is *manned* by two youths; young men, perhaps, and one girl. The girl and one of the young men row, the third steers, all are singing. The spirited refrain of the Canadian Boat Song reaches him where he stands:

> " Row, brothers, row, the stream runs fast,
> The rapids are near, and the daylight is past."

At the sound of the horn they turn simultaneously to look, and the traveler in his turn takes a long look at the girl, who handles her oar with a skill and ease that only long practice can have given. A pretty, fair girl in a suit of yachting costume of dark blue flannel, and broad white braid trimmings, a sailor hat of coarse straw, and a redundance of very light, very loose hair. She rests on her oar, after that look at him, and addresses the steersman. A brief discussion follows—the twain who row seem to urge some point, to which the third objects, but the majority carry the question. Instinctively the traveler feels he is the subject of the consultation; perhaps they know he wishes to visit the island, and are good-naturedly disposed to take the place of the tedious Tim. His conjecture proves to be correct; the pretty white boat is headed for the St. Gildas shore, is run sharply up on the sands, and the steersman, raising himself from his recumbent position, somewhat indolently touches his cap, and speaks.

"Beg pardon, sir. You want to go to Dree Island?"

"If I can get there—yes. The good lady who keeps the inn, blew a blast that might have raised the dead, but it has not raised the ferryman of this river."

"If you like to come with us, we will take you."

"Ah! thanks very much," availing himself with alacrity of the offer. "You are most kind. But will it not take you out of your way?"

"On the contrary, we were just going there. We have only been drifting about. Rush off, Johnny. If you like to steer, Snowball, I'll take your oar. You ought to be tired by this time."

Snowball! The traveler gives a great and sudden start, and sits down on the thwart with more precipitation than grace.

"Thank you, Rene, dear," responds the pretty girl, in the yachting suit, with much demureness. "I would row until my arms dropped off, I am sure, sooner than tire your poor dear muscles. No. Johnny and I will take *Boule-de-neige* home. Come on, Johnny."

Johnny comes on. The boat glides off like a great swan, out into the river, propelled by two pair of strong, willing young arms. The sun has quite dipped out of sight by this time, and the moon, "bright regent of the heavens," floats up in pearly luster. The long, mystic, silvery twilight of northern climes wraps them in its dreamy haze.

"A blazing red sunset, Snowball," says the young gentleman addressed as "Johnny," a strikingly handsome big fellow of eighteen or more, with a pair of large, deep, sea-gray eyes. "You will have a capital day for your trip to Moose Head to-morrow. Is Innocente Desereaux going?"

"Of course," responds the pretty girl, promptly, "and Armand—but he goes as a matter of course."

"Why a matter of course?" demands, rather peremptorily, the other young gentleman, darker, slighter, older than "Johnny." "You must be fond of the society of fools, Snowball, when you take so readily to the continual companionship of Armand Desereaux."

"A fellow feeling makes us wondrous kind," quotes

Mlle. Snowball, still demurely. "I get so overpowered with intellect and 'tall talking,' Rene, when you are at home, that, do you know, Armand's mild imbecilities are a positive relief. Besides, he is so very, *very* good-looking, poor fellow. Did you ever notice his dark, pathetic eyes?"

There is a disgusted growl from the austere-looking M. Rene—a smothered laugh from Johnny.

"Exactly like the eyes of a pathetic poodle, when he stands on his hind legs and begs!" this latter says. "I have noticed his dark pathetic eyes, Snowball, and always feel like taking him gently and sweetly by the collar to the nearest butcher's. They're ever so much, in expression, like old Tim's little terrier's, Brandy."

It is an impertinent speech, but, her back being turned to Rene, the young lady rewards it with her sweetest smile. And her smile is very sweet. She is, without exception, the prettiest girl, the stranger thinks, he has ever seen.

Whatever other opinion may be held of Snowball Trillon, there can be but one on the subject of her beauty. No eyes more coldly critical, better disposed to find fault, could easily be found; but fault there simply seems to be none. He sits at his leisure and takes the picture in. She appears to regard *him* no more than the thwart on which he sits. The head is small, and set with the much-admired "stag-like" poise on the fair, firm throat—a head crowned with a *chevelure dorée*, such as he has never looked on before. The figure is tall, very erect, very slender, as becomes sixteen years, its contour even now giving promise of getting well over *that* with a dozen more years. The face is oval, the eyes of turquois blue—blue to their very depths; fearless, flashing, fun-loving, wide-open eyes. A complexion of flawless fairness, white teeth, and a rounded dimpled chin. And—he thinks this with an inward shudder—it is also like a living likeness of a waxen, dead face, and rigid eyes of the same forget-

me-not blue, seen once and never to be forgotten, thirteen years ago!

As he sits and stares his fill, he is quite unconscious
that some one else is staring at *him*, and staring with a
frown that deepens with every instant. It is the young
man who steers, whose dark brows are knitted angrily
under the visor of his cap.

"Confound the fellow!" he is thinking, with inward
savagery; "one would think she was sitting to him for
her portrait! Hang his impudence! Snowball!" authoritatively; "you have handled that oar long enough.
Come and take my place, and give it to me."

Snowball looks at him, and reads in his face that he
means to be obeyed. In his place she will be out of eye-
shot of the ill-bred stranger, unless he has eyes in the
back of his head.

There are some tones of Rene's voice Snowball never
cares to disobey; this is one. Perhaps, too, she suspects.
She gets up obediently, smiling saucily in his darkling
face, and takes the stern seat.

Mr. Vane Valentine comes to himself at once, and is
conscious that he has given the dark and dignified young
Monsieur Rene cause of offense. He hastens by pleasant
commonplaces to make his peace.

"Very interesting town, St. Gildas — quaint, old
world, and that. Is that a Martello tower he sees over
yonder, on these heights? Ah! rare birds, these round
towers—built, no doubt, in times of French and British
warfare. Reminds him of Dinan, in Brittany, with its
Angelus bell, and its convents, and priests in the streets,
dressed in *soutanes.* Yes (to Johnny), he has been abroad;
has been a great traveler now for years. Charming
scenery, this! Is that Isle Perdrix, with the beacon
lights shining? A pretty island—very pretty, no doubt.
They know Isle Perdrix well?"

"Well enough, since we live there," Johnny answers,
with a shrug; "too well, we think sometimes. Life on

an island, be it never so charming, is apt to grow a stale affair after a score of years. We are Dr. Macdonald's sons, and he is at home, if you want to see him. It's not much of a show place, Dree Island, but tourists mostly do it. If you don't wish particularly to return to-night, sir, my father will be happy to offer you a room."

Johnny makes this hospitable proposal, in much simplicity, quite ignoring his brother's warning frown.

Rene has taken a sudden dislike and distrust of this dark, staring stranger, and his patronizing talk. He may spend his own shining hours—and he does spend a good many of them—in judicious repression of Miss Trillon, but he is singularly intolerant of any other male creature presuming to take the smallest liberty.

He sits absolutely silent, until they land, and then restrains Snowball, by a look, from leaving her place.

"We will row down as far as Cape Pierre," he says, peremptorily, "the evening is much too fine to go in. Tim," to that aged retainer, appearing on the shore, his pipe in his mouth, his hands in his pockets, his dog Brandy at his heels, "show this gentleman up to the cottage, will you?"

And then Mr. Vane Valentine finds himself on the shore of Isle Perdrix, old Tim inspecting him, with two rheumy, red eyes, Brandy smelling in an alarming manner at the calves of his legs, and the *Boule-de-neige* floating like a fairy bark down the moonlit stream.

"Two handsome young fellows, my friend," he remarks to Tim, following that faithful henchman up the rocky paths.

"Faix ye may say that. I'm sayin', ye may well say that. Divil their aquil ye'll find anywhere in these parts. Av ye want to stan' well wid the owl docther, ye'll spake a civil word for the byes. I say ye'll——"

"And a very pretty girl," interrupts the stranger, carelessly. "Their sister, I take it? although she doesn't resemble them."

Timothy groans.

"The gerrel! O well, thin, 'tis nothing bad I'll be sayin' av the gerrel, but upon me honor and conscience, 'tis nothin' good anybody *can* say! The divilment av that gerrel—the thricks and the capers av her—mortial man cudn't be up to. No, thin, she isn't their shister, not a dhrop's blood to thim, but a sort o' fonlin the ould docther's bringin' up. I'm sayin'—arrah shure here's the docther for ye himsel."

Dr. Macdonald appears, and Mr. Valentine approaches, and presents himself.

The presentation is not so facile a matter as he usually finds it, for the reason that he has made up his mind not to give his name. But the gentle, genial old doctor is simplicity itself—he sees a stranger at his gate, and asks no more. To give him of his best, and ask no questions, is his primitive and obsolete idea of hospitality. Mr. Valentine is invited in, is refreshed, and pressed to spend the night, and accepts graciously the invitation. Dr. Macdonald personally offers to show him over the island, seen at its most picturesque by this light, relates its history—a tragic history, too, of bloodshed once upon a time, of plague later, of terror and sudden death. Nine tolls from the steeples of St. Gildas; the little island, all bathed in moonlight, lies as in a sea of pearl—a sea so still that the soft lapping of the incoming tide has the sound of a muffled roar.

The hour, the light, the silence, has a strange, eerie charm even for this man, hard and sordid, and but little susceptible to charm of the kind.

"I cannot think what keeps my children," the doctor says, as they turn to go back; "they seldom stay on the water so late. The beauty of the night, I suppose tempts them. Ah! they are here."

His face lights. The white boat grates on the sand and the three young people come up the craggy slope

the gay voices and young laughter coming to where they
linger and wait.

"'Prithee, why so sad, fond lover? prithee, why so
pale?'" sings the girl, and slips her hand through Rene's
arm, and gives him a shake. "'Sure, if looking glad
won't win her, will looking sad avail?' .I don't know
whether I've got it right or not, but that's the sense.
Johnny, do you know if Innocente Desereaux has been
trampling on our Rene more than usual to-day? Because——"

"Hush! can't you?" retorts Johnny, giving her a
fraternal dig with his elbow, "don't you see? The Marble Guest!"

"*Con*-found him!" mutters Rene. "Snowball, have
nothing to say to him! Go up to your room and go to
bed. You must be up at dawn to-morrow morning, remember."

"Good little girls ought to be in bed at nine o'clock
anyhow," chimes in Johnny, severely, "do, Snowball.
Get some bread and milk in the kitchen, like a little
dear, and Rene will go up and tuck you in!"

Snowball receives this proposal with a shout of derisive laughter, which if a trifle louder than Mère Maddelena would approve of, is altogether so sweet, so joyous,
that the two men waiting smile involuntarily from sympathy.

"My little girl!" the old doctor says, and lays a
loving hand on her curls. She has snatched off her
sailor hat, and is swinging it as she walks. "My boys,
and my little Snowball, sir," he says to the silent man
who stands beside him, "but you have met before. You
rowed this gentleman over, didn't you, Snowball?"

Snowball drops the son's arm, and takes that of the
father. The stranger falls back with Johnny. Rene
walks on ahead, wishing his father and brother were a
little more discriminating in their unbounded hospitality.

"I don't like that fellow," he thinks, "and," rather ir-
relevantly this, "Snowball will be asked to play and
sing for his amusement, no doubt! Hospitality is a virtue, perhaps—but even a virtue may be carried to excess."

He is right—Snowball is asked to sing and play, and
does both, and quite brilliantly too for a schoolgirl of
sixteen, but then they are musical or nothing at Villa
des Anges. The instinct of coquetry is there, and flashes
out—no, let us be correct; not coquetry, malicious mischief, and *not* for the captivation of the stranger, but for
the aggravation of the silent and watchful Rene, who
sits in a corner, with a ponderous tome—*Lives of Artists and Sculptors*—held up as a shield, and keeps
watch and ward jealously behind it.

' Did you ever read the thrilling romance of the *Dog
in the Manger*, Snowball?" whispers Johnny, in a pause
of one of their concerted pieces; "just cast an eye at
Rene, and behold the tableau vivant!"

The stranger observes as well as the speaker. His
keen, half-closed, black eyes, take in everything. The
pretty, homely, lamp-lit parlor, whose only costly piece
of furniture is the piano, the white, benign head of the
doctor, the stalwart, handsome Johnny, like a model for
an athlete or a Greek god, as you choose, the silent,
grave, intellectual Rene, and the brilliant young beauty,
with the golden mane falling to her slim waist, the white
hands flying over the keys, and the blue eyes laughing
over at Rene's "grumpy" face.

"Is that glum-looking youth in the corner in love
with her?" Vane Valentine wonders; "if so, why should
she not marry him and stay here all her life? *That*
would be a way out of the difficulty; madam would
never trouble herself with the wife of M. Rene Macdonald. And he is handsome too, if he would only light
up a bit, in a different way, of course, from his brother.
Why no:?"

There seems to be no why not. It seems the most natural thing in the world, sitting in his room, later on, thinking it all over—that the girl should marry one of these Macdonald lads, and become socially extinct forever after. If left to themselves it will inevitably happen, but who is to tell whither this new craze may not lead Madam Valentine? She still retains the picture of the dashing little girl-soldier, still broods in secret over her new-found dream. The woman who hesitates is lost —she is but hesitating, he feels, before taking the final plunge that may ruin his every hope for life.

He is here now without her knowledge. He has found the spring heats down there at St. Augustine too much for him, and has come North, ostensibly to see that everything is gotten ready for her reception—in reality to pay a flying visit to Isle Perdrix, and behold for himself this formidable rival. He has seen her, and finds her more dangerous than his worst fears. If madam once looks on that winning face, that enchanting smile, that youthful grace, all is over—her old heart will be taken captive at once. She does not allure *him*—he is not susceptible, and his heart—all the heart he has ever had to give—went out of his possession many years ago.

He rises late, descends, and finds breakfast and the doctor awaiting him. It is ten o'clock. He apologizes, pleads late habits, and the evil custom of sitting up late. The doctor waives all excuses—his time is his guest's.

"I must be going before noon," Mr. Valentine remarks; "there is a train leaves St. Gildas about eleven, I find. I owe you a thousand thanks for your kind hospitality, my dear doctor. My visit to Isle Perdrix will long remain delightfully in my memory."

"Very pretty talk, but where the duse," he is thinking, "are the rest?"

The doctor sees the wondering glance.

"My young people started on an excursion down the

bay at daylight," he says, "and will not return before night. They left their adieux with me."

Which is a polite fiction on the doctor's part, no one having given the stranger within their gates so much as a thought. Well, it does not signify—he has seen her, and found her a foeman worthy his steel.

He departs. Old Tim prosaically rows him on the return trip, and he takes the eleven express, and steams out of gray St. Gildas, with the memory of a sparkling, laughing blonde face to bear him company, "a dancing shape, an image gay, to haunt, bewilder, and waylay" all the way he goes.

Two weeks later. Madam Valentine and her attendants are located with their *penates* in that luxurious domicile that is called for the time, "home." But the end of May has in store for Mr. Vane Valentine a still greater change. Sir Rupert Valentine dies. It has taken him many years to do it, but it is done at last.

The baronet is dead—live the baronet! Sir Rupert is gathered to his fathers, and other relations, and Sir Vane steps into his shoes—his title—his impoverished estate, his gray, ivy-grown, ancestral manor. It is sudden at last—is death ever anything else?—and Miss Dorothea writes him to come without delay. The family solicitor also writes, his presence is absolutely needed—things are in a terrible tangle—Sir Vane *must* come and see if the muddle can be set straight. He lays those letters—his brown complexion quite chalky with emotion—before his aunt and arbiter.

"Certainly, my good Vane, certainly," that great lady says, with more cheerful alacrity than the melancholy occasion seems to demand; "go by all means, and at once. Any money that may be needed, for repairs, &c., shall be forthcoming, of course. Remember me to your sister and Miss Camilla Rooth."

Time has been when Vane Valentine would have hailed this as the apex of all his hopes. That time is no more. He is torn with doubt. To leave Madam Valentine and her fortune for many weeks—months, it may be, who can, at this critical juncture, tell what may not happen in the interval? She may do as she has done—she may visit St. Gildas. Once let her see that girl and all is lost! What is an empty title, a handful of barren acres, a mortgaged manor-house, compared with the fortune he risks? But the risk must be run. Madam herself is peremptory in urging him to go.

"The honor of the family demands it," she says, severely. "You must go. Why do you hesitate?"

Ah! Why? He looks at her almost angrily, and would "talk back" if he dared. But discretion is the better part of valor—the risk must be run. With a gloomy brow, and a foreboding spirit, the new Lord of Valentine and his portmanteau depart.

And then, what he most fears, comes straight to pass. Ere the good ship that bears him has plowed half the Atlantic, Madam Valentine, attended by her maid, is on her way, as fast as express trains can whirl her, to St. Gildas, to see with her own eyes the original of the daring photograph she looks at every day.

CHAPTER XIX.

"LA REINE BLANCHE."

" LADY for you, *ma mère.*"

So says Sister Humiliana, and lays a card before Mère Maddelena, who sits busily writing in her bare little room. The mother looks up, and at the card, and knits her brows.

"Valentine?" she says. "We have no one of that name, my sister."

"No, my mother. Perhaps it is some one who comes concerning a new pupil. She is in the second parlor. It is *une grande dame, ma mère.*"

"It is well, *ma sœur.* I will go."

Mère Maddelena lays down her pen with some reluctance, for she is very busy. To-day there are the closing exercises of the school, distribution of premiums, addresses, graduation speeches, awarding of gold medals, wreaths, &c., with music, and a dramatic performance. And "His Grandeur" is coming, and many other very great personages, lay and ecclesiastical, among them a distinguished English "milor" and his lady. All these dignitaries Mère Maddelena has to receive and entertain ; her girls are to have one last drilling in their parts—a thousand things are before her. And now she is called to waste her golden moments, in futile talk, it may be, in the second parlor.

But she goes, with her slow, stately step, a very ideal lady abbess, serene of face, gracious of manner—a *very* gracious manner—quite the mien of a princess. And with some right, too, for Mère Maddelena once upon a time was a very great lady. So long ago, so like a dream it seems to her now, when it flits for a moment across her memory. In the days of the Second Empire, when the glory and the splendor thereof filled the earth, no braver soldier marched to the Crimea, among the legions of Louis Napoleon, than Colonel, the Count de Rosiere. Among all the brilliant ones of a brilliant court, few outshone Laure, Countess de Rosiere, either in beauty, in birth, or in high-bred grace. She let him go, and mourned for her Fernand, gayly—he would return with the Cross of the Legion, a Marshal of France. He did return—in his coffin, and his fair young wife took her bruised heart out of the world and into the cloister. At first she only entered *en retraite*, in those early days of death and despair, and there peace found her—a new peace, that no death could take away. That was in the

10*

dim past—Mère Maddelena is here now, but under the
serge of her habit, under the humility of the *religieuse*,
the old court manners, the old *air noble*, still remain.   It
is a very inspiring and graceful presence that enters the
"second parlor" and bows profoundly to the elderly
lady, so richly robed, who sits therein.

Madam Valentine rises, and returns that profound
obeisance, impressed at once by the stately mien of the
nun.

"Upon my word," she thinks, "these Frenchwomen,
whether nuns or society belles, have beautiful manners.
I only hope she has managed to instill a little of her
high-bred grace into this girl I have come to see."

"Be seated, madame," Mère Maddelena says, and
stands until her guest has done so.   "A grande dame,
truly!" she thinks, as their eyes meet, "and a handsome
and striking face."

"My name, perhaps, may not be unfamiliar to you,
reverend mother," begins the lady, glancing at the card
the mother still retains: "Valentine."

"It is unpardonable of me if I forget, but—Valentine?   No—I do not recall that, madame."

"And yet you have had a pupil here for many years,
bearing that name, have you not?"

"A pupil?   But no, madame—no one called Valentine."

"Perhaps then she is called," with some reluctance,
"Trillon."

"Trillon?   Stay!   Ah!   but yes, madame, it is the
little Dolores whom you mean.   The protegee of our
good Dr. Macdonald."

"Dolores?   She never was called Dolores that *I* knew
of.   Snowball if you like—a silly name."

"The same—the same !   But madame fails to recollect
—it was by madame's permission we christened her
Dolores.   She was written to on the subject '

"Was I? And when? Who wrote? I remember nothing of it," says Madam Valentine, rather abruptly.

"It is many years ago now, fully six at least. Madam Macdonald died, and the little one was sent to us. She had no name but the so foolish one of Snowball, and had never been baptized. Madame is aware," deprecatingly, "we could not tolerate that. Dr. Macdonald wrote to his very good friend M. Paul Farrar, then at Fayal, and M. Paul—he wrote to you did he not? Or a member of your family, perhaps, for the requisite permission."

"Ah-h! to a member of my family! I see," says madame's sarcastic voice.

"Permission came we might do as we pleased. And we called the child Marie Dolores. Is it possible, madam, that this is the first you have heard of it?"

"Quite possible—the very first, my good mother. But it does not signify at all. I prefer Dolores to Snowball, which, in point of fact, is no name at all. Well, it is your Dolores then, that I have come to see."

"Madame is——?"

"Her grandmother! I have never seen her in my life! You will wonder at that, my mother, but her father, my only son, married against my will, and to my great and bitter grief. He is dead since many years" (this conversation is carried on in French), "and his death I cease not to deplore. But toward his child I did not relent; I banished her from my sight. I sent her here. I fatigue you, I fear, my good mother, with all these family details."

She speaks with a certain coldness, a certain haughty abruptness of manner, that she is apt unconsciously to assume when forced to unveil ever so little of her heart to strangers. But Mère Maddelena's gentle, sympathetic face makes the task easy.

"Ah! but no, madame. I am interested. I am sorry, It's all very sad for you."

"I grow an old woman, I find." Madam Valentine resumes, still in that abrupt tone, "and I am lonely. She —this girl—is nearer to me than anything else on earth. It is natural I should wish to see her, at least. That's why I am here."

"Ah, madame?" in profoundest sympathy, "and once having seen her, you will love her so dearly. It is a heart of gold—it is a child of infinite talent, and goodness, and grace. A little wild and joyous, I grant you, but what will you—it is youth. And a paragon of beauty. We do not tell her *that*, you understand, but it is a loveliness most surpassing. All Villa des Anges will be *desole* if madame, *la bonne maman*, takes her away. And next year she is to graduate. Surely madame will not take her away!"

"If she is what you describe her, I surely will!" replies *la bonne maman*, decisively. "You paint a fascinating picture, my mother. Why, a girl like that, with a fortune such as I can give her, may have the world at her feet. Sixteen years old, you say?"

"Nearer seventeen, I believe, and tall and most womanly for her age. Ah! *ma chere petite!* how we will be sorry to lose you! Shall I send for her, madame, that you may see for yourself?"

She stretches out her hand to the bell, but the other stops her.

"No," she says, "wait. I do not mistrust your judgment, my mother, but I prefer to judge for myself. Let me see her, hear her, myself unknown, first. How can I do this?"

"Most easily. Honor us with your presence at the exercises this afternoon. She is to be crowned for excellence in music, and to receive the second medal. She afterward performs in a little vaudeville we have dramatized ourselves from history, "La Reine Blanche" we call it. When all is over, the pupils mingle with the guests in the parlors. You can there see and hear, and talk to her as much as you like.

"That will do admirably," madame says, rising ; "and now, as I am sure you are very busy, reverend mother, I will detain you no longer."

"Let me present you with one of our admission cards," says Mère Maddelena, rising also ; "so many wish to assist at the closing exhibition, that we are forced to protect ourselves against a crowd. Until this afternoon, then, madame, *au revoir.*"

The portress glides forward with her key, the big convent door opens and closes, and Madam Valentine is out, driving in her cab through the streets of St. Gildas to her hotel.

Her calm mind is almost in a tumult of hope, of fear. If this girl only proves to be what Mère Maddelena makes her out, or even half—what solace, what companionship may yet be in store for her ! For even in her reparation— and she honestly desires to make it—madam's first thought is of self. She grows, as she has admitted for the first time, very lonely in her desolate old age. Vane Valentine is no companion. She half fears, wholly distrusts him. She rebels against the sort of power he is beginning to exercise over her. His impatience is too manifest.

"I shall not die yet, my good Vane," she thinks, with a little bitter smile, "even to oblige you. How will you look, I wonder, when you hear in England that a graceful, golden-haired granddaughter has usurped your place ? George's child — George's little daughter ! To think that she is over sixteen, and I have never seen her yet !"

A pang of self-reproach passes through her—a pang that yet holds a deeper pity for herself.

"How blind I have been ! All these years—these long, lonely, wasted years, she might have been with me ; I might have won her love. What if now she refuses to come, or, if coming, comes reluctantly ? What if she prefers her friends here—this doctor and his family, who have cared for her always? It would be quite natural. But I would feel it! I would feel it! George's child!"

Still she does not fear it greatly. She has so much to offer—so much; they have nothing but love. And how often does love not kick the beam when gold is in the other scale? No one ever says "no" to Katherine Valentine. So she dreams on—of a future in which she will live over again her own wasted life, in the bright young life of this girl. How happy she will make her! How wholly she will win her heart!

"It will atone," she says, and her eyes fill with slow tears, " to the living and to the dead—oh! most of all, to the dead! What I refused the father shall be given, a thousand times over, to the child."

She counts the hours with impatience until the hour she can return to the villa. She does not wish to go too soon, and be forced to bear her impatience under the eyes of a hundred people. Her maid stares at her. Is this her calm, self-repressed, proudly silent mistress—this feverish, flushed woman, walking restlessly up and down her room?

The hour strikes at last; the distance is but short; a carriage is waiting. She descends, and is driven back to Villa des Anges. A stream of people and carriages for the last half hour has been setting in the same direction.

A waiting sister receives and escorts her, and several other arrivals, to an upper seat in the long and lofty hall. It is rather like going to the theater—there is the stage, the green drop-curtain, and silks rustle, and fans wave, and plumes nod, and an odor as of roses and violets abounds. Here is the ecclesiastical element, a bishop, and numerous priests; here is the British personage and his lady—an imposing assemblage as a whole. Sisters in black veils and white coifs, flit about, and all along one side, tier upon tier of innocence, white Swiss, blue sashes, and carefully arranged tresses, sit the " angels ' of Villa des Anges. Silent and demure they sit, wreaths on their youthful heads, white kids on their angelic hands, dancing light in their bright eyes. It is an effective picture altogether, and so thinks madam, taking it all in through her double eyeglass. The granddaughter of many Valentines might be in a very much worse place than this Canadian convent, after all. Madam has been given a conspicuous seat among the nobility and gentry, and in an excellent position to see everything. Bills of the performance, white satin, gold lettering, attar of roses, are distributed. She glances eagerly at hers, and sees the name for which she looks, " La Reine Blanche—A Drama in Three Acts ! *Marie Stuart*—MLLE. DOLORES MACDONALD !"

There is a list of other names—madame cares to read no farther. That name occurs in two or three other places, as performer of a " Moonlight Sonata," as soprano in a quartet, as second medalist. She hears the murmur of voices about her, she sees a sea of faces, but she takes in no details—cares for none. Yes, once she is slightly awakened. Two young men in a seat near her are discussing the coming entertainment in vivacious tones.

" Gilt lettering—ess. bouquet—white satin," says one, sniffing at his programme, " when Mère Maddelena does this sort of thing she does do it. Drilled the girls, too, in their parts, and you will see they will do her honor. She does not forget ; she once took part in private theatricals at the court of Napoleon Third."

" I see Snowball down for the ' White Queen,' says the second voice ; " she will look the part very fairly, at least, if she cannot act it. She is not unlike the pictures of the Queen of Scots—the same oval type of face, the same alluring sort of smile, I should fancy. Snowball will not make half a bad Marie Stuart. I saw Ristori in the part in New York not long ago."

" Well, Snowball won't equal Ristori certainly, but

my sister Inno says, she does herself and Mère Mad-
dclcna much credit by her rendering. Look at this
venerable party on our right," says M. Victor Desereaux,
the photographer, lowering his voice, "her black eyes are
going through us—you particularly—like gimlets."

Rene Macdonald, still half smiling, glances carelessly.
The "venerable party" looks both haughty and displeased—he sees that. Who are these young men who
are discussing her granddaughter—*her* granddaughter?
Our Snowball, forsooth! Then it dawns upon her—one
of these may be, must be, the doctor's son. What if—a
quite new and altogether unpleasant idea strikes her—
what if Dolores—pshaw! the child is but sixteen, and
with no thought, doubtless, beyond her piano-playing
and school-books. But her keen eyes linger on his face.
Is this young man handsome? Well, hardly, and yet it
is a fine face, a striking face, a clear-cut olive face, full
of promise and power.

"Who ever loved, that loved not at first sight?" quotes
Victor Desereaux. "It is a clear case, Rene, my friend.
The elderly party has snccumbed to your charms, she
can't take her venerable eyeglass off your too captivating face. If such is the havoc you work with a glance
upon sixty years, what—oh! what must it be when the
victim is but sixteen?"

The orchestra bursts forth at the moment, and drowns
his *persiflage*, and the performance commences. *Ces
demoiselles*, in airy white Swiss, flash on and off, "speak
pieces," sing songs, play the piano, make lovely courtesies to the audience, appear and disappear. Madam
Valentine sees them, and sees them not; they are not
the rose, but they grow near that peerless flower. She
is hot with impatience—her nerves are pulling hard.
Why does not this foolery end, and the drama begin? It
is the *piece de resistance* of the day, and is kept until lesser
matters are well out of the way. But its turn comes at
last, and Marie Stuart, the child-widow of the Dauphin,

in the snowy robes of her royal widowhood, "worn according to custom by the queens of France, hence called *reines blanches*," stands before them.

There is a murmur—a whisper—"*Snowball*"—a sort of vibration all through the audience, fairly taken by surprise at sudden sight of all that blonde beauty and grace. In those trailing pearly robes (white silk), her flaxen ringlets falling to her waist, with blue star-like eyes, but delicate rosebud face, those loosely clasped hands, she is a vision. Not Marie Stuart herself, in the days when her radiant loveliness was a world's wonder, could—it seems to those who look—have outshone this.

"My faith!" says the lowered voice of M. Desereaux. "That little sister of yours is a dazzling beauty, my friend, Rene! How is it? I have only thought her a pretty little girl, hitherto."

Is Rene Macdonald asking himself the same question?

He leans forward, his dark eyes kindling, watching every motion, drinking in every word.

Is this Snowball—little madcap Snowball, with whom he has been quarreling all his life; whom he has pelted blind with her namesakes, every winter; whom he has snubbed, and contradicted, and put down on every occasion? This fairy vision—this radiant Reine Blanche, the mocking, exasperating mischief-maker, whose breath he has half shaken out of her body erstwhile for her pranks, whose ears he has tweaked, whose misdeeds on the high seas he has reprobated! He feels dazed. Has he been blind—or is it the dress she wears—he has never seen her walking in silk attire before—is it his three months' absence in New York—*what* is it?

He has never seen this girl before, it seems to him, in his life—never, certainly, with the same dazzled eyes.

Will she be his commonplace, everyday Snowball to-morrow, and will this glamour have gone?

He almost hopes so; he does not know himself—or her—in this mood.

And still the play goes on—other people seem to be under the spell of the siren, too.

She is singing, now, with "tears in her voice," in a veiled, vibrating tone, that goes to the heart:

> " Adieu ! O plaisant pays de France,
> O ma patrie !"

And so on.

She is leaving that sunny land for bleak Scotland.

How low, how hushed is her voice! She seems to feel the words she sings. You may hear a pin drop in that long and crowded hall.

And now the curtain is down, and the music is playing, and the first act is over, and Rene Macdonald, like one who wakes from a dream, leans back and passes his hand across his eyes, as if to dispel a mist.

"My word of honor, Macdonald," says young Desereaux, "she is a marvel. She never looked like that before. How do you suppose she does it?"

The whole audience is in that flutter and stir that invariably follow the dropping of a stage curtain.

All are discussing "La Reine Blanche," her beauty, her surprising acting of the part, her vague resemblance to the lovely Scottish queen.

Rene Macdonald sits nearly silent, lost, in a sort of dream—waiting with a tingling of the pulses, a thrilling of the blood, a quickening of his calm heart-beats, altogether new and inexplicable.

Why should he care—like this—to see Snowball? He never has cared before?

The orchestra are playing something very brilliant— in the midst of it the curtain rises again. Yes—there is Mary Stuart, widow once more—exiled—imprisoned. She stands on the shore of Lochleven, and Willie Douglas kneels at her feet.

The white robes are gone—the floating curls are hid-

den away under a velvet " snood "—the face is sad and
pale. Willie Douglas kneels there, urging her to fly.

M. Victor Desereaux, with one eye on the play, keeps
the other well on other things, and notices especially the
rapt attention of the dignified elderly lady, whose hard
stare at Rene caught his attention from the first. He
sees her now, all through this act, sitting erect, a flush on
her thin cheeks, an eager light in her fine eyes.

All present are interested, but none to the same ex-
tent. Who is she? he wonders. Snowball has no relatives that any one knows of. Whosoever she may be,
she is vividly absorbed in the fair little heroine of the
drama.

And now it is the third and closing act—the very last
scene. She might be called la Reine Noire as she stands,
all in black—black velvet—(een)—that trails far behind,
and gives height and dignity to slim sixteen, a stiffly-
starched ruff, a dear littl♦ Marie Stuart cap on her blonde
head. In that sweeping robe, that ruff, that cap, Mlle.
Trillon feels a very important little personage indeed,
and treads the boards every inch a queen. She stands—
her queenly head well thrown back, her royal eyes flashing, her royal cheeks flushing, voice ringing—confronting and denouncing her great enemy, Elizabeth of England. One of the good sisters, with more love for the
memory of Mary Stuart than strict fidelity to historic
facts, has written this drama, and here, face to face, the
rival queens stand and glare at each other. Elizabeth, a
tall, stout young lady, in ruff and farthingale, and con-
spicuously flame-colored hair, cowers, strong-minded
though she be, before the outraged majesty of that glance,
and is altogether crushed and annihilated by the eloquent
outburst of regal wrath and reproach with which the
royalty of Scotland finally quenches her. But marry!
what avail reproaches? Marie Stuart is sentenced and
doomed to die.

The last scene: Dim light ; mournful music ; solemn,

expectant hush, and Marie Stuart, still in trailing velvet—black, wearing a long veil, carrying a crucifix, followed by her maids of honor, with lace mouchoirs to their dry eyes, is led forth to die. It is only a school play, but there is the block, sable, and suggestive, there is the headsman, in a frightful little black mask, and—most dreadful of all—there is a horribly bright and cutting-looking meat axe. It is only a school play, but Rene Macdonald is pale with vague emotions as he sits and looks. If it were real? How white she is, in that black dress—how tall it makes her look, how mournful are the blue, steadfast eyes, that never leave the symbol she carries. The low, wailing music of the orchestra gives him a desolate sense of loss and pain. He wishes they would stop. There is deepest silence. "Into Thy hands I commend my spirit." How despairingly the solemn words fall. She kneels, her eyes are bandaged, "with a Corpus Christi cloth, by Mistress Kennedy," saith history.

The sweet face droops forward, the golden head rests on the block. The headsman lifts in both hands the glittering axe! There is a sound—a sound as of hard-drawn breaths through the halls, then—it is the curtain that falls, and not the axe. Music and light flash up!

Marie Stuart has had her head comfortably off, and her manifold troubles are over!

"*Parbleu!*" says M. Desereaux, and laughs.

Rene falls back; he has been leaning forward in that almost painful tension—he is thoroughly glad it is over.

"Why, Rene, old fellow," his friend says, "how pale you look. If little Boule-de-neige were really getting her pretty head off, you could hardly put on a more tragic face."

"I find it close here," Rene says, with some impatience. "I wish it was over. What comes next?"

He looks at his satin slip, but when the next comes he hardly heeds. How lovely she looked! Who would have thought it was in her to throw herself into a power-

ful part like that? A clever little head in spite of its
wealth of sunny curls; odd he should never have found
it out before. She will appear again presently to play
—afterward to sing. She will do both. well; he knows
her musical power at least.

She comes—this time in the white Swiss and wreath
of the other *pensionnaires*—a school-girl—no longer a
white queen. She receives her crown and medal from
Episcopal hands, and has a few gracious words spoken
to her by that very great vice-regal personage, and that
other distinguished visitor, "my lady," by his side.

Then there follows the general distributions of prizes,
and the bishop and the personages are kept busy for
awhile, and literally have their hands full. This, too,
ends, and meeting and mingling in the parlors, and congratulations and mild refreshments are to follow.

Everybody rises and moves away. Sister Ignatia,
second in command, comes to Madam Valentine. Mère
Maddelena is of course devoting herself to her patrons,
and the personage and my lady.

"You will come to the parlors, madame?" asks
smiling Sister Ignatia. "I fear you must be tired. It
was rather long."

"I did not find it so. I have been deeply interested,"
replies madame, truthfully; "they acquitted themselves
excellently, one and all. The performance leaves nothing to be desired."

"And Dolores?" says the sister, gently; "pardon,
but reverend mother has told me all. How do you find
your granddaughter, madame?"

"So charming, my sister," says madame, smiling her
brightest in return, "that my mind is quite made up.
When I leave St. Gildas my granddaughter leaves with
me."

CHAPTER XX.

"ADIEU! O PLAISANT PAYS DE FRANCE!"

HREE long parlors, *en suite*, are filled with admiring, congratulating, pleased papas and mammas, as Sr. Ignatia with Madam Valentine make their way through. Many eyes follow curiously the distinguished-looking elderly lady, so elegantly simple of dress, so proudly severe of face—. a face that seems cut in old ivory—bearing unmistakably the stamp of "the world." There are introductions— the two titled people, the bishop, a few others of the more elect—and is then escorted to an easy-chair, slightly raised, whence, at her ease, she may sit and view the rooms. A very bright picture it is, very animated—all the smiling papas and mammas, and the "sisters, and the cousins, and the aunts ;" the pupils chiefly in Swiss and rosebuds, but the actresses all retaining their fancy dresses. The Empress Josephine, in the costume of the First Empire, her waist-belt under her arms, balloon sleeves and puffed hair, is sauntering arm in arm with that sanguinary young miss, who but now, in a scarlet blouse and black velvet mask, chopped off a royal head. Joan of Arc is present, in a helmet of shining silver-paper, a shield of the same invincible armor, a tin sword by her side, and valor on her lofty brow.

Marie Antoinette flits by pretty and piquant, and looking none the worse for her misadventures, all and sundry, in the temple. All the sugar-plums of French history are there—Blanche Castile, queen and saint ; Genevieve, peasant girl and patroness of Paris. And last, but not least—ever charming Marie Stuart, in full feather, black velvet cap, ruffs, and stomacher, all dotted over with sham pearls. Blue eyes sparkle, long ringlets flow, red lips smile—a dainty fan of black and gold flutters coquettishly—she looks to the full as alluring as her bewitching prototype.

Madam Valentine sits, unable for a moment to take her entranced eyes off this brilliant little queen of the revels.

"Shall I bring her up now, madame?" asks, defer-entially, Sister Ignatia.

"If you please, sister. Stay! who is that young man?"

"That is M. Rene Macdonald, the elder son of our good doctor, of Isle Perdrix, and the brother—*comprenez vous*—of mademoiselle."

"I see. Yes, bring her up."

The brother—*comprenez vous*—of mademoiselle has just stopped her, by catching one yellow curl and pulling it out to a preposterous length.

"Will it please your decapitated majesty of Scotland to cast an eye on the most unworthy of your subjects?" he inquires; and Snowball, turning quickly, gives a little ecstatic scream.

"*Rene!*" Both hands go out to him in a rapture of welcome. "Dearest boy! When did you come?"

"Dearest boy! Ah! happy Rene!" sighs M. Dese-reaux, and takes himself off.

"To-day, couple of hours ago," answers Rene, in-wardly much gratified by his reception, outwardly non-chalant, "just in time to see you beheaded. You did it very well, Snowball. I dare say we shall almost be proud of you one of these days. So Johnny's gone!"

"Yes," says Snowball, and a sigh, big, deep, sincere, heaves up from the very depths of her whaleboned stomacher, "Johnny's gone. And oh! how I have missed him. 'The heart may break, yet brokenly live on'—was it Byron who said that? It is dreadfully true, and I am a living example. My heart broke when Johnny sailed for Liverpool, and even the pieces went with him. Dear—dearest boy! (I mean Johnny this

time, not you.)   Life is a waste and howling wilderness
without him.   And to think he will not be back for two
long months to come!"

Another sigh, deeper, if possible, than the first.   And
a very real one; Snowball is as deeply desolated as
Snowball well can be, at the loss of her Johnny.   John
Macdonald has gone for a sailor, has accomplished the
desire of his heart to plow the raging main.   He is going
to do his plowing, however, under unusually favorable
circumstances—the captain is his cousin.   No duckling
ever took to water from its hatching more naturally or
lovingly than he.

"And it is but the beginning of the end—think of
that," says unsympathetic Rene, "now that he has got a
taste of tar and bilge-water, you will never be able to
keep him on land while he lives."

"As if I needed you to remind me of that!" reproach-
fully.   "As if it ever was out of my thoughts.   First
you went—although that was only a happy release—the
island was like paradise for awhile after.   And then came
Captain Campbell for Johnny, and he——"

"Jumped at it," says Rene, as Snowball falters, and
actually places a lace pocket-handkerchief gingerly to her
eyes, "only too thankful to get away from the ceaseless
hen-pecking — chicken-pecking, perhaps I should say,
that he has been suffering from all his life.   You see I
judge of his feelings by my own.   You don't ask me what
sort of time I have been having in New York, Snowball."

"Because I don't care.   Because I know selfish people, who only think of themselves, enjoy life wherever
they go.   Of course," resentfully, "you have been having a good time, while I have been breaking my heart!"

"Broken hearts become some people, I think," says
Rene, laughing, "and yours need be very badly broken,
indeed, to enable you to act Marie Stuart *con amore*, as
you did.   I know it nearly broke mine, to look at you.

Yes, Miss Trillon, I have been having a good time. I like New York; I like sculpture; I like my taste of Bohemia. And I am going back next week."

"Next week! Seven whole days—one hundred and sixty-eight hours! Do you mean to tell me we are to be afflicted with your society all that time?"

These little customary amenities have been going on while Sister Ignatia makes her way through the moving throng. She smiles and beckons to Snowball, at this juncture catching her eye.

"There! Sister Ignatia wants me. Come on."

She shoves her white kid hand through Rene's arm, and walks him captive in the direction of the sister.

"Sister Ignatia may want you; she may not want me. There is Innocente Desereaux, too, looking lovely as Queen Blanche. I haven't spoken to her."

"Oh, come on! Never mind Innocente Desereaux! She will survive, I dare say, if you never speak to her. I am sure you never have anything so agreeable to say. Sour things always keep well! Inno can wait."

Snowball may bicker with him, but she holds him fast, a not unwilling captive. Perhaps this sort of repartee is the spice of life to them, the sauce piquant, the leaven that lightens the whole. At this moment Snowball is proudly thinking there is not Rene's equal in the room.

"And how nicely he is dressed!" thinks this demoiselle of sixteen, though tortures would not have wrung the admission from her. "That is a most becoming suit —New York, I suppose. And that assured manner—his lofty way of carrying himself. A young man should always walk well. New York again. But no—Rene always had an air of distinction, the *air noble* Mère Maddelena says she likes. You beckoned to me, Sister!" (Aloud) "Did you not?"

"Yes, cherie. Do you see that lady yonder, in black, with the cashmere shawl and lace bonnet?"

"*My* old lady, by Jupiter!" ejaculated Rene. "Lady Macbeth returned to earth!"

"Looking all that there is lofty and unapproachable —yes, I see," replies mademoiselle. "Who is she?"

"She is Madame Valentine," answers the sister, looking attentively at her; "and she wishes very much that I should present you."

Snowball has many things at this moment to think of—the name conveys nothing to her mind; but it strikes Rene with a certain unpleasant consciousness—surely it is a name he has heard somewhere before!

"Wants to know me!" exclaims Snowball, with open-eyed surprise. "Now why, I wonder?"

"Come!" says Sister Ignatia, and leads the way. She still clings to her captive knight, who now makes a second effort to break his bonds.

"Let go, Snowball. The severe old lady in the gorgeous raiment doesn't want *me*. I will take you home whenever you want to go."

"Don't be foolish!" is Miss Trillon's only reply. "The old lady will not keep me a moment. 'Distance lends enchantment to the view.' She will be glad to dismiss me in about a second and a half."

They stand before her with the words.

"Dolores," says Sister Ignatia, briefly, "this lady is Madam Valentine."

Snowball drops her blue eyes under the fixed gaze of the piercing black ones, and makes a sliding school obeisance, without a word. The sister perforce presents the young gentleman.

"M. Rene Macdonald, madame."

Rene, standing very erect, clicks his two heels together, and bends his body forward profoundly. The whole performance is so French, that Snowball gives him a mischievous smile, and side glance from under her long lashes. Madam Valentine stretches out her hand, to the girl's surprise, and takes one of hers in a close clasp.

"My dear," she says, and in the resolute voice there is a tremor, "you do not know who I am ?"

Snowball is not embarrassed ; if she is, at least she does not show it. She lifts her eyes, and looks at the lady. Sister Ignatia, at the moment, feels a thrill of pardonable pride—the young lady's composure is admirable.

"No, madame," she says, "I have not that honor."

"My child—I am your grandmother !"

There is an exclamation from Rene—it all rushes upon him. He has heard the name from his father. Snowball's family are called Valentine. For her, she turns quite white.

"Madame !" she says, faintly, and stands—stunned.

"You are surprised, dear child. It is no wonder. Yes, I am your grandmother. I have come here expressly to see you. I remain to take you away."

She lifts her eyes to Rene standing beside her ; his olive complexion has blanched to that dead white dark faces take under the influence of strong emotion.

Involuntarily, unconsciously almost, her hand seeks his. But on the moment he turns, and with a low bow to the lady, goes hastily away. Sister Ignatia, too, turns and leaves them alone.

Madam Valentine looks, with a sudden sense of fear and pain at the face beside her, from which her words have in one instant driven color and life.

"Dear little one," she says, "you say nothing. Have I been too sudden, or is it—that you do not want to come ?"

Snowball wakes as from a dream. Sudden ! Yes. She feels as if for a moment her heart had stopped beating with the shock of the surprise. She draws a long breath, and the blue, wistful eyes look steadily into the dark ones bent upon her.

"Ah, madame !" it is all she finds to say for one

tremulous moment. " Yes—it has been sudden—sudden !
Mon Dieu! my grandmother! Oh, madame, are you
indeed that ?"

It is a very cry of orphanage. "I am sixteen and a
half years old," it seems to say, "and in all my life I
have known no one of my blood. Why do you come to
trouble me now ?"

"I love them so dearly," she goes on, without waiting for a reply, "so dearly, so dearly. They are all I
have ever known. They have been so good to me—so
good !" Her voice breaks.

"Whom do you mean by 'they'—that young man,
for example ?" asks madame, a touch of her old, cold
imperiousness in her voice.

"My brother Rene ? Yes, madame"—the fair head
lifts suddenly—"he as well as the rest. I mean all—
Papa Macdonald, Mère Maddelena, the sisters, the girls,
Johnny——"

"Who is Johnny, my little one ?" with a smile.

"My other brother—Rene's brother. I love them
with all my heart. I have been with them all my life."

"I know that. It sounds like a reproach to hear you
say so. It should never have been ; for you are mine,
Dolores—you understand ?—my very own !—my son's
daughter ! Ah ! my little girl, I am an old woman ;
there is no one in all the world so near to me as you.
See ! I plead—badly, I fear, for I am not used to words
of pleading—I plead for your love. Do not give it all
to these good friends, to whom I, too, am grateful.
Shall I ask in vain ? Look at me, dearest child ; give
me your hands ; let your heart speak ; say, 'I am looking at my father's mother, who wishes in her old age to
make up to his orphan daughter what she denied to him.'
It is reparation, my child. If you come, it must be willingly, else not at all. I could not take you with me a
reluctant captive. Speak, my child ; it is for you to say
how it shall be."

They are in a crowded room, but to all intents and purposes they are alone. No one observes them—if they do, what is there to see? An elderly lady in an arm-chair, holding the hands of a graceful girl in the dress of the Queen of Scots—both faces earnest, one pleading, one drooping, and startled, and pale.

"I shall not hurry you," the elder lady goes on. "I know that you are half-stunned by the surprise and suddenness of this, now. You shall have days—weeks, if you will. You shall consult your friends—this good doctor, this wise Mother Maddelena. I will not tear you from your dear ones; you shall always love them, and visit them; but you must not leave them all your heart. See! my Dolores, I am a very rich woman; but that is not to weigh with you. You are to be an heiress, and my darling. All that wealth can give you shall be yours —the pleasures, the brightness, the fairest things of life. Love, too—the love of these good people you possess already, and there awaits your acceptance all that *my* heart has to give. How strangely it sounds to me to hear myself plead! I, who, I think, never pleaded before. But you must come, my dear one, when I go, and willingly. The life you leave is good—you shall go to a better. The friends you quit are kind—you shall still find kinder. You shall travel the whole world over, if you choose; you shall see all those fair, far-off lands of which I know you must have dreamed. Your education shall be completed by the best masters. I am proud of my granddaughter to-day — I shall be far prouder of her years hence."

"Oh, madame!"

It is all poor little Snowball can say, overwhelmed by this torrent of persuasion. Her eyes are filled with tears, but it is not on the handsome, earnest old face bending over her they rest. They follow Rene's tall figure, far away in the crowd, and see him through a mist.

"I will not detain you now; you want to return to

your friends," madame says, very gently. She hardly knows herself in this mood; her heart melts as she gazes on this girl beside her, the last of her line. "Men, like pears, grow mellow before they drop off," says a wise and witty Boston poet; the mellowing process must indeed have set strongly in, when hard, haughty Madam Valentine can use such tones and words as these! But to this girl—George's daughter—it is easy.

"There is the doctor," Snowball exclaims. A tall, white head and benign face appear at the other end of the room, and she brightens at once.

"Ah! the doctor. Well, my dear, go then, and send him to me. I have much to say to him, and it may as well be said here as elsewhere."

Snowball darts off with alacrity, pauses, looks back.

"Shall I—" hesitatingly, "shall I return, madame?"

"Surely, child, before this company breaks up."

"Shall I—" the fair head droops again. "Shall I—have to go with you—to your hotel?"

"There must be no *have to* in the case. You shall do as you like best—quite freely, remember that. But I do not even wish it. If you come with me, it will be only when I go 'for good.'"

"And that will be, madame——"

"Say grandmamma, my little one. Oh! not for weeks to come, I foresee *that*. You must be thoroughly reconciled to the change before we leave St. Gildas. Now go and send your doctor."

Snowball goes, and the doctor comes and takes a seat beside madame, and it is a very prolonged and earnest conversation that follows. For Snowball, she goes to Rene, straight as the needle to the north star. He is leaning against a pillar in an angle of the room, and glances gloomily as she comes up. A small, pale face and two pathetic young eyes look up.

"Rene!"

"Yes, Snowball."

"Is it not awful—*awful!*"—a long, hard, tense breath "Oh ! Rene, *do* you suppose she is my grandmother ?"

"I see no reason to doubt it. I really cannot believe any old lady, however eccentric, would come, in cold blood, and claim *you*, if stern duty did not drive her to it."

Even in this supreme moment, Rene cannot quite lay aside the familiar style of snubbing, although his tone and look are unmistakably dreary.

"Rene"—pathetically—"don't be horrid. I know it is not in your nature to be anything else, but just for once, 'assume a virtue, if you have it not.' Do you know she is going to take me away ?"

"Poor old lady !"

"Rene——"

"I mean," Rene says, laughing, but ruefully, "I am awfully sorry, upon my word, I am, Snowball. Of course, I am going away myself, it may be for years, and it may be forever, as Kathleen Mavourneen says——"

"Kathleen Mavourneen says nothing of the sort. It was——"

"Well, the other fellow; the fact remains, whatever Irishman said it. But while away enjoying life in New York, and going in for sculpture as a profession, and anatomy as a study, and artists and doctors in embryo for chums, it would have been soothing to remember that you were pining in your loneliness here, the last rose of summer, a sort of vestal virgin on Isle Perdrix, growing up for me expressly, and counting the hours until my return. Now all that is at an end, and you are going to start in life on your own hook, and set up, I dare say, for an heiress. I don't wish your long-lost grandmother any harm, Snowball, but if we ever get her on Dree Island, she shall never leave it alive !"

A pause.

Snowball stands, a youthful picture of pallid woe; Rene stands nervously twisting the ends of a still inno-

cent and youthful looking mustache, and feeling sore
and savage, although his manner of expressing these
emotions is *degage* enough.

"I wish she were at the bottom of Bay Chalette!" he
bursts forth, at last. "Confound the old dame! After
deserting you all these years, and never concerning herself in the slightest degree to know whether you were
dead or alive, to come now and claim you! Snowball,
don't go!"

"I must," mournfully.

"When does she propose to take you?"

"Not until I am ready," she says, "which will be
never if I have my own way. You should have heard
her, Rene; one would think I was a prize—something
precious and peerless—to hear her go on!"

"Ah!" relapsing into cynicisms, "she'll get over *that*.
She doesn't know you, you see. I say, where does she
live when at home?"

"I don't know. I never asked. What does it matter?" despairingly.

"It does matter. If it is in New York I could see
you. Find out, will you, the next time you talk to her!
For me—I will address myself to her no more. I am
only mortal—my feelings might rise to the surface, and
there might be a tragedy. I am all at home in my anatomy, Snowball. I could run her under the fifth rib, and
she would be out of the world and out of mischief before
she knew what had hurt her——"

"Rene, don't talk in that dreadful way, please. Are
you going home after this is over?"

"Of course. You don't mean to say you are not
going, too?"

"Certainly I am going. I shall remain on the island
until—— Oh, Rene, *what* shall I do? I hate to go.
How shall I leave you all? And when Johnny comes
back——" emotion chokes further words.

"Never mind, Johnny! There are others in the

world, though you never seem to think so! Snowball,' earnestly, "if you really don't want to go, *don't* go. She cannot make you."

But Snowball shakes her head, and wipes her eyes.

"It is my duty, Rene; I belong to her, not to anybody here. But it b-b-breaks my heart——"

"It has been so often broken!" begins Rene, from sheer force of habit, then stops remorsefully. "Don't cry," he says, "I hate to see you, and you will make the point of your nose pink!"

A pause.

"You will write, I suppose?" gloomily.

"Oh, yes."

The pink suggestion has its effect. Snowball dries her eyes, and represses a last sniff or two.

Another gloomy pause.

"And, Snowball!" struck by a sudden alarming thought.

"Yes, Rene."

"There is that fellow—the nephew, or cousin, you know. M. Paul told us of him. He lives with this old lady—hang her! and was to be her heir."

"Yes."

"Well. He isn't married."

"No?" not seeing the drift.

"No, Snowball!"

"Yes, Rene."

"*You* won't marry him!"

"Oh-h!" a very prolonged "Oh?" of immense amaze. Then suddenly Snowball bursts out into her clear, joyous laugh.

"No, of course not," says Rene, not looking at her; "besides, he is as old as the everlasting hills. Very likely he will ask you, though. You had better not—not——"

"Well?" imperiously, "not what?"

"Marry any one, in fact! Fellows want to marry an

11*

heiress, don't you know—fortune-hunters and *vauriens* of that sort. But you won't, will you?"

"No!" says Snowball, and it is the old saucy, defiant Snowball all in a moment. "No, Rene, dear. Having known and loved *you* all my life, how could I ever look twice at any other man? I will wait for you, *mon frere*, until you grow up!"

And then laughing over her shoulder, Mary, Queen of Scots, turns her pretty shoulder to this darkling young Bothwell, and flits away to join her royal sister, Blanche of Castile—in every-day life Mlle. Innocente Desereaux.

.   .   .   .

It is the evening of the last day, two weeks later. Her boat is on the shore, and her bark *might* be on the sea, only they happen to be going by the 4.50 up express. And Snowball and Rene are pacing the sands of Isle Perdrix for the last time. All adieux have been made, everything has been arranged; Dr. Macdonald, with tears in his eyes, has bidden her go; Mère Maddelena indorses his words, her trunk is packed; *madame la bonne maman* waits impatiently, jealously, to bear away her treasure-trove. In these two weeks she has grown passionately fond of the child—it is Snowball's sunny nature to work her way into people's hearts.

For Rene—well, he has "looked at her as one who awakes"—looked at her with eyes new-opened from the moment she shone forth La Reine Blanche!

> "My path runs east, and hers runs west,
>   And each a chosen way;
> But now—oh! for some word, some charm,
>   By which to bid her stay!"

Something like this is in his thoughts, a cold ache and fear of the future fills him. She is going—going into a world, brighter, fairer than his, far out of his reach. She is to be an heiress, a belle, a queen of society. And he—well, he will have his heart's desire—

he will be a sculptor if it is in him—a marble-carver, at
the least, and dwelling in a world of which she will
know nothing. He may return here, but there will be
no Snowball to meet and welcome him with radiant eyes
and smile. And he feels he would give all his hopes,
the best years of his life, to keep her here, to know, to
know she remains waiting his coming, rejoicing in his
success—his very own. A selfish wish, it may be, but a
most thoroughly natural and masculine one. He thinks
of the story of the Arabian genie who carried his princess
about the world with him, safely locked up in a glass
box—he understands the genie, and his sympathies are
with him. After to-day, who is to tell whether he will
ever look upon her more? It is a jealous old grandmamma that, who waits, one who will know how to
guard her own.

They walk in silence, arm in arm. Old Tim and the
boat wait, their good-by will be here, where no eye,
unless the fish-hawks are on the lookout, can behold.
And they are silent. In life's supremest hours there is
never much to be said ; the heart is too full. The yellow
haze and hush of a sweet summer day lies over sea and
land, the bay glitters, the sky is deepest blue, the little
oily waves lap and whisper. Isle Perdrix looks a very
haven of peace and rest.

> " Adieu ! O plaisant pays de France,
>   O ma patrie !
>   La plus cherie,
>   Qui a nourre ma jeune enfance ;
>   Adieu, France, adieu !"

sings Snowball, softly, not knowing she sings. She
wears a traveling suit of pale gray, lit with ribbons the
hue of her eyes, a gray hat and feather, all the bounteous
pale gold hair falling free. She speaks, and her words
break the spell.

"It will be lonely for Johnny, when he comes," she
says, in the same soft voice, "you and me gone, Rene."

"Always Johnny," he says, impatiently. "I believe you care a thousand times more for Johnny than you do for—any one else in the world."

"I love Johnny," she says, gently; "don't be cross, Rene—now. I like you, too."

"Love — like! Snowball, you always cared for Johnny most."

"Did I? I care for you, too, Rene. Oh! Rene! Rene! I am sorry to go."

"Are you, Snowball? Really, truly sorry?"

He stops, and catches her hands, a swift flush rising over his dusk face, a quick fire flashing in his brown eyes, "sorry to go? Sorry to go from *me?*"

"Sorry, sorry, sorry? Don't you know I am? It has been such a good life, every day of it—all happy, all full as they could hold of pleasant things, and thoughts, and people. And I go from all that. Rene, nothing that can come—be it what it may—will be half as dear as what I leave."

"You mean that! Snowball, Snowball, you will not forget us—you will not forget me——".

"Never, Rene! Never while I live! You—you all —will be more to me than the whole world besides."

"Ah! you say so now, but you don't know. And people change. And it is such a different life you are going to. Snowball, if I thought you would forget——" He stops, his heart is passionately full, full to overflowing, but what is there he may say!

"I never will. I am not like that. I will write to you often—often. I will come back here, whenever I may. And we may meet, Rene—you and I—out in that world beyond Dree Isle. Give my dearest love to Johnny, when he comes back, if you see him before I do. And Rene—my brother—forgive me for all the things I have said, for all the times I have made you angry in the past. I liked you dearly, dearly through it all!"

Forgive her! Old Tim is waiting impatiently—it

will be full time to light the lamp before he gets back
from the other side. Will they never have done standing there, holding hands, and saying good-by. It is a
blessed release, Timothy is thinking in the depths of his
misanthropic old soul, as he sits and smokes his dudeen,
"sure there was iver an' always mischafe and divilment
wid that gerrel, and nothin' else, since she first set fut in
the island."

"An' her an' Master Raynay—sure they did be fightin'
like Kilkenny cats mornin', noon, an' night," ruminates
Tim, "an' there's for ye now, afther it—houldin' hans
as if it was playin' ring-a-rosy they wor, instid o' jumpin'
out o' their skins wid joy—in their sleeves. Dear knows
it's many's the dhry eye there'll be afther the same Miss
Snowball."

It is over. Snowball is here, running with red eyes
down to the boat, and Rene is standing where she has
left him—motionless in the twilight. Old Tim shoves
off ; the boat glides across the luminous river. St. Gildas side is reached, and grandmamma in a carriage awaits
her darling. One backward glance the girl gives. Rene
is standing there still, with that most desolate of feelings,
"left behind." She can just discern him, a lonely figure
on the island shore. Then she is in the carriage, in
grandmamma's arms, her tears being kissed away, and Isle
Perdrix, and Rene, and St. Gildas are already as "days
that are over, dreams that are done."

PART THIRD.

" With weeping, and with laughter,
Still is the story told."

CHAPTER XXI.

"NOT AS A CHILD SHALL WE AGAIN BEHOLD HER."

N old-fashioned Roman house, the *portone* entrance and stairs palatial in size, a great stone
court, where a fountain tosses its spray high
in the sunshine; groined arches, ablaze with
color, trees, vines, birds, butterflies; great pots, and
vases of flowering plants everywhere, and statues gleaming whitely through a glow of warmth and color, green
and gold. Between the draperies of one great window
there is a last glint of amber light. You see a loggia,
overrun with roses, a sky full of leaves, a glimpse of
orange trees, with their deep green leaves, and sprinkle
of scented snow, and jessamines, in profusion, rearing
their solid cones of flowery gold. An old-fashioned
Roman *sala*, with rather faded screens, of amber silk, set
in finely carved frames, walls nearly covered with dark
oil paintings, a great glossy cabinet, a miracle of wood-
carving, and that last pink and yellow glint of sunset
lighting up all.

A peaceful picture, a rustle of myriad leaves in the
beautiful twilight, whose air Italians so jealously shut

out and fear, a twitter of multitudinous sleepy birds, workmen and women going home, a crescent moon rising, like a rim of golden crystal, and *Ave Marias* ringing, until the evening is full of the music of bells, from storied campanile and basilica, to little arches set up against the sky. It is all a dreamy old-world picture, and the girl who stands heedless of the dangerous evening air, leaning against the tall arched window, gazes over it, with eyes that drink in with delight the quaint still sweetness of it all. She is the last and faintest touch of that fair picture, as she stands, tall, supple, straight as a dart, slender as a young willow and as graceful. The last light lingering there, in the fading west, falls full on her face, and fails to find in it a flaw, so fair, so fine is the luster of the skin, so delicate the small features, so perfect in its faint coloring, the tinge of rosy light in the oval cheeks. Her abundant hair, of palest gold, is drawn back from the broad forehead ; a few cloudy pearls, and a knot of jasmine, in the amber glitter. She is in evening dress, a trailing lustrous silk of so pale a blue as to be almost silvery—pink roses loop the rich lace of the square cut corsage, form shoulder knots, and drop in clusters here and there among the lace flounces. She wears no jewels, except the large starry pearls in her hair and in her ears, and clasping the girlish throat and large beautiful arms. Dress and woman are lovely alike, as she stands with loosely clasped hands hanging, leaning against the gray stone, the clustering vines framing her, dreamily listening to the music of the Ave Maria bells.

A servant entering with candles, arouses her presently. She looks up with a start.

"Already, Annunciata? Is it so late? And the signora—has she not yet returned?"

"Not yet, signorina."

The young lady moves away from the window, and the Italian servant closes the shutter and shuts out at once the exquisite evening picture and the malarious evening air.

"How very imprudent grandmamma is," the signorina says, glancing at the *pendule* on the chimney piece, "and in her weak state of health. Sir Vane at least should know better."

She begins slowly walking up and down the long sala, lit now by the wax-lights and one large, antique, bronze lamp. Her lustrous yard-long train sweeps behind her, her pearls shimmer with their milky whiteness in the amber strands of her hair, in the silvery blue of her dress. So pacing, in pretty impatience, she is a charming vision. Now and then she glances at the clock, and pauses anxiously to listen for carriage wheels in the court-yard.

"Grandmamma ought not," she says, half-aloud, half-impatiently. "Does she want a second Roman fever, before she is fully recovered from the first? Sir Vane is prudent enough where his own comfort and health are concerned—he might interest himself, a little at least, in hers."

There is a tap at the door.

"May I come in, deary?" says a voice, and the door is pushed a little way open, and a pleasant old face—not Italian by any means—peeps in.

"Oh, come in, Mrs. Tinker—come in, of course. It is too early to go yet, and even if it were not, I could not go until grandmamma comes back from her drive. She promised to return early, and here it is quite nine o'clock, and——"

"Eh? My maid, what is it you are saying? Not back? Bless thy pretty heart, my deary, she has been back these two hours, and is in the drawing-room with company. Leastways, maybe not company, so to say— it's her lawyer, Mr. Carson."

The young lady pauses in her walk to regard the old lady with blue, surprised eyes.

"Why, that is odd ! Back these two hours, and I——
Did she not go for her usual drive on the Corso with Sir
Vane, then, after all ?"

"Not wi' Sir Vane, my deary. She gave him the
slip, so to speak. Madame doesn't like to be watched
and spied on, you know. Yes, she went for her drive,
but not wi' Sir Vane, and not on the Corso. She went
to her lawyer's, and brought him back wi' her here. And
there they are in the drawing-room ever since."

"Well, Mrs. Tinker?"

The young lady says this interrogatively, for Mrs.
Tinker looks wistful and important, and as if charged
with a heavy load of information, and anxious to go off.

"Eh, Dolores, my maid?—can't 'ee guess what's the
business? Maybe I oughtn't to tell—but it's good news,
and I'm right glad to have it to tell. The madame"--
coming closer, and dropping her voice to a whisper—"is
making her will !"

"Her will !" The girl repeats the words, turning
pale. "Is—is grandmamma worse, then ? Oh, Mrs.
Tinker, surely she is not going to——"

"Bless thy tender heart, my deary ! No—it isn't that.
But she is old, you know, and, eh ! my dear, we none o'
us can go on living forever, and it's well to be prepared.
The last will left everything to *him*. It wouldn't do to
die sudden-like, and leave a will like that. So there's a
new one to-day, my deary, and me and the butler, we've
put our names to it. And seeing that I'm that long in
her service, and have tried to do my duty fairly by my
good mistress she's had it read to me. And, oh ! Miss
Dolores, my maid, thanks and praise be ! all's left to
you, or nearly all. And who has a right to your own
grandpapa's money, that he made himself in lawful trade,
if not his own son's child ?"

She lifts one of the slender white hands, and fondles
and kisses it.

"Eh, my sweet, but there'll be a great heiress, when

old Tinker's dead and gone. I've been sore afeard, my birdie, that death might come before I would see this day. I couldn't 'bide the thought of all that riches going to him. I never could 'bide *him*, from first to last. All for himself, my deary, and longing for the day to come that would make him master over us all. But that day will never come now, for which praise and thanks forever be !"

The girl listens, silent, startled, pale.

"And Sir Vane ?" she asks.

"Gets a share—not so much, but enough for *him.* But you are a great, great heiress, my bairnie. You are your grandmother's rightful heiress, and have what was left to him before. And right it is that it should be so. I don't hold with giving the children's portion to the——"

"Tinker !"

"To a far out cousin's son, then ! What rights has he, alongside o' yours, Master George's own bonnie daughter ? Don't 'ee look at me like that, honey ; it's the old madame's own, to do what she likes wi'."

"No, no, Mrs. Tinker, it is not. I mean this new will is unfair, unjust. What ! all these years Sir Vane has been led to expect that *he* will have the lion's share —has been told it should be so, and now, at the eleventh hour—— Tinker, I must go to grandmamma. It must not be."

"Eh ! my maid, that you can't. The lawyer is still there, and no one is to go in until she rings. And you would not get poor old Tinker into trouble, would you, my bairn, because she is too fond of you to hold her foolish tongue ? The madame did not mean me to tell you ; she wants to do that herself. Wait, my deary, until she does ; there is no such haste. But I say again, and will always say, that it is a right, and just, and proper will."

"There is the bell now !" the young lady exclaims

"Go, Mrs. Tinker, and tell her I want to see her. Tell her I *must* see her before I go out."

Some of the old imperiousness of Snowball is in the tone, and her "must" rules the household. Snowball it is, and yet no such person as "Snowball Trillon" any more exists, not even "Dolores Macdonald." This fair and stately young heiress, in pearls and roses, and silvery silk, is Miss Valentine, granddaughter and idol of Madam Valentine, a beauty and belle by right divine of her own lovely face, and a power here among the English-speaking circle of the Eternal City.

Three years have gone since that July evening, when Snowball's blue eyes looked through her tears on Isle Perdrix and St. Gildas. Three years, and those blue eyes have looked on half the world, it seems to their owner since, but never more on that childhood home. Three years, in which many masters, much money, great travel, polished society, have done all it lies within them to do for the island hoiden, the trapezist's daughter. This is the result : A beauty that is a marvel ; a grace that leaves nothing to be desired ; a well-bred repose of manner, that even an exacting madame can find no fault with. Sometimes the old fire and sparkle strike through, but rarely in grandmamma's presence. It savors of the past, and the past is to be forgotten—is to be as though it had never been—persons, places, all. She is to forget she ever was Snowball—ever was anything but a graceful blonde princess-royal, with servants and courtiers to bow down and do her homage ; an heiress, with the world at her feet ; the peerless daughter of all the Valentines, with the *sang azure* of greatness in her veins. And the girl does her best, not to forget, but to please grandmamma, by appearing as though she did. They love each other with a great and strong love—grandmamma's, indeed, waxes on the idolatrous. Since the loss of her son, hers has been a loveless life, a dreary and barren life, a sandy desert, without one green spot.

She has tolerated Vane Valentine, never, at the best, any more—of late years she has distrusted and disliked him. But this girl has come, and all has changed. She loves her with an intensity begotten of those many loveless years, and her pride in her is equal to her love. Even Vane Valentine profits by this softening change; she can look upon him with quite kindly and complacent eyes now. Perhaps a little of this is owing to a marked change in him. He has made up his mind to accept the inevitable, in the shape of this fair rival; he absolutely takes pains to conciliate and please. But that is within the last year only; he was literally furious at first. No word of the change had reached him, busied with a thousand things following the death of the late baronet—paying off mortgages, establishing his sister at Valentine Manor, making arrangements for having that ancient ancestral mansion repaired and renovated—four months had flown pleasantly away. Not once in that time had madame written. She scarcely ever wrote letters, certainly not to Vane Valentine. Then, the English business settled, in fine health and spirits, Sir Vane set out on his return journey. If madame would but make haste and die! He hardly knew where to find her, so unsettled and wandering were her erratic habits; but Mrs. Tinker was mostly a fixed star; he could always find her. He went to the house in the suburbs of Philadelphia, a sort of headquarters always. He found Mrs. Tinker there, vice-regent, awaiting him, and a letter.

Such a letter! Short as to the number of lines, brief and trenchant as to words, strong and idiomatic as to expression. She had gone to St. Gildas, and seen and been charmed by her granddaughter. They were together at present. Miss Valentine must see a little of the world. She loved her very dearly—more dearly than anything else on earth—already, and meant to part with her no more! As to their return, quite impossible to tell when that time might come. Her good Vane was

to amuse himself well, and not be anxious. He sits holding that letter—that cold, crushing, pitiless letter, that
blasted his every earthly hope. He was ousted! The
trapeze woman's girl won in his place. After his years
of waiting, hoping, scheming, this was the end !

He sat silent, still, the fatal letter in his hand. And
if any passing artist, wanting a sitter for Satan, had
chanced to look in, he would have found a model with
the right expression. A rage, a bitterness beyond all
words, filled him. To be beaten and baffled like this !
Of what use *now* the title of baronet, with nothing left
to keep it up ; of what use all these barren ancestral
acres, the ivy-grown, tunneled, half-ruined manor, with
the great Valentine fortune gone! For all will go to
this new idol—the wording of the accursed letter he
holds leaving little doubt of that. Farewell to all his
hopes—his hopes of that fair English home, freed from
the thrall of debt, restored and improved ; farewell to
those ambitious dreams of a seat in Parliament, a house
in London, fifteen thousand pounds a year, and Camilla
Routh for his wife. Adieu to it all—this girl, this
usurper, has mounted his pedestal ; he has been shamefully, cruelly deceived—swindled as no man ever was
before. Perhaps he has some right to feel all this rage
—it certainly is a frightful fall. What is worse, it is
impossible to pour out his wrath and wrongs upon the
head of the woman who has used and flung him aside
with such merciless ease. She has gone, her upstart
with her, whither no one knows. He strives in vain to
discover ; they might have vanished out of the world,
for all trace of them he can find.

Months pass in the quest, and these months do him
this good—they cool his first blaze of wrath, and bring
those second thoughts that we are told are best. He
thinks it over—he has ample time—and with a soul filled
with silent bitterness and gall, resolves on his course.
Nothing can possibly be gained by anger, much may by

resignation. He will accept disaster with the best outward grace he may, he will accept defeat with dignity,
he will resent nothing, he will conciliate the old woman
and the young one, he will warily bide his time. And
if that time ever comes !

Sir Vane Valentine sets his teeth behind his long
black mustache, and his eyes gleam with a passionate,
baffled light not good to see. They must return some
time—all is not lost that is in danger ; perhaps she may
be induced to yield him the larger share yet. It is his
right—this right in view of all these years of waiting and
expectation. If all sense of justice is not dead in Katherine Valentine, she must see it herself ; she must be
made to see it. And so in grim silence and resolution
Sir Vane establishes himself in the Philadelphia house,
and waits for them to come.

They come—fifteen months from the time they left
St. Gildas. And fifteen months of travel, of masters, of
madame's society, have done much for the wild girl of
Isle Perdrix. She has shot up, tall and graceful as a
stem of wheat, with hair like its pale silken tassels, all
that is best and brightest in her made the most of, the
blonde beauty enhanced—a lovely, womanly girl of
eighteen.

A vision this to dazzle any man—gilt as it is with
refined gold. Sir Vane Valentine looks on with un-
dazzled eyes. He is too defective in circulation ; too
cold-blooded, too wrapped up in self, to be a susceptible
man, and his heart—such narrow and contracted heart as
he ever has had—was given away, many years ago. The
immature of eighteen has no charms for him. The lady
who waits for him in England can certainly not be
slighted on the score of immaturity, but she has lost
her youth waiting for him. And to do him justice, his
allegiance never for one hour has waned. Still if in *this*
way fortune lies—if there is no other, he is prepared to
make the sacrifice even of Miss Camilla Routh ! The

best of his life has been wasted in the pursuit of this *ignis fatuus*—the Valentine fortune—without it the Valentine name, lands, title, are worse than worthless. No matter what the pride, it must be paid. Come what may now, it is a road on which there can be no turning back.

CHAPTER XXII.

"THERE CAME A LADDIE HERE TO WOO."

ND she is a pretty girl! He looks at her with those cold, critical eyes of his, and admits that much. She is a pretty girl at eighteen— at eight-and-twenty she will be a most beautiful woman. He might do worse! She will do him honor. And he prefers blondes naturally. All this fair, fresh, young beauty will fittingly adorn Valentine Manor; all men will admire his taste, and envy him his luck. Even if she had been ugly, she would still have been a gilded pill—to be taken with an inward grimace or two, perhaps, but still to be taken. And he and Camilla Routh need not part—quite. Her home is with his sister, as it has nearly always been; they are installed at Manor Valentine now, waiting for the golden age to come. Even if he marries this Dolores, it follows, as a matter of course, that Camilla will still remain as much a part of his home as the ancestral elms, or Dorothy herself. She has no other home, poor girl; it would be brutal to turn her adrift upon the world because the hard chances of fortune have forced him to marry Madam Valentine's heiress. His sister will manage the housekeeping as she has always done, even after Sir Vane and Lady Valentine return from their wedding tour. This petted beauty knows nothing, naturally, of the manifold duties of

house mistress. And Cousin Camilla will remain—prime minister. He grows quite complacent as he settles it thus—after all, matters might be worse; it is the consummation that will present itself as most desirable to the mind of Madam Valentine.

It has already done so. The truth is, madame, strong-minded though she be, has been a little afraid of the meeting with Sir Vane—her granddaughter by her side. But he has disappointed her agreeably—if there can be such a thing; he is dignified, it is true, and silent, but not sullen, and not more than the situation justifies.

"I do not pretend I was not indignant at first," he says to her, "and deeply disappointed. You see, I never thought of such a thing as your going to St. Gildas and falling in love after this fashion with the pretty girl there. She is charming enough to make almost any one fall in love with her, I admit, but then that sort of thing did not seem in the least like *you*. Still it is natural, I suppose," with a sigh, "and my loss is her gain."

"It need not be your loss — unless you wish," says madame. She is seated at a table, playing with a pearl paper-knife, and does not look up.

There is a pause.

"I think I understand," Sir Vane says, gravely. "Of course, I don't exactly claim to be disinterested in this matter—it would not be in human nature—and after all these years of waiting. The best of my life is gone—I am fit for nothing now, after yielding up all these years in the expectation of being a rich man in the end. Without wealth to support it, the title must sink; Valentine Manor and park must go. All this you know; compensation is due to me in justice. We might combine our interest, as you say. I might marry Miss Valentine."

"As *you* say!" madame retorts, quickly, almost angrily. "I have never said it."

"No? I thought that was your meaning. Does it

not strike you as the simplest—the only way of recon-
ciling the difficulty ?"

Another pause.

Sir Vane stands, tall, cold, dark, passionless, by the
mantel. Madame sits at the table, and taps with the
paper-knife. The thought has struck her before, but it ,
strikes her with a sort of chill now—a presentiment, it
may be, as she looks at the man. She shrinks from it
with a sudden aversion, for which she cannot account,
and his face darkens as he sees it.

"What is your objection ?" he coldly asks.

"There is a great disparity," madame says. "More
than twenty years. It is too much."

"You will be good enough to recollect I have spent
those twenty years in your service—by your desire. Do
you think it is the life I—any man—would choose, if left
to himself ?"

There is suppressed passion in his tone, fire in his
eyes, anger in his voice. Madame looks up. A spark
has been struck from the manhood within him, and she
likes him none the less for it.

"I forget nothing, my good Vane," she answers, not
ungently. "Compensation is due you. I admit it. My
granddaughter is young—she has seen nothing of the
world in one sense, in spite of her fifteen months of
travel—nothing of men. She is a child in heart and
years—a beautiful and innocent child. Give her time,
let her see a little of life before we trouble her with questions of marriage, or fortunes at stake. I love her very
dearly ; there is nothing so near to my heart now as her
happiness. If you can make it, I am willing—after a
time—to resign her to you. Indeed, in many ways, for
many reasons, I should prefer to see you her husband.
I know you. You are of one race—the honor of our
name is in your keeping—you two are the last of a very
old family. But in spite of this, I shall never force her
heart, her inclination. If—in a year from now say—

12

you can win her, do so. I shall favor your suit. Should she accept you, all questions of conflicting interests will be at rest forever. Should she refuse you, you shall not have wasted those best years you speak of in vain. But she is to be my heiress—that must be understood. The bulk of her grandfather's fortune shall go to her. As your wife, it will come to you indirectly, through her, but the income only—the fortune itself shall be settled upon her and her children. She is George's daughter; her interest must ever be paramount now. Meantime your chances are good; you will be with her; she will see you daily, and learn to care for you—I hope. For you—you remember the words of Shakespeare:

> " ' The man that hath a tongue I say is no man
> If with that tongue he cannot win a woman.' "

She rises with a smile as she says it, and holds out her hands, more gently than he has ever known her before.

"You have my best wishes, my dear Vane," she says kindly. "I believe it is in you to make a good husband; and my Dolores is a mate for a king !"

"Shall I speak to her, aunt?" he asks, holding the hand she extends, in both his, " or shall I——"

"No," she interrupts; "not yet—not for a year at least. Let her enjoy this one year of girlhood unfettered and free. Wait this one more year, and woo and win, and wear her there, if you can."

So the compact is made, and Sir Vane Valentine, with stately and old-time gallantry, lifts the jeweled hand to his lips, and so seals it. Indeed, Sir Vane is stately, and slow, and stiff, and solemn, and somber by nature, and walks through life in full dress, as though it were a per-petual court minuet.

Miss Valentine meets him, and gives him one slim white hand, and looks him over, with the frank imperti-nence of eighteen.

"Tall, lean, yellow, sourish; little bald spot on the top of his head; eyes like jet beads—don't think I shall like him," say the saucy, blue, fearless eyes. "Oh! to have Johnny here—my own ever dearest Johnny!—or even Rene! Life would be too delightful for anything if only it wasn't quite so prim and ceremonious, and if only I had my two boys."

"And it seems to me I have seen Sir Vane Valentine somewhere before," she adds, taking a second survey of the baronet. But she fails to place him. Indeed, she had but barely honored the passing guest of Isle Perdrix with the most careless and casual of glances.

Miss Dolores Valentine has certainly not got her "two boys;" but one cannot have everything. She has her fill of the good and pleasant things of this life. She does not include the professors who still visit her—her music, and German, and drawing masters—in that category, but she does her best to please grandmamma, and takes to dancing and singing by instinct, as a kitten takes to milk. French she is proficient in, of course; German and Italian follow in due order. She is apt and ready, a "quick study," and bids fair presently to be a very accomplished young woman indeed. Madame instills the habits of good society, the repose of manner becoming in the daughter of a hundred Valentines. She reads a great deal—history, travels, biography, fiction, poetry— she is quite ravenous in the matter of books; learns riding, and delights in daily gallops over the hills and far away, with a groom behind her. In a quiet way, she sees gradually a good deal of society; goes out more or less to youthful, innoxious evening parties, the theater, the opera; is admired wherever she goes as a beauty and an heiress, and leads altogether quite a charmed life. It is a very different life in every way from that old one, so far off now that it seems like a dream, but, in its different way, to the full as good.

Every day, every hour, is full to overflowing with

bright and pleasant life. She regrets her boys, and writes to them when she has time to think—to Mère Maddalena, too, and her friend Innocente Desereaux, but their memory is a trifle dimmed by time, and absence, and new delights. Even Sir Vane, seen with daily familiar eyes, grows less gruesome, less elderly, becomes indeed rather a favorite cavalier servant, a friend and cousin, without whom the smoothly-oiled wheels of life might jar a little. He so sees to the thousand and one little hourly comforts—the pleasant *petits soins* that go to make up life, that she finds herself wondering sometimes how she and grandmamma would ever get on without him. When he rides out with her, he is a much more agreeable escort than the groom ; he attends them everywhere ; half the good things she so much enjoys would be unattainable without him. And he is really not so elderly—and then he has a title, and is treated with deference, and is, taken as a whole, the sort of cavalier one can be rather proud of. And the summing-up of the whole thing is that Miss Valentine decides she likes Sir Vane very much, and that if he leaves them, and goes to England, as he talks of doing, she will miss him exceedingly.

How it comes about that the truth dawns upon her it would be hard to say. He adheres to his contract with the madame, and says nothing directly. But there are other ways of saying than in spoken words. In a hundred ways he makes her see his drift. The blue-bell eyes open very wide at first, in amazed incredulity, and a sort of consternation. Marry ! she has not begun to think of it. She has literally had no time—she has seen no one—to be looked at twice at least. She is busy thinking of a hundred other things. Marry Sir Vane ! he wishes it, bonne maman wishes it—she has found that out, too. Sir Vane looks upon the Valentine fortune as his right, and bonne maman means to give it to her. That she also learns—who is to say how ? If she marries him everything will arrange itself as everybody wishes; if she does not, there promises to be worry and disappointment, and a great deal of bitter feeling. Marry Sir Vane Valentine! Well, why not?

Why not? Miss Dolores Valentine has been brought up, as we know, in all the creeds and traditions that most obtain in French demoisellehood of the *haute noblesse.* First and foremost among these is the maxim—mademoiselle marries without murmur the *parti* papa and mamma select. To have a choice of her own, to fall in love— could anything be in worse taste, be more vulgar, more glaringly *outre* and indelicate? Papa and mamma decide the alliance, there is an interview at ten, under maternal *surveillance,* during which monsieur is supposed to sit, and look, and long, and mademoiselle to be mute and demure, and ready to accept the goods her gods provide. If monsieur be tolerably young, and agreeable, and good to look upon, so much the better; if he be old, sans teeth, sans hair, sans wit, sans everything but money, so much the worse. But appeal there can hardly be any from parental authority. There is always the cloister; yes, but what will you? We all cannot have a vocation for the nun's veil, and the convent grille. And these very old husbands do not live forever!

She has not thought much in all her bright summer-day life, she has never had occasion for anything so tiresome; others have done it for her. She knits her delicate blonde brows, and quite frowns her pretty forehead into wrinkles over this. She even writes, and lays the case—suppositionally—before her infallible oracle, Mère Maddelena. Mère Maddelena has been married herself, and knows all about it. The answer comes. But certainly, my child, says *notre mère,* it is all right— that. If the so good bonne maman wishes it, and great family interests are involved, and he is worthy as you say, and you esteem him, then why hesitate. A daughter's first duty is obedience, always obedience; *le bon Dieu* blesses the "dutiful child,"—and so on through four pages of peaky writing and excellent French advice. Esteem him? Well, yes. But the pretty penciled brows knit closer than ever. How about this love, her poets and novelists make so much of, lay such stress on ; positively insist on indeed, as the first and most important ingredient in the matrimonial dish! Is this kindly, friendly feeling she has for Sir Vane, love? Who knows? *Notre mère* says here, it is *not* necessary, it may be most foolish and unmaidenly ; esteem and obedience are best, and almost always, safe. And then what does it signify? She likes him well enough, better than any other. Since one must be married, better marry a gentleman one knows and likes than a stranger. A strange gentleman would be embarrassing; one would not know what to say to him after marrying him ? But one could always talk to Sir Vane. And he is never tiresome, at least hardly ever! Since marriage or convents are states girls are born to choose between, by nature, and as sparks fly upward, why make trouble and vex one's friends? Why not accept the inevitable and the bridegroom chosen ?

There is her friend la Contessa Paladine, only nineteen, the count nearly sixty, quite fat and gouty, and she does not seem to mind. And la contessa, who was altogether poor and obscure, and a little nobody before her marriage, is a personage of importance now, and sister-in-law to a great monsignore, who, in his turn, is a great friend of *il Papa-Re*. She lives in a big palazzo, and drives on the Corso every day, and says she did not begin to live until she was la contessa.

On the whole one might do worse, a Milordo Valentine, as they call him here, is far better than a Conte Guigi Paladino of sixty, all fat and gout. One need never be ashamed of him at least. Her decision, you perceive, is much the same as the bridegroom's own ; it is not what one would most desire, but it might easily be worse. So the fair brows unbend, and the inconsequent girlish mind is made up. Since it must be to please dearest grandmamma she will marry Sir Vane Valentine !

CHAPTER XXIII.

"TO LOVE OR HATE—TO WIN OR LOSE."

O matters stand on this bright evening, when Miss Dolores Valentine walks up and down the lamp-lit Sala in lustrous evening robe, and listens to Mrs. Tinker and her talk of the new will. No one has ever said to her directly one word on the subject matrimonial, but it is in all their minds, nevertheless, and mademoiselle knows it. Why not take the initiative herself, come generously forward, and put them out of their misery. It is through a sense of delicacy and consideration for her, no doubt, they hesitate. Well, she in turn will show them she is not lacking in nice perception. One must marry, it seems ; it appears to be a state of being no properly regulated young lady can hope to escape—since it must be done, then it were well 'twere done quickly.

Of late Sir Vane has been looking more than commonly black and bilious, and Eugene Aramish ; has talked in moody strains of returning to England, and rather committing social suicide, than otherwise. Bonnemaman has been rather silent and grave, a little perturbed, and as if in doubt, and has contracted a habit of regarding them both with anxious, half-closed eyes. The moral atmosphere is unpleasantly charged with electricity. Miss Valentine feels it incumbent upon her to apply a match and touch it off, and with one grand explosion clear away the vapors forever.

"Mrs. Tinker," she says, pausing in her meditative

walk, "go to grandmamma, please; see if the lawyer has gone, and if she will admit me."

Mrs. Tinker goes.

In all things, great and small, this young princess' will is autocratic. In a minute or two she is back. Madame is alone in the drawing-room, and bids her come.

Gathering up her lustrous, shimmering train, Miss Valentine sweeps away, bearing herself like the regal little personage she is—golden head well erect, slight figure held straight as an arrow.

"Bless you, my pretty—my pretty!" murmurs adoring Mrs. Tinker, "look where I will, among contessas, and marchesas, and then, I see no one fit to hold a candle to you."

Swinging lamps sparkle like fire-flies down the lofty length of this blue drawing-room. Madame, in black silk and guipures, sits enthroned in a great blue and gilded chair, with rather a weary, care-worn look upon her pale face. But it changes to a quick, glad, welcoming light, as her granddaughter enters.

"Dressed, my dear?" she says; "have I kept you waiting? It is still too early, is it not?"

For they are due at a party at the big, grim, palazzo of the laughing contessa—not one of the great Paladino state balls, Miss Valentine not being yet properly "out" —a rather small reception—madame's weekly At Home.

"Too early? Yes," Dolores answers, absently. She draws up a low seat, sits close to madame's side, folds her small hands on the elder lady's silken lap, looks up with two wide, blue, utterly unembarrassed eyes, and plunges at once into her subject.

"Grandmamma, Mrs. Tinker says you have been making a will."

"Mrs. Tinker is a foolish old gossip. But it is true. Mr. Carson has just gone."

" Mrs. Tinker says it is a will in my favor, leaving me almost all your money.":

"Tinker is worse than a gossip; she is an old fool. But it is true again. I have."

One jeweled old hand rests lovingly, lingeringly on he fair head. She looks down with worshiping eyes on the fair, upturned, sweet young face.

" My pretty Dolores," she says, "you will be—you are —a very great heiress. You are dowered like a princess, do you know it?"

"I know that you must be very rich, grandmamma."

"And it is a very fine thing to be very rich, my dear. It brings the world to your feet. Have you found that out in these last two years? All our English circle here in Rome—ay, and these titled Italians also, talk of the rich and beautiful Signorina Valentine. And you have known poverty, too, there on your island. Which do you think is best?"

She puts back the strands of yellow hair with a complacent smile, and waits, sure of the answer. But that answer is not quite to order when it comes.

"I was very happy there on my island, grandmamma —ah, happy! happy! Everybody was good to me—so good. And I loved them all dearly. I never wanted for anything. I never thought of being rich—never wanted to be. But, yes, I suppose it is a fine thing; it gives me music, and books, and pretty dresses, and jewels, and handsome horses and carriages, and parties, and pleasant people, and it makes the beggars shower one with blessings ; but somehow, I think I could be quite happy without so much money. It's not everything. I suppose I am not ambitious. At least," seeing madame's brow darken, "it is not worth quarreling over, and having hard feelings about. And I am afraid," nervously, "there may be much hard feeling about this new will."

"What do you mean, Dolores?" a little sternly.

12*

"Don't be displeased, grandmamma. Only is it quite fair to Sir Vane?"

"It is quite fair—it is perfectly fair. My money is mine to do as I please with ; to dower hospitals, if I see fit. I see fit to give it to my granddaughter. What more right or natural than that ?"

"Yes, grandmamma, but still you know Sir Vane expects——"

"My dear," sarcastically, "Sir Vane expected I would die some fifteen or more years ago and leave him my ducats. I believe he considers himself a wronged man, that I have not done so. Perhaps he is no more mercenary and selfish than the majority; perhaps it is natural enough he should wish me out of the way, and my fortune his, but you see even Sir Vane Valentine cannot quite have everything to suit him. I do not think he has much to complain of, on the whole. I do not fetter him in any way. If he remains here constantly, it is his own wish. I think he finds me liberal in all ways. And if I have re-made my will, and left you my heiress, I have not forgotten him. Something is due him—much is due him. I grant that, after all these years of waiting and expectation. *Noblesse oblige*, my dear—I forget nothing. I am as desirous as he is to see Valentine restored, and the old name, a power in the land, once more. Your inheritance would amply do that. Dolores, you plead his cause—plead against your own interests. Is it possible—child, let me look at you—is it possible you *care* for Vane Valentine?"

Red as the heart of a June rose, for a moment, grows the upturned face, but the blue, frank eyes neither falter nor fall.

"As my very good friend and yours, grandmamma—yes. I see him every day, you know," naively, as though that was a reason. "I am sure I don't know half the time how we would get on without him. Oh, yes, *madre carissima*, I like him very much!"

"Ah!" grandmamma laughs a sarcastic little laugh, "in that way—I understand. As you like the family cat! Vane *is* a tame cat in his way too. But as a husband, petite, we have not time to mince matters—it grows late. As a husband, how does Sir Vane strike you?"

The blush fades, the little hands fold resignedly—a deep sigh comes from the pretty lips.

"Oh, grandmamma, I don't know. It is very tiresome to have to marry. Why need one—at least until one is quite, quite old—four-and-twenty say? Grandmamma, I wish—I wish, very earnestly, this, that you would destroy this last will. Let it be as it was before—let Sir Vane have the great Valentine fortune, and then it will not be necessary for me to marry him, or anybody. Money makes so much trouble—it is so hard to make enemies, and bitterness, and family quarrels just for its sake. If I am not an heiress, no one will want to marry me. I could live with you, for years and years to come, this pleasant life of ours, and then—may be—by and by——"

"Well? and by and by?" says grandmamma, half amused, half provoked. "Oh! you great baby! how differently you will think when you come to that antiquated age—four-and-twenty! You would hardly thank me then if I took you at your word to-night. No, my dear, as it is, so it shall remain. You are my heiress—it is your birthright. If you have a mind to marry Vane Valentine, well and good; you might easily do worse, and great interests will then be combined. It is what I would decidedly prefer. If you have not a mind, then there is no more to be said—your inclinations will not be forced, and he must take what I give and be content."

"But he will not be," says the young lady, ruefully, "that is the worst of it. And he will look upon me as his rival and enemy, and be bitter and angry, and feel wronged. If I have a mind to, indeed! I wonder at you, grandmamma! Of course, I have no mind to him, or any one else, but right is right, and if you wish it——"

" I do wish it."

" And he wishes it—why, then——"

" You consent, my dearest Dolores, is that your meaning ?"

Mademoiselle rises hastily to her feet, with a little foreign gesture of both hands, palms downward, but she makes no answer in words, for at the moment enters Sir Vane, ready to escort them to the party.

They go in silence. The Corso is all ablaze with light, and thronged with people and carriages, as they drive slowly through. Overhead there is a purple sky. golden stars, a shining half-ring of silver ; and Dolores, lying back in a corner, wrapped to the chin in snowy cashmere and swan's-down, looks up at it, and thinks of the moonlight nights long ago. Bay Chalette, one great sheet of polished silver ; the black crags of Isle Perdrix, tipped with shafts of radiance ; the little white cottages, looking like a miniature ivory temple. Where are they all—they who dwell together on lonely Isle Perdrix, now? Old Tim is there still in his light-house ; Ma'am Weesy dwells alone in her cottage ; Johnny is among those who go down to the "great waters" in ships ; and Rene is—somewhere—studying his beloved art. It is more than a year ago since she heard from him. He too was traveling ; and that reminds her, she has never answered that last letter. Mère Maddelena is still at Villa des Anges, and Dr. Macdonald—ah ! Dr. Macdonald's name is written in marble, and he has gone to be a citizen of that City whose maker and builder is God.

The great, grim stone front of the tall palazzo is all a glitter of light ; music comes to them as they enter. A dashing young officer, in the glittering uniform of the Guardia Nobile, meets them on the threshold, and devotes himself with *empressement* to the fair Signorina Inglese from that moment. He is a handsome lad, and a gallant, a cousin of the Paladini, and deeply, hopelessly in love with Meess Valentine. A dim suspicion that it is so dawns on Miss Valentine's mind this evening, but she is not sure; she is quite pathetically innocent, for eighteen, of the phases and workings of the *grande passion.*

"May I, grandmamma?" she says, looking over her shoulder gayly, as, permission granted, she flits away by his side.

For Sir Vane—he is distinctly cross. He takes his stand near madame's chair, with folded arms and moody brow, looking darker and thinner, and older than usual, and frowning rather on the gay company before him. He watches with jealous eyes the golden head, pearl-crowned, of his youthful kinswoman, with her glittering Noble Guard by her side. Is this to be the end? The young fellow will be a marchese one day; he is just five-and-twenty; he is handsome, and he is in the deepest depths of the sovereign passion. It is patent in his liquid Italian eyes for all the world to read. Is this to be the end? And Carson was at the house to-day, and a new will was made—a final one this time, no doubt, and the Valentine fortune has been left irrevocably to this amber-haired girl. After all his wasted years, his lost youth, his hopes, is this to be the end?

"Is there anything the matter with you, my good Vane?" madame asks at last, struck, as no one can fail to be, by the dark look his face wears.

"There is nothing the matter with my health, if that is what you mean," he answers, shortly enough.

"Ah! that is satisfactory. Your illness then is a mind disease, I take it."

"Does it follow," still curtly, "that I must be ill at all, because I do not choose to talk in this din?"

Sir Vane has often been irritable—so distinctly as this, never before. But she is in exceptionally good humor herself, and great allowance is to be made for Sir

Vane, she is aware. "If you do not choose to talk that is another thing," she says, coolly ; "when you do I have a word or two to say to you, you may like to hear."

"Indeed?" coldly ; "anything pleasant will be rather a welcome change. My letters from home to-day were all most confoundedly unpleasant. Everything is going wrong, everything from the manor to the cottages tumbling to pieces. I must go over, Dorothy says, if anything is to be done. I can go, of course, although I fail to see of what particular benefit my going can be. I feel rather hipped, I must confess, in the face of all this. And *that* does not add to one's comfort." He motions to where Dolores, still on the arm of the Noble Guard, is waltzing over the waxed floor, to the music of Gourond.

"It is of that I would speak. Come closer, my good Vane, we can talk here as securely as at home. You saw Mr. Carson at the house to-day, I infer?"

"Yes," curtly.

"I have made a will—a new will—my final disposition this time. The bulk of my fortune is left to my granddaughter—naturally."

"Naturally," he repeats, with a half sneer, setting his teeth behind his mustache, and biting back a sullen oath.

"Dolores discovered, and, strange to say, objected. She wished *you* to have the larger share. She considered it due to you. She pleaded your cause most urgently."

"I am infinitely obliged to my fair cousin—the future Marchesa Salvini."

"She is not your cousin—at least, the cousinship is so remote that it need not count. I object to the marriage of cousins. And there is a question of marriage here, Vane. We spoke of it, she and I. I told her I wished it, you wished it, and she——"

"Well?"—breathlessly.

"Consents. Dolores will marry you, my good Vane."

There is silence. He stands erect, and for a moment

draws his breath in hard. It is a moment before he can quite realize what he hears. Marry him! Then that tall fellow in black and gold is no favored lover after all. He looks at her with kindling eyes, triumphant eyes. At last! The fortune is secured! And she is pretty— very pretty—yes, beautiful—a bride to be proud of! And she is dowered like a grand-duchess! Only a moment ago all seemed lost—and now—— Lamps, flowers, waltzes, music, surge around him as things do in a dream. "You say nothing," madame says, suspiciously, and in some anger. "Am I to understand——"

"That a man may be dazed, stunned, speechless, from sheer good fortune—yes. There are shocks and shocks, my dear aunt. You have just given me one. I was in despair—I may tell you now—one moment ago. I meant to throw up everything to-morrow, to go back to England, and return here no more. I thought she cared for that fellow. And now—to know this——"

"Do you mean to say," demands madame, and looks up at him earnestly, "that you care for the child apart from her fortune—that you love her, in short?"

"You need hardly ask that question, I think," he answers, calmly. "Could any man see her, in her beauty and sweetness, as I do day after day, and *not* love her? You hardly compliment our lovely Dolores by the doubt."

"Pardon. I thought—I mean—well, I am very glad. Yes, she is lovely enough to inspire love in any one. There is a great disparity of years," with a sigh; "but that must be overlooked. You will be good to her, Vane?—my poor little tender one!"

And Sir Vane protests, and takes a seat by her side, and while the music swells around them, and the dancers dance, and the rosy hours fly, they two sit there and plan, and talk of the future, and the restored fortunes of the house of Valentine.

CHAPTER XXIV.

"NOTHING COMES AMISS, SO MONEY COMES WITHAL."

HERE is a picnic, three days after, and they go to the Villa Ludovisi. It is lovely picnic weather, and the gay little contessa is never happy but when in the midst of something of the sort. To-day they are a *parti carré*—Sir Vane, madame, la contessa, and Dolores. And to-day Sir Vane determines to put his fate to the touch—to speak to Dolores definitely. Not that there is any real need of such a proceeding, but Sir Vane is not a Frenchman, and believes in doing this sort of thing properly and in order, and in English fashion. They drive through the sunny streets, where hooded capuchins, and picturesque artists, and flower-girls, and fruit-sellers, and friars of orders gray, and cavalcades with jingling bells, and brown beggars, lie in the sun, and the sharp chirp of the cicala cracks through the green gloom, and flowers, and orange trees, and roses, and Roman violets, and Victor Emanuel's soldiers are everywhere. Overhead, there is a hot, hot sun, but with it there is a breeze, an air like velvet, the streets are a blaze of light, and life, and color. It is not the old picturesque, papal picture, of cardinal's carriages—*il Papa-Re*, benign and white-robed, in their midst—but a glowing vista of moving life and color still. They ascend to the heights among ruins, and the red petticoats of *condatina* into the dense green gloom of olive and ilex woods, where luncheon has been ordered, and waits them. There is hard brown bread, and crisp, silvery lettuce, and figs that are like globes of gold, and ice-cold wine. And after dinner, as they stand under the shade of the ilex for a moment alone, Sir Vane finds his opportunity, and speaks.

She is looking very fair, and very young—too young the man of forty beside her thinks—impatient of those forty years. She is dressed in white, crisp, gauzy, silky, as spotless as her own maiden heart. The amber hair falls long and loose over her shoulders in girlish fashion, tied back with a knot of pale pink ribbon. Her cheeks are flushed with the heat, to the same rose pink glow. That glow deepens to scarlet as she stands, with white drooping lids, and listens.

She wishes he would not—she shrinks from what he says. His words of love and passion sound forced, cold; they repel her. No answering sympathy awakes within her—she shrinks as she hears. Was it necessary to say this? Grandmamma has told him. Love? no, she feels none of it—she does not believe he does either. She is relieved when he is silent, and looks about her, half inclined to run away. But he has caught one of her hands, and so holds her. "Dear little hand," he says, clasping it between both his own, "when is it to be mine, Dolores?"

"Grandmamma will arrange all that," answered mademoiselle, and hastily withdraws it; "it is a matter in which I desire to have no choice. I should like it to be as far off as possible——"

"Ah! that is cruel—the first unkind word you have spoken to-day."

"Otherwise," quite calmly, ignoring the interruption, "I am prepared to obey. And, meantime, I should be glad, Sir Vane, if you will not speak of this again. It is not needed, and—I find it embarrassing." There is no necessity to say so; her deeply flushed cheeks speak for her.

Sir Vane promises with alacrity. He is not at all sorry to be rid of the bore of wooing. Her wish renders it easy to make a merit of his own desire. He lights a philosophic cigar, and strolls off to enjoy it, as la contessa comes up with madame.

Later that afternoon, strolling down the hillside, Do-lores finds herself alone; the others have paused to ad-mire a ruin farther up. Where she stands is just beneath a shrine—a shrine set in a tall, precipitous, flower-crowned cliff—a Madonna, in a little blue grotto, with clasped hands and upraised eyes, and a tiny lamp burn-ing like a star at her feet. Some devout client has wreathed the feet with flowers, but they are withered now and drooping, after the noontide glare. It occurs to Dolores to say a little prayer and remend the floral offering. Wild roses are in abundance; she breaks off some long, spiky branches, wounding her fingers in the effort, and mounts some loose large rocks to reach Our Lady's feet. Standing so, two white arms uplifted, the gauzy sleeves falling back, both hands filled with rose branches, she is a picture. So the young man lying quietly on the tall grass a few feet off, watching her at his ease, himself unseen, thinks. She stands on the stones, and essays to twine the roses round the base of the statue. But her footing is precarious, the topmost stone—loose always— slips, fails her. She tries to grasp something, fails in this too, and is toppling ingloriously backward, when the unseen watcher springs from the grass, and with one leap catches her in his arms. She drops into them with a gasp, a horrified "Oh!" then draws precipitately back.

"*Scuse!*" begins the rescuer, trying to uncover, but at the sound of his voice, with a second look in his face, there is a quick little scream of ecstasy; two milk-white arms are flung round his neck, and hold him tight, tight, and a voice brimful and running over with transport, cries out.

"Rene!"

"Rene! Rene! Rene!" cries this ecstatic voice, "don't you know me? Oh! Rene, how glad—how glad I am!"

"Snowball!" he says, blankly. Intense surprise is his first feeling—his only feeling for a moment—mingled with doubt. "*Is* it Snowball?"

"Snowball, of course. Oh! my dearest, dearest Rene! how good it seems to see you after all these years once more!" She loosens her arms by this time and looks at him again. He stands, half laughing, half embarrassed, wholly glad, but not gl d in the same effusive way. And with that second look, it dawns upon this impulsive young person that she has been embracing a Rene very different in appearance from the Rene of old. This is a tall young gentleman, and, in a dark way, an exceedingly good-looking one. And he wears a mustache. And he is a MAN! And all the blood of all the Valentines rises up, in deepest contrition and confusion, in the fair, pearl-like face.

It is Rene, and not Rene. And he is laughing at her —that is to say, there is a smile in his dark eyes, and just lurking at the corners of that new mustache, though he is evidently making a decorous effort to efface it. What would grandmamma, and oh! *what* would Sir Vane say if he had seen! Red as a rose is she—the sweetest, the prettiest, the most charming picture of confusion—and Rene longs to take her in *his* arms this time and return the hug with compound interest. Only he does not, you understand. On the contrary, he stands, hat in hand, and looks as though he could never grow weary of looking.

"It is Snowball!" he says; "and to think that for ten full minutes I have been watching your efforts to decorate that statue, and never knew you. How you have changed!"

"Not half so much as you, I think. I haven't grown a mustache. But you always were rather stupid about recognizing your old friends, Rene."

He laughs outright—her tone is so exactly the dis-putatious tone of wild Snowball Trillon. "Have you never given up your habit of vituperation?" he asks; "or is it only me you favor with it? I am glad if you keep anything exclusively for me—even your trick of finding fault. But my dear little Snowball, how glad I am to see you."

"O-h-h! it has taken you some time to find it out. You are like the man who had so much mind, it took him a week sometimes to make it up. I knew I was glad to see you at first sight."

"You don't quite sound so," still laughing; "*ma foi!* how tall you are, and how——"

"Well," imperiously, "what?"

"Pretty. Pardon me my outspokenness. We never stood on ceremony with each other you may remember."

"I remember. I am sorry I cannot return the compliment," gravely. "You have not grown up at all pretty, Rene."

"No?" laughing once more. "Ah! how sorry I am to hear that. I never regretted being ugly before. But handsome is as handsome does, you know, Snowball, and *I* am doing most handsomely, I assure you."

"Are you? At sculpture, I suppose. Do you know, I don't think much of sculptors and artists. One sees so many of them. And they are all alike—smoke grimy pipes, wear blouses, and never comb their hair."

"Mine is cropped within half a quarter of an inch of my head. I have none to comb, my dear Snowball."

"And Johnny," says Miss Valentine, "where is Johnny? Ah! how homesick I have been many a time for Johnny. I never can sleep stormy nights thinking of him. Does he still go to sea?"

"Still goes to sea—happy Johnny! Gone for a three years' cruise to China. I don't see how you can reconcile it to your conscience — if you have any — to like Johnny so much better than me. He never liked *you* best?"

"Oh! but he did," cries Miss Valentine, warmly, and flushing up, "a great deal the best. You never cared for anybody in your life — well, perhaps, except Ma'am

Weesy, when she was cooking something particularly nice !"

"How unjust," says Rene, "how extremely unjust. I may have concealed my feelings, but I always had—I have at this moment," lifting two dark, laughing, yet earnest eyes, "the very friendliest regard for you."

"Your power of concealment then, past and present, do you infinite credit, monsieur. · I rejoice to be able to congratulate you on anything. What are you doing in Rome?"

"What do all who aspire to carve their names among the immortals in sculpture do in Rome?"

"Among the immortals ! Let me congratulate you once more ; this time on your modesty. Since when are you here?"

"Since four months ago."

"Did you know *I* was here?"

"My dear Snowball, there are some fortune-favored people, who can no more hide themselves than the sun up yonder. You are of these elect. Even to my obscure workshop the fame of the fair, the peerless, the priceless Signorina Inglese has been wafted."

"How priceless, please?"

"Need you ask ? Need the heiress of the great Begum——"

She stops him with a motion, and a rising flush. "And, knowing I was here, you never came, never cared to see me all this time ! Was I not right when I said you were made of the same stuff as your own statues ? You never cared for anybody, my friend Rene, in your life."

"But, Snowball, think. You are—what you are ; I am Rene Macdonald, obscure and unknown to fame, with the poverty of the proverbial church mouse, and——"

"And the pride of Lucifer ! Yes, I understand. Ah ! they have missed me ; here is grandmamma."

Grandmamma ascends the slope, and exclaims somewhat at the sight of her missing granddaughter, stand-ing quietly here, in deep converse with a "rank" stranger.

Dolores springs forward, and offers her strong young arm. "See, grandmamma! an old friend—the oldest of old friends. You have heard me speak of Rene Mac-donald? This is he."

"I know M. Rene Macdonald very well," says ma-dame, smiling, and holding out her hand. "I have heard his name on an average ten times a day for the last three years. I think I may claim him as an acquaintance of my own, however. I am almost certain I have met him before."

"Very likely, madame. I have been in Rome several months."

"Not in Rome—at a certain school fete, at a certain quaint little Canadian town. A young person we both knew played the *role* of Marie Stuart, and two young gentlemen, sitting near a certain elderly lady, very fully and freely discussed the actress."

"Pardon," Rene says, laughing; "I recollect. Ma-dame has excellent ears and eyes, to remember so long and so well."

"Grandmamma never forgets a face or a name," says Miss Valentine, quite proudly; "she is gifted with second sight, I think. Dear me! how very, *very* long ago that day seems now."

"Life has dragged so wearily, you see, monsieur," says madame, pinching one rosy ear, "with this young lady since she has been torn from her island friends. Three years appear like a little forever, do you hear? But *I* know to my cost, that, 'though lost to sight to memory dear,' Johnny, Rene, Inno, Weesy, *notre mère—* the changes have been rung on those beloved names every day, and many times a day, since."

"And madame has been bored to extinction by us all," says M. Rene. "I fear so much of us in the past will naturally prejudice you against us in the present."

"It will not be difficult to make you an exception, young sir," grandmamma says, graciously. She is in high good-humor with herself, her heiress, and all the world to-day. "Here come Sir Vane and la contessa."

They come up, surprised in their turn, but in a moment la contessa has recognized an acquaintance. "*Il Signore Scultore !*" she exclaims. "My dear Dolo, I told you I was having a bust of myself done, did I not? No! Then I am. I go to the signore's studio every day. You must come with me to-morrow and see it. The signore does the most exquisite things, I assure you."

Sir Vane, standing a little apart, comes forward at this moment, and there is .a presentation. Rene bows rather stiffly, and in a moment recognizes the dark, nameless stranger whom he, and Snowball, and Johnny rowed over from St. Gildas that evening years ago.

"So *you* are the man," thinks Rene, eying him with but half-hidden disdain ; "and you came as a spy."

They meet there, on the mountain side, and the Valentines go home, through the lovely starlit dusk. Rene Macdonald stands and watches them out of sight, pleasure, pain, he hardly knows which, the stronger feeling within him. It is the half-forgotten emotion, awakened for the first time on that night madame has recalled, stirring its nearly extinct embers into a glow once more. How lovely she has grown—but was she not always lovely? He used not to see it in those old days, blind mole that he was. And she has not changed—it is the old Snowball, with the life and sparkle, as of yore, in those starry blue eyes, with sweetness, and truth, and repartee still on her lips. Her words are not very sweet —never have been—but too much sweetness cloys, a little acidity flavors the flatness of life's nectar. Who would not prefer lemonade to *eau sucree?* Underneath it all, sparkle, and malice, and retort, he has seen joy—

deepest, fullest joy at meeting him. Her arms have clasped and held him, her first words have been words of gladdest greeting. Dear, dear, dearest little Snowball! unspoiled by flattery, by wealth, by adulations, by the world. What a prize she will be for the man who wins her! And that reminds him—he dislikes and distrusts Sir Vane Valentine. To come to the island, to accept its hospitality, as a spy! A chill feeling of repulsion fills him. Will they—dare they think of giving Snowball, fresh, bright, pure, a child in heart, to *him?* Faugh! the thought sickens him. He has heard of this Milordo Valentine, that he is a screw in money matters, a man not liked by men, a toad hunter, a tame tabby. He is old, too, fully twenty years her senior. Oh! it would be monstrous. Surely Snowball would never consent. In a very meditative mood, indeed, *il Signore Scultore* betakes himself to his lodgings and his atelier. It is an *appartamento* not far from the grand Palazzo Paladino, a studio on the ground floor, and two or three private rooms *al secondo*. He can see the long rows of windows of the *Palazzetto*, sparkling like great diamonds, hear its sonorously sweet music swelling in the soft night air. La contessa gives one of her balls to-night. He descends to his studio, deserted now by the workmen, lowers a swinging brass lamp, uncovers a marble figure, and looks at it.

It is a girl, standing on a windy headland, her hair blown back, her face bent eagerly forward, one hand shading her eyes, gazing over the sea. The face is full of impatient expectation, every curve instinct with grace —the grace of youthful strength and symmetry in repose. An Italian girl has been his model for the figure, the arms, the pose of the head—the face has been wrought from the model of a face in his mind. How often he has seen Snowball stand on Point Lookout, with the sunset lights in her face, her flaxen hair streaming like a yellow banner in the gale, waiting for Johnny and the

Boule-de-neige to come in. He stands, half smiling, and gazes long, then, with an impatient sigh, recovers it, and goes over to one of the windows. He leans with folded arms on the gray stone, and gazes thoughtfully and a little troubled, at the flashing lights of the Palazetto. How wildly sweet those Strauss waltzes peal! Many carriages flash by and draw up in line. Is the Valentine equipage among them, he wonders; is she entering those "marble halls" at this moment, on the arm of the odious milordo.

Next day, what he has hoped for, but hardly dared expect, comes to pass. When la contessa arrives to sit for the bust, Miss Valentine is with her. But—his workmen around him, the double doors of his studio open to the world, the sculptor at his work is a dreamer of dreams no more. On the contrary, he is rather a despotic young autocrat. He places la contessa, gives her her directions, requests Miss Valentine rather peremptorily to amuse herself with a volume of designs in the recess of a window, and not talk. That young lady opens her blue eyes at the tone—it is one she has not been used to of late—then smiles a little to herself, and proceeds to examine every article in the studio. In due course she reaches the statue called "Waiting," and twitches off the covering unceremoniously. There is a faint feminine exclamation. Rene, chipping and cutting in silence, is thrilled by it. Then she stands, as he did last night, a very long time looking at it. She glances at him once, rather shyly, but his eyes—dark and stern they look to-day—are fixed on the marble features of the Contessa Paladino. At last she obeys his first command —goes to the window recess, takes up the big book and tries to interest herself in the pictures. But she cannot —her thoughts interest her more. She lies back dreamily, and looks out of the window instead. A flood of quivering sunbeams, the sound of bird voices, the flutter of multitudinous leaves, an odor of roses and jasmine, the

13

plash of a fountain down in the stone court—that is
what she sees and hears. She is in a dream. Rene is
yonder—the brother she loves; she wishes she could sit
here and go on dreaming forever!

The sitting ends. A shower of silvery chatter from
the vivacious young countess proclaims it as she rises,
and flutters her silky skirts. She admires il Signore
Scultore very much—la contessa. He is handsomer, she
thinks, than any work of art in his studio—she admires
those lustrous, beautiful, dark, grave eyes of his, that
reticent, stately manner. If only one could have all this
and that, too, she sometimes has thought. ‾All this means
the glory of the world, and the splendor thereof—a big
palazzo, family diamonds, weekly balls, all that comes
when one accepts a noble husband with sixty years and
much gout. *That* stands for a tall, slender artist *sposo*,
with handsome eyes and grave glances, a dark Saint
Sebastian sort of face, and a perfect manner. Only these
things never go together, and one must take which one
likes best—no mortal is so favored by the gods as to
have all.

Madam Valentine, going home from her afternoon
outing on the Corso, drives up in state, presently, for
her granddaughter, Sir Vane in attendance as a matter of
course, and offers him a commission. Will he make her
a bust of Dolores? She has wished for one a very long
time, but never could induce the restless child to sit.
She exclaims at the beauty of la contessa's, and some
others, for though Rene dislikes portraits, he accepts
commissions as yet, being much too poor in fact to decline. One or two rather great people have sat to him;
he is beginning to be known and talked of, and to swim
away to the golden shore of success. Will he execute a
bust of Miss Valentine, and will he be so *very* good——?
It is a blank check madame offers in her most empress-
like manner, "and M. Rene will fill it up to suit himself."

An angry glow suffuses the olive pallor of his face for a moment; then his eyes lift, fall on the young lady in question, and the reply on his lips—a rather haughty reply, too, dies. What business have impecunious young marble carvers with pride? it is a sin for their betters. Let him take his blank check, fill it in handsomely, and put it in his pocket. If madame deals with him as a queen, is she not the Great Begum he called her? Does she not so deal with all tradesmen whose wares she purchases? Let. him pocket his pride and his price, do his work, take his wage, and be thankful. Snowball will be here daily, and for many hours each day; she looks as if she would like the sittings to begin this moment.

And so M. Rene Macdonald bows in that *grande seigneur* manner of his la contessa so much admires, and which would be much more in keeping with the eternal fitness of things, madame thinks, if he wrote his name *Don* Rene; and it is settled that Miss Valentine is to be immortalized in marble, and that the sittings are to commence at once.

----•----

CHAPTER XXV.

"WHATEVER'S LOST, IT FIRST WAS WON."

IR VANE VALENTINE stands a little apart, and strokes his mustache, and looks cynical. What a fool the old grandmamma is, after all! And the fellow is so picturesque in that dark green working-blouse, with his four-and-twenty years, and old acquaintanceship too! Well! it is not a question in which he is going to interfere. He is not in love—let her take care of herself. She has promised, and will keep her promise—he knows her well enough for that. What does the rest signify?

The sittings begin. Sometimes la contessa comes,
and plays propriety; sometimes Mrs. Tinker; sometimes
grandmamma herself. There is nothing to alarm anybody; they seem on the verge of an open quarrel half
the time, these two. Dolores is especially and perversely
contradictory and disputatious. Monsieur Rene does
not say much; he smiles in exasperating superiority at
her perpetual fault-finding. But the sharpness, the acidity,
is only surface-deep; la contessa, at least sees that. Even
Mrs. Tinker has an inkling that the feud between them
is not deadly—that it is not absolute hatred that flashes
out of the blue eyes when they meet the brown.

"My pretty!" that good old person says, "what a
handsome pair you two do make! Eh, my dearie, if it
was only him, and not t'other one!" For Mrs. Tinker
does not like "t'other one," does not approve of the
coming alliance. "Eh, my maid, 'tis but ill always to
mate May and December," she says, with a dismal shake
of her old head. Never in her life has she liked Sir
Vane Valentine; never has she forgiven him for step-
ping into the place of her lost Master George; never has
she swerved from her first affection. He is in love with
old madame's money, not with this sweetest maid under
the sun, and she could find it in her leal old heart to hate
him for it.

"Don't 'ee, my lovey! don't 'ee, dearie!" she has said,
over and over again—"don't 'ee marry Sir Vane! He is
no match for thee, my pretty; he is old enough to be thy
father; and he is *dour* and dark, inside and out. Don't
'ee, my maid!—don't 'ee marry him!"

"I must, old lady," Dolores answers, sighing; "it is
kismet—it is written. Grandmamma wishes it; I must
please grandmamma, you know. And I have promised
—it is too late now. Sometimes——"

"Yes, my maid. Sometimes——"

"Sometimes," dreamily, half to herself, "I have wished

—of late—I had not. If I had only waited another day even——"

"It was the day you promised like, you first met Mr. Reeney?" says, with artful artlessness, Mrs. Tinker.

And Dolores starts up from her dreams, flushing to the roots of her fair hair. "Hush, nurse! What am I say-ing? You must not talk of such things. It is wrong—wrong!" She lays her hand on her heart, beating wildly. "You must not say harsh things of Sir Vane. He is very good, and—and I have promised. It is too late now." There is a pathetic ring in these last words; they end in a stifled sob, as she hurries from the room. But it is only that she is very tired, perhaps; she was up at a party, the largest she has yet attended, last night, and the weather—Lent is drawing near, and the weather grows oppressive. It is so oppressive, indeed, that she does not go out at all that day, although M. Rene Mac-donald expects her, and la contessa, who is more than willing to do chaperon duty, drives up punctually for her. She has a headache, she says, and lies in her dark-ened room, and sends away grandmamma, under pre-tense of trying to sleep, and lets Tinker sit beside her instead, and bathe her hands and forehead with cologne. She does not go to the studio for a week, although the bust is nearly completed now, and only a few more sit-tings are required. Weeks have passed since that meet-ing on the hill-side, and madame is talking of quitting Rome immediately after Easter, and going to Florence. They have lingered, indeed, more on account of this work of art than anything else; and this last whim of Dolores is rather trying in consequence. It is not quite all whim, though. The girl really droops this warm spring weather, and all her bright, wild-rose color deser**s** her.

Grandmamma is very impatient for the completion of the work. To have this marble likeness of her dar-ling will be such a comfort to her when Dolores is far away. It is not a bust, as was at first intended ; the idea and the figure have grown, and the sittings have been mostly standings. It is called " At the Shrine." It is a slender girl, with uplifted arms, hands filled with rose branches, head thrown back, face upraised, trying to reach and adorn a shrine of the Madonna. The pose is grace itself ; every outline of the beautiful hands and arms, every curve of the slight, supple form, is there in the marble. The fair, youthful face, like a star, a flower, a rose is filled with a sweet seriousness of whispered prayer. Madame is charmed—is lavish of praise.

" You have caught her very trick of expression when she is in church—or looking at a holy relic—or listening to the grand music of a mass. I can never thank you sufficiently, my dear·M. Rene, for this treasure."

" M. Rene has all the talents," cries la contessa. " I think *I* like best our Dolores when she is a little mutinous—coquettish—what you will. Not with that look of the angels. She is everything there is of the most charming, but she is only a girl after all."

She glances keenly at the silent artist. " How say you, M. Rene?" she demands, gayly ; " is our Dolores most charming as an angel—a saint like this," tapping the marble face with her fan, " or as we know her—a bewitching, alluring little coquette?"

" A coquette," repeats grandmamma, not best pleased. " Dolores is never that. The child is a perfect baby where *that* fine art is concerned—who should know that better than you, contessa *mia*—past mistress as you are of the profession."

But the little countess only laughs at the rebuke, still looking at the sculptor. " Signore Rene declines to commit himself. Well, he is very wise. You will have an exquisite likeness at least, madame, of our dearest Dolores when—by the by," innocently, " when is it to be ?"

" In the autumn," madame answers, absently, her

glass still up examining critically the statue, "they will
spend the winter in travel, and go to England in the
spring. I shall remain in Rome, I think." She sighs
and drops her glass. "When will you send me my
treasure, Mr. Macdonald?"

"In a very few weeks now, madame." He answers
gravely, but la contessa still keenly watching, is not
much the wiser. He is always so grave, this austere
young M. Rene; it becomes him, she thinks. One cannot figure him frivolous, or frittering his time away in
foolish small talk and feeble platitudes. Silence is
golden on such lips as his. But all the same he is hopelessly, irretrievably, despairingly in love with Dolores
Valentine.

It chances—for the first time in all those months of
meeting—that next day Miss Valentine and M. Rene
find themselves alone, together, in the studio. Mrs.
Tinker is there, it is true, in the flesh—in the spirit she
is countless worlds away in the land of dreams. It is a
very warm afternoon, there is that excuse for her. And
the slumberous rustle of the leaves, the twitter of the
birds, the heavy perfume of the flowers, outside the open
window, are soporific in their tendencies. The sitting is
almost over; Rene has chipped away in the drowsy stillness, without a word, Miss Valentine too is half asleep
in the perfumed greenish hush. It is near the hour of
Ave Maria, near the time to go. And there is to be but
one more coming after this. "Only one more," he says,
aloud, as if in answer to her thought. "Can you realize
that it is almost three months since we met there at the
villa Ludovisi? When have months so flown before?"

She sighs, and is silent. Yes, they have flown—life's
best days always do fly.

"You leave Rome soon?" Rene asks.

"Next week," another sigh. "I suppose you stay on,
Rene?"

"At my work—yes. I have all I can do. Snowball,"

suddenly stopping in his chipping and looking at her full, "you are going to be married?" It is the first time the very first, that the subject has ever been alluded to Sir Vane has been there many times, of course. And it is no secret, and la contessa has discussed it freely. Of course he knows, has always known, but no syllable has ever passed his lips before. His eyes, his voice, are stern now; she feels arraigned — guilty. Her head droops, her eyes fall before his.

"Yes, Rene."

"To Sir Vane Valentine?"

"Yes."

A pause. He works again; Mrs. Tinker sleeps. Slanting sunbeams quiver about them; Dolores droops a little in her chair.

"Do you remember," he says presently, "the day we parted on Isle Perdrix? Do you remember our last walk—our last talk? I asked you then not to marry this man, and you——"

"Rene!"

"And you said you would not. Even then, you see, I was among the prophets. I felt it would come. Snowball," suddenly again, in deepest, tersest tones, "why do you marry him?"

"Rene——"

"Why do you marry this man? You do not care for him; he cares nothing for you. There is the fortune— yes. Is money everything, then? are you, too, mercenary, Snowball?"

"Rene, listen——"

"Ah, what is there to say? I know—I know. Your grandmother wishes it—you owe her much—*he* wishes it; a fortune is at stake. Yes, I admit all that. But there is something else in marriage besides money; there is love. Where is the love here? There is love of riches; Sir Vane has that, I grant you. But are you to be so bought and sold, Snowball?"

Her answer is a sob; she covers her face with her hands. He leaves her nothing to say. Love! What is this rapture that fills her as she listens—fills her with ecstasy and agony at once? He throws down chisel and mallet, and comes and stands beside her, pale with all that is in his heart.

"Is it too late?" he asks. "Snowball, listen to me—look at me. My heart's darling, don't you know that I love you? How can I see you given to this man—so old, so cold, so mercenary, so unworthy, and not speak? I have no right—no, I am poor, a struggling artist; you are an heiress, but you are my Snowball too, whom I have loved always—always, always!"

"Always?" she repeats, and tries to laugh; "how can you say so? We have been quarreling all our lives."

"Ah, there are quarrels and quarrels. I have loved you always. How can I stand by in silence and see you given to this loveless marriage—this unloving man? It is never too late, Snowball; draw back while there is yet time."

"There is no time; it *is* too late. No one urged me, only I knew it would please them all. That very day of our first meeting, not an hour before you came upon me, I gave him my word."

"One hour before—one hour too late!" he says, bitterly. "Well, perhaps there is a fate in these things. What hope could there be for me, at the best? Your grandmother would never have given you to me. If he were but worthy—if he but cared for you, you for him, ever so little, I would die before I would speak. I would have bidden God to bless you, and gone on my way, my secret in my heart, to the end. But it is because I know you will not be happy. Happy!" he starts up, and begins walking up and down, with flashing eyes; "you will be miserable! That man is capable of any baseness—of being brutal, even to *you!*"

"Rene, hush! You frighten me. You must not. Oh,

13*

how wrong all this is! Do not say another word! How can you make me—make me——" She covers her face again, and cries aloud.

"Forgive me!" he says. He is by her side in an instant, stricken with remorse. "You are right. I will say no more; I should not have spoken at all. But your happiness is so near to me—so dear! I would give my life to secure it. And after to-morrow we may meet no more. The thought of that has been maddening me all these weeks; the thought that so soon—so soon you will be that man's wife, and gone out of my life forever! Fate deals hardly by some of us, Snowball." There is silence for a little. He stands by her chair. Has the weeping ceased? The drooping face is hidden still; the loose bright hair veils it, and falls across his arms, as he leans lightly on her chair-back. "Snowball," he says, "little friend, tell me this. I will ask no more, and it will be something—everything—in all the years without you that are to come. If I had been sooner that day on the hill-side—that fatal first day——"

He breaks off; he can see the quiver that goes through the bowed figure as he speaks, but man-like, he will not spare her. "Tell me," he pleads, "one word only, it is so little—so little, *Mon Dieu*, and I lose so much——"

But the word does not come. There is a movement instead, a small cold hand slips into his, the slender, chilly fingers clasp his close. He is answered.

"Miss Dolores, my maid," murmurs a sleepy voice, "is it nearly over? I've been dozin, a bit, I'm afeard, in the stillness like and the heat. There's them evening bells; it must be time to be going."

So Mrs. Tinker brings them back to the world, and out of their dangerous dream. *Ave Maria* is ringing from campanile and belfry, up against the purple Roman sky, and it is time to go home to grandmamma and dinner, and Sir Vane. It is very warm still, the air quivers with a sort of white after-glow, but the girl shivers as she rises. It is going straight out of paradise to—well, to a gray, grim, old-fashioned house, and gray, grim, old-fashioned people. But duty calls, and there is a silent hand-clasp, and she goes. The carriage is waiting outside the wide stone court, and they enter and are driven away. Long after they have gone, long after the workmen depart, long after Ave Maria ceases ringing, long after golden clusters come out, and burn in the purple, Rene Macdonald stands there, with folded arms, and stares out at the gemmed, flower-scented twilight with blank eyes that see nothing of the beauty, with blank mind that holds but one thought—a thought that keeps iterating itself over and over again with the dull persistence of such things, putting itself into words of its own volition, and ding-dinging through his brain. "One hour too late! One hour too late!"

CHAPTER XXVI.

"FIRE THAT IS CLOSEST KEPT, BURNS MOST OF ALL."

ADAME'S treasure, "At the Shrine," comes home duly, and Miss Valentine goes no more to the studio. Whether la contessa has dropped a hint, whether madame herself suddenly awakens to a sense of latent danger, whether Sir Vane has sneered audibly in spite of himself, who knows? Miss Valentine goes no more to the studio, and by grand-mamma's express desire. She looks rather keenly at the young lady, and madame's looks at all times are exceedingly keen, piercing, sidelong—none may hope to escape them—as she speaks, but she sees little. The girl

is very pale, she looks a trifle fagged and weary, and out of sorts, but it is oppressive spring weather, and what is to be expected in these sultry weeks? She says nothing —nothing at all, except in a spiritless voice, strangely unlike the clear, ringing, joyous tones of Dolores. "Very well, grandmamma," and so turns and walks slowly and listlessly up to her room.

Grandmamma decides she is not in love with the dark and picturesque M. Rene, the fortuneless sculptor with the Vandyke face, and grave brown eyes, but all the same the child needs change, needs it badly, and must have it at once. So they prepare to go.

On the day but one before their departure for fresher fields, and breezes new and cool, a surprise comes to good Mrs. Tinker. She accompanies the family of course. Madame goes nowhere without her, and she is busy in the midst of much packing, when she is summoned to her own particular sitting-room, to see a visitor. Going in haste, and rather breathless, she finds awaiting her a young woman, whose face and dress proclaim her nationality before she speaks a word. That first word puts it beyond doubt. "I guess you've forgot me likely, Mis' Tinker," says this young woman, in a nervous tone, rising as she speaks. "It's a pretty considerable spell sence we met afore—nigh onto fifteen years, I reckon."

"Why, lord bless me!" exclaims Mrs. Tinker, adjusting her spectacles in direst amazement. "I do declare if it isn't Jemima Ann!"

"Yes, Mis' Tinker; I'm awful glad you ain't forgot me. I'm over here with a family; Bosting folks they be, and now, the lady, she up and died. She was sort o' peaky and pinin' like all the passage. An so I'm out o' place, and hearing you was here, Mis' Tinker, I thought, for old time's sake, and poor Aunt Samanthy——" Here Jemima Ann puts her handkerchief to her eyes, and Mrs. Tinker sighs responsively. Aunt Samantha has gone

the way all landladies, even the best, must go some time
—the way of all flesh.

At this moment the door opens suddenly, and a young
lady—an apparition, it seems to Jemima Ann—in gray
silk and amber ringlets, comes in, and pauses at sight of
the stranger. "Oh, come in, my 'dearie!" says Mrs.
Tinker. "I was just going to you to ask your advice.
You've often heard me speak of Jemima Ann, who was
so good to you when you stopped for a week at her aunt's,
and who waited on"—lowering her voice—"your poor
ma? Well, this is Jemima Ann, Miss Dolores, my lovey,
and she is out of place, and——"

But the young lady waits for no more. Her fair face
flushes up, she crosses the room, and holds out both
hands. "And you are Jemima Ann! Oh! I have heard
all that—of your goodness and affection—all that you
did for me, for my poor mother, in the past. I was a
baby then, too young to know or thank you, or feel
grateful ; but I feel all now. I thank you with my
whole heart. If there is anything we can do for you—
anything—you may be sure it shall be done."

Jemima Ann gasps, stands, stares. "You!—you!—
why, Lor'! *You* never air little Snowball, grown up like
this!"

"Little Snowball—no one else—to whom you were
so very, very good. Not so little now though, you see.
And what are you doing in Rome, of all places, Jemima
Ann?"

Jemima Ann explains, with considerable confusion,
caused by the shock of finding little Snowball in this
graceful young lady. Aunt Samanthy died, the boarders
dispersed, Jemima Ann went down to Bosting (strong
nasal twang on the first syllable), took service there with
a lady out of health. Be'n livin' with that lady right
along sence. Lady ordered to Europe by doctors for
change of air. Took Jemima Ann with her as kind o'
nurse-tender. Up and died, here in Rome, a week ago,

after all her trouble crossin' over. And Jemima Ann finds herself a stranger in a strange land. By chance she had heard the Valentine family were here, and allowed Mis' Tinker might be still with them. On that chance has come, and—is here.

"And here you shall stay!" cries impetuous Miss Valentine. "Why should you think of going back all that way, and friends who owe you so much, here? Some day I will go back myself, if I can,"—a wistful, longing, homesick look comes into the blue eyes—"and I will take you. Meantime,"—gayly—"consider yourself my maid."

"And that is little Snowball!—little Snowball! So peart, and chipper, and sassy, and cunnin'-like, as she used to be! Little Snowball growed up into such a beautiful and elegant young lady as that!" says Jemima Ann, still dazed. She accepts the offer, of course, "right glad to get it," as she says, and is especially detailed off into Miss Valentine's particular service.

Sir Vane puts up his glass, and stares at her, the first time they chance to meet, as though she were a monster of the antediluvian world come to light here in this Roman household. Certainly she is as unlike as possible their Italian servants. He has forgotten, of course, the slipshod handmaid of the Clangville boarding-house, but Miss Hopkins has not forgotten him.

"Oh! you may stare," she remarks, mentally; "you ain't so much to look at yourself, when all's said and done. You never were a beauty the best o' times, and fifteen years standing to sour ain't improved you much. I'm awful sorry to hear my Miss Snowball is going to throw herself away on you. Don't know what she sees in you, I'm sure. *I* wouldn't hev you if you was hung with diamonds—though you mayn't think so."

Madame lifts her eyebrows over this latest whim of Dolores, but laughs and makes no objection. She will be an unique maid certainly, but if it is the child's fancy

—and a servant more or less in an establishment like this matters little. She is an American, friendless in a foreign land; it is like the dear girl's gentle, generous heart to compassionate and care for all such. But if madame *knew*—knew that this stolid, homely, rather clumsy Yankee woman had closed the dying eyes of Mlle. Mimi Trillon, had ministered to her for days before, knew the whole well-hidden secret of the trapezist's life and death—be very sure the massive *portone* of the old Roman house would never have seen her pass in, and many leagues of blue water intervened between her and the fair, stately daughter of the house. But grandmammas are not to know everything; the long, long conferences of the past are held with closed doors, in the dim, fragrant dusk of mademoiselle's boudoir. Lying back, her slim figure draped in those pale lustrous silks and fine laces madame loves to deck her darling in, her fingers laced behind her golden head, Miss Valentine nestles in the blue satin depths of her low chair, and listens by the hour to Jemima Ann Hopkins telling of that time so long ago, when little Snowball Trillon came suddenly into her life to brighten its dull drab, and of the beauty and brightness, and tragic death of the young mother. Of the belated suppers, of the many lovers, of the hilarious state in which poor Mimi sometimes came home, she discreetly says nothing. Jemima Ann has a delicacy and tact of her own, under her ginger-colored complexion and down-East drawl.

"At the Shrine" comes home, and is placed in madame's most private and particular sitting-room, with a pink silk curtain so draped as to throw a perpetual rosy glow over it, and friends come and gaze, and admire, and other orders flow in upon the talented young artist. Only the young lady herself says nothing—she stands and looks at it, with loosely clasped hands, and a misty far-away look that madame has an especial objection to in her great star-like eyes.

"Well, Dolores," she says, sharply, "are you asleep —in a dream—that you stand there, and say nothing? Do you not admire this exquisite gem?"

"It is very pretty, grandmamma."

"Very pretty, grandmamma!" mimicking the listless tone, "and that is all you find to say. I must tell this to my clever Mr. Rene, that you are the only one who has not seen his statue and not been charmed. I say he has caught your very expression—it is the most perfect thing of its kind I ever saw. It will be a great—the greatest comfort to me, when I—when you are gone."

"Dearest grandmamma!" The girl comes and puts her arms about her, as she sits, and the fair head droops in her lap. "You are too good to me. You love me too much. No one will ever care for me again like that. It is not well to be spoiled. Grandmamma, I wish I were not going away."

"Nonsense, my dear. An old grandmother, however fond, cannot expect to keep her little one to herself always. And what do you mean by no one loving you again? Sir Vane——"

"Ah!" says Dolores, and something in the sound of the little word makes madame pause a moment.

"You doubt it? You need not, my dear. He is fond of you—very fond of you, believe me. He is reticent— reserved by nature—it is not his way to show it, and he is older than you—it is the one thing *I* object to in this union, but, for all that, my dearest, I am confident he loves you with all his heart."

"Ah!" repeats Miss Valentine, and laughs, "has he told you so, grandmamma? It is more than he has ventured to tell me. With the best inclinations in the world to be credulous in such a point, I fear the effort would be too great. But what does it matter after all," a sigh here, that is half a sob, "it will be all the same fifty years hence."

"My darling, that is a dreary philosophy from youth.

ful lips. Why are you so sad—so listless, of late, so weary of all that used to set you wild with delight? Is it that you are out of health—that this heat——"

"Oh, yes, grandmamma!" rather eagerly; "that is it—this heat. Any one would wilt, with the thermometer up among the nineties. And the spring is so long, so long. I grow tired of this perpetual staring sunshine, and the smell of the roses and orange trees. I would give a year of my life for one day of poor old Isle Perdrix, and its sea fogs, and bleak whistling winds." And then, to madame's infinite dismay and distress, all in a moment, the fair head is buried low, and the slender form is rent and shaken with a very tempest of sobs.

"My child! my child!" is all madame can say in her deep consternation. "Oh! my little one, *what* is this?"

But with a great effort, the summer tempest ends as quickly as it began; a few hysteric sobs hurriedly suppressed, and then a great calm. "Forgive me, grandmamma—dear, dearest, best grandmamma that ever was in the world—forgive me for this! I did not mean— only I am so tired, so tired out with it all. If I were away, I would be better. Take me away from Rome, grandmamma."

"*Is* there anything in it?" thinks madame, in dire dismay, a little later, and alone. "*Did* she go too much to that studio? He is very handsome, and she knew him always. How foolish, how extremely foolish and rash, I have been!"

But it is not too late yet—at least madame thinks so; one may always hope so much for young persons under twenty, and time and distance are such capital cures. They depart at once, with their maid-servants and their man-servants, and the house in Rome is shut up for the present. Madame proposes, drearily enough, to occupy it with her faithful Tinker this winter alone.

M. Rene Macdonald, among his clay casts, and plaster

figures, and brown, dark-eyed Roman models of saints
and brigands, works away alone these sultry May days.
He does not mind the heat, he likes it ; he is absorbed
in his work, feverishly so, indeed. He grows thin in
these long, lonely, hard-working hours ; his brown eyes
—"eyes like golden Genoa velvet," la contessa has once
said—take a deeper, darker orbit ; his olive cheek grows
hollow. So la contessa, who flits in and out at times,
like the bird of Paradise she is, tells him gayly. But he
grows no less handsome, she thinks—pining, pouf ! for
la bambinella. Pretty ? Yes ; la contessa could make a
prettier face in pink and white wax, any day ! And it is
for her this Signore Rene, who looks like one of his own
gods, and carries himself like a king ; who has the face
of a Raphael, and the genius too—grows thin, and silent,
and stern, and shuts himself up like a hermit in his cell.
La contessa does *il Signore Scultore* the honor to be deeply
interested in his case, introduces him to half his patrons,
lavishes invitations upon him, and meets with the usual
reward of goodness in this world—indifference, ingrati-
tude. M. Rene wishes, irritably enough sometimes, this
flirting little painted butterfly would spread her gorgeous
wings, and fly off to other victims and leave him alone.
But la contessa thinks otherwise—she can plant her sting
like a wasp, butterfly though she be. If this artist—
marble like his own creation—will not fall down and
admire, she will at least awake within him some other
feeling. He must be human at least in some things—
human enough to feel pain. All she can inflict he shall
have as his punishment. She flutters in to tell him in
her vivacious way when the Valentines leave Rome ; she
flutters in to tell him one sparkling October day, just five
months later, of a fashionable marriage at Nice.

He has spent these months in the solitude of his
workshop, and sculpture, at its best, is not a sociable art.
He has been working hard, commissions have been plentiful enough, and a fair guerdon of both fame and gold

has been won. He might have won friends, too, friends well worth the winning, had he so chosen　But he is unsocial in these days ; even among his brothers of the chisel he cares to cultivate few friendships. But he is in fairly good spirits on this particular day, for the early post has brought him a letter from a friend, long living in Russia, but now en route for Rome.

Paul Farrar is on his way to Italy, and it is to Pau͞l Farrar Rene owes everything, the recognition and culti-vation of his talent—his studio in Rome, his first success. In a couple of weeks at most Paul Farrar will be here.

So Rene is whistling cheerily as he chips, and for once the haunting ghost that seldom leaves him is laid— a ghost in " sheen of satin and shimmer of pearls" with bright hair and blue-bell eyes. Then, like a scented, silk-draped apparition, the Contessa Paladino is before him.

She is not alone—a Neapolitan marchese and a Brit-ish attache form her body-guard. She has been absent from Rome nearly all summer, and is full of sparkling chatter and silvery small talk as usual.

" And the wedding is over—milordo's—but you have heard *that*, of course, signore mio ?" she says, gayly, apropos of nothing that has gone before.

" I hear nothing, madame. News from the great world never pierces the walls of my workshop, except what you are good enough to tell me."

The little touch of sarcasm in the last words are not lost on la contessa. Neither is the quick contraction of eyebrows and lips, and a perceptible paling of the dark face. " Che ! Che ! then it is for me to give you the good news. But I surely thought—such friends as you seemed —that she would have done it herself. And it is all quite two weeks old, and you have not heard. She has her victim, as naturalists impale beetles, on a pin, and watches with dancing, malicious eyes the effect of her words.. But he works on, and gives no sign.

'La Signorina looked lovely, exquisite—every one said so; and *Dio mia!* how she was dressed! It was the wedding-robe and jewelry of a princess. The bridemaids—eight of them—were all English; four in pink, and four in blue. *Milordo* was solemn, and stiff, and black as usual—blacker than usual, I think. They are to travel until spring, and then return to their native fogs. Bonne-mamma comes here, you know. Of your charity, go to see and console her, Signore Rene; the poor grandmamma! She is *desole sconsolato.*"

He says something; it is brief, and sounds indifferent, and still works on.

"I saw Sir Vane and Lady Valentine," says the Englishman, who is examining the figure called "Waiting" through his glass. "She is very beautiful, quite the most beautiful person I have—" he checks himself just in time, for la contessa's eyes are already looking daggers—"this face resembles her, I think. Is it a portrait?"

And Rene works on, only conscious of one thing—an unuttered wish that they would go. But they do not. They linger, and look, and admire, and criticise, until he feels as if the sound of their voices were driving him mad. La contessa remains until she is absolutely forced to depart, and goes with a petulant sense of disappointment under her gay "Addio, signore." She really cannot tell whether this exasperating young sculptor, as cold, as hard, as any of his own blocks of marble, cares or not.

Cold, hard! If she could only but have seen him, when, the atelier doors closed, locked, he stands there alone with his love, his loss, his despair! Married, and to Sir Vane Valentine! Ah! la contessa, even your outraged vanity, from feminine spite—the hardest thing under heaven to satisfy—might have had its fill and to spare, could you have looked through those locked doors and seen.

CHAPTER XXVII.

"FORTUNE BRINGS IN SOME BOATS THAT ARE NOT
STEERED."

T is the afternoon of a raw and rainy October
day. An express is thundering rapidly Rome-
ward in even more of a hurry than usual, for
it is trying to make up half an hour of lost
time. In a compartment there sits by himself a man,
bearing upon him, from head to foot, the stamp of steady
travel. He is big, he is brown, he has dark resolute eyes
—eyes at once gentle and strong, kindly and keen. The
mouth suits the eyes; it is square-cut, determined-look-
ing, with just that upward curve at the corners that tells
you it would not be necessary to explain the point of a
joke to him. His hair is profuse and dark, sprinkled a
little with gray, though he looks no more than forty, and
is inclined to be kinky and curl. His square, broad
shoulders and erect mien give him a little the look of a
military man. But he is not; he is only a successful
speculator, coming to Rome after a prolonged sojourn
in Russia and the East. A few days ago he landed at
Marseilles, now he is speeding along at a thundering
rate toward the Holy City, and a certain greatly esteemed
young friend he expects to find there.

"Rene won't know me with all the beard off," he
thinks, stroking from custom the place where a heavy
mustache used to be. "It was a pity, but it had to go.
It was so confoundedly hot there in Cairo I would have
taken off my flesh as well, if I could, and sat in my
bones. Let us hope no one who ever knew me in the
old days will be loafing about Rome. If so, I shall be
found out to a dead certainty."

For it is Paul Farrar, minus that silky black-brown

beard and drooping mustache that became him so well.
The change alters him wonderfully. It is the George
Valentine of two-and-twenty years ago ; somewhat bigger, somewhat browner, much more manly and distinguished-looking, but otherwise so much the same bright,
boyish-looking George that any one who had ever known
him in those old days—before he was drowned in the
Belle O'Brien—must have recognized him now, despite
that melancholy fact, almost at a glance. "If I were
going to the New World now," he thinks, half smiling,
as they fly along, "instead of the very oldest city of the
old world, it would never do. I don't covet recognition
at this late day. No good could come of it. I am un-
forgiven still, and everything is disposed of, as it should
be, to the little one. Pity she married Sir Vane—never
will be half good enough for her, let him try as he may.
But I don't think he will try. Rene would have suited
her—pity, again, they could not have hit it off. Not
that madame would ever have consented—her hopes and
ambitions are the same to-day as they were when her
only son disappointed her, like the headstrong young
fool he was. Ah, well, these things are written in Allah's
big book—it is all Kismet together. Whom among us is
stronger than his fate ?"

The train stops at a station and Mr. Farrar gets out
to light a cigar and stretch his legs. A drizzling rain is
falling, a chilly wind is blowing, he pulls down his felt
hat, pulls up his coat collar, and strides up and down the
platform during the few minutes of their stay. Doing
so he glances carelessly into the carriages as he passes.
One, a first-class compartment, holds two elderly women,
a lady, evidently, and her maid. The lady, a grand-
looking personage, of serene mien, and silvery hair and
face, rests against the cushions with eyes half closed.
The servant sits near the window and gazes out. At
sight of these two Mr. Farrar receives such a shock that
for a moment he stands stock-still, a petrified gazer,

His face pales startlingly under his brown skin, he looks as though he could not believe his own sense of sight. The woman looks at him, sits up, looks again, with a low, frightened ejaculation, and glances at the mistress. A second later, she looks out again—in that second he is gone

"What is it, Tinker?" asks, wearily, Madam Valentine.

"Oh, madame! my dear mistress, I saw a man, only a glimpse of him, but it made me think of—of——"

"Well?" pettishly.

"Master George. It was that like him. Dear heart! what a start it did give me, to be sure."

"Nonsense," madame says, sharply. "How can you be such an old idiot, Tinker. You should have more regard for my feelings than to speak that name in that abrupt way. Does it still rain?" wearily. "Tinker, I wonder where my dear child is by this time?"

"In better weather than this, poor lamb, wherever it is," responds Mrs. Tinker, with a shiver. "Lawk! my lady, I feel chill to the bone. I do hope now Anselmer will see to the fires all through the house. It would be the very wust thing that ever wus, for you to go into damp rooms after such a journey as this."

"Do you think she looked happy, Tinker, when we left?" pursues madame, unheeding the weather, absorbed in thought of her resigned treasure. "She cried, of course, at the parting, but do you think she looked happy, and as a young bride should? I grow afraid sometimes—afraid——"

"Well, ma'am, to speak plain truth, Sir Vane ain't neither that young, nor that pleasant as he might be. I always thought him a molloncholy and sad gentleman, myself. But tastes differ. *Maybe* Miss Dolores is happy." Mrs. Tinker's face, as she says it, is dismal beyond expression. "I'm sure I hope and pray so, poor sweet young lamb—no more fit to be used bad than a baby.

But——" She breaks off as her mistress has done—un-finished sentences best express their fears. Both are filled with foreboding and vague regret, now that the deed is done beyond all recall. Her darling is not happy—she sees that at last. And the fault is hers—she who would give the remnant of her old life to make her so. She has, indirectly at least, forced her into a love-less marriage, with a man double her age, a man ill-tem-pered and mercenary, a man no more capable of valuing the sweetness, beauty, youth, he has won, than he is of doing a great, a generous, an unselfish deed. Her child wished to remain with her, and she forced her from her —thrust her into the arms of Vane Valentine. And now that remorse, and sorrow, and fear, come upon her, it is too late—for all time, too late !

The train rushes along on its iron way ; evening is closing, foggy, and windy, and wet. She dozes a little as she lies wearily among the stuffy cushions, but she is too filled with unrest to sleep. It is three weeks now since the wedding-day, and she and her faithful old friend are journeying back to Rome, there to spend the winter. Next spring the newly-wedded pair are to go to Valentine ; in the summer she is to join them for a pro-longed visit. That is the programme, if all is well. But all will be well, be happy. The look of pale, shrinking *fear* of him, with which her darling clung to her, just at the parting, haunts her—will haunt her night and day, until they meet again. Is she afraid of Vane Valentine?

"Oh ! my dearest, my sweetest !" the poor old lips murmur in the darkness, "if I had you back—all my own once more—no man should take you from me, unless you went with a glad and willing heart." And then there rises before her a man's face—a dark, delicate head, a grave smile, deep, serious brown eyes, a slender, strong young figure, a broad, thoughtful brow, altogether a face unlike Sir Vane's, a fitting mate, even in beauty, for the golden-haired heiress.

"She loved him," madame thinks, with a pang ; "and he is worthy of her. If I had given her to him, she would have been happy. And I might have had her near me always—always! What will life be like without her? Poor? Yes, he is poor ; but he has talent ; he will win his way ; and as she said to me with her pretty, baby wisdom—is money everything? My little love! why did I give you to Vane Valentine? But he will not dare to be unkind to her. No ; the fortune is hers ; there is too much at stake."

But this is sorry comfort, and her heart is very heavy, as they speed along through the wet, wild night, and the windy darkness, toward the many towers, and palaces, and bells of Rome. Suddenly—what is it? There is a swaying of the carriages, a dull, tremulous vibration, the sound of many voices, of women's screams, a shock that is like earth and heaven striking together, and then —nothingness.

. . . .

"Clear the way ! let me through!" cries out an impetuous voice, and a man strides between the affrighted throng, suddenly huddled here on the wide Campagna.

Overhead there is the black, wind-swept sky ; beneath there is the sodden, rain-swept grass, the wrecked train, women and children, terrified, hurt, talking, sobbing, screaming—confusion dire everywhere. Those who are safely out are trying to extricate those who are still prisoners, foremost among them this tall, sunburned man, who forces his way to one particular wrecked carriage, and wrenches open the door.

" Mother !" he cries ; " Mrs. Tinker ! Are you here ? For God's sake, speak !"

There are groans ; they are there, but past speaking. Mrs. Tinker is not past hearing, however. Through all the shock of pain and fright, she hears and trembles at that call. Help comes, they are brought out, both hurt, Madam Valentine quite insensible. Mrs. Tinker looks

14

up through the mists of what she thinks death, and tries to see the face on which the lamp-light shines, the face that is bending over her mistress.

"Bid him come," she says, faintly; "bid him speak to me again before I die! It was the voice of my own Master George!"

He is with her in a moment, holding her in his arms, bending down with the handsome, tender face she knows so well. "My dear old friend!" is what he says.

"Master George! Master George! my own Master George! Has the great day come, then, and the sea given up its dead, that I see and hear you this night?"

"Dear old nurse—no. I never was drowned, you know. It has been a mistake all these years—it is George Valentine in the flesh. Do not talk now—lie still—we will take care of you. I must go back to my mother."

"My dear mistress! is she much hurt?"

"Very much, I fear; she is senseless. Take this stimulant, and keep quiet. You are not going to die—do not think it."

But Mrs. Tinker only groans and shuts her eyes. She is bruised, and broken, and crushed, and hurt, but no bones are broken, and her injuries are not serious. She is so stunned and bewildered with fright and pain, that she can hardly wonder or rejoice to find her Master George after all these years alive.

The accident, after investigation, turns out to be comparatively slight. A few persons are hurt more or less, all are badly scared. Madam Valentine appears to be the only one seriously injured. That she *is* seriously injured there can be no question. She lies, while they travel slowly into Rome, in her son's arms, without signs of life. They reach the great city, and she is driven slowly through the streets to the Casa Valentine, but all the while she lies like one dead. Mrs. Tinker so far recovered already as to be able to sit up, chafes her hands, and cries and moans dully to herself, and alter-

nately watches Master George. "Grown such a fine
figure of a man, God bless him!" she thinks admiringly.

Anselmo, the major-domo, awaits them; the rooms
are warm, beds are aired, all is in order. Madame is
undressed and put to bed, the best medical skill in Rome
is summoned, and when the sun is two or three hours
high, she opens her eyes and moans feebly, and struggles
back painfully out of that dim land of torpor, where she
has lain so long. Struggles back to life, and pain, and
weariness, and a sense of stifling oppression that will not
let her breathe. Madame's life is drawing to its close—
"it is toward evening, and the day is now far spent."
She will never look upon her darling's face in this world
again. Mrs. Tinker sits by her side—it is on that tear-
wet face her eyes first fall. A glint of sunshine steals in
between the closed jalousies—it turns the rose silk curtains to flame, and bathes in a ruby glow the marble face
of the figure, "At the Shrine." Her eyes leave Mrs.
Tinker, and rest on that.

"My darling!" she whispers, "never again—never in
this world again." For she knows the truth. She is
quite calm, and a sort of smile dawns on her lips, as she
looks at the weeping servant by her side.

"My good old friend," she says, "you will see the
last of me, after all. I used to wonder sometimes, Tinker,
which of us would go first."

"My dear mistress, my dear mistress!" the old servant sobs.

"A hard mistress, I am afraid, sometimes—an imperious mistress." She sighs, glances at the statue, looks
back wistfully. "I should like to see that young man
before I die," she says, "I liked him."

"Mr. Raynay, ma'am? The young gentleman that
made that?"

"Yes; send for him, Tinker, will you? Tell me"—a
painful effort—"how long—how long do these doctors

give me? I see them in consultaticn in the room beyond."

"Oh! my dear mistress," crying wildly, "not long, not long—till to-morrow, they say," sobs choke Mrs. Tinker, "till to-morrow, maybe."

A spasm crosses the strong old face. She shuts her eyes, and lies still. Then she opens them again with the same earnest, wistful gaze. "Tinker, it is strange, but just at that time, when the crash and the darkness came, I seemed to hear a voice, and it called me—it said *mother!* It was the voice of my son, Tinker—my dear dead son."

Mrs. Tinker is on her knees by the bedside, with clasped hands and streaming eyes. "Not dead, mistress! Oh, praise and thanks be. Not dead—not dead! Living all this time, and with us now. It was his voice you heard call—his own dear living voice. Mistress! mistress!" with a scream of affright, "are you dying? Have I killed you?"

She has fallen back among the pillows, so white, so death-like, that Mrs. Tinker starts from her knees with that ringing shriek. The doctors fly to the bedside. It is not death, but a death-like swoon.

"I told her, Master George, I told her, and the shock killed her a'most. Oh! do'ee go away, before she comes to again. The sight of you will kill her outright for sure."

"But George does not go. His mother's eyes open at the moment, and rest on his face—rest in long, solemn, silent wonder. "Mother," he says, gently, "dearest mother, it is I—George. Do you not know me? Mother!"

"My son." She lifts one faint hand by a great effort, and lays it in his hand. She lies and looks at him with wide, dilating eyes, that have in them as yet only solemn, fearful wonder—no joy.

"Dear mother," he kisses the other hand lying on the quilt, "are you not a little glad. I love you, mother,

I have wanted to come back all these years, but I was afraid—I was afraid I was not forgiven. Dearest mother, say you forgive me now !"

"His eyes, his voice, his words. It *is* my George—my George—my George !"

"You are glad then, mother? You will say it, will you not? If you only knew how I have longed all these years for the words 'I forgive you.' Let me hear you say them now."

"Forgive you !" she repeats. "Oh ! my God, it is I who must be forgiven. I have been the hardest mother the world ever saw. Forgive you ! My best beloved, I forgave you long ago. I forgive with all my heart. Oh ! to think of it, to think of it ! a wanderer and an exile all these years, and all the while, my own son, my heart has been breaking for the sight of your face. If it is death that has restored you to me, then death is better than life. My son ! my son ! kiss me, and say *you* forgive *me !*" He does as she bids him, and his tears fall on her face. "I can die now," she says; "tell them all to go, while we bless God. 'For this my son was dead and is alive again, was lost and is found.'"

It is noontide of another day. They are again together, there in that darkened room. The rose light floods the pure, passionless, marble face of Dolores. The dying woman so lies, propped up with pillows, that she may see it to the end. For even the son who sits by her side cannot drive out of her heart her other darling.

"And then it is only loving you in another way, for she is yours," she says. "I love her for your sake as well as for her own, my George."

He says nothing. His brows contract a little—there is something he would like to say, but the end draws very near now, she is fitted for no new shocks. And she loves the child. No, he will not speak.

"That reminds me," she says, faintly, "*you* are the baronet, not Vane. I did not think of that before."

"Do not think of it now. What does it matter. Let it go."

"It does matter. It shall not go. Right is right," some of her old imperious command flashes in her dim eyes, rings in her feeble voice. "You are the baronet, not he. You must claim your right, George. Promise me you will when I am gone."

"Mother, is it worth while——"

"It *is* worth while—a thousand times worth while. Right is right, I say. He is a just man with all his faults; he will acknowledge your superior right. He has no shadow of claim on the title while you live. And the fortune is yours too—your daughter will resign it. It must be so, George—promise me."

"Mother——"

"Promise me, if I am to die content. Through my fault, through my cruelty, you have lost both title and fortune. Let me do what I can to repair it. Before those doctors in the next room, before my lawyer, my servants, I have already acknowledged you; promise me you will make the world acknowledge you, that you will resume your rightful name and rank, your place in the world. Promise me before I die. You cannot refuse the last request of a dying mother."

No—he cannot, but he looks infinitely disturbed as he reluctantly gives the pledge. "I promise—to let Dolores know," is what he slowly says.

"You hear this?" she asks, appealing in terrible earnestness to the two silent witnesses of the scene—Mrs. Tinker, kneeling beside her, Rene Macdonald, standing at the foot of the bed. "You are listening, Monsieur Rene? You will witness for me that he keeps his pledge? He must assert his rights. Dolores is your friend—I commission *you* to tell her this. She will do what is right I know—it is a heart of gold. And it is her own father. How glad the child will be. You will love her very much, George, and care for her? Do not let her husband be unkind to her. He is a just man—Vane—but hard, and a little grim. When I am gone, Monsieur Rene, go to England, and tell the little one. She will gladly give up a fortune and a title for her father's sake."

"My dear mother, you do wrong to agitate yourself in this way. Do not talk. Rene is going now. Will you say good-by to him, and try to sleep?"

"To sleep, to sleep," she murmurs, heavily. "I shall sleep soundly soon, my son—soon, soon. I am sorry to leave you. Do not go away, stay here with me until the end."

"I am not going, mother—it is Rene."

"Addio, signore," she says, with a wan smile, "I like you, I always liked you. And you will tell my little one when I am gone. She liked you, too—she liked you best. I know it now. Do not tell Sir Vane; he would not like it. Yes, she liked you best."

"Her mind is wandering," her son says, hurriedly, but he glances questionly at Rene as he says it. In the dim gray-green light of the death-room, he sees the profound pallor of the dark face. So, poor Rene!

They watch by the bedside during the long, slow hours of the afternoon. She rambles sometimes, and murmurs broken sentences—generally, though, her mind is quite calm. George sits by her side, holding her hand, administering stimulants and medicines, watching every breath. And so death finds her when it comes, quite peacefully and painlessly, her last smile, her last look, her last word for him. When *Ave Maria* rings out in the pearly haze of twilight, Katherine Valentine lies dead.

CHAPTER XXVIII.

"IN HIS DREAMS HE SHALL SEE THEE AND ACHE."

HE studio, the late afternoon lights filling gayly its high chill length. The sculptor stands busy, his fingers deep in molding wet clay, two swinging bronze lamps sparkling like fire-flies in the half light. The autumn day has been damp and dark, the sky out there, seen between the wet vines, is the color of drab paper, a fog that London could not surpass shrouds the Eternal City. Looking rather moodily out at it, sits George Valentine, ensconced in a great carved and gilded chair, and encircling himself with a second fog of his own making— the smoke of his cigar. Both are silent, the younger absorbed in his clay cast, the elder in his thoughts. A week has passed since the funeral. Presently George Valentine leaves off staring at the yellow fog, and turns his attention to the artist, still busily absorbed in modeling his wet clay, and stares at him.

"What an odd fellow you are, Rene !" is what he says.

Rene looks up. It strikes Mr. Valentine, as it has not struck him hitherto, that his young friend is altogether too worn and hollow-eyed for the number of his years, and that he has grown more taciturn than he ever used to be. "What is it you say?" Rene asks.

"I say you are a queer fellow. Why, look here. For the past sixteen years or more you have known me as Paul Farrar. All in a moment, as it must seem to you, I start up, like the hero of a melodrama, not myself at all, but somebody else ; not Paul Farrar, but the long-lost son of a lady you very well know—a Tichborne Claimant No. 2. You are summoned suddenly to a death-bed ; you meet me there, under another name and

identity, and you accept the metamorphosis without
question or comment. Over two weeks have gone since
then, we have met daily, still not a word. It may be
delicacy of feeling, it may be indifference, it may be
good breeding—I don't know what name you give it, but
it is queer, to say the least."

"It is good breeding," says Rene, laughing. "I have
always been taught that it is impolite to ask questions.
Besides, *mon ami*, how could I intrude on your secrets—
painful recollections, perhaps? You knew me; when
you saw fit, you would tell me. Meantime——"

"Meantime, absorbed in secrets of your own, you
don't burn with curiosity to hear those of other men.
You look hipped, my lad, as if fate had given you a
facer of late. You work too hard, and you don't eat
enough. I've watched you. No wonder you grow as
thin as a shadow. No touch of Roman fever, I trust,
my boy?"

"Well—who knows? There are so many kinds of
Roman fever. Yes," Rene says, half jestingly, half seriously; "I suppose I may call it that. I certainly caught
it here in Rome. Never mind me," impatiently; "I will
do well enough. I am a tough fellow, lean though I be.
I'll pull through all right. Tell me of yourself, *tres cher.*
You give me credit for less interest in you than I possess, if you do not see I am full of curiosity—though
that is not the word either—to hear your story. It should
be a romantic one. As to being surprised—I don't
know. You always seemed a man a little out of the
ordinary to me—a man with a history. No; I was not
much surprised to find you were somebody besides my
father's friend, M. Paul Farrar."

George Valentine has gone back to his scrutiny of
the weather; he watches it through the blurred panes
with dreamy, retrospective eyes. There is silence; he
smokes, Rene plunges his fingers into the soft clay,
and an angel's face breaks through. The elder man's

14*

thoughts are drifting backward to that other life, that seems now like a life lived in a dream.

"What a little forever it is to look back upon!" he says, "and yet like yesterday, too. That old time at Toronto, when I led the luxurious, idle life of a youthful prince, as spoiled, as flattered, as headstrong, as self-indulgent as any prince—how it comes back as I sit here, and I am no longer the George Valentine of forty years—battered, world-worn, gray—but the lad George, who rode and danced, and dreamed, and thought life a perpetual boy's holiday, and who fell in love at nineteen with a trapeziste, and ran away with her and married her."

Half to himself, in the tone of one who muses aloud, half to Rene, who listens and works in sympathetic silence, he tells the story—the story of the one brief love idyl of his life. "I came back to my senses more quickly than I lost them," he says, "as I suppose most people do who make unequal marriages. I had simply made utter wreck and ruin of my life. She is dead, poor soul, this many a day—she was Snowball's mother. I will say nothing about her that I can leave unsaid. Only—when I left her, after ten months of marriage—you may believe me when I say I was justified in doing it. She was not in love with me. I found *that* out soon enough; she was not of the women who fall in love. She was so utterly wrapped up in herself, she had no room in her poor little starved heart for any other human creature. Perhaps she may have been fond of her child, but I doubt it."

"You left her after ten months," Rene repeats. Something in the statement seems to fit badly with some other fact in his mind. He regards his friend with a puzzled look.

"Just ten months, my young friend—we parted thus for our mutual benefit. I never saw her again until I saw her fall from the slack-rope in Badger's circus, one day some six years after."

"Six years after," again repeats Rene, the puzzled look deepening in his face. "And Snowball was but three years old then!"

"Precisely. It's a deuce of a business, Rene——"

"Well?"

"Snowball is not my daughter."

A stunned pause. And yet—Rene could not tell you why—the shock of astonishment is not so great as it ought to be. "I thought you would say that," he says, in a hushed tone. "And your mother—we all, she herself, her husband—have been deceived."

"It's a bad business, old fellow, I don't deny, and all owing to the false report of my death. By the merest accident—a slip on the ice, a sprained ankle—I did not sail in the fatal Belle O'Brien. Another man took my place—a poorer devil even than myself—so poor that to keep him from freezing to death that bitter winter weather I shared my scanty wardrobe with him. He, George Valentine, as his clothes led all to think, perished that stormy night, and the Paul Farrar who lived, and had a hard fight with fortune for many a year, was a castaway about whom no one was likely to be concerned. I did not know I was forgiven. I only knew another heir had been found for the great Valentine fortune. I did not know Mimi, my wife, had married again, in good faith enough, Tom Randal. I was engaged in a hand-to-hand fight for bread in those early days. When I did know, it was too late. I came to Clangville, honestly resolute to see my mother, and obtain her pardon. Time might have softened her, I thought, and condoned my offense. It was an extraordinary thing that Mimi, my wife —Tom Randal's widow, if you like—should be there at the same time. There she was, with little Snowball, and I soon discovered, from Vane Valentine, that he knew all about her (except the fact of her second marriage ; *that*

very few people ever knew) ; that she had visited my
mother, and threatened to make public her marriage with
me, unless bought off. Vane Valentine only knew me
as Paul Farrar, of course. I had met him at Fayal some
time before. A new thought struck me. Without pre-
senting myself in person I could judge of my mother's
feeling toward me by her conduct toward the child supposed to be mine. If, after Mimi's tragical fate, she
showed pity for the child, I would have come forward at
once, and revealed myself. I longed for her forgiveness,
Rene ; I longed to be back in the world of living men,
from which for years I had seemed to be thrust out ; I
longed to be once more my mother's son. One kindly,
womanly act toward the child—I would have asked no
more—I would have come forward, pleaded for pardon,
and striven in the future to repair the past. But that act
never came. The child—unseen, uncared for, as though
she were a dog or a pet bird of the dead woman's—was
banished, and given over to the hands of strangers. She
thought her her grandchild, and still banishered her unseen. Perhaps it was the doing of Vane Valentine—
Heaven knows ! It sufficed to kill my last hope forever.
The heart that could be so hard to the child was not
likely to soften to the father.

"I accepted the decision in silence and went my way,
taking the little one with me. Of course I fell in love
with the child at sight—every one did that. She was the
most bewitching baby in the world ; but you remember
her, no doubt. You know my life since then, the life
of a wanderer always. But for the accident that night
on which we met there never would have been either
reconciliation or forgiveness. I had made up my mind,
you see, after the episode of Snowball, that there was no
hope for me. But it has been decreed otherwise. My poor
mother ! hers was a lonely life. She wrapped herself in
silence and pride, and shut out the world. Can a mother
forget her child ? On her death-bed she told me I had

been forgiven always. It will comfort me when I am on mine to remember that."

Rene stands silent. After a pause George Valentine goes on : "Perhaps there, just at the last, I should have told my mother the truth. I think I would, but that I knew the explanation would be too great a shock for her to bear. And she loved the girl so dearly, as I do, as you, as we all do. Dear little Snowball ! what does it matter? If she were my daughter in reality I could never be fonder of her than I am."

"It matters a great deal," Rene answers, "and so Vane Valentine will think, and say, when he hears it. It robs him at a word of title and fortune. How do you think he will take that ?"

"He had better take it quietly, or it may be worse for him. If he is harsh to that child he shall rue it. And you, too, my friend—you have become involved in this family tangle. It will devolve upon you, I suppose, as you have already promised, to go and tell Snowball. I wish—I wish my mother had not insisted upon that. The *exposé*, if it must come, will be the deuce and all to stand."

"Right is right," says Rene.

"To be sure ; but if a man prefers the wrong ? Supposing he is the only one to suffer ? It is rather a nuisance, isn't it, to be forced into a court of appeal, whether or no ? Look here, Rene, Vane Valentine will not resign what he has waited for so long, gotten so hardly, without fighting it out to the bitter end. Do you know what that means for me ? It means taking the whole world into my confidence—telling it what a confounded ass I have been, all my life,—seeing my name, and *hers*, and my mother's in glaring capitals in every English and American newspaper I pick up. Do you know what it means for Snowball? The exposure of her birth, as the daughter of a lawless circus woman—an heiress under false pretenses—a wife whom Vane Valentine no more would

have married, knowing the truth than—— Good
Heaven ! Rene, don't you see the thing is impossible ?"

Rene stands silent. Right is right—yes, but to hold
fast to the right through all things, simply because it *is*
right, sometimes requires a courage superhuman.

"It will break her heart, it will brand her with
infamy, it will blight her life, it will compel her to face
an exposure, for which a crown and a kingdom would
not repay. No, no, Rene ; go over and tell her, if you
like, since the promise was extorted on a death-bed, but
there we will stop. Sir Vane shall be Sir Vane to the
end. It shall be no new Orton and Tichborne affair,
this, with the same ultimate ending, no doubt. It is a
thousand pities it must be told at all—it will make the
child miserable all her life. Rene, *need* it be told ?"

"Undoubtedly, since I have promised. Better be
miserable, knowing the truth, than happy in a fool's
paradise of ignorance."

"A fool's paradise ! Ah ! poor little Snowball ! I
doubt the paradise, even a fool's, with Vane Valentine.
If he is unkind to her—*then*, Rene, I will face all things,
and have it out with him. Let him look to it, if he is
harsh with her. Come what may, I shall not spare
him."

Still Rene is silent. He stands with folded arms
and knitted brows, staring moodily out at the pale flood
of moon-rays silvering the stone court. George Valentine has risen, too, and is pacing up and down.

"You will see for yourself," he says, "when you go
there. There need be no haste ; they do not return to
England, I believe, until spring. Go over then, and see,
and tell her. For myself, I shall remain in Rome this
winter. One look at her will tell you more than a score
of letters, whether or no she is happy. I seem to have a
sort of presentiment about it, that she is not—that she
never will be. I distrust that fellow—I always have.
He has the soul of a miser, grasping, sordid, cruel ; and

he was in love with another woman, a cousin. Snowball never cared for him, I feel sure. How could she ?—old, cold, self-centered, unfitted for her in every way. Dear little Snowball! so fresh, so bright, so joyous—how soon he will change all that ! It is a pity, a thousand pities, *mon ami*, that you——"

"For Heaven's sake, hush !" Rene Macdonald cries out, fiercely. "Do you think I am made of this ?" striking passionately the marble against which he stands— "that I can listen to you? Do you think there is ever an hour, sleeping or waking, in which she is absent from me ? I try to forget sometimes—I force myself to forget, lest in much thinking of what might have been but for this fortune and that man, I should go mad."

George Valentine lays his hand on his shoulder, and stands beside him—mute. Something of this he has suspected. How could it be otherwise ? But he speaks no word. The voice that breaks the silence is the voice of a girl singing, to a piano, in the apartment above. An English family have that second floor. The voice of the girl, singing an English song, comes to them though the open windows, through the slumbering sweetness of the night.

> " In the daytime thy voice shall go through him,
> In his dreams he shall see thee, and ache,
> Thou shalt kindle by night, and subdue him
> Asleep or awake."

"If you would rather not go," George Valentine says, at last, "it may be too hard for you——"

"I *will* go," Rene answers, between his teeth ; " I must see for myself. If he makes her happy—well, I shall try and be thankful, and see her no more. If he *is* what you think him—what I think him—let him look to it ! Say no more, *tres cher*, there are some hurts that simply will not bear handling ; this is one of them."

PART IV.

"Marriage is a desperate thing. The frogs in Æsop were extremely wise; they had a great mind to some water, but they would not leap into a well, because they could not get out again."

CHAPTER XXIX.

MY LADY VALENTINE.

 SPRING evening—April stars beginning to pierce through the blue one by one; a silvery haze over yonder above the firs, showing where the moon means to rise presently. An air like velvet, a soft southerly breeze stirring in the elms and chestnuts, and bending to kiss the sweet hidden violets and anemones as it flutters by. Down in a thorn-bush near the keeper's gate a nightingale is singing, and everything else that flies and twitters, holds its breath to hear. So, too, does the stout, unromantic-looking woman, who leans across the gate, watching and waiting and rather anxious, but charmed as well by the wonderful flow of bird-music.

Anxiety, however, soon gets the better of her again, and she peers down the long white strip of wood, bending her ear to catch the sound she listens for. But only the nightingale's song breaks the sylvan stillness of the sweet spring evening.

"Late again," she says to herself; "I guessed she

would be. And Miss Valentine she's such a one to nag if the poor dear is five minutes past the time. I wish the cross old cat was furder—I do."

She glances apprehensively over her shoulder as she says it, not quite sure that Miss Dorothy Valentine may not pounce upon her, as rapidly and soundlessly as the feline to which she has compared her. But she and Philomel seem to have it all to themselves. The lofty trees and broad acres of the park spread around her; down here it is a lonely spot where even Miss Valentine, who is omnipresent, never comes. Over yonder peep the gables of the house, Manor Valentine, sparkling all along its somber brick front, with many lights.

It is an ugly, old-fashioned mansion of Queen Anne's time—once red, of a dull, warmish-brown tint now, that contrasts very well with the green of the ivy that overruns most of it, and softens and tones down the gaunt grimness of its stiff and angular outlines. It has pointed gables, and great stacks of chimneys, and quaintly-timbered porches—in summer time, very bowers of wild-rose and honeysuckle. It has old-fashioned, prim Dutch gardens, kept at present with care, but left to run riot in the days of the late baronet, and all the old-fashioned, sweet-smelling flowers that ever bloomed, grow in beauty side by side. And here in the park are magnificent copper beeches, great green elms, branching oaks, and a world of fern and bracken waving below.

This primeval forest of untouched timber is the delight of Sir Vane Valentine's life. Poor as Sir Rupert ever was, all these wonderful woods of Valentine were undesecrated by the axe. He held these family Dryads sacred, and left them in their lofty beauty unfelled. Fallen from its once high estate no doubt it is, but even in these latter days of decadence, Manor Valentine is a heritage to be proud of. Its present lord *is* proud of it—of every tradition of the old house, of every black and grim family portrait, of every tree in the stately demesne, of every queer, unfashionable flower in the Queen Anne gardens. These quaint gardens shall grow and flourish undisturbed; he has decreed it. There may be orchid houses, and an acre under glass, and ferneries to the heart's content of his sister and cousin, but all else shall remain, a standing memorial of by-gone days, and dead and buried dames. And here in the park, leaning over the gate, looking at the moonrise and listening to the nightingale, stands faithful Jemima Ann waiting for her sovereign lady to come home. Something of the fidelity of a dog, of the wistfulness of a dog's eyes, looks out of hers as she stands, with her face ever expectantly turned one way; and all the loyalty, all the love without question and without stint, of a dog, is there.

"I wish she would come," she keeps whispering to herself. "Miss Valentine will jaw, and Sir Vane he'll scowl blacker'n midnight, and that there dratted Miss Routh, she'll sneer and say, 'Bogged again? Ah, I thought so!' and laugh that nasty, aggravatin' little laugh o' her'n. An' scoldin', an' scowlin', an' sneerin' is what my precious pet never was used to before she went and throwed herself away—worse luck!—on sich as him." Again she glances back apprehensively over her shoulder. Miss Valentine has an uncomfortable way of pouncing upon her victims at short range, at inopportune moments, and in the most unlikely places. Jemima Ann would not be surprised to see her glide, ghost-like, out from among the copper beeches down there, all grim and wrathful, and primed with rating to the muzzle. An austere virgin is Mistress Dorothy Valentine, even with her lamp "well trimmed and burning," and the household here at the Manor is ruled with a vestal rod of iron.

A stable clock, high up in a breezy turret among the trees, strikes nine. But it is not dark. A misty twilight, through which the moon, like a silver ship, sails, vails the green world. Jemima Ann, however, hears, and anxiety turns to agony. "I wish—I *wish* she would come," she cries out, in such vehemence of desire, that the wish seems to bring about its own fulfillment. Afar off, comes the rapid tread of horses' hoofs down the high road, and in a moment, dashing up the bridle path, the horse and rider she looks for comes. She has just time to dart back when both horse and rider fly over the low gate, then with a laugh the big black horse is pulled down on his hind legs, there is a flourish in space of two iron front hoofs, then the rider, still laughing, leans over to where, under the trees, Jemima Ann has sought sanctuary.

"It *is* you, Jemima Ann," she says.

"Me, Miss Snowball," answers a panting voice, "it's me. I thought you'd never come. I wish you would not jump over gates, Miss Snowball. You'll kill yourself yet. I declare, it gives me such a turn every time you do it——"

The young lady laughs again, springs lightly down, and with the bridle over her arm, gathers up her long riding-habit with the other hand. "Bogged, as usual, you see, Jemima," she says, ruefully, "and in for black looks, as usual, if I am caught. I *won't* be caught. I'll steal up the back way, and into your sanctum, you dear old solemn Jemima, and you shall fetch me down an evening dress, and I will repair damages, and no one be the wiser. Have you been waiting long?"

"Nearly an hour, Miss Snowball. It's just gone nine."

"Is it! You see I carry no watch, and—" glancing up with a quick look of aversion at the house—"I am never in a hurry to come back. Have I been missed?" carelessly.

"Yes, Miss. Miss Valentine asked me where you was, and looked cross."

"It is Miss Valentine's *metier* to look cross, my Jemima. Any one else?"

"Well," reluctantly, "Sir Vane——"

"Yes. Sir Vane—go on."

" He kind o' cussed like, between his teeth sorter,
when he heerd you'd gone without the groom. He said
folks hereabouts would think he'd up and married a wild
Injun—always a-gallopin' break-neck over the country,
without so much as a servant. He said," hesitatingly,
" he'd put a stop to sich goin's on, or know the reason,
why."

" Ah !" slowly, " did he say all this to you ?"

" Kind o' to me—kind o' to himself. But I allowed he
wanted me to hear it, and tell you."

" Which you are faithfully doing," says Sir Vane's
wife, with a laugh that has rather a bitter ring. " And
Miss Dorothy—was she drinking in all this eloquence ?"

"She was there. Yes, Miss Snowball."

" And Miss Routh ?—the family circle would not be
complete without the lovely Camilla."

" Miss Camilla was in the drawing-room. She has
company—the kirnal.   Don't you see all the front windows lit—and hark to the singing—that's her at the
pianner. I guess that was why Sir Vane was put out at
your being away—the kirnal came promiscus with some
other officers, and it made him mad 'cause you wan't in to
dinner. The gentlemen is in the dining-room yet, drinking wine."

" Officers—Miss Routh's friends—odd that Sir Vane
should invite them to dinner. How many are there,
Jemima ?"

" Three. I heerd Miss Routh call one of them 'my
lord.' If you dress in my room, Miss Snowball, what
shall I bring you down ?"

" I don't care a pin, Jemima—it does not matter
With the beauteous Camilla to look at, my most ravish-
ing toilet would be but love's labor lost. Bring down
anything you chance to light on—the dress I wore yes·
terday, for instance. But first, as I have missed my
dinner, it seems, and am hungry, you shall bring me
some coffee and chicken, or *pate*, or anything good you

can get—there is no use in facing misfortune starving. Lock your door, and admit no one for the next three-quarters of an hour, though the whole Valentine family should besiege it in force."

She takes a side entrance, runs lightly up a stair, along a dimly-lit passage, and into the small sitting-room reserved for the use of my lady's maid—for the use of my lady herself. Often enough it is her harbor of refuge in troubled times, the only room among the many the big house contains, in which she ever feels even remotely "at home." In the long and frequent hours of heart-sickness, home-sickness, disappointment, sharply wounded pride, bitter regret, she comes here, and with all the world shut out, bears the bitterness of her terrible mistake, her loveless marriage, in silence and alone.

It is but a small room, cozy and carpeted, and there are books, and flowers, and pictures, and needle-work, and the few relics of the old life, Dolores, Lady Valentine, has brought with her from Rome. It is all the cozier now, for the wood fire that burns and sparkles cheerily, and the little rocking-chair that sways invitingly before it. Miss Dorothy has uplifted voice, and hands, and eyes in protest against so luxurious a chamber being given to a waiting-maid, but though Miss Dorothy is the supreme power behind the throne, and mistress of the Manor, Sir Vane's young wife has shown she can assert herself when she chooses.

"Jemima Ann is my friend. You understand, Miss Valentine? Something more than my maid. Her sitting-room—mine, when I feel like it, as well—is to be pretty."

And pretty it is. As a rule, Lady Valentine lets things go; it is not worth while, she says, wearily; life will not be worth the living if it is to be lived in a perpetual wrangle. Let Miss Dorothy do as she pleases. When one has made direst shipwreck of one's life, it is hardly worth the trouble of quarreling over the flotsam and jetsam. And Miss Dorothy *does* do as she pleases with a very high hand. And so it comes that Sir Vane's bride flies here as to the "shadow of a great rock in a weary land," oftener and more often, or mounts her black horse and flies over the hills and far away, out of reach of Miss Dorothy's rasping tones. Safe in this harbor of refuge, Jemima Ann leaves her mistress, locking the door after her according to orders, and goes for the coffee and accompaniments. Dolores stands by the fire, holding her riding-whip in her hand, her long, muddied habit trailing behind her, her eyes on the fire. She has thrown off her hat, and the fire-shine falls full upon her, standing quite still, and very thoughtful here. Look at her. It is seven months since her wedding day—as many years might have passed, and not wrought so striking a change in her. She looks taller than of old, and, it seems, even more slender, but that may be due to the long, tightly-fitting habit. Her face is certainly thinner, with an expression of dignity and gravity that it never used to wear. All the old spark- ling, child-like brightness is gone, or flashes out so rarely as to render its absence more conspicuous. A look, not quite of either hardness or defiance, and yet akin to both, sets her mouth—the look of one whom those about her force to hold her own, the look of one habitually misunderstood. All the bounteous *chevelure dorée* that of old fell free, is twisted in shining coils tightly around the small, deer-like head. The golden locks, like the fair one who wears them, have lost their sunny freedom forever. She has tasted of the fruit of the tree of knowledge, and found it bitter. The old sparkle, the old joyous life of love, and trust in all things and crea- tures, is at an end forever. Snowball Trillon—Dolores Macdonald—have gone, never to return; and left in place this rather proud-looking, this reserved and self-poised Lady Valentine. The fair head holds itself well up— defiantly, a stranger might think ; the blue eyes are watchful, as of one ever on guard. But pride and defiance alike drop from her as she stands here alone—a great fixed sadness only remains. The blue eyes that gaze at the leaping light are strangely mournful, the sensitive lips lose their haughty curve and droop. She has made a great, a bitter, an irreparable mistake. She has bound herself for life to a tyrant, a harsh, loveless household despot, a man whose heart—such as it is—is now, and ever has been, in the keeping of Camilla Routh. She has made her sacrifice, and made it in vain, that a man, mercenary and money-loving, might have the Valentine fortune. She has thought to learn to love him, she has thought that he loved *her*—she knows that love never has, and never will, enter into the unnatural compact. She has made, as many women before her have made, a fatal mistake ; she has done a wrong in marrying Sir Vane Valentine that her whole life long can never undo.

CHAPTER XXX.

"FULL COLD MY GREETING WAS, AND DRY."

STANDING here, waiting for Jemima Ann, her thoughts go back—back over these last seven months that have wrought so great a change in her, that she sits and wonders sometimes if "I be I." Those months rise up before her, a series of dissolving views in the fire, the slow, first awakening to the fact that she has made a life-long mistake, that Sir Vane has married her fortune—only her fortune—that in his secret heart his feeling for her is more akin to hate than love. Two months of marriage suffice to show her this much ; slowly but surely it has come home to her, through no one particular word or act, but simply from the fact that truth, like murder, will out. **The** innate brutality of the man has shown itself in spite of him, through the thin outer veneer of good manners, from the very beginning. The first overt act was upon the news of the death of Madam Valentine in Rome. Stunned by the suddenness of that tragic death, wild with all regret, Dolores' first impulse was to fly back at once—at once. But Sir Vane, quite composedly, quite authoritatively, put the impulse and the hysterics aside.

"Nonsense, Lady Valentine," he says, coolly, "she is buried by this time, or is certain to be before you can get there. If your friend, Macdonald, the marble carver, could not have sent you word in time to see her living, he need not have sent you word at all. And she was a very old woman—it was quite to be expected, even without the intervention of the railway. You did not suppose she would live forever, did you? Though 'gad," Sir Vane adds, *sotto voce*, "it is the conclusion *I* had about come to myself."

There are tears, a very storm of wild weeping, prayers, supplications—an agony of grief. "Oh, grandmamma! grandmamma!" the poor child sobs—a sense of utter desolation rending her heart. It is a vehement scene, and Sir Vane is extremely bored. He bears it for awhile in silence, then the temper that is in the man asserts itself suddenly. He throws down the English paper he has been reading, and speaks loudly and harshly. "Enough of this," he says; "don't be a baby or a fool, Dolores. Madam Valentine is dead, and you are her heiress. What is yours is mine, and I have waited for it for twenty years. One may buy even gold too dear—I sometimes think I have had to do it. It is mine at last, and it is a noble inheritance, and I am not disposed to grieve, or let you grieve, too deeply, over this accident that has taken her off. It was quite time she went. When people get into a habit of dragging

out life over sixty, they seldom know where to stop
Dry your eyes, Lady Valentine ; there is the dinner-bell.
We are to dine at the *table d'hote ;* it is less expensive, I
find, than dining in one's own apartments, and a great
deal less dull."

That is how the death is received. Indignant fire.
dries the tears in Lady Valentine's blue eyes. She
shrinks in a sort of horror from the man she has married,
the man who has spoken those brutal words. From
thenceforth her tears flow in secret, they trouble Sir
Vane no more. But from thenceforth, too, a strong
repulsion, she has never felt for him before, fills her,
makes her shrink from his touch, with a sensation that
is little short of loathing.

Her second repulse is on the subject of her mourning. Lady Valentine naturally wishes to order it at
once ; it seems to her she can find no black black enough
to express the loneliness, the sorrow, that fills her at the
loss of her best friend, who loved her so well. Here,
too, marital authority steps in. "I hate black !" Sir
Vane says, petulantly ; "I abhor it. Crape and bomba-
zine, and all the other ugly trappings of woe and death.
I'll have none of them ! I object to mourning garments
—on—conviction. I consider it wrong, and—er—flying
in the face of Providence, who—er—must know best
about this sort of thing, of course—when to remove
people, and all that. It would give me the horrors to
go about with a lady looking like an ebony image, a
perpetual *memento mori.* You shall not do it, Lady Valentine ; it is of no use firing up, or looking at me like
that. I am not easily annihilated by flashing glances,
and I mean to be obeyed in this and all things. And if
people make remarks I'll explain. And a mourning
outfit," this added inwardly, "costs a pot of money, so
Camilla writes me."

The decree is spoken from which there may be no
appeal. Dolores *does* appeal, passionately, vehemently,

15

angrily it is to be feared—it *cannot* be that Sir Vane
means these merciless words. He does mean them. As
vainly as waves dash themselves against a rock, she beats
her undisciplined heart against the dogged obstinacy of
this man " I never change my mind, Lady Valentine,"
he says, grimly, ' when once I am convinced I am right.
I am convinced here. And tears and reproaches are
utterly wasted upon me—you had better learn that in
time. Let us have no more of these ridiculous, under-
bred scenes—these hysterics, and exclamations, and red-
dened eyes. It is all exceedingly bad form, and coarse
and repulsive to a disgusting degree. You shall not
return to Rome, you shall not put on black. If you
force me to use my authority in this way, you must take
the consequences. ' Be so good as to dry your eyes, and
let all this end."

And Dolores obeys—fiery wrath dries up the tears in
the blue eyes, and in her passionate heart at that moment
she feels that she abhors the man she has married. The
feeling does not last, it is true ; Dolores is not a good
hater—it is a loving little soul, a tender, child-like, confiding heart, that must of its nature cling to something ;
that would cling, if it could, to the man who is her husband. Duty points that way, and Dolores has very
strong instincts concerning duty, but try as she will she
cannot. On every point she is repulsed. He wants
none of her love, none of her confidence, none of her
wifely duty. He has married her because otherwise a
fortune would have slipped his grasp ; he has been compelled to marry her, and he hates everything by which
he is compelled. " She cared for that other fellow—the
marble carver in Rome," so run his thoughts, contemptuously, and he is base enough to set *that* down as the
mainspring of her desire to go back. Without caring
for her, himself, one jot, he is yet wrathful that it should
be so. She married him to please her grandmother,
against every girlish inclination of her own ; he will

make her feel that to his dying day. He bears her a bitter grudge ; she came between him and the fortune for
which he had served for a weary score of years—let her
look to it in the days to come ; let her not hope that he
will ever forget, or spare, or yield, or forgive !

And so alone, forced ruthlessly to wake to the bitter
truth, Dolores has had the fact that her life is spoiled
brought home to her well, before the first two months of
her " honey moon " are over. Alone ! A dreary, a despairing sense that she will be, must be, alone for the
rest of her life, fills her at times with a blank sense of
horror and fear. Alone ! with Sir Vane Valentine, till
death shall them part. Alone ! a stranger, in a strange
land, an intruder in her husband's house, a home without
love, without one friend. A panic of terror seizes her when
she thinks of it, a fear that is like the fear of a child left
alone in the dark. She clings to Jemima Ann, at such
times, with a passionate clinging that goes near to break
that faithful creature's heart.

"Do not leave me, Jemima," she cries out ; "promise
me you will not ; promise me you will stay with me as
long as I live. I have no one, no one, no one left but
you." And Jemima fondles, and soothes, and promises
as she might a veritable frightened child. She sees, and
understands, and resents it all, but she is especially careful not to let this resentment appear. Sir Vane eyes
her, has eyed her from the first, with sour disfavor,
mingled with contempt ; he has striven to dissuade his
wife from taking with her so *outre* a maid. Her honest
heart aches for her pretty young mistress, who grows
paler, and thinner, and sadder, and more silent day by
day, who never complains, and who clings to her as the
drowning cling to the last straw. It *is* her last straw,
her last hold upon love ; every one else seems to have
slipped forever out of her life. She stands alone in the
world, at the mercy of Vane Valentine.

All these months of post-nuptial wandering, Sir Vane

keeps up a voluminous correspondence with tne ladies of Manor Valentine. Lengthy epistles from his sister and cousin come to him with each post. His wife, of course reads none of these; she has no desire to read them. His womankind must of necessity be like himself. She looks forward with unspeakable dread to the return to the house that is to be her home. The present is bad enough; with a sure prescience she feels that any change—that most of all—will be for the worse. Now, at least, there is the excitement of new scenes, new faces, kindly stranger voices; *there* a monotony worse than death will set in. There, there will be three to find fault with her instead of only one. For Sir Vane seems to take a rancorous, venomish pleasure in girding at his young bride. If she is silent, she is sullen; if she laughs aloud, as from pure youth she sometimes does, she is a hoiden; if she talks to Jemima, she is addicted to low and vulgar tastes. In all things her manners lack repose, and are childish and *gauche* to a degree; altogether un-fitting the dignity of that station in life to which it has pleased Providence to elevate her.

What wonder that she looks onward in blank dismay and affright to the dismal home-going to Valentine Manor! With eyes of passionate longing and envy she looks at the peasant girls in the streets; at the grisettes, who go to their daily work; at the wandering gypsy women, with their brown babies at their backs. Oh, to be one of them—to be anything free, and happy, and be-loved again! She looks back in a very passion of long-ing to the life of long ago—the life of Isle Perdrix, with her boys, and her boat, and her hosts of friends, and the gentle old doctor—to that other later life, with grand-mamma—grandmamma indulgent and best loved—and even Sir Vane—a very different Sir Vane from this—the suave, guarded, deferential suitor. A strange, mournful, incredulous wonder fills her. Was that man and this the same? And Rene—but she stops here; that way mad-

ness lies She covers her face, and sobs rend their way
up from her heart; tears, that might be of blood, they so
scar, and blister, and burn, fall. Rene! Rene! Rene'

> " I have lived and loved, but that was to-day;
> Go bring me my grave-clothes to-morrow."

Her heart breaks over Thekla's sad song. Life
seems to have come to an end. It came to an end for
her on the day it begins for other girls—her wedding-
day.

And now the revolving lights in the fire change;
another series of pictures rise. It is a rainy March afternoon, and the express is thundering along the iron road
to the station where the carriage from Valentine is to
meet them, with the sister and cousin so much dreaded.
Sir Vane has telegraphed from London. He is in a
fever of nervous, restless impatience; his sallow cheeks
wear a flush; his black eyes glitter; his lean fingers
twist his mustache. He can only constrain himself to
sit still by an effort-; he cannot read his *Times;* he keeps
putting up and letting down the window, until the other
people in the compartment look at him in exasperated
amaze. Lady Valentine sits back in a corner, and a
more utter contrast to his restless fidgettiness it would
be difficult to find.

She is very pale, she is cold; the March breeze blowing in through the window Sir Vane opens at intervals
chills her through, in spite of her furs; a silent great
dread looks out of her eyes. She sits quite silent, quite
motionless, quite white. The wind goes by with a
shriek, like a banshee's, she thinks, with a shiver; the
rain falls in long, slanting lines. It is all in keeping
with her heart—this dark and weeping day—her heart,
that lies like lead in her breast. This is to be all of life
for her, coldness, darkness, storm, and—Sir Vane Valentine' They rush into the station. Her hour has come,

"Is the carriage from Valentine waiting?" Sir Vane demands, authoritatively, and the reply is crushing :

" No, there ain't no carriage from Valentine."

Nothing is waiting but one forlorn, dejected, bedraggled railway fly. The baronet is furious, but the fact remains. His telegram has been unheeded, no carriage is in waiting; the lord of the land, and his bride, must perforce go in the stuffy fly, or walk through the rain. Sir Vane swears—anathemas " not loud but deep "—it is another of the objectionable things he never used to do, or if he did, "it must have been in his inside," as Jemima Ann puts it. Dolores shrinks within herself, more and more repelled. There is no help for it, the fly it must be ; he helps her in, follows, and so, through mire and rain, in silence and gloom Sir Vane and Lady Valentine ignominiously return to the halls of their ancestors.

Within those halls it is worse. No one awaits them —no one expects them. No train of retainers is drawn up in the entrance-hall to bid their lord welcome, no fires blaze, no smiling sister or cousin receives them with open arms. Black fire-places, cold rooms, surprised faces of servants alone meet them. What the —— does it mean ? Where is Miss Valentine? Where is Miss Routh ? Where is his telegram ? Sir Vane is savage beyond all precedent. Then it appears that the telegram is lying on Miss Valentine's table, still unopened, and Miss Valentine and Miss Routh went up to town yesterday, and are not expected back until to-morrow. Direst wrath fills Sir Vane, but it is wrath expended on empty air. The servants fly to do his bidding, fires are lit, dinner is laid, my lady is shown to her room—a very pallid, and spiritless, and fagged my lady.

The servants look at her furtively and are disappointed. They have been told that master married a great beauty and heiress—she looks neither in the wet dreariness of this dismal home-coming. Left alone, she sinks down in the nearest chair, lays her arms on the table, droops her aching head upon them, and so lies—too utterly wretched even for the relief of tears.

Next day the ladies of the Manor return, full of dismay and regret at the contretemps. Sir Vane is bitter and unreasonable at first, but these being the only two creatures on earth he really cares for, he allows himself to be softened gradually, and forgives them handsomely. A prolonged family colloquy ensues. Dolores takes no part in it, but from a distance she has seen the meeting—seen Miss Valentine kiss her brother primly on the forehead, seen Miss Routh offer first one cheek, then the other, seen her husband stand with both her hands clasped in his, a look in his dark face that is altogether new in his wife's experience of him. She dreads the ordeal of meeting these two women, and wishes it was over—it is something that *must* be, but it is an ordeal that sets her teeth on edge.

She dresses for dinner in one of the pretty trousseau dresses—that she has grown to hate, since she never puts them on without feeling it should be black instead, and goes down stairs. It is a cool but fine March afternoon, and meeting no one, she gathers up her train, and descends to a terrace that commands a wide view of the country road and the village beyond, and paces to and fro, mustering courage for the coming ordeal. The ordeal comes to her in the person of Miss Dorothy Valentine, in sad colored silk, *not* a confection of Madame Elise —Miss Dorothy Valentine, as grim as a grenadier and as tall. She is upright as a ramrod, and nearly as slim—she is a duplicate of Sir Vane, in slate-colored silk, and false front. She is lean like Sir Vane, she is yellow like Sir Vane, with a mustache that the very highest breeding cannot quite overlook ; she has small black eyes like Sir Vane, she has a rasping bass voice, and a rigid austerity of manner, and she has—at first glance—some seven and fifty years. On her false front of bobbing black ringlets she wears an arrangement of lace and red roses. And she holds out two bony fingers in sisterly greeting to her brothers's bride. "How do you do, Lady Valentine?" is what she says.

The black eyes go through the shrinking figure before her — they read every quivering, nervous, tremulous throb of her childish heart. "You are nothing but a baby," that stern, black glance seems to say. "You will need a great deal of bringing up, and keeping down, and training in the way you should go, before you are fit for your position as my brother's wife. You are a spoiled baby—a foolish, frivolous, flighty young thing; it shall be *my* business to change all that."

The black, grim eyes say all this, and a chill of despair creeps over the victim. She feels crushed, as the captive in the iron shroud may have felt, watching with hopeless eyes the deadly walls of his prison closing, ever closing, down on his devoted head.

"Shall we go .n to dinner?" is Miss Valentine's second austere remark; "that is the last bell. We are always punctual, *most* punctual, at meals in this house. It is one of my rules, and my brother approves."

"And do you presume to be late at your peril, young woman," add the black, snapping eyes. In silence Dolores turns to follow. What is there to say to this terrific chatelaine? She feels she will never be able to talk up to her awful level as long as she lives.

"We are very sorry—Camilla Routh and myself— at our misfortune in being absent yesterday when the telegram arrived. It was our duty to be here, and welcome home my brother and his wife. My brother, with his customary goodness, has consented to overlook it. I trust, Lady Valentine, you do likewise."

Lady Valentine bows. She would like to gasp out something—something conciliatory—but the command of language seems to have been frozen at its source. If she lives for a hundred years, she thinks desperately, she will *never* be able to talk to this terri⁙le Miss Dorothy Valentine. A gay voice is singing blithely. a merry lilting Scotch song, as they go in. They are in time only to catch the refrain :

> " Then hey for a lass wi' a tocher,
> The bright yellow guineas for me !"

Sir Vane is standing beside the piano. a smile on his face, as he looks down at the gay singer. *She* is looking up at him—mischief, malice, coquetry in her uplifted eyes. She rises as the two ladies enter, and comes forward—a small person in pale pink silk, with a most elaborate train, and a still more elaborate structure of chestnut puffs and ringlets on her head—a small, rather plump young lady—that is to say, as young as something over thirty years will permit—with a pink and white complexion, and the very palest blue eyes that ever looked out of a blonde woman's face.

" My Cousin Vane's wife," she exclaims artlessly, and holds out the small, very ringed hands, " *so* very happy, I am sure !" The pink lips touch, the slightest touch, the pale cheek of Cousin Vane's wife ; the light, small eyes take in one comprehensive flash Cousin Vane's wife from head to foot. Then Sir Vane comes forward and offers her his arm, and they all go in to dinner.

It is dinner in little but name and form to the bride. She sits in almost total silence, seldom addressed ; the talk of the other three is of places and people unknown to her. There is a good deal of laughter and badinage on the part of Miss Routh, who is fairy-like and kittenish, as it is in the nature of some young things of thirty odd to be, and Miss Dorothy ballasts her with a solid and unsmiling observation, now and then. All through ʾhe long evening it is the same. Miss Valentine retires to a corner and a table, and adds up accounts, with a pair of spectacles over the black eyes, that glitter across the room in quite an awful way. Miss Routh, who, it

15*

appears, is extremely musical, adorns the piano-stool, and soothes them with silvery sounds. Sir Vane enthrones himself in an easy-chair near by, and listens, and reads that day's *Times* at intervals. Dolores shrinks away into a seat, as remote from them all as possible, in the deep embrasure of a window, and looks out with eyes that are blind with tears. She is lonely, homesick, heart-sick—she is far away, kneeling beside a new-made grave in Rome. Oh! dearest grandmamma, friend of friends—generous heart that poured out love upon her lavishly, and without stint!

It is a dark, moonless night; outside the window there is little to be seen but a patch of cloudy sky, and tall trees rocking to and fro, in a rising gale, like black phantoms. Miss Routh's singing, more shrill than sweet, if truth must be told, pierces drearily through her sad dream.

> " Old loves, new loves, what are they worth ?
>   Only a song! Tra-la-la-la!
> Old love dies at new love's birth,
>   Give him a song. Tra-la-la-la!
> New love lasts for a night and a day,
>   Cares not for tears,
>   Mocks at all fears,
> Flies laughing away!
> Then what is love worth
>   At death or at birth ?
> Only a song. Tra-la-la-la!"

The song is a foolish one—it cannot be that—perhaps it is the desolate sighing of the night wind, but a hysterical feeling rises and throbs in the girl's throat. Her heart is full—full to overflowing, of loneliness, and heart-break, and pain. She bears it—as long as she can —then with a hysterical feeling in her throat, she gets up, passes swiftly from the room, and runs down to Jemima Ann's sanctum. There, alone, Jemima Ann sits, placidly sewing by the light of her lamp, and there her youthful mistress flings herself down on her knees beside her, in all the bravery of her silk dinner-dress, and buries her head in her lap, and cries—cries as if her very heart were breaking.

"Jemima! Jemima! Jemima!" she cries wildly out. And Jemima holds her fast, and kisses the golden hair, and murmurs broken words of fondness and caressing between her own tears of sympathy.

"There, there, there, my lamb, my pretty, my sweet young lady, don't, don't cry like that. I know you're homesick—and they're all old, and hard, and not what you're used to. And you're thinking of your grandma, and you ain't nothin' but a child when all's said and done, and *he's*—oh! my dear! my dear! my dear!"

That is Lady Valentine's coming home.

CHAPTER XXXI.

"FOR ALL IS DARK WHERE THOU ART NOT."

HE last picture fades out of the red glow, as Jemima's key again turns in the lock, and she re-enters from her foraging expedition. Lady Valentine wakes from her dream with a sigh, that ends in a smile, as she looks at the laden tray. Chicken, raised pie, toast, tart, jelly, fruit, cream, coffee—it is a melange, but Jemima Ann knows her young mistress had a headache at luncheon, and ate nothing, and has indulged in a ride of many hours since then.

"The gentlemen have gone up to the drawing-room," she says, panting under her load, "and Mr. and Mrs. Eccleman, and the two Miss Ecclemans, has come, and that there young Squire Brooghton."

"Indeed," responds my lady, lifting her eyebrows, "well—they say there is safety in numbers—among so

many, I will not be missed. Besides, is not the charming Camilla present to do the honors? Neither she nor
Sir Vane really want me—all the same, I am certain of
a reproof for my absence. I am glad Mrs. Eccleman is
there, good motherly old soul. I can shelter myself and
my sins, for an hour or two, under her broad, maternal
wings."

She says this to herself, as she partakes of Jemima's
spoil. Mr. Eccleman is the rector. Mrs. Eccleman is
everything that's true, is most plump, and genial, and
matronly, and with both the rector and his wife Sir
Vane's pretty, graceful, youthful, half foreign wife is a
pet and a favorite.

"And now to dress," she says, getting up, "and to
face my fate. What a bore it all is, Jemima Ann. I
would much rather spend the evening here alone with
you."

"But it would not be right, Miss Snowball. They
talk as it is, in the house, about your spending so much
of your time with me, and bein' so free and friendly like
with your maid. Sir Vane don't like it, and Miss Valentine gives me black looks whenever I meet her, and
Miss Routh——"

"That will do, Jemima; we will leave Miss Routh's
name out. Button my dress, please, and keep out of
Miss Routh's way. *She* is not my keeper, at least. Now
fasten this spray of honeysuckle in my hair. How old
and ugly it makes me look, wearing my hair twisted up
in these tight coils. Miss Dorothy would have a fit, I
suppose, if I ever let it loose as I used."

"Ah! very old and ugly!" assents Jemima Ann,
standing with folded hands, and loving eyes, and gazing
at the fair, girlish beauty before her; "even Miss Dorothy looks young and lovely beside you. How *can* Sir
Vane have eyes for that simperin' white cat up stairs,"
she thinks, inwardly, "with that to look at. And
yet——"

But even to herself she is loth to put her thought
into words. Sir Vane's partiality for his cousin, his
coldness for his wife, are patent to all the household.
And Jemima Ann is not the only one who wonders. For
they know Miss Routh in that establishment, and she is
not a favorite. "A green-eyed, spying, tattling cat!"
that is the universal verdict below stairs. "And what
Sir Vane wants either her, or t'other old 'un for, now
that he's got a pretty young wife, nobody knows." In
their eyes she is neither useful nor ornamental ; my lady
is the latter, at least, and as gentle and "haffable" as
she is pretty. But Sir Vane is in love with Miss Routh,
has always been in love with her, and can see neither
beauty nor any other charm in his wife, now that she *is*
his wife.

> " How is it under our control
> To love or not to love ?"

he might have demanded with the poet.

For Miss Routh—well, *she* is in love with the excellent *menage* and *menu* of Manor Valentine, with the allowance Sir Vane makes her, with her pretty rooms and
"perquisites," with being franked over the road whenever
she travels, with the old, ivy-grown, ponderous Manor
House in every way as a home.

"Will I do, do you think, Jemima?" demands Jemima's
mistress, looking at herself in rather a dissatisfied way in
Jemima's mirror. "I am dreadfully tanned riding in this
March wind and sun, and Sir Vane will be sure to notice
and disapprove. And I don't think this *eau de Nil* dress
becoming. Perhaps we had better go up to my own
room, and do it all properly ?"

"You look as pretty as pretty, Miss Snowball," cries
Jemima, warmly. "Go up jest as you be. Miss Camilla
will have to be born again, I reckon, before she takes the
shine off *you !*" And Jemima is right. Dolores is in
great beauty this evening, despite sunburn, and *eau de
Nil* green. The pale, lustrous train sweeps far behind

her ; its trying tint is toned by a profusion of tulle and lace. A little knot of fairy roses is twisted with the woodbine spray in her hair ; she wears a blushing breast-knot of the same sweet flowers. It is a combination that only first youth, a perfect complexion, and golden hair can carry off. So, in her fresh, pearly loveliness, bringing her silken tail of lace and flounces behind her, like Little Bo-Peep's sheep, the culprit ascends to face the foe.

She means to enter by a *portiere* that opens from a cool, green fernery, filled just now with silvery light, and twinkling with the fall of a fountain in its marble basin. The tall, green fronds nod to her as she passes. Within, the piano is going ; Miss Routh, as usual, is charming the company with a song. She has not much voice—what she has is thin and shrill—it is " linked sweetness long drawn out." Dolores' hand holds back the heavy curtain, while she takes a preparatory peep, but a pair of lynx eyes note even that. In a moment her husband stands before her, his hand hard on her wrist, and she is drawn backward into the fernery, and Sir Vane's dark, hard face looks down upon her, darker, harder, than ever.

" Well !" he says, and his voice rasps every nerve in the girl's body, " what have you to say for yourself, *now ?*" She uplifts two blue, pleading eyes to his, eyes so innocent, so youthful, that they might have moved even him. But Sir Vane Valentine is not easily moved. " Do you know you have been missed—your singular absence commented on, your long, lonely rides wondered at ? Do you know I am looked upon with suspicion because of them ? Do you know people say you are unhappy—have something on your mind—that it is because you are wretched as my wife, that you go careering over the country like a mad woman ? Do you know you neglect every social and household duty for these insane rides ?"

She is in for it with a vengeance, and her spirit rises to meet the assault. "Social and household duty! she repeats. "I did not know I had any. I am relieved from all cares of that sort, in this house."

"Do you know, in a word, that your conduct is disgraceful—disgraceful?" goes on Sir Vane, twisting his mustache with those long, lean, nervous, brown fingers of his.

The color flushes up in Dolores' face. The blue eyes uplift again, very steadily this time, and meet the irate black ones full. "Disgraceful!" she repeats once more, the slender figure very straight, the white throat held very high, "that is a strong word, Sir Vane Valentine. Since when has my conduct been disgraceful?"

"Since I have known you! In Rome you spent half your time in the workshop of that marble cutter Macdonald—a fellow in love with you, as you very well knew—as he took care to let you know, no doubt. And you—how was it with you in those days? Here, you contemn my sister, ignore my cousin, set at naught my wishes, slight my guests, spend your time in the saddle, or by the side of that atrocious Yankee woman, the very sight of whom—with her nasal twang and gorilla face— I have always detested. You defy me and public opinion by galloping breakneck across the country, heaven knows where, without so much as a groom. By what name are we to call such conduct as this?"

The flush has faded from her face, faded and left her strangely pallid and still. She stands, her hands clasped loosely before her, her steadfast, scornful gaze still fixed upon him.

"You make out a strong case;" there is a quick catch in her breath, but her voice is quiet. "Is the indictment all read, Sir Vane, or is there more to come?"

"Your bravado will not avail you, Lady Valentine. It is time all this ceased. It shall cease from to-night, or I shall know the reason why."

She bows. "As the king wills! What are your wishes? It is not in form to lose your temper, is it? Be good enough to signify what you desire—no, command—me to do, distinctly, and I will endeavor to obey."

"Yes, I am aware of the kind of obedience I may expect. Why have you dismissed Lennard, the groom?"

"Simply because if I must creep along at a snail's pace, to accommodate Lennard's rate of riding, I prefer not to ride at all. Appoint a man who can keep me in sight, and I shall submit to his surveillance. I can give up going out altogether, though, if you prefer it."

"And have the country set me down as a tyrant, keeping my wife under lock and key. The *rôle* of martyr would suit you, no doubt. No, you may ride, with a groom, but *not* at the pace you indulge in, nor till such outrageous hours. For the rest, I desire you to dismiss that woman."

"What woman?" startled. "You do not mean—no, impossible!—Jemima Ann?"

"I mean Jemima Ann. Her presence is odious to me. It always was. You have had her from the first, in open defiance of my express wishes. And only to-day she insulted Miss Routh."

"Insulted Miss Routh! Jemima Ann insult any one! Oh! pardon me, Sir Vane, I cannot believe that."

"Do you insinuate that Miss Routh says what is not true?"

'I think Miss Routh quite capable of it," retorts Dolores, calmly, though her heart is beating passionately fast "Miss Routh is capable of a good deal to injure a person she dislikes. And I know she dislikes poor Jemima. If she says my maid insulted her, I believe she says a thing deliberately untrue."

"Upon my soul," the angry baronet exclaims, "this is too much. To my very face you tell me my cousin lies! But this is no time nor place for such a discussion. We shall settle this matter later. At present, if you mean to appear among my guests at all this evening, it is high time." He holds back the *portiere*, smooths, as well as he can, the black temper within him, and follows her in. She is perfectly pale, but the blue eyes are starrily bright, the delicate deer-like head held high. She is in a dangerous humor at this moment ; she holds herself as a princess born might. All timidity has vanished ; she stands at ease, and surveys the long room. And she is a picture as she stands. One of the Eccleman girls has the piano now, an attendant cavalier, the extremely young Squire of Broughton, beside her. Miss Dorothy and the rector's wife sit on a sofa and wag their cap ribbons in concert over ponderous household matters. Miss Routh, in a shadowy recess, if shadow exists in such brilliant light, lies back in a dormeuse, and looks up with that artless, infantile smile of hers into the face of a rather dashing-looking military man beside her. He is a handsome man, and a distinguished one, of Sir Vane's age, and as swarth as a Spaniard. Miss Routh is improving the shining moment with blue-green glances, and alluring smiles, and sweetest chit-chat—in the very depths, indeed, of a most pronounced flirtation.

Sir Vane looks, and his gloomy eyes grow baleful. Miss Routh is lost to him, true ; all the same he glowers at her and this other man. He knows she is only here, pending what time she may bring down a golden goose of her own and fly away to another nest. She is quite ready to say " Yes, and thank you," at this or any other moment Colonel Deering may see fit to throw down his heavy dragoon glove. And Sir Vane knows it, and is gloomy, and wrathful, and jealous accordingly. Standing here, Dolores sees it all ; her husband's frowning brow ; Miss Routh's absorption ; the careless smile with which the dashing officer attends. What if she tries her hand at reprisal—plays at Miss Routh's own game, and beats her on her own ground? She is in a dangerous mood. She is younger than Miss Routh ; she is quite as

pretty; what if she show her husband she can be as attractive in the eyes of other men as even the captivating
Camilla? She is no coquette; the game is beneath her,
and she feels it, but she is sore, stung, smarting, hurt to
the very heart. And Camilla Routh is the mischief-
maker and direct cause of it all. Very well, let Camilla
Routh look to it! for this one evening, at least,

> " They shall take who have the power,
> And they shall keep who can."

Her fixed gaze perhaps magnetizes the handsome
colonel. He looks up, across, and sees—a goddess! As
it chances, although he has been here before, it is the
first time he has seen this face. A face! it looks to him,
in the sparkle of the lamp, a radiant vision, all gold and
green, and starry eyes, an exquisite face. He looks and
fairly catches his breath. "Good Heaven!" he says,
under his thick trooper mustache, "what a perfectly
lovely girl!"

Then he turns to Miss Routh, too much absorbed in
her own vivacious tittle-tattle to have noticed, and says,
in his customary tones:

"There is a new arrival, I fancy. Who is that young
lady in the green dress?"

Camilla looks, and her face changes for a second; a
sort of film, it seems to Colonel Deering, comes over the
green eyes. "That," she answers, coldly, "is Lady
Valentine."

"Lady Valentine? Ah!" in accents of marked surprise, "Sir Vane's wife?"

"Sir Vane's wife. A wild American who ousted him
out of a fortune, and whom he married after to—secure
it," says Miss Routh, and some of the bitter hatred
within her hardens her dulcet voice. "Her youthful
adorer, Harry Broughton, is leading her to the piano;
we are to hear as well as see her, it seems. She spends
her time galloping over the country, like the Indians on

her native plains ; that is why you have not seen her on any previous call. She is called pretty," carelessly, "do you think her so?"

Colonel Deering's reply is of course to order ; he is much too mature a bird to be caught with Camilla's smiling chaff. His answer smooths away the rising frown ; he does not even take the trouble to glance a second time at the group surrounding the piano. Maud Eccleman has given place to her hostess. She, as well as the youthful Squire of Broughton, is the ardent admirer of Lady Valentine.

"Sing that lovely thing of Adelaide Procter's, you sang at the rectory the other evening," says Miss Eccleman ; "the plaintive air and exquisite words have been ringing through my head ever since."

"' Where I fain would be' ?" asks Dolores.

The smile leaves her face, lost in a sigh. In a moment the long, lamp-lit drawing-room fades away, and the sunny shore of Isle Perdrix rises before her. Rene is standing clasping her hands, trying to say good-by, the boat waits below that is to bear her away to her new life. All her passionate, sorrowful heart is in the words she sings :

"Where I am the halls are gilded,
    Stored with pictures bright and rare ;
Strains of deep melodious music
    Float upon the perfumed air.
Nothing stirs the dreary silence,
    Save the melancholy sea,
Near the poor and humble cottage
    Where I fain would be.

Where I am the sun is shining,
    And the purple windows glow,
Till their rich armorial shadows
    Stain the marble floor below.
Faded autumn leaves are trembling
    On the withered jasmine tree,
Creeping round the little casement,
    Where I fain would be.

Where I am all think me happy,
    For so well I play my part,

None can guess, who smile around me,
  How far distant is my heart—
Far away in a poor cottage,
  Listening to the dreary sea,
Where the treasures of my life are
  There I fain would be."

There is silence. Something in the song, in the voice
of the singer, in the suggestions of the words, holds all
who hear, quite still for a moment. In that moment she
rises—in that moment Colonel Deering, stroking his
heavy mustache with his hand, thrilled by the song and
the singer, sees the brow of Sir Vane black as night, sees
the malicious smile and glance Camilla Routh flashes
across at him, and in that moment knows that Sir Vane's
wife is as miserable as she is beautiful. "God! I don't
see how it could be otherwise," he thinks, "married to
that death's-head. Miss Routh," he says, aloud, but still
carelessly, "Lady Valentine has a voice, and knows how
to throw soul into words. Do me the favor—present
me."

Miss Routh rises at once—it is no part of her plans
to show reluctance. She casts a second mocking, malicious glance at Sir Vane as she sweeps by—he is seated
beside the elder Miss Eccleman, but, Camilla knows,
loses not one sight or sound that goes on.

Colonel Deering is presented in form, and bows
almost as profoundly as he does to her Majesty, when he
attends a drawing-room. "You sang that song with
more expression than I ever heard thrown into a song
before," he says. "We are all fortunate in having caged
a singing bird at Valentine. I wish I could prevail upon
you to let us hear it once more."

"Sing a Scotch song, Dolores, dear," chimes in Miss
Routh, sweetly, "Sing Auld Robin Gray."

The malice of the suggestion is lost on Dolores.
Harry Broughton adds his entreaties, and she goes again
to the piano, guarded by Colonel Deering. She strikes
the chords, and sighs forth the sweet old song:

" And Auld Robin Gray was a gude man to me. "

"She means nothing personal, I hope, Vane," laughs the artless Camilla, fluttering down by his side. "Nineteen and forty-three—it is a disparity. I wonder you were not afraid. It is a pity—it is so suggestive coming after the other.

" ' Far away in a poor cottage,
Listening to the dreary sea,
Where the treasures of my life are
There I fain would be !'

That means the island, of course. 'Where the treasures of my life are,' chief among them the handsome boy lover of those blissful days. He *is* handsome, Vane. I saw his picture, by chance, one day, in her album ; his name underneath—Rene. He was her first lover ; Colonel Deering bids fair, from his looks, to be her latest. Now, there is really no need for you to scowl in that way, my dear cousin, I am but in jest, of course. Of course she cannot help being pretty, and exciting admiration wherever she goes.

" ' I dinna think o' Jamie now,
For that wad be a sin.' "

She laughs ; it is a laugh that makes her victim writhe and grind his teeth, and rises to flutter away. Sir Vane twists his mustache in the old angry, nervous fashion, and looks up at his tormentor, and makes a feeble effort to strike back.

"Are you jealous, Camilla ? I *do* see that Deering is evidently swerving in his allegiance. Land him, Camilla, if you can, he is a fish worth even *your* bait ; he has ten thousand a year, and will write his name high in the peerage when his uncle goes."

"It would suit me very well, ten thousand a year," responds Miss Routh, coolly ; " whether it suits him or not, *cela depend*. At present Lady Valentine seems rather to have the game in her own hands; you perceive she is going with him to visit the orchid house."

The blue-green eyes flash balefully, then she laughs. " Suppose we too go and look at the orchids, Vane?"

They go, Sir Vane still moodily gnawing his mustache, irritated with his wife, Colonel Deering, Camilla Routh, all the world. "Have you spoken to your wife about the impertinence of her maid?" she asks, as they cross the room.

"Yes. She declines to credit it; her maid is incapable of impertinence to any one. So she says."

" Which is equivalent to saying I have told a falsehood. Am I to endure that, Cousin Vane?"

" What do you wish me to do?" sulkily.

"If that insolent servant remains in this house, *I* shall quit it. Insults from persons of that class are not to be endured. I shall not remain under the same roof with her. My mind is made up."

" What the deuce did she say?"

"I made some remark, a harmless one, of course, about her mistress. She resented it at once, in a manner insolent to outrage. She said," the words coming sharply between Miss Routh's closed teeth, " that when ' Miss Snowball'—ridiculous name!—was *my* age, she might perhaps be as ' set like and settled.' It wasn't to be expected "—Miss Routh grows dramatic, and snuffles in imitation of unfortunate Jemima Ann—' that a gal of nineteen could be as solid and prim as an—*old maid!*' Those were her odious words; she did not mean me to hear them, but I did. Do as you please, Vane, but—if she stays, I go."

" What the—what's the use of losing your temper, Camilla! You know she will go. I dislike her as much as you do. Say no more about it. She shall leave."

" Thanks, dear Vane." Tears fill Camilla's pale eyes, she presses so gratefully the arm on which she leans.

"I am foolishly proud and sensitive, I know. And you are, as you ever were, the best and dearest of cousins."

The tall colonel, and the *eau de Nil* robe, are away in the midst of the orchids, like "Love among the Roses," when the other pair enter. Dolores' clear young laugh greets them—she is in greater beauty than ever, her cheeks flushed, her eyes sparkling, a sort of reckless gayety in every look and word. Why not? She has done her best up to this night, and her best is a signal failure. Why not? Life's roses and champagne are here—why not take her share, and defy the fates she can not propitiate? She has made shipwreck of her life— the ruin looks to her so dire to-night, that no reckless act of her own can ever work greater woe. A fatal doctrine, and one quite foreign to all the instincts, all the training of her life, to every innocent and pure impulse of her heart. The past is dead and done with, the future is hopeless, the present is a dire anguish and pain. Why not try at least to laugh and be merry, and forget.

"I have put my days and dreams out of mind—days that are over, dreams that are done," she thinks, with a pang of cruelest pain. Colonel Deering looks at her at least with human, friendly eyes—eyes that admire and praise, and that soothe. One grows weary of the stony stare of gorgons after awhile. Colonel Deering is agreeable, and Miss Routh is piqued. Alas, poor Dolores! That suffices for to-night. But when it is all over presently, and the Colonel, more deeply *épris* than he has been for many a day, has said his reluctant good-night, she goes wearily up to her room, trailing her sheeny silk and lace as though it weighed her down, and sinks into the depths of a downy chair, with a long, tired, heart-sick sigh.

"It was all dismally stupid, Jemima Ann," she says; "I would have been a great deal happier down in the snuggery with you."

"I heerd you singin', Miss Snowball," Jemima says, letting down the long hair. "I hoped you was enjoyin' yourself. But I see easy enough you do look jest as white and wore out as——"

"Send this woman away, Lady Valentine," says an abrupt voice, "I have a word or two to say to you." It is Sir Vane, forbidding and sullen.

Jemima Ann gives him a glance of unmistakable fear and aversion, and goes.

"Wait in the dressing-room," says the sweet, clear voice of her mistress; "I shall want you again, Jemima. Now, then, Sir Vane?"

She looks up at him with the same steadfast glance of a few hours earlier. If it *must* be war to the knife, she thinks, is she to be blamed for trying to hold her own?

"I desire you to dismiss that woman!"

"I have dismissed her. We are alone."

"I mean out of the house, out of your service. Why do you pretend to misunderstand? She has insulted Miss Routh. Her presence is not to be tolerated."

"I am sorry if she has insulted any one. She must have been very greatly provoked. I shall speak to her about it, and if Miss Routh has not made a very great mistake, Jemima Ann will apologize."

"I want no apologies. My cousin has given me her ultimatum. Either your maid leaves or she does."

"That would be a pity—Valentine without Miss Routh—one fails to imagine it! But I do not think you need be seriously alarmed by that threat. Believe me, Miss Routh will think twice before she quits your house."

"We do not require your beliefs. I have not come to discuss this question, or to ask a favor. I demand that you send away that woman, and at once."

"And I distinctly refuse!"

"Madam——"

"Sir Vane," she says, rising, "listen to me. I have borne a great deal since I became your wife. I have yielded in all things since I came here, to your sister and

your cousin, for the sake of peace. But even peace may
be bought too dearly. You ask too much to-night, or
rather the mistress of your house, Miss Routh, does !"

"Lady Valentine," furiously, "do you know what
you say ? The mistress of my house ! Take care—take
care ! You may go too far !"

"She is that, is she not ?" his wife responds, proudly,
not quailing, standing pale and erect. "You do not
mean to imply for a moment that *I* am. Jemima will
apologize to her if she has offended her, she will keep as
much as possible for the future out of her way, and yours.
More than that I cannot promise. She is my one friend,
I cannot part with her. I cannot—I will not !"

"By Heaven, you shall ! Your one friend ! And
what of the marble cutter in Rome, to whom you were
so anxious to return a few months ago ? What of your
new lover of to-night ? Your one friend ? She shall go
—I swear it—though you go with her !"

He turns from the room, hoarse with passion, and
confronts Jemima in the dressing-room door. "I give
you warning," he says ; "do your hear ? You leave this
house, and at once ! Pack up and go, and, until you *are*
gone, don't let me have to look at you again !"

"Oh, Miss Snowball ! dear Miss Snowball !" gasps
the affrighted Jemima, " what—whatever have I done ?"

"Nothing—that is, you have displeased Miss Routh.
Sir Vane is excited to-night ; keep out of his sight and
hers for a few days, until this storm blows over. He
will forget it—I hope. Go to your room, Jemima, dear ;
I shall not want you again."

"And you will not send me away ? Oh, my own
Miss Snowball ! how could I live away from you, my
own dearest dear ?"

"And I—oh !" the girl cries, catching her breath with
a sob, " what—*what* have I left in all this world but you ?
No, you shall not go. Leave me now—yes, do, please—

16

I would rather. Never mind my hair; I will twist it
up. Good-night, good-night."

Jemima goes, crying behind her apron. Her mistress
locks the door, and drops on her knees, and burying her
face in the cushions of her chair, "Rene!" she cries
aloud, "Rene! Rene!"

His name breaks from her lips in despite of herself.
His image fills her heart as she kneels his voice is in
her ears; his eyes look upon her. She loves him! she
loves him! In shame, in misery, in remorse, she realizes
in this wretched hour, how utterly, how absolutely, how
sinfully.

"Rene! Rene!" For this she gave him up, her
heart's darling! for this man she resigned the heaven on
earth, that would have been hers as his wife. Lower and
lower she seems to sink, in the passion of impotent longing, and love, and regret within her. Her loose hair
falls about her; great sobs tear their way up from her
heart and shake her from head to foot; the velvet is wet
with her raining tears. And so, while the dark hours of
the sighing April night drag away, while the household
sleeps, Sir Vane Valentine's wife keeps her vigil of tears
and despair.

CHAPTER XXXII.

"OH! SERPENT HEART HID WITH A FLOWERING FACE!"

"LADY VALENTINE," says a somber voice,
"be good enough to let me say a word to
you."

Dolores, leaning over the wire rail that
separates one of the stiff Queen Anne gardens from the
park, turns her head carelessly, but does not otherwise

move. She holds in her hands a great bunch of garden
roses and heliotrope. Her straw hat lies on the grass
beside her, her glorious hair falls in its old unconstrained
fashion, rippling down her back. She wears a crisp
white dress, for the May morning is warm and sunny,
and in the blue ribbon that clasps her slim waist, is
thrust a second great bunch of pink and purple sweetness. In this muslin dress, with all that feathery hair,
she looks so girlish, so fair, so much of a child, that
even grim Mistress Dorothy Valentine pauses, for
a moment, struck by it with a sort of pity and compunction for what she is about to say. Still she will
say it—that way duty lies—and Mistress Dorothy would
march up to the stake and be broiled alive, sooner than
forego one jot or tittle of duty. It is mid forenoon—
eleven o'clock—and these two ladies seem to have the
place to themselves. Sir Vane and Miss Routh are exceptionally lazy people, and rarely appear before
luncheon, to the silent exasperation of Miss Valentine.
To her silent exasperation, for whatever she may be
nominally, she is no more mistress of the house than is
Sir Vane's wife. She stands in very considerable awe of
the baronet, and, if the truth must be told, of Cousin
Camilla also.

"Good-morning, Miss Valentine," my lady responds,
going back to her roses; "yes—say on." But the ease
of manner is but surface deep, an impatient sense of
pain and irritation fills her. Can she *never* be free,
morning, noon, nor night? Is she to be nagged at,
girded at, taken to task, on all sides? What is her
crime now? Miss Valentine wears the expression of
the judge on the bench, at the moment of rising and
putting on the black cap.

"And the sentence of the court is, that you be taken
hence, and hanged by the neck until you are dead,"
thinks Dolores, filled with dismal apprehensions. "I
wish they would—it would shorten the misery, and not

hurt half so much as this perpetual fault-finding from dawn till dark."

"Lady Valentine," resumes the somber voice, " do you know how many days it is since you met Colonel Deering first ?"

"Oh-h !" thinks the culprit, "*that* is the indictment." Aloud. " No, Miss Dorothy, I do not. I take no note of time. In this house the days fly on such rosy wings, that they come and go before I am aware of them. And I never could count worth a cent, as they say over in my country. You are more correctly informed, no doubt. How many is it ?" It is a flippant speech ; it is meant to be so. She is stung, reckless, at bay. Miss Valentine looks and feels unaffectedly shocked. She adjusts her spectacles more firmly on her polished aquiline nose, with its shining knob in the middle, and regards her young sister-in-law through them, with strong and stony disapproval.

"You take this tone with *me*, and on such a subject? Dolores, I felt inclined to be sorry for you, a moment ago, you looked so young, so——" Miss Valentine clears her throat, "so child-like, I may say, so almost irresponsible. If you answer me like this, I shall regret what I am obliged to say no longer. It is precisely nine days, then, since Colonel Deering first saw you in this house, and in those nine days how often, may I ask, have you and he met?"

"You may ask, but I doubt if I can answer ;" her tone is still light, but a deep flush has risen to her check. A flush of conscious guilt, it looks to Dorothy Valentine, of impotent anger in reality. "Let me see. That night, next day out riding, the following evening at Broughton Hall, yesterday at the rectory—oh ! I really cannot remember, but quite frequently. Why?" She looks up with an innocence, an unconsciousness, so deliciously *naive* and true to life, that the exasperated spinster tingles to box her ears.

"Why? You ask *that!* Lady Valentine, you are playing with me, with the truth. There is not a day of those nine days you have not met Colonel Deering in your rides. Do not attempt to deny it."

"Why should I deny it?" The blue eyes meet the stern *lunettes* with a quick, fiery flash. "I have met Colonel Deering daily in my rides. And what then?"

Something in her look, in her challenging tone, disconcerts her inquisitor. Miss Dorothy clears her husky throat before speaking again. "If my brother knew," she is beginning.

"What? has not Riddle, the groom, his spy, told him? That is strange. I took it for granted that was his mission, and thought it such a pity he should have nothing to tell for all his trouble. I believe I allowed the colonel to escort me for the very purpose. And he really only has told you? Now, I wondered Sir Vane had not taken me to 'task. However, it is not too late. You can inform him at any time."

"Child, what do you mean? What an extraordinary tone you take—what extraordinary things you say. Are you altogether reckless—altogether mad?"

"Another difficult question to answer. I sometimes wonder I do *not* go mad under all I have to endure. Oh, Miss Valentine, leave me alone. It is a pity to waste your time scolding me, when you may be so much more usefully employed over your account books, and tracts for the poor. I have not been brought up properly, you see—no one ever found fault with me in my life until I was married. Since then there has been nothing *but* fault-finding, and that sort of thing does not seem to agree with me. I never could assimilate bitter medicine. Reckless! Yes, I am that! Leave me alone, Miss Dorothy; you, at least, have no right to insult me. Do you think," turning on her with sudden, hot passion—"do you dare to think I am in love with Colonel Deering?"

"Dolores—no! I never thought so. You are foolish, hot-tempered, impulsive to rashness, but a flirt, a married coquette—no! Do not look at me with such fiery eyes, child. I am sorry for you—I mean this for your good. You are unhappy—I see that, and I regret it. I may seem stern to you. I cannot pet you as your grandmother used, but I like you—yes, I honestly like you, and believe, with judicious training, you have it in you to be a noble woman—an excellent wife."

Dolores laughs—a sad, incredulous little laugh enough. "Thank you, Miss Dorothy. And this is your idea of judicious training. Well, such a wretch as I am should be thankful for even small mercies. And you like me! Now, I confess," with a second short, bitter laugh, "I should never have found that out. If I am not in love with this dashing and dangerous heavy dragoon, where is the guilt of an accidental meeting?"

"They are not accidental, Lady Valentine," solemnly; "no, do not fire up again—hear me out—on his part, I mean. You are not in love with-him, but *he* fell in love with you the first time he ever saw you."

"Indeed!" There is something so suddenly funny in the grim Dorothy's perspicacity on this tender point, that she laughs outright through the passionate tears that fill her eyes.

"You have an eagle glance, Miss Valentine."

"I have," with increased solemnity; "I watched him that evening. He looked at you, and at no one *but* you, from the moment you came into the room. He left Camilla Routh, and lingered by your side, like the most devoted lover, all the rest of the time."

"Ah!" exclaims Dolores, "*now* we come to the head and front of my offending! He deserted Camilla Routh for me! Yes, and I meant that he should! Her motto is 'Slay, and spare not'—I made it mine for that once. And I won, Miss Valentine. There would have been no fault found, if I had failed—if Miss Routh could have kept her captive."

"That is beside the question. Camilla Routh is single—you are a married woman——"

"*Helas!*" sighs Dolores, under her breath, but the other hears.

"Do not make me think you wicked as well as weak," she says, harshly. "You *are* married ; you have nothing to do with Colonel Deering, or any other man. You will be talked about—you *are* being talked about already. My brother has not yet overheard—you can imagine how he will feel when he does."

"Ah ! I can imagine. I have seen Sir Vane in most of his moods and tenses. Does it ever occur to him—to you—that I may feel too ? I am not in love with your brother," cries Dolores, now utterly and altogether reckless, "but I am his wife. Do you think his very pronounced devotion to Miss Routh is an edifying or agreeable sight ?" Miss Valentine winces—the ground is suddenly cut away from under her feet. She takes off her spectacles, and wipes them, and clears her throat, and is silent. "You say nothing, Miss Dorothy. You do well. It is a poor rule that will not work both ways. But I have nothing to do with that. You may mean well—kindly—I do not know. This I will say. I met Colonel Deering first in my husband's house. I infer then he is a gentleman, and I may know him. I have met him in my daily rides, purely by accident, on my part at least, and he has been agreeable and courteous as any gentleman may be to his friend's wife—no more. I am no coquette, I never will be, please Heaven—not for your brother's sake, understand, Miss Valentine—for my own. And now what is it you will have me do ? Give up my daily ride altogether ? I will do it if you say so."

"I think it will be well, for the present," responds Miss Valentine, more softly. "Cæsar's wife should be——"

"Oh !" cries impatient Dolores, "do not quote that, I beg ! Cæsar's wife ! If she was not above reproach for her own womanly pride's sake, for her own soul's sake, why should she be for Cæsar, or any other man? No doubt Cæsar amused himself well in his own way. Had he a cousin, I wonder, with green eyes, like a cat? Is my lecture over, Miss Valentine?" wearily ; "there is the sweet Camilla beaming on us through the window, in India muslin and pink ribbons. Colonel Deering comes to breakfast, by the bye, does he not? If you have quite said your say, I will go in."

"You are a strange young woman, Dolores," says Miss Valentine, looking at the flushed, fair face, more in sorrow than in anger. "I think it is a pity you married Vane."

"So do I. Oh! *Mon Dieu!*" the girl cries out, clasp·ing her hands with sudden passionate despair. "So do I. A pity, a pity, a pity!"

"What I mean is," says Miss Dorothy, half alarmed, half angered, "that there is an—hem—incompatibility of temper, of age, of thought, of——"

"Heart, soul, mind—yes, everything. It has been a deadly, desperate mistake—who should know that better than I? Here is your *bete noir* coming, Miss Valentine, singing, too, as though no guilty passion for a married woman consumed him. Until we meet at table, then, *au revoir.* I fly before the wolf." She laughs as she goes. Colonel Deering, sauntering up the path, switching the flowers, and singing to himself as he saunters, sees the white flying figure with the amber hair, and grim Dor·othy Valentine blocking up the path like any other dragon, guarding an enchanted and enchanting princess. He smiles to himself, and uplifts his fine tenor voice a little for Miss Dorothy's benefit. These are, to Miss Dorothy's suspicious ears, the sinister words he sings :

"' I will gather thee,' he cried,
       ' Rosebud, brightly blowing.'
     ' Then I'll sting thee,' it replied,
     ' And you'll quickly start aside,

With the prickle glowing.'
Rosebud, rosebud, rosebud, red,
Rosebud brightly blowing."

"How do you do, Miss Valentine?" says this audacious dragoon, cheerily. "I am not behind time, I
hope? You look as if you might be waiting." He takes
off his hat, bows to Miss Routh at her window, and goes
with Miss Valentine into the house. Everything that
there is of the most chilling and austere is Miss Valentine's greeting, but Miss Routh amply makes up for all
that, by the warmth and cordiality of hers. Sir Vane,
too, seems a shade less sour than usual, which fact is ac-
counted for by some letters lying near his plate, inform-
ing him of a marked increase in the yield of certain
Cornish coal-mines that have been rather unproductive
lately. "I must run down to Flintbarrow," he says, "and
see about it, presently. A little fortune lies in these
mines, properly worked. I shall attend to it at once."

"Not quite at once, I hope, Vane," says Camilla,
"there is Lady Ratherripe's ball, to-morrow night. You
must not miss that."

"I don't greatly care for balls; still, as we have accepted—yes, I will stay and run down the following day.
I may be detained some time in Cornwall;" taking up
his letters again. "Challoner speaks glowingly of what
can be done, with very little expenditure, either."

"I petition for to-morrow night's first waltzes, now,"
says the colonel. "Miss Routh, you have already promised. Lady Valentine——"

"I am not sure that I shall go," indifferently.

"Not go?" Sir Vane looks sharply up. "And offend
Lady Ratherripe! Nonsense, Dolores. Certainly you
will go."

"Then may I entreat——"

"I shall not dance," brusquely; "at least, I do not
think I shall. And I never pledge myself ahead of time.
Unto the day, the day." Colonel Deering's dark, bright

16*

eyes look across and regard her for a moment. Something wrong, he sees. Have these confounded old maids been nagging at her? They both look as if they could nag with a vengeance, by Jove! She must lead the deuce and all of a life in this dull old house, with these three old women! Poor girl!—what a casting of pearls before swine, when she was given to this latter-day Othello. And the dry, elderly prig is in love with this middle-aged, simpering, insipid Miss Routh. In this disrespectful way does the gallant colonel stigmatize the blonde Camilla, and the dignified baronet. He has decidedly lost his head over Sir Vane's fair girl-bride, but he has sense enough to leave her alone just now, and devote himself to Miss Routh. He will meet her at the ball, and have these waltzes, or fail where he wishes to win for the first time.

The night comes. Sir Vane and Lady Valentine are there. And Dolores is lovely. She wears white taffetas, embroidered in silver, diamonds and lilies of the valley in her hair, a collar of diamonds, with a great star-like pendant, clasping the slender throat, lilies of the valley everywhere about her. She is a glittering, bride-like figure, looking almost unreal in her extreme fairness and translucent robes. People stand, and look, and admire—audibly even; introductions are demanded. She is a bride and a beauty, and, beyond compare, the fairest of all the fair women in the rooms. There is something almost dramatic about this dazzling last appearanc.—it is commented on afterward. For it is the last time—the first for many, the very last time for all, that they ever see her thus. She has flashed upon them like a meteor, to vanish after into outer darkness and be seen no more!

Some feeling—not of course that it will be so, but some instinct that it will be well to take the goods that the gods provide, and enjoy herself if she can, comes to her as she stands here, the center of many eyes. She

has not desired to come, her husband has angrily insisted ;
she has not wished to dance, he has irritably told her not
to be an idiot, not to attract attention, to do as others do.
Very well—she will take him at his word. It is a wife's
duty to obey. Colonel Deering scribbles his name on
her tablets many times—there are dozens of aspirants—
she might dance every dance three times over if she
chose.

She is only a girl—and the music sets every young
nerve tingling. Colonel Deering is past-master of the
art of waltzing, and she floats like a fairy or a French
girl. She floats—a dazzling creature—all silvery taffetas,
flashing diamonds, fragrant lilies, golden hair, and blue,
blue eyes. Colonel Deering is not the only man conquered to-night—she might count almost as many cap-
tives as names on her tablets. But she thinks nothing
about it, or them ; they are her partners in the dance, one
the same as another. Life holds some bright moments
still, when one may laugh and forget, even though it be
spoiled as a whole.

The Valentine ladies are all three there, the stony
Dorothy as Medusa-like as ever, looking grimly at all
this foolish gyrating disapprovingly through her spectacles. She disapproves of her sister-in-law most of all,
of this glamour, this dazzle of uncanny beauty—this
flashing sort of radiance fit to turn the heads of all these
frivolous men. What does she mean by it ? She is only
a pretty, fair-haired girl on ordinary occasions—she is a
beauty to-night ! And Colonel Deering's infatuation is
distinctly indecent—is atrocious ! He takes no pains to
hide it ; it looks out of his bold black eyes for all the
world to read. It is altogether wrong, and to be reprobated, and she hopes that Vane——She looks round for
Vane ; he is just quitting the ball-room, with Camilla
Routh on his arm. And Camilla Routh's face wears a
look Dorothy Valentine knows very well, and has
quailed before very often, strong-minded vestal that she

is. The green eyes burn with a baleful glow ; jealousy, hatred, rage—many evil passions look out of them as they glitter on her cousin's wife. His two duty dances over, Colonel Deering has not once come near her, and even during those duty dances his eyes were with his heart, following his neighbor's wife. And Miss Routh's impotent jealous fury is not to be put in words.

"Take me out of this room, Vane," she says, almost in a gasp, "I stifle in it. Take me out of the sight of your wife."

"My wife is not here," says Sir Vane, looking round.

"Nor Algernon Deering !" she cries, with repressed passion. "No doubt they are happy somewhere together. Take me out on the balcony—the heat here is unendurable."

He does as he is told—together they go out on the bal-cony. The ball-room windows give on it, and they stand under the stars, the cool wind of the May night blowing upon them, tall pots of flowering shrubs on every hand. "You will catch cold," he says ; " I will go and get you a wrap."

"I wish," she answers, between her set teeth, "I could catch my death ! Better be dead than alive—a miserable, neglected, disappointed woman !"

Sir Vane stands silent. He has been through this sort of thing before, and does not like it. " What is the matter with you, Camilla?" he asks, sulkily. "What is wrong *now ?*"

"Do *you* ask !" she cries, panting—"you, for whom I have wasted my life, for whose sake I have grown into what your wife's odious servant calls me—an old maid !" He stands with folded arms, and gazes moodily before him at the dark, star-lit stretch of garden and lawn. " You are but a poor creature, after all, Sir Vane Valentine ! You ordered this woman to go, and she defies you to your face—she and your wife ! She is at Valentine still, and means to stay——"

"She shall not stay," sullenly, "she will go. I have said it, and I keep my word."

"And to-night," goes on Miss Routh, still in that tense tone of fierce anger, " did you watch your wife to-night ? She has been with Colonel Deering the whole evening ; her conduct has been scandalous—you hear?—scandalous ! For me—but what does it matter for me ? I gave up my girlhood—my youth—to waiting for you. You were my lover ; you were to return to marry me ; you made me swear—almost—to be true to you. And I kept my word—fool, fool that I was ! How did you keep yours, Vane Valentine? You returned with a bride of nineteen, and I and my years of weary waiting were forgotten—forgotten—forgotten !"

"Not forgotten, Camilla—never forgotten ! By my sacred honor, no ! I loved you then—only you ! I love you still—you alone ! She is younger—fairer, it may be, than you, but not in my eyes—I swear it ! You are the one woman in all the world I have ever wished for my own ! You know why I married her—why I was forced to marry her, with no love on either side. By all my hopes, if I were free to-night, I would marry you to-morrow !"

There is no one to hear this impassioned speech; they stand quite alone on the balcony—this modern, middle-aged Romeo and Juliet—with the peaceful stars looking down, and the tall acacias and syringas screening them. Cautious even in her excess, Miss Routh looks round to make sure. But though Miss Routh's eyes are as sharp as that of any other cat in the dark, they cannot pierce the satin draperies of the open French window, where, enjoying the cool freshness of the night, a lady and gentleman stand. And the gentleman is Colonel Deering, and the lady is Dolores—Lady Valentine.

They hear every word; they see Camilla Routh drawn, half reluctant, half yielding, into a quick embrace. They have had no time to fly, it has all been so rapid. Colonel

Deering starts up, honestly shocked for her sake. For her—is she in a trance of white horror, that she stands frozen here, looking, and, for the moment, feeling absolutely unable to stir. "There are times when I hate her," Vane Valentine is saying, and no one can hear his strident voice and disbelieve, "since she stands between me and you. I love you, Camilla! I could not bear my life if I lost you!"

"Shall we go, Lady Valentine?" says Colonel Deering in a smothered voice. It is growing too much even for him, and the stone-white face of his companion frightens him. He touches the gloved hand on his arm, and it is like ice. She does not seem to hear him; she looks as though she were stunned into a trance by the atrocious words that fall on her ear. "Lady Valentine," he gently repeats, and draws her with him back from the window.

The motion awakes her; she looks at him with two dull, blind eyes—eyes that see, but, for the moment, do not seem to know his face.

"Shall we go back, Lady Valentine?" he asks, still very gently, motioning toward the brilliant ball-room. And then she seems to come back with a shock from that stunned torpor into which her husband's brutal words have struck her. "Do come," he says, uneasily ; "you are cold ; you are whiter than your dress."

"Come?" she repeats ; "where? Oh, back there," with a gesture of indescribable repulsion. "No ; not yet. Leave me alone, Colonel Deering, I like it best here." There is that in her face that compels him to obey. He goes, but reluctantly, slowly, and looking back. Of all the unutterable asses it ever has been his fortune to meet, commend him to this pig-headed baronet, he thinks. The music of the Strauss waltz floats to her—a sigh in its gay sweetness. She stand alone, and looks out at the stars, at the tall plants, at the balcony, deserted now.

A marble goddess is beside her ; the chill, pale gleam of
the stone face is scarcely stiller or paler than the living
one. She has read the whole truth—at last !

CHAPTER XXXIII.

"TIRED OUT WE ARE, MY HEART AND I."

T is the afternoon of another day—two days
later. My lady's carriage waits before the
stately portico of Manor Valentine, and my
lady herself, in silk attire, comes down the
broad stone steps. Miss Routh follows, Miss Valentine
last of all, in a stiff, rustling moire of melancholy, dead-
leaf tint, and all three enter the carriage. Sundry boxes
and parcels are stowed away. Miss Routh's maid ascends the rumble, and Miss Routh is in a state to be best
described by the undignified word "fuss," lest any of her
belongings be left behind.

"Are you sure everything is here, Partlett?" to her
maid ; "are you certain the gray wig, the apron, the
shoes, are all packed? I suppose your maid has attended
to *your* things, Lady Valentine?" rather sharply. "She
looks stupid enough to have forgotten ; and it will be
rather awkward at the last moment if any necessary
article is forgotten. You are not asleep, I hope?" more
sharply still.

"I am not asleep, Miss Routh; I hear. I presume
Jemima has attended. I have not looked. I dare say
the dress and adjuncts are all right." She answers
coldly ; she does not look at Miss Routh as she speaks ;
she does not look at Sir Vane, standing, hat in hand, on
the steps. She looks out of the opposite window so listlessly as to give Miss Routh some grounds for her query
whether she is asleep.

"And you really will not come, Vane ?" Camilla says. "Well, of course, if you *must* hurry down to Cornwall, you must. Business before pleasure, I suppose, though it is an odious motto, and one *you* need never subscribe to. It seems a pity to miss the private theatricals, and not to see Lady Valentine as the peerless Pauline. Colonel Deering will play the love-struck Melnotte *con amore*, no doubt. Love-making under false colors is rather in his line, on the stage, and off. Well, good-by ; I shall write you a full and detailed account of the Lady of Lyons, and her goings on."

"Good-by, Brother Vane," says, austerely, Miss Dorothy. "Do not overwork yourself about those mines. When may we expect you home ?"

"Do not know—not for weeks, it may be. I shall expect an exhaustive detail of all that goes on, Camilla." He glances at his wife as he says it. "Good-by."

"Good-by," Miss Routh and Miss Valentine simultaneously answer. His wife alone sits silent. She bows slightly in adieu, but even this without lifting her eyes to his face.

"Humph !" says Miss Valentine, sharply, "you do not bid your husband farewell, Lady Valentine." She makes no motion, no answer. She might be deaf as she sits there, for all sign she gives. She is pale ; dark shadows encircle her eyes ; those blue eyes look singularly large and somber in her small, colorless face. "Humph !" says Miss Valentine again, and glances at Camilla Routh. Something is wrong, very wrong, growing more and more wrong every day, and very likely Cousin Camilla is at the bottom of it. Her thin lips wear a faint smile at this moment, that Dorothy Valentine knows of old, and distrusts. She gives it up, and the trio sit in perfect silence, while the carriage bowls over the high-road in the direction of Broughton Hall.

Broughton Hall, the family seat, where boyish Harry Broughton reigns lord of the land, is eleven miles from the manor-house, and is at present in a state of internal commotion over sundry private theatricals, to come off presently, under the auspices of Mrs. Broughton and Colonel Deering. The " Lady of Lyons " is, as usual, the play to be done, and Lady Valentine has been chosen by acclaim as the Pauline of the piece. Whether she possesses the slightest histrionic ability is altogether a secondary matter—she is the prettiest woman in the county, she is a bride and a stranger, and young Harry Broughton was beside himself with love for her ever since he saw her first—three incontrovertible reasons. He burns to play the Claude to her Pauline, but extreme youth, a bad memory, and some boyish diffidence, stand in his way. Colonel Deering, an old hand at the business, and troubled with none of these drawbacks, does Claude, instead.

Of course the usual trouble and heart-burnings have obtained over the cast, but all is settled, more or less satisfactorily, the rehearsals are well over, and to-night is *the* night big with fate. The ladies of Manor Valentine are not to return until to-morrow. The drama is to be followed by a dance. Miss Routh has been cast for the Widow Melnotte, which part she intends to dress in pearl-gray silk, and a point-lace cap and apron—not exactly perhaps in keeping with that elderly person's station in life, but decidedly becoming to Miss Routh. And it will enable her to keep a watchful eye upon the fascinating Claude and the too-trusting Pauline.

The eleven miles are done in profound silence—three Carmelite nuns vowed to life-long speechlessness could not have kept it more rigidly. The two actresses study their part ; Miss Valentine studies *them* through her spectacles with a severe cast of countenance. She disapproves of them both. The May sun is setting as they drive up the noble avenue that sweeps to the Hall, the dressing-bell is clanging out, and young Squire Broughton, flushed and eager, runs down the steps to meet and greet them.

He blushes with delight as he gives his hand to his enchantress.

"I have been on the lookout for the past hour," he
says. "A little more, Lady Valentine, and I would have
mounted my 'dapple gray' and ridden forth in search of
you. But what is the matter? You are not ill, I hope?
You are as pale——"

"Oh, no! I am quite well." Her tone is as listless as
her look, her smile so flitting, her manner so utterly without its customary youthful brightness, that the lad looks
at her in real concern.

"I am afraid you are not. You do not look at all well
—I mean, not like yourself. Perhaps, though, you are
only tired after the drive."

"What is that?" asked Mrs. Broughton, coming forward, "somebody ill? Not Lady Valentine, surely!
Why, this will never do—our Pauline as pale as a ghost!
What is it? The drive! Nonsense, fifty miles would not
blanch Lady Valentine's roses. Surely you are not such
a foolish child as to let Sir Vane's absence prey upon
your spirits?"

Miss Routh, sweeping down the wide oaken hall,
laughs softly her silvery tinkle. "That is it, dear Mrs.
Broughton! I did not like to betray trust, but your sharp
eyes have found it out. Consider! a bride of little more
than half a year! and this is the first separation."

The blue-green eyes glanced backward over her shoulder, as she turns to ascend the stairs.

"Cheer up, Dolores, *cherie.* You look as dismal as your
name. What will your adoring Claude say presently, if
he finds his radiant Pauline all in the downs? For his
sake, if not for ours, forget the absent lover for the
present."

Dolores looks up at her—blue eyes and green meet, in
one long, level, defiant gaze—the gaze of two swordsmen
on guard.

"You are right," she says. "You are always right, Camilla. I will take you at your word."

She does. By a great effort she throws off her languor, her gloom, and gives herself up to the spirit of the hour. This is no time for memory, no place for cruelly-stung and spurred hearts. Eat, drink, and be merry. "Gather ye roses while ye may." Vane Valentine is out of her sight, she will shut him out of her thoughts as well. *Facilis est descensus Averni*—this poor Dolores can go the pace as rapidly as the rest. Presently life and color return to her, the flush of excitement to her cheeks, its fire to her eyes—the last trace of bitterness is gone.

"That is right," says Harry Broughton, in an approving whisper. "I knew you would be in first-rate form when the time came. Gad, how I wish I was to be Claude instead of that lucky beggar, Deering."

"That lucky beggar does not look particularly jubilant at this moment," retorts Lady Valentine, laughing.

"That is because he is half a hundred miles from you, at the other end of the table, with only Miss Routh—the Widow Melnotte—his mother, by Jove!" with a grin. "Filial affection ought to suffice. He can't expect to monopolize you all the evening, even if he *is* to marry you presently. Miss Routh is smiling at him like an angel, and still he doesn't look grateful. He looks bored. He really hadn't ought to, as our transatlantic cousins have it."

"I am a transatlantic cousin, Mr. Broughton, if you please. Be careful."

"By Jove! so you are. But then you are a Canadian, aren't you?" looking puzzled. "Do you know, I never got it straight somehow. And it is a matter about which I don't like to be muddled."

"Naturally!" laughing. "It is a matter of moment."

"But *which* are you? Yankee, Canadian, French—which?"

"I don't know," still laughing. "I get muddled my-

self when I try to make it out. A little of all three, I
think, with a sprinkling of English extractions thrown
in. See Miss Valentine watching us—*we* really hadn't
ought to, Harry. Miss Valentine disapproves of laugh·
ter, and we are laughing shamefully—I am sure I do not
know at what—and we are shocking her to the deepest
depths of her being."

Squire Broughton makes a feeble effort to adjust a
glass to one eye, and stares across at the stern virgin
down the table. "Rum old girl," he thinks, for in his
inner conscience this youthful heir is slangy. " I wonder
what it feels like to be a venerable fossil like that, and
ugly enough to be set up in a corn-field. What business
has *she* with a mustache when other fellows can't raise a
hair ! Should think you would find it rather—aw—flattening," he says, aloud, looking with compassion at his
fair friend, "to see much of that lady. Elderly parties
of that stripe prey on *my* spirits, I know. But then,
of course, you have always Miss Routh."

"I have always Miss Routh," assents Lady Valentine,
and the smile that goes with the words puzzles the simple
brain of young Broughton. "*Au revoir*, Harry ; your
mamma gives the signal. Don't stay long," she whispers,
coquettishly, as she rises to go.

There is no time for staying—the gentlemen speedily
follow the ladies, and the stage is cleared for action.
A last hurried rehearsal is gabbled through, while the
guests gather ; there is no time for anything but the play.
Everybody runs about, chattering their speeches franti-
cally, with little books in their hands. The roll of car·
riages is almost continuous now; there will barely be time
to dress before the hour. A very large gathering are
coming ; every seat in the amateur theater promises to
be full. The rehearsal ends ; there is a long interval
during which the audience talk and laugh, and flutter
into their seats, and read their bills. Fans languidly
wave, jewels brilliantly flash, music fills the air. The

orchestra, at least, is all it should be ; it remains to be
seen whether the amateurs are.   The hour strikes, the
bell tinkles, the drop-scene goes up, the play begins.
All the world knows what the "Lady of Lyons," performed by amateur actors and actresses, is like.   Young
ladies and gentlemen, stricken dumb with stage fright at
sight of all those watchful eyes, losing every atom of
memory at the first sound of their own voices ; arms and
legs horribly in their owners' way ; quivering voices that
refuse to be heard beyond the first row of seats.   The
prompter and Colonel Deering are the two most audible
men of the troupe.   For the ladies—Pauline does fairly
well, speaks her words audibly, lets Claude make love
to her, as though she were quite used to it, and does not
seem to find her hands and arms an incumbrance.   It is
not her first appearance, it will be remembered ; the
recollection of that last time, when she wore the dress of
" La Reine Blanche," and Rene and grandmamma sat and
watched, rises before her with a cruel pang more than
once.   But it will not do to think of old times, or old
friends, to-night ; the present is all she can attend to.
She is received and rewarded with great applause, and
many bouquets, and much soft clapping of gloved hands.
On the whole, the Pauline and Claude of the evening
are a success, and the leaven that lightens the whole
play.
"But for Lady Valentine and Colonel Deering it
would be a signal failure," is the universal verdict.
"And a handsome pair, are they not? Colonel Deering
speaks and looks his part to the life. One would think
he meant it every word." "Perhaps he does," is the significant answer. "Deering has been hard hit for some
time, and makes no secret of it. Watch him when the
dancing begins, and you will see."
But there is not much to see.   Lady Valentine does a
few duty dances, one with "Claude Melnotte," of course,
but no more.   She pleads a headache, sits out, to the

unutterable chagrin of at least half a score of *soupirants.*
Colonel Deering follows her lead, and dances as little as
possible also. He keeps near her, but "not at home to
admirers" is written legibly in my lady's eyes to-night.
She keeps close to Miss Valentine—and the man who
could make love within ear-shot of the austere Dorothy
would be something more than man. It is all over at
last—she is glad when it is, and she can go up to her
room, trailing the white silk bridal bravery of Madame
Col. Melnotte after her. Perhaps she is losing her zest
for these things—or is it a presentiment of evil to come
that weighs upon her to-night?

Next day comes, and brings with it Colonel Deering,
and sundry of his brother officers. The ladies Valentine
were to have departed after breakfast, but their host and
hostess urge them to remain until after luncheon. Miss
Routh yields gracefully, so perforce the others follow,
she is ever leader in these small social amenities. Dolores does not care. Here, or at Valentine, what does it
signify—it is equally *triste* everywhere. So they remain
until afternoon, and then, attended by a strong military
escort, set out on the return march, home. That dull
feeling of impending evil weighs upon Lady Valentine
still. She cannot talk, she sits silent, listless, languid,
the gay chatter of Miss Routh falling without meaning
on her ears. She hardly cares what may happen; it seems
to her life can be no more bitter, no more hopeless, than
it is. Her heart lies like lead within her—the brief, ficti-
tious sparkle of last night has vanished like the bubbles
on champagne. Life stretches out a dreary, stagnant
blank once more.

She goes up to her rooms the moment she arrives.
Jemima Ann, for a wonder, is not there to meet her.
"Send my maid, please," she says to one of the house-
maids, and the girl looks at her with almost startled eyes.

"Oh, if you please, my lady, Jemima ain't here!"

"Not here?" pausing and looking. "What do you mean? Not here? Where is she, then?"

"Please, my lady, she's gone away."

"Gone away!"

"Yes, my lady, with Sir Vane. And if you please, ny lady, I think she's gone like for good." She has been standing—she sits suddenly down at the.e words, feeling sick and faint. "There's a letter for yoa, my lady," the woman goes on—"there's two, please, on your dressing-room table. She cried when she was going away. She went last evening about an hour after you."

Without a word my lady hurries into the dressing-room. There, on the table, two letters lie—one all blurred and nearly illegible with tears, and blots, and blisters.

"MY EVER DEAREST, DEAR MISS SNOWBALL—He says I must go away. He says I must go this very hour, and without bidding good-by to you. I hope you will be able to read this, but I am so blind with crying, I can hardly see to set down the words. If I make trouble, it is better for me to go. My own dear, sweet Miss Snowball, good-by. I am going to London first, and I will write to you from there. And I hope you will answer— I cannot go back home without a word from you. I hope you will be happy, and not forget your poor Jemima Ann. I have plenty of money, so don't worry about that. Good-by, my own best and dearest darling. I will never serve any one again as long as I live that I will love like I do you. Your ever faithful JEMIMA ANN."

She takes up the second letter; it is shorter.

"DOLORES—You refused to obey me and dismiss the woman, Jemima. As I am determined to be obeyed in all things, great and small, I remove her this evening. Do not attempt to go after her or have her back. You will defy me in this, or in anything else, at your peril.
"Your husband,   VANE VALENTINE."

A shadow comes between her and the sunshine. She looks up from these last merciless words, and sees standing on the threshold, a sneering smile of triumph on her face, Camilla Routh.

CHAPTER XXXIV.

"NOT THUS IN OTHER DAYS WE MET."

T is four hours later. The down express from London leaves one traveler at the village station, and thunders away again into the yellow sunset. A foreign gent, the loungers at the station set him down ; very dark, with a long black mustache, and a certain undefinable air of cities and travel about him. His only luggage is a black portmanteau, also of foreign look, and well pasted with labels. He inquires, in perfect English, with only the slightest possible foreign accent, the way to Valentine Manor. A barefoot rustic lad undertakes, for sixpence, to show him thither, and afterward carry his bag to the Ratherripe Arms, and together they set out.

It is the hour "between the gloaming and the mirk," the hour of *Ave Maria* in the fair, far-off land whence this stranger and pilgrim has come. The fields across which his guide takes him, by a short-cut, lie steeped in sheets of gold-gray light ; overhead there is a gold-gray sky, flecked here and there with crimson bars. The sleepy cows lift slow, large eyes and regard them as they pass. A faint, sweet, warm wind stirs in the tree-tops, and the dark, watchful eyes of the stranger drink it all in—the quiet beauty of the twilit landscape.

"At the eventide there shall be light," he dreamily thinks. "One might be happy here, if rural peace and loveliness were all.'

They pass a last stile, and the youthful guide pauses and points to the zig-zag path between the trees.

"Keep straight up yon," he says, "t' house is at the t'other end."

The traveler hands the promised sixpence, and the lad scampers away. The footpath is a continuation of the short-cut across the park, and ends at one of the Queen Anne flower gardens. The Manor is in sight now, and he pauses to look at it, something more than mere curiosity in his gaze. With the full flush of the crimson and gold west upon it, gilding climbing rose, and trailing ivy, and tall honeysuckle, softening its decay, mellowing its ugly angles, it is a quaint and picturesque old house indeed, from an artistic point of view, with its top-heavy chimneys and mullioned windows, and antique-timbered porches. Hitherto he has met no one, now the flutter of a lady's dress catches his eye. A robe of soft "hodden gray" color, dear to the artist eye, a touch of deep crimson, a gleam of creamy lace, the sheen of braided yellow hair, a face in profile under a straw hat—that is what he sees. And for a moment the man's heart within him stands still.

"Therewith he raised his eyes, and turned,
And a great fire within him burned,
And his heart stopped awhile—for there
Against a thorn bush fair
His heart's desire his eyes did see."

She is seated on a knoll, her head resting against the rough brown boll of a tree, her white hands lying loosely in her lap, without work or book, and so still that at first he thinks she is asleep. But coming closer he sees that she is not ; the blue eyes are looking with a strange sort of vacancy straight before her, at the red and amber light in the sky. She does not hear him ; he treads lightly, and the elastic tur. gives like velvet ; she does not see him, she seems to see nothing, not even the lovely sunset light on which her blank eyes gaze. He is by her side looking

17

down on her as she sits, his whole passionate heart in his eyes. "Snowball!" he says. She almost bounds, soft as the sound of his voice is. She springs to her feet, and stands looking at him, her lips apart, her eyes dilated, mute with amaze. "Snowball!" he says, and holds out both hands, "I have startled you. But I had no thought of coming upon you like this. I was going to the house when I chanced to see you here." He stops. She does not answer, does not take the eager hands he holds out; she only stands and looks, too dazed by the shock of surprise for welcome or for joy.

For Rene, a terrible pang pierces him. *Is* this Snowball—bright, laughing, radiant Snowball—so full of impulsive gladness and happy greeting always—this pale, silent, stricken shadow?

"Rene!" she says, at last, almost in a whisper, "Rene!"

And then, slowly, a great gladness fills the blue eyes, a great welcome, a great joy. She gives him her hands, and tears well up and fill the blue, sad eyes. "Rene! Rene!" she says, and there is a sob in the voice; "I never thought to see you again."

He clasps the hands, wasted and fragile, and looks at her, and says nothing. He thinks of the last time when he came upon her thus suddenly, among the Roman hilltops. How brightly beautiful had been the joyous young face then!—how impulsively eager and joyful her greeting then!—how different from this! Now—he has it in his heart to invoke a curse on the head of the man who has changed her like this. "How white you are!" he says—"like a spirit here in the gloaming, my Snowball. You do not look well. Have you been ill, *Carina?*"

"Ill? Oh, no," she answers, wearily; "I am never ill. Do not mind my looks—what do they signify?—tell me what has brought you to England?"

"Sit down again, then," he says. "You do not look fit to stand."

She obeys him, sinking back on the grassy knoll, hardly yet believing the evidence of her ears and eyes. "Rene, Rene—here—how strange!"

"What is it?" she asks. "You look as if you had something to say. Why are you in England—at Valentine? It seems so strange."

"That sounds slightly inhospitable, Lady Valentine," smiling. It is an effort to call her by this name her husband has given her, but it helps to keep in his mind, what there is some danger of his forgetting, looking in that pallid, wistful, too-dear face, but even while he says it, he hates it and him.

"You know what I mean?" she says, simply. "I am not afraid of being misunderstood by you, Rene. You did not come all the way here simply to see me. You would not have come for that. It is something else—something important. What is it?"

"Shall I tell you?" he looks at her anxiously, in doubt. "You do not look well, and it will--it must—shock you, Snowball. Yes—I have something to tell you, something distressing, and very, very strange. I hardly know how you will believe it—you may not--and yet it is true. I have felt it rather hard from the first, that *I* should be the one chosen to bear the evil tidings, but fate has thrust it upon me. It is a long story, and I should like to tell you immediately. Are we likely to be disturbed here?"

"No in the least likely. No one ever comes here. It is the most secluded spot in the park. I choose it always for that reason. Now what, I wonder, is this amazing revelation you have to make?"

"It *is* amazing. It is the story of the dead alive. Dolores, listen—here—George Valentine has risen from his grave!"

"What!"

"He never was drowned, you know. It was all a

mistake--that old story of long ago. **He** was not drowned. He is alive to-day !"

She sits and stares at him, trying to take this in. A flush sweeps over her face, "Rene! Oh, Rene, think what you say! My father——"

"And he is not your father—that is where the trouble comes. He left his wife—your mother—within a year of their marriage. For five years she heard nothing of him —when she did it was what others heard—that he was drowned. And she married again. Your parents are both dead, as you always, until of late years, thought but George Valentine lives. You are no kin of his—no drop of Valentine blood flows in your veins."

She sits and listens, and looks pale with consternation and amaze—though slowly it dawns upon her, this that she hears. "Then grandmamma was deceived, I was not her granddaughter after all—not her heiress. Oh, Rene! Rene! if she—if I—if he—Sir Vane—had but known that!" She stops and covers her face for a moment with her hands. Not Madam Valentine's heiress—if she had but known that! She might have been free to-day, or— Rene's wife.

"If we had but known," Rene echoes, sadly. "It has been a fatal mistake. It would have been better, I some-times think, if, at this late day, it were unknown still. But George Valentine lives, and what he has lost may be his again. It was Madam Valentine—not he—who commissioned me to come here and tell you this. Nothing short of a pledge to the dying could have made me do it. It is a singular story, this, I have come to tell."

And he tells it—the story of Paul Farrar, the change of name and identity, the escape from shipwreck, the after life, the return to Rome, the railroad tragedy, and the recognition. He softens every detail that he can—of her mother, of her father, of course, there is nothing to tell. *His* biography is of the briefest. He was—and he died. He repeats Madam Valentine's dying words—her conviction that Vane Valentine will resign the fortune and the title to which he has no shadow of right. And Dolores listens to it all, with a half dazed sort of comprehension, feeling giddy with the effort to take it in, but convinced that it is true, because Rene is convinced, and because M. Paul is the lost heir, and because "grandmamma" wished it on her dying bed.

There is silence for a little when he has done. The gray evening shadows are creeping up, and the ruby fires of the sunset are paling fast. She sits and looks at that dying light, some of the rising gray shadows seeming to darken her face. Is she sorry—is she glad? She hardly knows ; she feels apathetic ; poor or rich—what does it matter? George Valentine's daughter, or the child of this unknown man whose name was Randall— what does it signify now? She is still—come else what may—Vane Valentine's wife. No change can change that. Other things are nothing, less than nothing. For her the world has come to an end—such things as Rene tells her of are outside the one vital interest of her life. If she could but be free again? But she is in bonds and fetters for all time. Let rank and wealth then come and go as they list.

"Well," Rene breaks in upon her dreary reverie, after a long pause. "You are silent. You look strangely— like a ghost, almost, in this half light. What is it, *Carina mia ?"*

"I can hardly tell you," she answers, dreamily, "it is all so strange. I am trying to realize it. M. Paul Farrar —George Valentine ! Well it is easy to believe anything of M. Paul—he was always like an exiled prince. And his mother knew and forgave him at the last ! and he made her dying hours happy ! Ah ! *that* is a good hearing. But the fortune—the title—does he think—his cousin will give them up ?"

" No, Dolores ; he does not."

" Nor do I," she says, simply, and her large eyes look

at him earnestly; "I am sure he will not. Will the law
compel him, Rene?"

"I think so. I feel sure it would eventually, if George
Valentine should choose to resort to law. But he will
not?"

"No! Then why——"

"He has no hope, Snowball, of getting his own back
again; and he does not much care, I think. If you were
happy as mistress here—as that man's wife——"

She makes a sudden motion, and he stops. She feels
she cannot trust herself on this ground; it is best not to
tread on it at all.

"Leave me out of the question," she says; "it is a
point of honor—of simple right and honesty—not of
feeling. If George Valentine lives, we—I have no right
here. Perhaps I wrong my husband—who knows? At
least we will not prejudge him. He shall know all,
and thus——"

They sit silent; they know so well what Vane Valentine's decision will be.

"Is M. Paul in England?" she asks.

"He is not; he remains in Rome. He is strangely
sensitive and abhorrent of all notoriety. Half a score of
fortunes would not make up to him for the pain of telling his story to the world. That is why a question of
birthright, easily enough proven, I should fancy, becomes
a question of honor. If, in the face of the evidence he is
prepared to show, Vane Valentine persists in keeping
what he has got, through you, then keep it he must.
George Valentine will never tell the story of his reckless,
erratic life to the world through the medium of an end-
less Chancery suit."

"It is like him," she says. There is another pause.
"Where are you stopping, Rene?" she inquires, suddenly.

"At the inn in the village. I am going up to London,
however——"

"No," she interrupts ; "do not for a day or two. My husband is in Cornwall; I will write to him to-night, and tell him what you have told me. Wait here until I receive his answer. Who knows? We may wrong him. When the truth is fully known to him——"

"Who is that lady ?" asks Rene, abruptly, "there between the trees—in the pink dress. She has been watching us for the last five minutes."

"In a pink dress ? Miss Routh then, of course," her delicate lips curling; "it is her *metier* to watch me always. Yes, it is Camilla Routh, and she sees that we see her."

The pink dress emerges, its wearer advances. Who is this olive-skinned, dark-mustached, extremely handsome young man, with whom her cousin's wife talks so long, so earnestly, so secretly, under trees, in hidden places in the park ? It is her duty to see into this, and curiosity is nearly as powerful as sense of duty with Miss Routh. So she comes forward, gathering field flowers and ferns as she comes, humming a little tune—fair, sweet, artless, unconscious, a picture of blonde, patrician British beauty. But she is not destined to be gratified— it is the rudest repulse, perhaps Miss Routh has ever received in her life. As she draws near, Lady Valentine deliberately rises, eying her full, passes her hand through the arm of her picturesque-looking cavalier, and turns her back upon her enemy. Rene is rather aghast, but there is nothing for *him* but to follow Dolores' lead. It is the most cutting of cuts direct. Miss Routh stops— stunned.

"Do not come up to the house, Rene," Dolores says, her pale cheek flushing painfully. "I cannot ask you. And do not come here again either. I fear that woman. When I hear from—him—I will let you know. *I* believe what you tell me—say so to Paul—whatever the result may be. Until then—adieu and *au revoir*."

Miss Routh, watching afar off in speechless, furious anger. sees her hold out her two hands, sees him take them, and hold them in a clasp that is close and long. Oh ! that Vane, that Dorothy, that Colonel Deering were but here now ! She cannot hear a word they say—more is the pity—making a second assignation, no doubt. Before she sleeps Vane shall be written to of this, shall hear it with all the additions and embellishments that malice and hatred can add. A dull glow of horrid triumph fills her in the midst of her rage. Let her look to it after this ! It is the young French-Canadian sculptor, no doubt, of whom Vane is already jealous. She has lost no time in sending for her old lover, now that her husband is out of the way ! It is a coarse thought, but the fair Camilla's thoughts are mostly coarse. Let her look to it ! the insult has been deadly—the reprisal shall be the same.

They .part. Rene returns to the village—the two ladies, by different paths, to the house. Miss Routh does not appear at dinner ; she is busy over a letter, every word of which is freighted with a venomous sting. She likes her dinner, and has it brought up to her, but she likes her revenge better. My lady writes a letter too, before she sleeps, also a long one ; it takes her until past midnight, and is a carefully and minutely-worded repetition of the story Rene has told her under the trees. There is more than the story—an earnest protestation of her belief in its truth, and her perfect willingness to resign the fortune, to which she has never had a shadow of right.

" I do not fear poverty," she writes, " trust me, Vane ! I was never born to be a lady of rank and riches—both have been a burden to me, a burden I will lay down, oh ! so gladly. This ' burden of an honor unto which I was not born ' has weighed upon me like an evil incubus from the first. Oh, my husband, let us give back to George Valentine his birthright. He will act generously—more than generously, I know, for I know *him*— and for me, I will go with you, and be in the day of disaster more faithful, more fond, more truly your wife, than

I can ever be weighted down with wealth to which neither of us has a claim."

But while she writes—her whole heart in her pleading words—she *knows* she writes in vain. More of her woman's heart is in this letter than she has ever before shown to the man she has married. Apart from the misery of dwelling under the same roof as Camilla Routh—with the right done nobly for the right's sake—far away from this place in which she has been so wretched, poor and obscure, if it must be, she feels that a sort of happiness is possible to her yet. If her husband is capable of an action at once honest and noble, then her heart will go out to him—freely, fully. The very thought of his doing it seems to bring him nearer to her already. If he will but do the right—if he will but let her, she may care for him yet.

Next morning, by the earliest mail, two very lengthy, very disturbing epistles, in feminine chirography, go down to Sir Vane Valentine, Bart., among the mines of Flintbarrow.

CHAPTER XXXV.

"IT WAS THE HOUR WHEN WOODS ARE COLD."

HERE come times in most lives when, after long depression and wearing worries, a sort of revulsion, a sort of exaltation of feeling sets in. Such a time comes now to Dolores. There is a revulsion in favor of her absent husband. Perhaps the fact that he *is* absent has something to do with it. Looking in his gloomy face, it would seem a difficult thing for any woman wife or otherwise, to get up much sentiment for Vane Valentine. Her ideas, after all, of the sacrifice demanded are vague. If Manor Val-

17*

entine and the fortune are resigned to their lawful owner, she knows very little what will remain to them She doubts greatly if the sacrifice will be made ; it will never be, at least, until proof "clear as Holy Writ" is placed before him—that is to be expected. He will be enraged and unbelieving, beyond doubt. Still, once convinced— and she is sure such conviction must be possible since M. Paul is the claimant—he *cannot* be so glaringly dishonest and dishonorable as to retain what will no longer be his. Dolores, reasoning on these points, is primitive and of another world than this ; the distinction between mine and thine stands out with almost startling vividness in her unworldly mind. To retain, knowingly, the goods of another is to resign hope of salvation here and hereafter —that is her creed, sharp and clear. It is quite in her to regard with horror and aversion such a one. For a husband capable of such a crime she feels that even the outward semblance of regard and duty must come to an end —that for him, for all time, nothing but contempt could live in her heart. And to drag out life by the side of a man one despises—well, life holds for any woman few harder things.

But if he does the right—oh ! then how gladly will she go with him, to poverty if need be.; how she will honor him, how hardly she will try to win him back. She does not fear poverty—was she not poor on Isle Perdrix, and were not those the best, the very best, days of her short life? She would like a cottage, she thinks, where she might reign alone, far from stern Miss Dorothy, sneering Miss Routh, and with her husband alone, who knows? —she *might* learn to love him; he even might learn a little to care for her. She would so strive, so try, so pray ! Anything—anything would be better than this death in life here, this most miserable estrangement, this loveless house, these cold, hard faces. Any change, be it what it may, must be for the better. She will try, at least—the opportunity being given—she will do her utmost to soften and win the man who is her husband.

With hopes like these in her girl's mind, Dolores waits through the long day that follows. She does not go out ; she has a feeling that she would rather not meet Rene again until she has seen her husband. She must be loyal . of heart, even to the shadow of a shadow, and to sit by Rene's side, look up in Rene's eyes, listen to Rene's voice, and remain thoroughly true to Vane Valentine, is no such easy task. If she goes abroad she may meet him, so she remains at home.

The evening post brings her a letter from London, from Jemima Ann. She has half forgotten this faithful friend, in thinking of other things; she feels self-reproachful for it, as she reads. Jemima is stopping, for the present, in an humble London lodging, and proposes remaining there until her "dear sweet Miss Snowball " writes good-by. Then she will go back to New York and resume life in her native land. It is not quite so easy to think wifely thoughts of Sir Vane and make generous resolutions, after reading this, and remembering how treacherously and stealthily this humble friend was forced away.

Another night; another day. This day certainly will bring the absent seigneur. A strange nervousness, begotten of waiting and expectation, hope and dread, fills her. She can rest nowhere; she wanders aimlessly about the house, starting at every heavy footstep, at every opening door.

Miss Routh watches her with malicious, smiling eyes. *She* has seen Rene, at least ; has walked down to the village on purpose, and chatted for five minutes condescendingly with the hostess. No, they have not many strangers at the Arms this spring, the landlady says, dropping a courtesy. Only one just now; a Mr. Macdonald, a foreigner, by his looks, and ways, and talk, in spite of his Scotch name. No, she does not know when he is going away ;

he does not say ; he is a real gentleman in all his ways,
and gives very little trouble. Mr. Macdonald appears at
the moment, walking briskly up the road, with his sketch-
book and cigar, and keen dark eyes, and Miss Routh
hastily pulls down her vail and departs.

The day wears on. Sir Vane comes not. It brings no
answer to her letter either, and Dolores' fitful exaltation
of feeling vanishes as it came. A dull depression, a fear
of the future, fills her. How blank and drear that long
life-path stretches before her, here in this silent, dark,
moldering old home, with the faces of these two women
who dislike her, before her every day, and all day long !
Insulted, distrusted, unloved, *how* shall she bear it to the
bitter end. And she is but nineteen, and life looks so
long, so long !

Perhaps it is the unusual confinement to the house
that is telling upon her ; it is now two days since she
has been out. A half-stifled feeling oppresses her ; she
must get out of these deathly-silent, gruesome rooms,
or suffocate. It is after dinner ; the last ray of twilight
is fading out ; there is a broad May moon rising, and a
star-studded sky.

She leaves the house and wanders aimlessly for awhile
between the prim beds and borders of one of the stiff
Dutch gardens. Now and then she stoops to gather the
old-fashioned, sweet-smelling flowers, but almost without
knowing what she does. A nightingale is singing, in a
thorn-bush near, a song so piercingly sweet, so mournful
in its sweetness, that she stops, and the tears rise to her
eyes as she listens. And in that stop and pause to listen
something more than the nightingale's song reaches
her ear—the soft, cooing tones of Camilla Routh pronouncing her name.

"Dolores' lover ? Was he really a lover of your wife's,
Vane, before you married her ?" she is asking. "Anything more lover-like than they looked when I surprised
them it would be difficult to find. And he is *very* hand-

some—there can be no mistake about that—with the most beautiful Spanish eyes I think I ever saw."

There is a grumbling reply; it sounds like, "Devil take his eyes!" and it is in the voice of the lord of Val- entine.

Dolores stands quite still, thrilled and shocked, feel- ing all cold and rigid, and powerless to move. A tall, thick hedge separates them; she wears a dark, dun-col- ored dress, and in this shadowy light, among the other shadows of trees and moonlight, she can hardly be seen. They are walking slowly up and down a secluded avenue known as the Willow Walk. In the deep evening hush even Miss Routh's subdued tones are distinctly and pain- fully audible.

"He is still in the village," again it is Miss Routh who speaks; "how often they meet, where they meet, I do not know. That they do meet is certain, of course. Yes, Colonel Deering has called twice; but she has de- clined to see him; one lover, I suppose, at a time, is as much as she can attend to.

> '"Old loves, new loves, what are they worth ?
> Old love dies at the new love's birth.' "

hums the fair Camilla, and laughs softly.

"Signor Rene is far and away the handsomer man of the two."

"Are you too deserting Deering and going over to this sallow, black-eyed boy, Camilla?" retorts, with a sneer, Sir Vane.

"No," lightly. "Like your pretty wife, I am true to my first lover. She *is* pretty, Vane—really pretty. I al- ways doubted it—being a blonde myself, I seldom admire blondes—but the other evening, when I came upon her by his side down there in the park, you should have seen her—transfigured by gladness, love—who knows what? Yes, she is pretty—when she likes. I confess the woe- begone expression she puts on for *us* hardly becomes her,

People are beginning to talk—many were whispering the other night at the Broughton's how wretchedly ill and worn Lady Valentine was looking. It would be well to speak to her on the subject, I think, Vane. It may be pleasant for her to pose in the part of the heart-broken wife, but it can hardly be agreeable for *you*." ﹁

Something—a sulky and stifled imprecation it sounds like—ground out between closed teeth, is the answer. Miss Routh is an expert mouser, and knows how to torture her victim well.

"But about this extravagant story—what of that, Vane?"

Miss Routh appears to have the ball of conversation in her own hands, and to unwind at her pleasure.´

"Something must be done, and at once. *We* may disbelieve it, but we cannot afford to ignore it. And others will not, if we do. Once let it get abroad that you are not really the rightful baronet—the rightful—— "

She is interrupted, sullenly, angrily, by her companion. "I do not propose that it shall get abroad," he says.

"No? But that is this Macdonald's purpose in coming here. How are you to prevent it? Your wife will see him—— "

"My wife will *not* see him. She shall never see him again !"

"What do you mean ?" breathlessly.

"Nothing that you need take that startled tone about," sulkily, "nothing but what I have a perfect right to do. I mean to remove my wife out of his way."

"Yes ?" eagerly. "How—where ?"

"To Flintbarrow. My mines will keep me there, off and on, for months—years, if I like. What more natural," grimly, "than that an adoring young wife should wish to remain with her husband ? It is a dismal place, I admit : all the more reason why she should enliven my enforced exile there. The old stone house is out of repair,

but we can furbish up two or three rooms, and for two
loving and lately united hearts, what more is required?
And I doubt if M. Rene Macdonald's beautiful Spanish,
French, Italian—what was it?—eyes will illuminate the
gloom of Flintbarrow for her, though they were twice as
as sharp they are."

There is silence for a moment ; they pass out of range
in their slow walk, and the sweet song of the nightingale
fills up the pause. For Dolores—the world is going
round, the stars are reeling ; she catches hold of the
hedge, but fails to hold herself, and half falls, half sinks
in a dark heap in the dew-wet grass.

" She will not go ; I tell you, she will not go," are the
words of Camilla she hears next. " She has a great deal
of latent force and resolution, once aroused, and she
fears and dislikes and distrusts us all. Here she has
friends—Colonel Deering, the rector's family, the
Broughtons, Lady Ratherripe—to whom she *may* appeal
if she chooses. There she will have no one. She will
not go !"

" Will she not?" says the hard, metallic tones of the
baronet. " Ah, we shall see ! You taunted me before
with my impotence in my own house—I could not compel
the woman Jemima to leave. I have banished the maid ;
I shall banish the mistress exactly how, and when, and
where I please. Meantime, tell Dorothy nothing of this ;
I don't want to be maddened by her questions and com-
ments. For this Macdonald——"

There is another break; they pass down under the
willows. She who crouches under the hedge, prone
there on the wet grass, makes no effort to overhear. She
has heard enough.

" I shall take high-handed measures with *him* "—it is
the voice of Vane Valentine, on the return walk.
" There is a law to punish scoundrels who conspire for
purposes of extortion and fraud. This Farrar—a clever,
clear-headed rascal as I know him of old, a vagabond by

profession—has addled his brains reading up Roger
Tichborne. George Valentine was drowned, beyond all
doubt, a score of years ago. Men don't rise from the
dead after this fashion, except in the last act of a Porte
St. Martin melodrama. I don't fear them with my credulous fool of a wife out of the way. If it got wind that
she believed the story and was on their side—well, I can
hardly trust myself to say what I might not do in such a
case. At Flintbarrow she will be safe; at Flintbarrow
there are no long-eared neighbors to listen, no prying
eyes to see. There she will be, perforce, as silent as in
her coffin. And there, by Heaven, she shall remain
until she swears to me to resign all complicity or belief
in this plot—ay, though it should be until her hair is
gray !"

"She will not go," retorts the quietly resolute voice of
Camilla Routh ; "she will suspect your intentions, she
will see your anger against her in your face——"

"*That* she shall not," grimly ; "she shall suspect
nothing. It shall be made a family affair. You will all
come down." They pass by again. A long moment,
then returning steps and voices. ——"in this way. I
shall use *finesse* until I get her there," with a laugh that
makes even Camilla shiver. "I shall doubt the story, of
course, decline to see Farrar's ambassador, refuse to listen to a word, scout the whole impossible romance.
Meantime I must at once return to Cornwall, and it is
my desire that you, and my sister and my wife come
down after me to see the place. What can be more natural ? and once there——"

The pause that follows is more significant than any
. words. Camilla's low laugh comes through it softly.

"An excellent idea, Vane—I did not give you credit
for so much strategy. Of course Dorothy is to be kept
in the dark ?"

"Of course. She has a sort of liking for my wife

and might blurt out something. She will like to see the old place again ; she spent her youth there, you know."

"How long are we to remain, she and I, I mean ?"

"A week or two—as you like. Of course I would be very glad to keep you there, Camilla, but you would not like it. It is deadly dull ; the nearest hamlet is five miles off ; nothing but moors behind, stretching up to the sky, and the sea in front melting into the horizon. A week, I dare say, will be as much of it as you will be able to exist through. No one will wonder at Lady Valentine's remaining ; it is surely the most natural thing in the world that she should remain with her husband under the circumstances. Now, perhaps, we had better go in. I have not dined. After dinner I shall speak to Dolores, and—the rest will be easy."

They pass out of sight and hearing—this time there is no return. The nightingale, on the thorn-bush near, has the night to itself and its sweet love-song.

Dolores lies where she has sunk—her face hidden in her hands, the chill, fresh-scented grass, cool and grateful to her heated head. She is numb and aching, full of a cold, deathly torpor—"past hope, past care, past help." Life has come to an end—just that. "And now I live, and now my life is done"—done—done forever and forever !

After a time—not long—though it seems long to her, a physical sense of discomfort and cold makes her get up. Once on her feet she stands for a moment dizzily—then turns mechanically and walks back to the house. It is late and she will be missed ; she does not want to be missed, she is hardly conscious of more then that. If she suffers she hardly realizes it—in soul and body she is benumbed. Much pain, many blows, have dulled for the time all sense of agony.

They are all three in the drawing-room when she enters, Miss Valentine bending over her never-ending account books, Miss Routh at the piano. Her fingers are

flying over the keys in a brilliant galop, she laughs up
in Sir Vane's face, and chatters gayly as she plays. She
looks over her shoulder, keenly, at the new-comer, her
mocking smile is most derisive.

"How pale you are, Lady Valentine," she says:
"whither have you been wandering until this unearthly
hour? See! our truant has returned in your absence. She
has pined herself to a shadow, as you may see for yourself, in your absence, Vane. You must take her with you
to Cornwall, I think!"

Sir Vane rises and comes forward, quite like the old
Sir Vane of Italian days, courteous, if cold, and takes her
hand.

"You do look pale, Dolores. You should not stay
about in the night air. And see—your dress is quite wet
with dew. I have returned to answer your letter in person. Naturally it annoyed me. How can you credit such
a cock-and-bull story? Come here and sit down, and
let us talk the thing over."

He leads her to a chair—wonderful cordiality, this!
—and takes another near her. It is quite a lover-like
tableau—Miss Routh's gray-green eyes gleam derisively
as she glances. Dolores takes up a screen and holds it
before her face.

"The light dazzles my eyes," she says, without meeting his glance.

He looks at her suspiciously. She is singularly,
startlingly pale ; her eyes look wild, and dark, and dazed
—what is the matter with her? Has this story and Macdonald's coming turned her brain? But his voice is
smooth, suspiciously smooth and gentle, when he speaks
She sits, the screen held well before her face, her eyes
fixed upon its frisky Japanese figures, but seeing none of
them. His voice is in her ear, as he talks steadily on and
on—she hears its tone, but is scarcely conscious of his
words. Miss Routh's gay playing fills the room ; she
plays the "Beautiful Blue Danube"--his monotonous

words set themselves to the gay, bright music, and blend and lose themselves in the melody—all mingle themselves together in her mind ; nothing seems clear or distinct.

Is she assenting or answering at all to what he says ? Afterward she does not know. He seems to be satisfied, at least, when he rises at last, and leaves her, crossing over to Camilla Routh.

" Well ?" she asks.

" It *is* well. I knew it would be. She says yes to everything. She will go."

" I don't believe she knows what she is saying," thinks Miss Routh, glancing across at her. " She sits there with the fixed vacant look of a sleep-walker. She had it when she came in. What if she heard us talking out there ? It is very possible. Suppose she has—what then ?"

She looks once more, trying to read her answer in that pale, rigid face. As she looks Dolores rises, and without glancing at any one, or speaking, quits the room.

" H'm !" muses Miss Routh, thoughtfully, resuming her performance, " something odd here. The end is not yet. Your wife is not in Cornwall yet awhile, Sir Vane Valentine."

"How long do you stay with us ?" she asks him, aloud.

"Until to-morrow only. Apart from this affair, my presence is necessary there. By being on the spot I save no end of money, and hurry on the work. You, and Dorothy, and Dolores will follow—say in two days. I suppose it would look a trifle abrupt to hurry you off with me to-morrow. Meantime, watch her ; no more secret meetings with Macdonald, if you can by any means prevent them. Come to Flintbarrow without fail on the third day."

" *I* will come," responds Miss Routh. " But whether your wife will accompany me or not, cousin mine," she adds inwardly, "that third day only will tell !"

CHAPTER XXXVI.

"ADRIFT, AS A LEAF IN THE STORM."

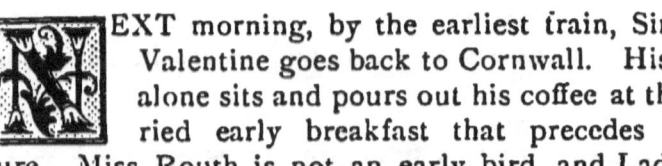EXT morning, by the earliest train, Sir Vane Valentine goes back to Cornwall. His sister alone sits and pours out his coffee at the hurried early breakfast that precedes departure. Miss Routh is not an early bird, and Lady Valentine, usually up as early as Dorothy herself, does not appear. Sir Vane does not seek to see her to say goodby. He is nervous and ill at ease, and has no appetite. This "fraudulent plot," this "trumped-up conspiracy" disturbs him more than he cares to show. If they persist in it, and drag it before the world, a horrible exposure will be the result. And even if their defeat is ultimately secured, the legal expenses will be something he shudders to contemplate. With what it feeds on, Sir Vane's love of wealth grows. If their defeat should *not* be secured—but even in thought he cannot imagine so wild a possibility as that. Once let him get his credulous, romantic wife out of the way, safely down in the lonely, sea-girt seclusion of Flintbarrow, and the first step toward safety will have been taken. She is as wild and shy as a partridge—as ready to take flight. He will not disturb her this morning ; she will come the more readily and unsuspiciously with his sister and cousin, if he does not seem too eager. After that he will know how to deal with M. Rene Macdonald. Silence reigns at the hasty meal. Miss Valentine is pleased at the invitation to return to her native Cornish wilds for a little, but Miss Valentine is not diffusive by nature, and sits grimly and silently behind the coffee-pot. Desolate, lonely, shut out from the world by far-stretching moors and leagues of dark and stormy sea, she yet loves those "thundering shores of Bude and Boss," and would willingly resign

her position as housekeeper of Manor Valentine to return thither to her peaceful life. But Vane rules it otherwise, and Vane's will has ever been her law.

"You think your wife will be willing to go, Vane?"
she asks, rather abruptly, just before he departs.

"Certainly; why not?" he returns, sharply. "A
wife's place is beside her husband. She needs a change,
too, and bracing air—the visit will do her good. Sea
air is native air to her; she was brought up on an
island."

"Yes," Miss Dorothy assents, thoughtfully, "she looks
as if she needed a change. She eats nothing, and fails
away to a shadow. Still I doubt if Flintbarrow will help
her, or if she will like the place. It is a gloomy spot,
you must admit, for a young girl like her, Brother Vane."

"She will have to accustom herself to its gloom. I
shall be there to bear her company. Do you wish to leave
her behind, to amuse herself flirting with Deering, Dorothy? Be kind enough not to be a fool. Here is the
trap—good-by. I shall expect you all without fail,
remember, on Friday afternoon."

He leaves the room, banging the door angrily after
him, jumps into the waiting trap; the groom gathers up
the reins, and they drive off. Three pairs of feminine
eyes watch the departure, with very different looks—Miss
Dorothy Valentine, grimly, through her glasses; Miss
Routh, with an inexplicable smile; and two somber blue
eyes, dark and heavy-lidded from a sleepless night. Miss
Routh, in the freshest and crispest of morning toilets,
indulges in a stroll through the village before luncheon,
and makes a call, in her gracious way, on the hostess of
the Ratherripe Arms. As she sits by the open parlor
window, framed in woodbine and roses, Mr. Macdonald,
sketch-book in hand, the inevitable cigar between his
lips, passes, and glances in. So! he lingers still, then!
She must watch well, and discover whether another secret
interview takes place before the departure for Cornwall

She hastens home and makes inquiries. Her maid, in structed for the purpose, has kept an eye on my lady's doings. But there is little to report. My lady has not appeared at all ; some tea and toast have been taken up to her, and she has declined to receive a call from Miss Valentine, under the plea of headache. The maid is positive my lady has not quitted the house the whole morning ; she has sat, with her sewing, the whole forenoon in one of the rooms near, the door open, and has heard my lady talking to the housekeeper in her own sitting-room.

Luncheon hour comes ; still my lady appears not. Miss Routh and Miss Valentine partake of that meal in profound silence. Miss Routh never needlessly wastes her energies in conversation with her own sex ; she eats her luncheon with excellent appetite, and thinks her own thoughts, a half smile hovering around her lips. What is my lady about in the seclusion of her own room ? She has no faith in the headache. The conviction is forcing itself upon her that her talk with Vane in the Willow Walk has been overheard. Dolores looked as if stricken by some desperate blow when she came in—what else could have given her that white, wild face ? Well, and what then ? If she goes, it means imprisonment for an indefinite period in the dreariest old house in the world ; if she refuses to go, it means, of course, secret meetings with her old lover, open meetings with her new one, Colonel Deering, either way destructive for her rival. On the whole, perhaps, she half hopes it may mean refusal to go. A few of these stolen assignations in secluded nooks in the park, and—it may be possible for Vane to procure a divorce. Lucy, her maid, is a spy by nature, and the only servant in the house who dislikes Lady Valentine. Lucy will watch well, and who knows —who knows——

' He is *very* handsome," Miss Routh thinks, a greenish, evil glitter in her brooding eyes, " and she loved him long before she knew Vane, and would have married him but

for old Madam Valentine. Of course she is in love
with him still, and of course, also, she hates her husband.
If she overheard their conversation what more natural
than that she should wish to see him again, and tell him,
and seek sympathy and consolation. And Lucy will
watch. How will it sound?—her old lover comes to
Valentine—I surprise them in the most secluded nook of
the park-land ; she refuses to join her husband in Cornwall, though Dorothy and myself go ; she and this lover
still have private meetings in our absence. Will it be
enough, colored as Lucy will color it? A divorce would
free him—he hates the bond as much as she does, and
once free he will marry me. As for the dead-alive story
this Signore Macdonald tells, I do not believe it. Camilla, Lady Valentine ! Well, since Colonel Deering is
not to be captured, it must suffice. For her—she will go
back to the outer darkness, with her Spanish-eyed, handsome young lover, and be heard of no more !"

Colonel Deering calls before dinner, and is invited to
stay and dine *en famille*. He accepts—he has come for
that, indeed, and for a glimpse of his enchantress. Miss
Routh is maliciously willing to accommodate him. But
will she appear? Yes—just as dinner is announced,
Lady Valentine comes in and takes her accustomed
place.

Camilla Routh looks at her curiously. She is dressed
in pale pink, and if she is whiter than usual, the delicate
rosy tint of her robes lends a sort of illusive glow, to
eyes not too inquisitively alert. But she is very pale,
and except when directly addressed scarcely speaks
throughout the meal. The conversation turns on the
trip to Cornwall ; the colonel is profuse in his regrets
that even for a few days they are to lose the ladies of
Valentine, but Camilla notices that Lady Valentine holds
aloof from the subject, and expresses no feeling in the
matter, one way or the other. All Colonel Deering's
efforts to draw her into the general talk fails ; her replies

are monosyllabic, her eyes scarcely leave her plate.
What is she thinking of? Camilla Routh wonders, with
that pale fixed, unsmiling face.

After dinner they stroll out into the grounds, silvery
and sweet, in the starry dusk ; that is to say, Colonel
Deering and Miss Routh do. Dolores does not join
them. She sits by one of the open windows, her hands
lying listlessly in her lap, the somber look that never
used to be there, that is growing habitual to them, in her
blue eyes. Miss Dorothy, at another window, goes prac-
tically over the week's housekeeping, and checks the
tradespeople's accounts. Later, when they return, Camilla goes to the piano, according to custom, but all
through the musical storm that follows, and until the
colonel perforce departs, she never quits her place, her
eyes never leave the dim starry landscape, the whispering
trees, the falling night. She is pressed by him to sing,
but refuses, still in the same listless way, and the hand
she gives him at parting is cold and lifeless. "It is good-
night, you know," he says. holding it in his close clasp
"I shall ride over to-morrow, and the day after I shall
at least have the pleasure of coming to say good-speed."

She makes no answer, and when his briefer adieus
have been made to the other two ladies, and he turns for
a last glance at her, he finds she has already gone.

Thus far the watchful Camilla has been foiled; there
have been no further meetings with lovers, in public or in
private. All next day she keeps up her system of private
espionage, but with the same result. She can obtain no
clew to Dolores' hidden thoughts, and she certainly
leaves the house to meet no one. Colonel Deering calls
according to promise, but my lady is engaged, and does
not see him. Her conduct these last two days is decorum
itself. Well, time will tell ; to-morrow at nine they start,
and Camilla, by this, has worked herself into a fever of
curiosity to know how all this is to end.

This last day is spent in packing. Lady Valentine

has no maid ; she has declined all successors to Jemima
Ann. Miss Routh kindly presses upon her the services
of Lucy ; the offer is declined with cold thanks. Still not
a sigh, a hint, a look to show whether it is to be Cornwall or not.

The last night comes—goes, and the morning is here.
An early breakfast has been prepared. At eight o'clock
Miss Routh and Miss Valentine, "booted and spurred"
for this trip, appear in the breakfast-room. One hasty
glance from Camilla's green eyes, her heart quickening
expectantly its calm beating—Dolores is not there.
"Where is Lady Valentine?" demands Miss Dorothy;
"is she not ready? Go up, Dobson, and see. Tell her
we have but just fifteen minutes for breakfast as it is.
Make haste!" Dobson goes—returns, and alone.
"Well?" Miss Dorothy demands, with asperity.

"Please, 'm," says Dobson, breathless, "my lady's
compliments, 'm, and she ain't a-goin' !"

"What !"

"Which it's a bad headache, 'm, and she ain't
hup. She says don't wait for her, if you please, 'm.
She says she ain't able to go nowheres to-day, please, 'm."

Miss Dorothy adjusts her double eye-glass more firmly
on her Roman nose, and glances sternly at Camilla Routh.
That young lady shrugs her shoulders and sips her tea,
a gleam of exultation in her cat-like eyes. "What does
this mean, Camilla?"

"You had better go and ask, Dorothy. You need not
glare at me in that blood-freezing fashion—*I* have nothing to do with it. Impossible to account for the vagaries
of our charming Dolores. Go up and see for yourself,
if you are curious. It *may* be as she says, she *may* possibly have a headache. Meantime I will finish my breakfast."

She pours herself a second cup of tea. But her hand
shakes, and her pulse beats quick and high. Not going,
after all ! Miss Dorothy, much perturbed, takes the ad-

18

vice, and marches up to the chamber of her sister-in-law
Entering, she finds Dolores in semi-darkness, and Dolores
herself, lying pale among her pillows.   Her eyes are
closed, her hands are clasped above her head, her fair
hair is tossed about—so lying she looks so wan, so worn,
so really ill, that Dorothy is startled and alarmed.

"My dear Dolores," she exclaims, "what is this?   Is
it possible you are really ill?"

The blue eyes open, and look up at her.   The dark
circles that tell of sleepless nights surround them.

"Not really ill, only out of sorts and altogether unfitted for a railway journey.   My head aches.   You will
please start without me.   It is impossible for me to go to
Cornwall to-day."

"But Vane said——"

"I know," quickly, "he could not foresee this.   Indeed
my head aches horribly ; I was awake all night.   Do not
stay for me—with a few hours' perfect quiet I shall do
very well.   There is no reason why you and Miss Routh
should disappoint him.   Do not lose your train by waiting here.   A few hours' repose, and I will be quite well
again.   Your brother will be angry if you disappoint him,
you know."

This is so true that Miss Valentine winces.   She stands
more thoroughly at a loss than ever before in her life.   To
go, or not to go, that is the question.   Which will anger
Vane most—to go to him and leave Dolores behind, or
to remain with her, and disappoint him?   His irritation
is certain either way.   While she stands irresolute,
Camilla comes fluttering gayly to the rescue.

"Ill, Lady Valentine?   So sorry.   So very inopportune.
Cousin Vane will be *so* disappointed.   Still, Dorothy, it
will not do for *us* to disappoint him as well.   His wishes
were most positive, you may remember, to go to-day without fail.   You had better not linger.   We will tell him of
Dolores' indisposition, and of course he will come for
her to-morrow.   So sorry to leave you quite alone—such

a bore for you—but it is only for one day. Come, Dorothy, we shall certainly miss our train."

"You really think, then, Camilla, that Vane would prefer us to go and leave Dolores?" asks the perplexed Dorothy. She has much faith in Camilla Routh's opinion where Vane is concerned, much faith in her influence over him.

"Certainly I do," Miss Routh responds, promptly, "I not only am sure he would prefer it, but that he will be alarmed, as well as angry, if we do not. Adieu, Dolores, *cherie*—be ready to come with Vane to-morrow. Now, Dorothy!" Her tone is sharp, she moves away impulsively, she hurries off the still doubtful, still disposed-to-linger Dorothy before there is time for further discussion. The carriage is at the door, they are in, and whirling rapidly to the station. There is time to get tickets, to take their places in the compartment, and no more. The door shuts upon them, the whistle shrieks, and they are flying along Cornwall-ward almost before Dorothy Valentine has had time to catch her bewildered breath.

"We have done wrong to leave her, Camilla," she gasps, flurried and breathless. "We might have telegraphed to Vane, and waited until to-morrow. We have done wrong. Vane will be very angry."

Miss Routh laughs—a laugh neither mirthful nor pleasant to hear. "Yes, Dorothy," she says, sweetly, "I think he will. But not with us. *We* have obeyed orders. Yes, he will be angry, and I think—I think with reason."

"Then why," demands Miss Valentine, with acerbity, "did you urge me to come? I would have stayed with her, but you said——"

"I said Vane had ordered us *not* to stay, and I said truly. We have done as commanded—he has no right or reason to find fault with us. To-morrow is but one more day—to-morrow he will return for her, and then——"

"Well—and then?" says the elder woman, struck by the strange look Camilla Routh's face wears.

"And then he will bring her to Flintbarrow—*perhaps*," answers Camilla, with her most suggestive smile. .

* * * * * * *

Dolores' excuse has been something more than a mere excuse ; her head does ache with a dull, persistent pain. But as the carriage rolls away she gets up and dresses— not in one of her pretty, much-embroidered morning robes, but in the plainest traveling suit her wardrobe contains. For she is going on a journey to-day, though not to Cornwall—a very long journey, and Manor Valentine is to know her no more. This is the end. All she can bear she has borne ; flight alone is left. Death were better than what awaits her in that desolate house down by the Cornish sea. Life by the side of Vane Valentine is at an end for all time. Outrage, insult, sneers, neglect, have been her portion from the first in this hated house—this house to which neither she nor the man who is her husband has any longer claim. To-day she quits it to return no more. She has thought it out, over and over again, during these two silent, secluded days ; no one shall know whither she goes, not even Rene —least of all Rene. He is still at the village inn, she is aware ; but she will neither see him nor write to him. She is going to her one faithful friend, Jemima Ann, waiting for the answer to her letter in her London lodgings, and with her she will return to America. What she will do when she gets there she does not yet know ; time enough for that ; at present she has but one thought, escape, before her husband comes. To-morrow night he will be here, angry, suspicious, more sullen and despotic than ever ; her escape must be secured before that time. And once away, no power on earth shall compel her to return. Come what may—death itself—she will never return to this life from which she flies.

She dresses. She packs a satchel with some needful things ; she takes the jewels given her by Madam Valentine, and money sufficient for all present needs. If these

things are not hers, they are not at least the property of
Vane Valentine. If M. Paul is their rightful owner, M.
Paul is her true and generous friend. Then she rings
for tea and toast, and makes an effort to eat. Strength
is necessary—courage, presence of mind. Hope is rising
within her. Once free, once with Jemima, once far
from this house, once across the ocean, once fairly out
of the power of her tyrant and Camilla Routh, and she
fears nothing—neither work, nor poverty, nor homeless-
ness. She will be free! Her heart beats at the
thought. A few weeks more of this life would drive
her mad.

The house is very still, in its long forenoon repose.
The servants are engaged in their various duties—the
watchful Lucy has gone with her mistress. No one
notices the quiet figure that, vailed and cloaked, with
hand-bag and shawl strap, leaves the house by a side
entrance, and disappears amid the thick growth of the
park-lane. She takes the short cut to the station, along
which Rene came, and found her the other day—there is
a London up-train at eleven-fifty. At the turn where
the path branches off and the house disappears, she
turns for a moment, aversion, hatred, strong in her face,
and looks back. It is a leaden, sunless day, threatening
rain—the gray old Manor looks grayer and more gruesome than she has ever seen it. How utterly miserable
from the very first she has been there! With a shudder
she turns away, pulls her vail over her face, and hurries
on.

She is in excellent time. She takes her ticket, and,
hidden behind her thick vail, waits. No one she knows
is at the station—the village folks have seen very little
of her during her brief reign at the Manor House.
Presently the train rushes in; she slips into an empty
carriage ; a moment more and she is speeding on her
London way—flying from Valentine—free !

CHAPTER XXXVII.

" AFTER LONG GRIEF AND PAIN."

HE close of a murky London day. Over the chimney-pots a sky of dullest drab is settling down ; from the court below the voices of women and children come up. In her room —bedroom and sitting-room in one—Jemima Ann leans out of the little window and tries to catch a breath of air, where air in this pea-soup atmosphere there is none On her knees, her folded arms on the sill, dejection in her face, she watches the matrons laden with babies in arms, comparing notes concerning the 'eat of the past day, and the tattered children at play on the flags. For she is homesick and lonely, and longing for a word of farewell from her darling ere she starts on her long return journey across the Atlantic. That answer was due two days ago, and has not yet arrived. She is sufficiently well provided with money—Dolores has ever been a generous mistress—but she feels this week must perforce bring her waiting to a close.

She so longs to get away from the sights and sounds of this great grimy city, from these innumerable strange faces, from the land that holds the one being she loves best on earth, and yet keeps her so far away. She will go home—nay, she has no home—but to New York—it will seem home to her after London—and take a new service there. If Miss Snowball would but write that good-by she so hungers to hear. All day long she has been listening for the postman's knock—listening in vain. Even the illustrated " penny dreadful " she has gone out and bought, with its four pages of thrilling narrative, has failed to interest her. And now, disappointed and discouraged, hope has left her for the day.

She does not blame her young lady—it is the doing of Sir Vane and those two cantankerous old maids. Only she feels it will go nigh to break her heart altogether if she has to leave London without a word.

The gray evening grows grayer; the leaden sky threatens speedy rain. The mothers and most of the children go indoors to supper. Boys from the nearest public-house flit about in the obscurity with pots of beer. There is a savory odor in the thick air as of toasting muffins, and fizzling sausages, tripe and onions, and other dainty dishes to go with foamy flagons of bitter beer. Jemima Ann absorbs sights, and sounds, and smells, dreamily, and opines that she will light her candle, and have a cup of tea, and another try at the illustrated penny work of light literature. The sound of wheels; of a cab drawn up at the entrance of the court fails to attract her notice; it is only the sight of a lady entering, and making her way in the dingy dusk down the court, that rouses her out of her apathy.

A lady, even in that murky light—slender and tall—who pauses to ask her way of the children. Jemima Ann hears the answer, "Up them stairs—three pair front—there she is at the window," and starts wildly to her feet. Is it—can it be possible that *this* is the answer to her letter? She dashes to the door, opens it, and encounters on the landing a slender young lady, dressed in dark gray. An oil lamp swings in the passage; its dim light falls on the face of her visitor—a very, very pale and weary face, but a face whose like, Jemima Ann rapturously thinks, the wide earth again does not hold.

"Oh, my dear, my dear, my dear Miss Snowball!" she cries out, in a transport of amaze and joy. She has her in her little room, the door shut, seated in a chair, she herself kneeling at her feet, her arms clasped about her crying, hugging, all in a breath.

"Oh! my dearest darling Miss Snowball! To think of your coming yourself all this long way, of finding out poor Jemima Ann, of traveling hundreds and hundreds of miles to say good-by to your poor girl who loves you so much."

"Dear Jemima," her young mistress says, her head drooping wearily on Jemima's shoulder, a stifled sob in her tired voice, "not good-by. I have come to stay, if you will have me, Jemima Ann."

"Miss Snowball! My sweetest Miss Snowball—to stay!"

"To stay. I have run away, Jemima. I am not going back—never, never, never more! No—do not ask me questions to-night; I am tired, so tired. I cannot talk. Give me some tea, please, if you can, and let me lie down somewhere and rest. To-morrow I will tell you everything." Utter weariness, heart-stricken pain, are in her voice. Jemima Ann starts up, full of concern and repentance. In a moment the candle is lit, and she is removing her young lady's hat and mantle. Now she sees how thin she has grown, how pale, how worn—a very shadow of the brightly beautiful "Miss Snowball" of hardly a year ago.

"Oh, my poor dear," she murmurs, tears rising to her eyes, as she kisses Dolores' listless hand. "What a hard hard time you must have had."

"Yes, hard—heart-breaking," Dolores answers in the same spiritless way, "but I am only tired out now, Jemima, for all that is over—over forever; I am here with you, and we will part no more my one true and loving friend."

She drops her head against the side of the upright wooden chair, and rests so, with closed eyes, pallid, spent. Full of a great compassion, Jemima bustles about, upstairs and down, brings tea, sets the table, goes out and returns with a crusty loaf, a pat of fresh butter, watercress, and a cold roast fowl. These refreshments she arranges in the old deft, neat way, and then gently summons her beloved guest. In her hard, stiff-backed chair, Lady Valentine is half asleep, thoroughly fatigued and worn out. The little supper looks tempting, and she is hungry, and eats with a relish she has not felt for weeks. She is free—her Bastile is left behind—that is the thought that gives zest to the viands. After supper, refreshed and invigorated, she is ready for a talk, but Jemima, with gentle insistance, puts it off until to-morrow.

"There is plenty of time, Miss Snowball; I am in no hurry to go now that you are here; to-morrow will be time enough. Have a good sleep to-night, and tell me all about it after breakfast. Mine is a harder bed than you are used to, but it is as clean as clean, and after ten there is no quieter or respectabler court in London than this. So undress and lie down. You do look just fit to drop."

Dolores obeys passively. She is completely wearied with her journey, and she slept none last night. She lies down on the little hard, clean bed, and holds out her hands, like a child, to her faithful attendant.

"Dear Jemima," she says, "what would I do without you? Kiss me good-night."

"My own, own darling Miss Snowball!"

Jemima says "Oh!" under her breath, watching the sweet, wan face, the tired blue eyes slowly closing, "to think there should be a man in the world hard and cruel to you! But Sir Vane Valentine is not a man—he is a brute!"

And thus the answer to Jemima's letter comes.

Next day dawns foggy and raw. The rain is pattering on the window-panes, when, quite late, Dolores opens her eyes on this mortal life in the "three pair front." Outside there is wind, and wet, and mud, and fog; inside, a brisk little fire blazes in the grate—a glow of hospitable warmth, and welcome, and sunshine, in itself—an aromatic odor of coffee perfumes the air, hot rolls are on the table, and her clothes, all brushed and fresh, lie on a chair beside her. No one is in the room, as she gets up, half-bewildered at first by the strangeness of it all, but

wonderfully strengthened by her long sleep, and proceeds
to dress. She has nearly finished when Jemima enters,
rosy with rain and rapid walking, laden with eggs, and
marmalade, and cool, pink radishes.

"Now, now, Jemima," Dolores remonstrates, laughing, the matutinal greeting over, "this will never do.
What sort of a gourmand do you take me for, that you
must run out in the rain like this in search of delicacies?
I shall need no tempting after this, remember—my appetite has not been left behind at Manor Valentine. And
you are not to waste your substance in riotous living for
me. We are going to get on plainly and economically,
you know, and save our money and return to dear New
York as soon as may be. And I shall wait upon myself
after this—we are friends from henceforth, recollect,
friends and equals—no more mistress and maid. I shall
never be any one's mistress as long as I live again. 'My
lady' is dead and buried down there in the dreariness of
Valentine. *This* is Snowball—your friend—who has no
friend in the world to whom she can turn but you, dear
old Jim!"

Jemima Ann laughs gleefully. To see her darling
with the old brightness in her face, the old blitheness in
her tones, to know she is to part from her no more—it is
bliss—she asks no more of fate.

They breakfast well and leisurely. Over the coffee
and rolls Dolores tells her story—all of her story at least
that she can, or may ever, bring herself to reveal. There
are things she will never be able to think of, much less
speak of, without a pang of the old bitterness and cruel
pain. Jemima listens—lost in a medley of wrath and
pity, and anger and love. Dearest dear Miss Snowball!
that brute Sir Vane! green-eyed cat, Miss Routh! that
sour old Tartar, Miss Valentine! Ah! it is a blessed
escape to have cut the cord, and got away from that dismal old house.

Miss Snowball has done right—of course she has done

right. What ! go and be buried alive in a drearier dungeon even than Manor Valentine, with Sir Vane for her jailer, and Miss Routh exulting and triumphant ! Better poverty, better hard work, better the worst that life can bring than such death in life as that.

They sit together through the long, dull rainy day, and discuss their plans. It will not do to depart at once —they are safer, hidden away here, in this obscure nook of the great city, than in seeking further flight. Sir Vane will search for his wife, will leave no stone unturned in his efforts to trace her. He will move the whole detective force, and spend his beloved money lavishly to capture her if he can. If he can ! Dolores' eyes flash, her hands clench at the thought.

"I will die first !" she cries, and she means it. Death holds no terror so great as the terror of returning to that horrible life. "I will never go back !" she exclaims ; "he may do what he likes. The law that takes the part of the husband always against the wife, may do its utmost. I will bear all things, but I will never go back."

They decide, therefore, that for the present masterly inactivity will be savest. After an interval of a month or so, under assumed names and more or less disguised, they may go to Liverpool, or cross to Havre, and take passage for New York. Once there life will begin anew, a life of labor and much privation, no doubt, of loneliness and discomfort very likely, but they will be together and free. That is everything after the life of the past year. Work ! Work is nothing, Dolores thinks, with eagerly flashing eyes ; she is young, she is strong, she is full of confidence in herself, her tastes are simple, her wants few. In New York, and together, they will be quite, quite happy again. If only the good time were nearer, and they were on their way.

"Some people are born to be obscure, and some have obscurity thrust upon them," she says, laughingly, to Jemima. "I am of the former. The happiest time of my life was on Dree Island, in a Holland frock, helping Ma'am Weesy to shell peas and toast the bread, and digging for clams, and scouring Bay Chalette in a batteau with the boys. What a lifetime ago all that seems now. To go back and live in the little white cottage, with the solitude of the little white cottage shutting us in, and all this big, turbulent, troublesome world shut out, listening to old Tim croak and Weesy scold, with you to chatter to, and Inno Desereaux and Pere Louis, my only visitors. Oh, *that* would be a foretaste of heaven!"

> " Where I am the great and noble
> Tell me of renown and fame,
> And the red wine sparkles highest
> To do honor to my name.
> Far away a place is vacant
> By an humble hearth for me,
> Far away where tears are falling
> There I fain would be."

She sings the words under her breath, then sighs impatiently, and get up, pushing back all the soft rings of fair hair, and walks up and down, a lofty, slender, gray-clad figure, in the narrow, dingy room.

"If one could forget! If I could but shut out the last horrible year, with all its hateful remembrances, its bitter · humiliations, its heart-burnings, its shame, its insults. But I will carry it with me always, a plague-spot in my life, down to its very end. And though I have snapped my chain, I shall carry my half clanking with me to my grave. What latent possibilities of evil lie undreamed of within us. I am afraid of myself when I think what a few months more of that life might have made me. I don't wonder women go wrong so often through sheer desperation. I have felt the capability within myself. Thank God! all these evil thoughts of hatred and vengeance have been left behind. I am conscious of nothing now but an unutterable longing to be out of England. Go where I may, endure what I will, I can never suffer again as I have suffered here."

And now the days of waiting begin—weary days, when they sit in the dull little three-pair front, and never stir out except in the very early dawn, when only the milkmen and market people are abroad. Under assumed names and characters, keeping always aloof from the matrons and maids of the crowded court, yet finding their best security in that very crowding, the long summer days drag themselves out one by one. No one disturbs them, no suspicion follows them, that they can see. Hope buoys them up, and enables them to bear the depressing confinement without much harm to health. Only at intervals profound depression, deadly apathy, passionate regret for her wrecked life, lay their hold upon Dolores, and for the time she sinks and droops. What is there left worth living for? She is a slave who has escaped, but a slave her whole life long none the less, and liable to capture any day. She is Vane Valentine's wife—no power on earth can alter that. Life or death—what do they matter? All that makes life best worth living—love—has gone forever. She grows hollow-eyed, silent, wan; she fades away before Jemima's affrighted eyes like a shadow. These moods do not last, of course; the natural vigor and elasticity of blessed youth reassert themselves. The days, weeks of waiting drag themselves out; the time approaches for their second flight, and the excitement rouses Dolores to new life and hope.

Early one morning they take the Havre steamer, thinking this route safest, and cross to France in safety. By the first steamer that leaves that port they take passage to New York. No one pursues them; nothing happens. They shut themselves up in their cabin, and watch with glad eyes the receding land, the leaping waves of the wild ocean, that is to sever them for all time from Vane Valentine. "And now, my own sweet Miss Snowball," cries Jemima Ann, clapping her hands gleefully, "we are free, and off at last, and all the world is before us to seek our fortunes, like the princesses in a fairy tale ! And good-by to Sir Vane Valentine and his Cornwall prison, and his two sour old maids, forever and ever !"

But *we* cannot quite say good-by to Sir Vane Valentine, after Jemima Ann's summary fashion. On the evening of the day of my lady's flight, Sir Vane comes up from Cornwall, black with disappointment, and fiercely angry with his wife for her unexpected defection. That she would dare refuse to come at the last moment, he has never for an instant thought, and in her sudden and violent headache he has no faith. No idea has ever entered *his* mind that she has chanced to overhear his interesting little plot in the park. He has been disposed to vent his wrath on Miss Dorothy and Miss Routh for coming without her, but Miss Routh has a way of putting him down that never fails. Drawing her small figure up to its tallest, looking him full in the fiery black eyes with her coolly gleaming green ones for a full minute in silence, he is cowed and mesmerized into sullen silence before she speaks a word.

"Be good enough to reserve your abuse for your wife—when you see her, Sir Vane Valentine," she says, haughtily, "we do not deserve it, and decline to take it. We have obeyed your orders, and are here. There is a return train at six, I am told ; we can go by that, if you like."

But the baronet does not like. He mutters a sulky apology, and will go back for his wife himself instead. He takes the train ; "nursing his wrath to keep it warm," and reaches the Manor House in the cool of the evening. He finds the servants gathered out of doors, enjoying the fresh beauty of a very fine moonrise. They disperse precipitately at the first sight of his scowling face, at the first harsh sound of his imperious voice. Where is my lady ? He wishes to see her at once. Let her be told he is here, and waiting for her in the drawing-room. They look at one another a moment in startled silence. Then Watkins, the oldest and most confidential servant there, advances.

"If you please, Sir Vane," rather tremulously, "my lady is—is not here."

"Not here!" with a start and a stare, "where then is she?"

"Sir Vane, we think she has gone. Almost as soon as Miss Valentine and Miss Routh left this morning, she dressed and left the 'ouse. None of us saw her go, but we missed her at luncheon time, and a couple of hours ago——"

"Well?" he says, blankly ; "well?"

"A couple of hours ago I was down at the station, if you please, Sir Vane, and I heard there——" another nervous pause, and a furious stamp from Sir Vane.

"Go on, you staring fool !" he cries out.

"I heard there," said Mr. Watkins, turning red and defiant, "that my lady had taken a ticket for London, and left by the arf after ten express. And there is a letter for you, Sir Vane, in my lady's dressing-room."

"Bring it here," he says, "and go."

He stands dazed—stunned—his fierce temper quieted by the very force and unexpectedness of this crushing blow. Run away, he thinks, blankly. He has never thought of that. Watkins brings him the letter—yes, it is in her hand. He tears it open and reads :

"I hope to have left Valentine forever, hours before you receive this. Search for me if you will—find me if you can, but no power on earth shall compel me to return to the life I now leave—life with you. Leave me in peace to work my own way, and hidden from all who have ever known me, I will trouble you no more. Let me be dead to you who hate me, as I shall be to the few friends who still care for me—I ask for no more than that. Hunt me down, and it shall be at your peril. I

will throw myself on the protection of George Valentine, and proclaim to the world with him that you hold
illegally his title and estate.   DOLORES."

He stands with the letter in his hand—silent, overwhelmed by this blow, this total overthrow of all his
plans—filled with fury and disappointment. Fled—escaped! She has suspected then, has perhaps overheard.
He reads the letter again and again. If he leaves her in
peace her lips are sealed; if he seeks her out she will
claim the friendship of the man he hates—ay, and fears.
He does not for a moment doubt what she says here, he
knows that she is true as truth itself. But what of her
lover in the village—is he in ignorance of her flight too?
He puts on his hat and goes straight to the Ratherripe
Arms. There, standing on the threshold, enjoying the
starry beauty of the night, Rene Macdonald stands—as
he is convinced he would *not* stand if he knew of to-
day's work. He passes by without entering, and walks
moodily back to the Manor. Here further confirmation
meets him in the shape of a note, brought by a boy from
the village, in his absence. It is addressed to Lady Valentine. He opens it at once; it begins abruptly:

"DOLORES—I have had a letter to-day from George
Valentine, summoning me to London, where he awaits
me. Can I not see you for one moment before I go, if
only to say good-by?   RENE."

"The boy is waiting, if you please, Sir Vane," the
servant says who delivers it; "there is an answer, he
says."

"Tell him Lady Valentine left for Cornwall this
morning, and that you do not know when she will be
back," responds Sir Vane.

The answer is delivered, and the boy goes.

That night Sir Vane spends perforce at the Manor;

next morning he takes the earliest train for London, and his first action is to drive straight to Scotland Yard and set a clever detective on the track of his runaway wife.

"I'll find you, my lady, if skill and money can do it." he says, with a vicious snap of his white teeth, "and I'll take the consequences, and, by ——, so shall you !"

That same early train bears away another passenger, the dark, foreign-looking young artist who has been stopping for the past week at the village inn. The two men meet, and eye each other in no very friendly fashion at the station. No greetings are exchanged ; they are enemies to the death, and they read it in each other's glance. Rene Macdonald turns away, a chill sensation of repulsion filling him, and thinks, with a shudder of pity and love, what Dolores' life must be like beside this man. Her pale, pathetic young face, so worn, so altered, rises before him as he saw it that evening in the park.

"And I am powerless to help her," he despairingly thinks. "I would give my life to save her from one sorrow, and I must stand aside and yield her up to be tortured to death by this sullen scoundrel. Oh, my darling ! my little love ! if only the past could be undone what power on earth should be strong enough to force me to yield you up to Vane Valentine ?"

And so, with the falling night of Dolores' first day in London, the train that comes thundering in through the dismal twilight disgorges among its crowd of passengers the man who hates and the man who loves her. At the moment her thoughts are with both—with fear for one, with longing for the other—as she drearily sits at the window of Jemima's dingy little lodging, watching, with blue, melancholy eyes, the ceaselessly-falling rain.

CHAPTER XXXVIII.

"FOR SAD TIMES, AND GLAD TIMES, AND ALL TIMES PASS OVER."

T is the afternoon of a wild and tempestuous winter day—a day for glowing coal fires, and drawn curtains, and easy chairs, and cozy ingle nooks. Long lines of sleet lash the windows sharply as steel, the wind whistles shrilly down the streets, half beating the breath out of the unwary, and goes whooping through the streets of New York like a March wind gone mad. Shutters bang, loose casements rattle, ancient tenements totter before the face of the blast. Few are abroad—the pavements are brittle and slippery as glass, street lamps twinkle gustily athwart the sleet and wind. Stores are closing early— only the lager-bier saloon at the corner, with it's dazzling display of gas, looks brisk and cheerful, and seems to drive a thriving trade.

"And I hope to goodness gracious she'll take a stage down town, and not get her death trying to save ten cents," murmurs a watcher, flattening her nose anxiously against a window-pane ; " it's an awful afternoon."

It is. The wind sweeps by with a whoop and a howl as she says it, a fresh dash of sleety rain beats noisily against the panes. The watcher leaves the window, and gives an admonitory poke to an already brilliant coal fire, another touch here and there to a trimly-set table, places the small cane rocker more geometrically straight in the center of the hearth-rug, and turns the lamp up yet a trifle higher, for it is nearly dark at five o'clock. It is a comfortable little room, with a warm-looking red carpet, some cane chairs, white curtains, a piano in a corner, a litter of books and magazines, and a pile of

needlework in a basket. It is an apartment big enough
for two, for three, perhaps fitting tightly—no more. But
as only two persons are ever in it, this is hardly an
objection. "And less coal does to warm it," says,
sagely, Jemima Ann. It is Jemima Ann who moves
about now, in a flutter of nervous unrest, waiting for
her young lady, who has not yet returned from her day's
work. And no queen recently come into her kingdom
was ever prouder of that dominion than is Jemima Ann
of this furnished "floor through" in the third story of a
third-rate New York house, in a very third-rate street.
For it is their own, their very own, and they are
together, and happy, and free, and she helps to keep it—
is not only sole housekeeper and manager, but also part
bread-winner. That pile of white plain sewing there
in the basket is hers, thrown down while she gets
tea. And hard and trying times have come and gone
ere they found themselves safely moored in this small
haven of rest.

They have been adrift for weary months in New York
city before fortune steered them here, and into safe and
pleasant work. True, they have never known want, nor
anything approaching to it, but suspicious eyes have
looked at them, insolent voices have spoken to them;
they have been unprotected, and lonely, and full of fear.
But all that is past, and hardly to be regretted now, as
they look back. It was one phase of life, imagined before,
but never seen; it is over, and not likely to return.

Eight months have gone since they left Havre—
nearly ten since Lady Valentine fled from her husband—
and in all that time she has heard little of the life and the
people left behind.

"What be you a-goin' to call yourself when we get to
New York?" said to her, one day on shipboard, Jemima
Ann.

"Call myself?" Dolores says, vaguely, looking up
from the book she is reading.

"What name will you go by? Not Lady Valentine,
I hope," says Jemima, laughing. "No one will believe
that."

"Lady Valentine! No," Dolores says, with a shudder; "I hate that name. No. Let me see. I might take
yours, only Hopkins is *not* pretty. Let me think." She
looks at Jemima half smiling. "Suppose I go back to the
old name I had as a child—Trillon? It will do as well
as any. How many I seem to have borne in my time.
Yes; the name by which you knew me first, my Jemima,
you shall call me by again. I am, from the hour we land,
Mrs. Trillon."

The sea voyage does her a world of good. Depression,
melancholia, drop from her as a garment; she brightens
in spirits, gains in health and strength, looks like her
own blooming self once more. The relief is so unutterable of this almost accomplished escape. For now that
the Atlantic flows between them, she fears Vane Valentine no longer. To discover her in New York will be a
difficult task, even for him; to force her to return to him,
an impossibility. And she is scarcely more than twenty
years old—and life so easily puts on its most radiant face
when one is free, and twenty years old! They land, and
try boarding at first—Mrs. Trillon, and her friend, Miss
Hopkins—there is to be no more the distinction of mistress and maid. They find a boarding-house, and, after
a few days' delay, begin to look about them for work.
Both are failures. Life in a noisy, gossiping second-rate
boarding-house is not to be endured; a month of it is as
much as Dolores can bear. Neither is work to be had
for the asking; they are not adapted, these two, to many
kinds of work.

"Let us try housekeeping, Jemima Ann," suggests
Mrs. Trillon, looking up one day from the big daily, whose
page of advertisements she is poring over with knitted
brows. "Here are no end of furnished apartments for
'light housekeeping.' Let us try light housekeeping

Jemima Ann. I fancy it will cost us no more than we are paying here, and it will certainly be more private and more clean."

Jemima Ann hails the happy thought; she puts on her bonnet and sallies forth in the quest. But New York is a large city, advertisements are deceptive, and land-ladies sour.

Another week goes by, much shoe-leather is worn, many door-bells are rung, and many, many weary stairs mounted before anything is found suitable to limited means and rather fastidious tastes. Then references are demanded, and references they have none. At last the tiniest of all tiny French flats is discovered—a minute parlor, two dimly-lit closets, called bedrooms, a micro-scopic kitchen, and dining-room—all neat and clean, and at a high price, but within their united means. Best of all, the janitress—a pleasant-faced matron—consents to take her month's rent in advance and waive references. She likes the looks of her, she smilingly tells Jemima Ann. Here they come early in September, and here they have been ever since. They find it agreeable enough at first ; it is like playing at housekeeping in a doll's house Jemima Ann cooks the most delicious little dishes, and proves herself a very jewel of a housekeeper. Lady Val-entine is charmed with everything—the dots of rooms, the wonderful little kitchen range, that seems hardly too large to be put in her pocket—the absolutely new life that begins for her. Even the street is not without a charm of its own—a dusty, stuffy street enough, with a commingled odor of adjacent breweries and stables hang-ing about it, a sidewalk noisy with children all the day long, a favorite haunt of organ-grinders, with weary ma-trons holding babies, and sitting on door-steps in the cool and silent eventide. The charm is surely in nothing but its entire novelty, but Dolores likes to sit behind the Nottingham lace curtains of the little parlor, and take it all in. Life in this phase she has never seen before, and

she is among them, if not of them, for all time now. But
still work comes not, and work they soon must find.
Their united hoard, increased by the sale of Dolores'
jewels, is melting away—let Jemima Ann cater never so
cautiously. Their rooms are secured for this month at
least, before it ends work *must* be found. Winter is approaching, and " winter is no man's friend."

"We must keep together, come what may," says
Dolores, decidedly, "*that* at least is as fixed as fate. Work
or no work, part we shall not, my Jemima."

"No, my pretty, I hope and pray not."

"Let me see," says " Mrs. Trillon," tapping her pretty
chin with her pencil, that reflective frown, so often there
now, knitting her brows, " my work must be teaching if
I can get it. I can teach music, vocal and instrumental
—that is my one strong point. French, of course, German after a fashion, and I could give lessons in crayon
and pencil drawing, and water colors. Embroidery, too,
ef every kind, we were thoroughly drilled in at *Villa des
Anges.*" Here her gravity suddenly gives way over the
list of her accomplishments, and her joyous young laugh
rings out. " It sounds ridiculous, doesn't it, cataloguing
my wonderful ·talents after this fashion. I ought to
make out a list of terms for to-morrow's *Herald*, and
inform the public that the highest bidder can have me
cheap. Heigho ! one laughs, but it is no joke after all.
I *will* advertise, Jemima Ann, and try my fortune twice."

She does ; after a score or more attempts an advertisement is drawn up. It is a repugnant task, this cold-
blooded chronicling of, what she can do ; it sounds boast-
ful and blatant, read over. One is written at last, that
Jemima Ann pronounces perfection, and which Mrs.
Trillon finds the best she can do—and it is sealed up in
an envelope, and dropped; before Jemima seeks her vestal
couch in the nearest letter-box.

There follows an interval which Jemima Ann em-
ploys in looking out for work for herself. Dolores tries

to dissuade her. "If I get a situation as governess," she says, "it will suffice for us both. Your work will be to keep this little house bright and cozy."

But Jemima is as resolute when she likes as her young mistress. "No, Miss Snowball," she says earnestly, "that would never satisfy me. I must do something for my keep—sewing if I can get it—as well as you. I will have plenty of time for the housekeeping. There ain't no kind of plain sewing I ain't up to, I guess, and Mis' Scudder, our landlady, has took a kind o' fancy to me from the first, and she reckons she can get me something to do, pretty soon."

Mrs. Scudder proves to be as good as her word. She gets Jemima Ann "slop" shirt making, and plenty of it; coarse work, and wearily unremunerative prices, but still a help; and from thenceforth Jemima is as busy as a bee and as happy as a queen.

But Dolores' ambitious advertisement seems as bread cast upon the waters. Many days elapse and it does not return. Answers there are, and terms are stated, and applications are personally made; but, somehow, nothing comes of these negotiations; the reference question stands in the way again. Pretty young widows, highly accomplished, without references, are not desirable preceptresses for innocent youth, and a fair, sweet face, and gentle, graceful manners, fail to compensate.

At last, in November, when blank despair is coming upon her, one impulsive lady falls in love at sight with her pathetic pale face and great wistful blue eyes and low, sweet-toned voice, and braves fate and references, and engages her as French and music teacher to her two boys on the spot. Even without a reference she can do no particular harm to Willy and Freddie, aged ten and twelve. She is closely watched for a little, and is found to be a painstaking teacher, even more gentle and winning than she looks.

"Nothing succeeds like success." Her first employer

speaks of her pretty paragon to her friends, and speedily three other engagements follow. And now, all day long, behold Dolores, draped in waterproof and vail, a roll of music in her hand, fully established as a "trotting governess," and adding dollars and dollars monthly to their humble *menage*.

About Christmas she is engaged as finishing governess to Miss Blanche Pettingill, sole daughter of the house and heart of Peter Pettingill, Esquire, of Lexington avenue, millionaire and woolen manufacturer, the wife of whose bosom literally hangs herself with diamonds, and blazes with them at her big parties up in the brown-stone palace in this one of New York's stateliest avenues. There is a villa at Newport, a homestead up the Hudson, a winter place in Florida, and the enchanted princess who is to have all this one day is nineteen years old, and rather an ignoramus than otherwise, and has suddenly wakened up to that fact, and made up her mind to atone for lost time by studying under the pretty, and gentle, and obscure Madame Trillon.

"Pa says he would give ten thousand dollars to have me able to play, and sing, and talk French as you do, Mrs. Trillon," says the princess, with a despairing sigh ; "I wish to goodness he'd have thought of it half a dozen years ago. He has been so busy making money ever since I can remember, and ma's been so busy spending it, that they neither of them had time to attend to my education, and here I am an heiress and everything, and hardly an accomplishment about me. And when a person is nineteen, and in society, studying languages, and doing pianoforte drudgery, is no end of a bore."

Mrs. Trillon sympathizes, does her best, and spends three hours daily in the Lexington avenue mansion, secluded in Miss Blanche's boudoir. For it is to be a profound secret from all the world that this polishing is being given to Miss Blanche.

"That is what I like Mrs. Trillon for," remarks Miss

Pettingill to Mrs. Pettingill, "she knows how to hold her tongue. And yet she is sympathetic, you can see she appreciates the situation, and is trying to do her very best for me. And she has the most elegant and aristocratic manners. I only wish I could ever be like her."

"Mrs. Trillon is a person, I guess, who has seen better days," responds mamma.

"I should rather think so," Miss Blanche cries, energetically. "She plays and sings perfectly splendid, and talks French like a native. She never speaks of herself, but I know she must have a story, and a romantic one, if a person could only get at it. But I never can ask questions of Mrs. Trillon."

It is at the Pettingill mansion that Dolores is this wild and blustery March afternoon, while Jemima Ann stirs the fire and looks expectantly out of the window, and waits for her coming home. It is late when she comes, neither wet nor weary from the howling storm, but all laughing, and with cheeks and eyes bright with the frosty wind.

"Oh, my own dear," cries Jemima, "you are half dead, I know. I do hope you rode down town in the stage."

"No, I didn't," returns Dolores, laughing. "I rode, but not in the stage. They sent me in the carriage; Miss Pettingill would have it so. They are really the best-natured people in the world. They wished me to stay all night, and as I would not, insisted on the carriage. Is supper ready? for I am hungry, although I had tea and cakes at five o'clock. It must be nearly nine now."

"Jest twenty minutes to," says Jemima, bustling about. "Take off your things, my deary, and sit here in the rocker and warm your feet. Supper's all ready, and it will be on the table in ten minutes."

"How cozy it is here," Dolores says, with a delicious sense of rest well earned, and of the long evening to come, with two or three new magazines to speed its flight. "What a dear little home we have, and what a queen of

19

housekeepers is my Jemima Ann. It is very splendid up
there in the Pettingill palace, but I really do not think I
would care to exchange. I like our duodecimo edition
of housekeeping best."

Supper is served—two or three delicate little dishes,
and tea brewed to the point of perfection. Outside, the
whistling and lashing of the March night accents the
sense of comfort and warmth.

"There is to be a prodigious party up at the Pettingill's next week," says Dolores, as they sit and discuss
their repast. "Quite a mammoth gathering of the plutoc-
racy of New York, and I am to. go and play the accompaniments of Blanche's songs. She has not much courage
about performing in 'public, although she really has a
very nice voice, and absolutely insists that I shall play
the accompaniments. I do not like it, but I cannot refuse, they are so extremely nice to me, and Blanche is
such a dear, simple-minded, good-natured little soul.
The piano is to be placed in a sort of bower of tall flowering plants, and I shall be pretty well screened from the
company. I must get a dress for the auspicious occasion
—white trimmed with black, I suppose, and jet ornaments, to keep up my character of a widow in half
mourning. I find the whole thing rather a bore, but I
cannot disappoint Miss Pettingill."

So, in the lamp-lit, fire-lit little parlor they sit
together and chat over the doings of the day. These
evening home-comings are delightful to both—Dolores
snugly ensconced in the rocker, Jemima with her sewing
at the table. There is talk, and music—and the shrill
beating of rain and sleet without, and perfect peace,
monotonous perhaps, but very grateful, within.

"If it will only last," Dolores says, looking dreamily
into the fire ; "at times it seems almost too good.
Peace is the best thing in all the world, Jemima Ann—
better than love, with its fever, better than wealth, with
its cares. If it will only last !"

  *   *   *   *   *   *

It is the night of the great ball up on Lexington avenue. The big brown corner house is all a-glitter with gas, a lengthy row of carriages wind down the stately street, a little crowd has gathered to see the guests go in, music resounds. Mrs. Pettingill, all alight with those famous diamonds, like an Indian idol, receives her friends. Miss Blanche, in a wonderful dress from Paris, stands near, looking flushed and nervous, and wishing, more than ever before, pa's wealth could buy for her Mrs. Trillon's beautiful, gracious, graceful manners. Mrs. Trillon is up-stairs in the boudoir, where, by her own desire, she is to be left until summoned for those songs. Miss Pettingill has had but one flurried moment with her.

"It will be even worse than I thought," she exclaims, in a panic of nervous apprehension, "there is an Englishman coming, somebody very great, a nobleman, I believe, and I wish he was safely back in his own country. He is coming with the Colbarts—he is their guest while in New York. It was bad enough before, goodness knows; it will be dreadful—*dreadful* to have to sing before him."

Dolores laughs.

"I really do not see why. Let us hope the nobleman is no musical critic. What is his name?"

"There is ma calling," cries excitable Miss Pettingill. "I wish—I wish ma wouldn't insist upon my singing, but she does, and I know—I feel I shall break down and disgrace myself forever."

She flies away, and Dolores settles for a quiet hour or two over a new book. The swelling music floats up to her, sounds of laughter and gay voices reach her now and then, but the story she reads absorbs her presently, and when at last the message comes that it is time to go down, she starts up, surprised to find it so late.

"And you need not go through the crowded room," says Miss Pettingill's maid, who comes for her, "although," with an honest admiring glance at the crisp new dress and ornaments, the golden curled hair and flower face, "there is not a lady down there that looks prettier than you, Mrs. Trillon. I can take you right to the piano without passing among the people at all."

"Yes," Mrs. Trillon says, "that will be best."

They go, and manage to make their way almost unnoticed to where the big Steinway stands. Tall shrubs, and a very bower of ferns and lofty plants, almost completely screen the instrument and the performer. Blanche comes up in a flutter of apprehension and nervousness.

From where she sits Dolores can see far down the dazzling vista of light, and flowers, and thronged rooms, herself invisible.

"Courage!" she whispers, brightly; "imagine we are alone, and it is our daily music lesson."

She strikes the first chords of the symphony, and Miss Blanche bursts into song.

A little group follows the heiress and listens to her song. Dolores glances through her verdant bower as she plays, thinking of other nights and scenes like this in far-off lands, when *she* was queen of the revels. Of that other ball that seems so far off now, at Lady Ratherripe's, where Colonel Deering was her devoted slave, and she came upon that never-to-be-forgotten scene between her husband and Camilla Routh. A chill, creeping feeling makes her shiver in the perfumed warmth as she recalls it; some of the shame, the pain, the anger, the hunted feeling of that night returns to her.

And yet it is as a dream now—a bad dream, that is over and gone. *That* life is at an end forever. There is no longer a Dolores, Lady Valentine—only a Mrs. Trillon, who teaches for a salary, and walks the New York streets in shabby dresses, and lives in a poky five-roomed flat, and plays Miss Blanche Pettingill's accompaniments for so much per night. That life has come and gone like a dream, and she is quite content—or tries hard to think she is—to let life go on indifferently like this.

The song ends, and with no disastrous breakdown. There is a soft murmur of thanks and pleasure, and Blanche breathes again. But the respite is only for a moment.

"Here is——"

Dolores does not catch the name, lost in the last vibrating chords she strikes, but a flutter goes all at once through the little circle behind her.

"Oh!" cries Blanche, with a gasp of very real horror, "it is the Englishman and ma! Now I *know* she will make me sing again!"

Dolores half laughs at the anguish of the tone, the tragic terror of the look, and peeps with considerable curiosity through her leafy screen. She sees coming down the long, brilliant room Mrs. Pettingill, in her diamonds and moire antique, on the arm of a tall, dark gentleman, who does not look in the least like an Englishman. And as she looks the room spins round, the gas-lights flash out and blind her, a mist comes before her eyes, her heart absolutely stops beating.

For the man on whose arm Mrs. Pettingill leans, the English "nobleman" coming straight to where she sits, is—Sir Vane Valentine!

CHAPTER XXXIX.

"FOR TIME AT LAST MAKES ALL THINGS EVEN."

HE sits for one dizzy moment, stunned, bewil-dered, motionless. Her husband!—and here. —drawing nearer, his head a little bent, lis-tening to what his hostess is saying, with something of a bored look in his sallow, dissatisfied face.

She holds her breath, and sits gazing, held by some·
thing of that subtle, horrible fascination with which a
serpent holds its quivering victim. They are already
within five yards of her; a second or two and they will
be face to face!

And then—what will he do then? He hates a scene—
will he make one before all these people? As she thinks,
her brain whirling, some one meets them, and Mrs. Pettingill pauses for a moment to introduce the some one
to the lion of the night.

, And then, like a flash, Dolores awakes from her
stunned torpor. He has not seen her; it is not yet too
late; no one is looking at her; Blanche is watching, in
a flutter of apprehension, the approach of ma and her
nobleman.

She starts to her feet, slips between the tall plants, flies
out of the room, down a long hall, up the stairs, and into
the room she so lately left. Her hat and mantle lie
where she threw them upon entering; she snatches them
up, breathlessly, and puts them on. No time to stop, no
time to think, no time to falter or hesitate. Flight!—
that is her one idea; to get away from this house—from
him—without a second's loss of time. A sickening fear
of him fills her—a blind, unreasoning fear, that bids her
fly and heed no consequences. A clock on the mantel
strikes two. It is an unearthly hour to be out alone in
the streets of New York; but she never heeds that—
nothing that can befall her can be as terrible as meeting
Vane Valentine.

With the thought in her mind, she is down the stairs,
and out of the house, and hurrying rapidly down the
silent street. It is moonlight, bright and cold. There is
no wind, and the cold, keen air she does not feel. If it
were blowing a hurricane she would not feel it now.
She is filled with but one idea—to get home, to hide herself, to fly to the uttermost ends of the earth, if need be,
from this man. Of course he is here in search of her

Will her sudden disappearance to-night create comment, and come to his ears ?—quick and suspicious ears always. Will he ask questions, and get a description of her, and recognize her at once ? Will he set the city detectives on her track, and hunt her down ? It will not be difficult —an assumed name is but a thin disguise. And when he has found her, what then ?

" I will die before I return to him," she says aloud, as she flies breathlessly on. " No law, no power on earth shall compel me ; I will never go back—never !" She is panting and breathless with her haste ; once or twice a passing " guardian of the night " tries to stop and accost her, but she is past like a flash before he can frame the words. She may be pursued—she does not know—they will be fleet walkers who will overtake her to-night. At last, without harm or molestation, but spent, gasping, fainting with fatigue, she unlocks her door, and drops in a heap on the little parlor sofa.

Jemima Ann is in bed and asleep ; she is not expected back until to-morrow. She does not wake her, she lies there in a sort of stupor of exhaustion, and at last drops asleep. And so, still sleeping, when with the morning sunshine Jemima Ann rises, she finds her—dressed as she came in, with the exception of her hat, which lies on the floor beside her. Her exclamation of surprise and alarm, faint though it is, arouses Dolores—she sits up in a bewildered way, and looks with wild eyes at her friend.

" Jemima," she cries, " he has come."

" Lor !" says Jemima Ann, and sits down flat. She needs no antecedent to the pronoun ; there is but one *he* for these two in the universe—their arch enemy. "Lord's sake ! Miss Snowball, you never mean that !"

" I saw him last night. He was at Mrs. Pettingill's party. I got up and fled. I ran out of the house at two in the morning, and never stopped to draw breath, it

seems to me, until I fell down here. Jemima—oh
Jemima ! *what* shall we do ?"

" Lord sake !" exclaims Jemima Ann again, stunned.
Maid and mistress sit gazing blankly and fearfully at
each other—altogether stupefied by the magnitude of the
blow.

" We must leave here, Jemima—we must go to-day.
He is here to search for me ; he will never rest until he
finds me. We must fly again. And we have been so
happy here," she says, despairingly.

But Jemima's wits are beginning to return.

" Wait a minute, Miss Snowball," she says ; "let us
think. It's of no use flying—this big city is the safest
place we can hide in, it seems to me. If he finds us out
under false names here, in a crowded part of the town
like this, why, he will find us go where we may. I don't
believe in flying ; it ain't a mite o' good. Let us just
stay here, and face it out."

" Jemima Ann, it would kill me to see him, I think—
just that."

" Bless you, my deary, no, it wouldn't. It takes a
sight more to kill us than we reckon for. Besides, you
can refuse to see him—you can fly, you know, when it
comes to that. What is he goin' to do to you ? Sir Vane
Valentine may go to grass ! This is a free country, I
guess ; there ain't no lor as ever I heerd on to make a
wife go back to a husband as ill-treated her, if she's a
mind to work for her own livin'. He can't carry you off
like they do in stories, and you wouldn't stay carried
off if he did. We can't run away—we ain't got no money,
and we're settled here like, and making a nice livin'. We
ain't goin' to let Sir Vane Valentine spile all that. No,
Miss Snowball, my pretty, don't you be skeered—he
won't find us, and if he does then we'll clear. *I* will
stand my ground, and face him if you will let me, and
that for Sir Vane Valentine ! I ain't married to him,
thank the Lord, and he can't carry things with such a

high hand here in New York city, as over there at Valentine. But I don't believe he'll find us anyhow. No one knows our real names, and the Pettingills don't know where you live. Don't you be scared, Miss Snowball, my deary. I don't believe he'll ever find us out at all."

Jemima Ann has reason on her side, and as she says, they cannot afford to fly. Whatever comes, they must perforce stay and face it out. So Dolores lets her first panic be soothed, and yields. But it is settled she is to go on the street no more at all for the present, and their doors are to be kept locked to all the world.

"I shall lose Miss Pettingill, and all my other pupils," she says, mournfully; "and I had so much trouble getting them. I hardly know what we are to do, Jemima Ann. Mrs. Pettingill and Blanche will think I must suddenly have gone crazy."

"They must think what they please for awhile, I reckon. In a week or two I might go up early some morning with a note from you, to say you was kind o' ailin' or somethin'; for gettin' along, we will get along, never you fear. I have saved something, and I mean to work double tides until you get about again. The worst thing about it all is, that you will fret, and the confinement to these close rooms will hurt your health."

But fretting and confinement must be borne. And now for the second time a dreary interval of waiting and watching, and daily dread sets in. Behind the closed blinds Dolores sits all day long, anxiously peering into the street, drawing back whenever a passer-by chances to glance up, seeing in every man who looks at the house a detective on her track. Jemima Ann does her errands at the earliest hour of opening the grocer's, and sews by her mistress's side all the rest of the day. Dolores essays to help her, but it is little better than an effort; the dread of discovery paralyzes all her energies. She cannot settle to sew, to read, to practice; she sits through the long

19*

hours, silent, anxious, pale. It is an unreasoning dread, morbid and out of proportion with its cause ; she simply feels, as she has said, that if she meets him she will die. Five days go by, very, very slowly, but without a word or sign of discovery. Then a shock all at once comes.

It comes in the shape of a letter, delivered by the postman, and addressed to Mrs. Trillon. She turns quite white as she receives it. "Hast thou found me, oh, mine enemy ?" is the cry of her heart. No one knows her address ; this is the first letter addressed to her since she has been in New York. It is in a man's hand—not her husband's, but what of that?—and is correctly directed both as to street and number. She sits with it in her hand, in a tremor of nervous affright that shakes her from head to foot.

"Open it, my deary, don't you be afraid. Lor—Sir Vane Valentine can't eat you. Open it ; he ain't inside the envelope, wherever he is," says, cheerily, Jemima Ann.

She obeys, with shaking fingers. It is dated New York, and the day before. She glances at the signature, and utters a cry, for the name at the end is George Valentine.

"Read it, Miss Snowball—read it out aloud !" cries Jemima, in a transport of curiosity, and Dolores obeys. It is short.

"NEW YORK, March 27, 18—.

"MY DEAR SNOWBALL :—I may still call you by the old name, may I not?—the dear little pet name by which 'M. Paul' has so often called you. It will not alarm you, surely, to know that I am here, and have found you ? My dear child, you know you may trust your old friend. I have crossed the ocean in search of you, and am most desirous of seeing you at once. I will call upon you this afternoon. I send this as an *avant-courier*, to break the shock of the surprise. You are living in strictest seclusion, I know but you will see me, I feel sure. Are you aware that Vane Valentine is also in this city, also in search of you? He has not found you, and departs, I am told, in a few days. You need not fear him, I think. At present he is about starting with one Mr. Lionel Colbert on the trial trip of the latter gentleman's yacht down the bay. I shall call at your lodging at three this after-noon. Until then, my dear Snowball, I am, as ever,

"Your faithful friend, GEORGE VALENTINE."

"Thank the Lord for all his mercies!" ejaculates, piously, Jemima Ann.

"But do you believe it?" asks Dolores, the glad flush fading from her face, and the anxious contraction growing habitual there, bending her brows; "it may be a ruse. It may be the work of Sir Vane himself, or of his emissaries. Oh, Jemima! I am afraid—afraid!"

"Now, Miss Snowball, there ain't no reason. That sounds like an honest letter, and I believe it. At three this afternoon I'll be on the watch down at the front door, and if it ain't Mr. Valentine—well, then, the party that comes will have some trouble in getting into this room. Don't you be afeared. Just put on your prettiest dress and perk up a bit, for you do look that pale and thin, Miss Snowball, that it's quite heart-breakin' to see you; and trust to me to keep him out if it's the wrong man. If it's the right one, as I feel sure it is, all our troubles is at an end. A man's *such* a comfort at times when a body's in a muddle, and don't know what to do. I wonder," says Jemima Ann, stitching away diligently, and keeping her eyes on her work, "if Mr. Rayney is with him?"

There is a sound as of a sudden catching of the breath at mention of that name, but no reply. Indeed, Dolores hardly speaks again for hours. She sits silently at her post by the window, in a fever of alternate hope and dread, watching the passers-by. She makes a toilet, as Jemima Ann has suggested, she tries to read, tries to play, walks up and down, and has worked herself into a feverish and flushed headache long before three o'clock.

It strikes at last. She resumes her place by the window, and clenches her hands together in her lap, as if to hold herself still by force. At the moment the bell rings.

"There!" cries Jemima Ann.

Both start to their feet. Jemima Ann hurries down stairs, locking the door behind her, and Dolores stands pale, breathless, her hand still unconsciously clenched, her heart beating to suffocation. It seems to her the supremest hour of her life. She hears a joyful cry from Jemima, and the maid rushes joyously in.

"Oh, Miss Snowball! dear Miss Snowball! it's all right—it's him! it's him!"

And then before her, tall, strong, handsome, bearded, resolute, good to see, comes George Valentine.

The quick revulsion of feeling, the sudden joy, takes away her last remnant of strength. She holds out both hands, and would fall, so dizzy does she grow, but that she is in his arms, held against his loyal, loving heart.

"My little Snowball! my dear little girl!" he says, and stoops and kisses the pale, changed face, more touched by that change than he cares to show.

"I—how foolish I am," she says, and laughs, with eyes that brim over; "forgive me, M. Paul. I have been wretched and nervous lately, and the shock of seeing you——"

She breaks off, sinks back in her chair, covers her face with her hands, and, for a little, utterly breaks down.

"Oh, I beg your pardon," she says, "do not mind me, pray. I will be all right in a moment. Only it so brings back the old times, and—oh! how good, how good it is to see a friendly face again."

"That is a pleasant hearing," he says, cheerily; "so you were afraid my letter was all a ruse? My dear child, I have known for over a week you were here. If you had been discovered by *that other*, I was always ready to come to the rescue. My poor little Snowball! Life has gone hardly with you, I fear, since I saw you last."

Tears, hard to hold back, spring to her eyes once more; they fill, they overflow.

"I am very weak; I never used to be a crying animal," she says at last, trying to laugh through the falling drops. "Yes, life has gone hard, but I did not mind so greatly until I found him here after me. We were getting along so nicely, I was almost quite reconciled before that. But, M. Paul—I may call you by the old name, may I not?—I would rather die than go back. You will not let him force me, will you?" she says.

"My dear girl, you shall not go back—no," he answers, "no one shall force you against your inclinations. You have nothing to fear, I think. He certainly has been in search of you; he certainly, also, has not as yet found you. He traced you, as I did, to London, to Havre, to this city; but I have been more fortunate than he here, and have discovered you. He is not in New York to-day. The yacht started on her trial trip this morning, to be absent a week; so your enforced imprisonment may end for the present. I mean to take you for a drive this afternoon—oh, you must! I will have no refusal. I am quite alone in New York; our good friend, Rene, is in Rome, back at his work. He wanted to come. For obvious causes, it was better he should not accompany me. I dispatched to him the moment I discovered you. I am to write to him at length to-night. Have you any messages, Snowball?"

No; Snowball has none—her remembrances, and she is well—nothing more.

"You have done nothing in the matter of your claim to the title and estate?" she asks, after a pause.

"Nothing! and mean to do nothing, for the present at least. Rene told you that, you know. The exposure of my life to the world would be no easy thing for a thin-skinned fellow like me to bear; I doubt if any fortune could compensate for it. There would be a prolonged contest, no end of names of the living and the dead dragged through the mud of a public court and a confoundedly public press. No ; Sir Vane must remain Sir Vane, I suppose, until my moral courage grows a good deal stronger. Now run, and wrap up ; it is a jewel of a day. Your imprisonment has lasted long enough ; we are going for a drive to the Park, in this fine frosty air."

She obeys. Oh ! the relief of feeling her great enemy is no longer in the city—the relief of feeling she is free to go out once more.

"And I will have supper ready when you come back," calls after them Jemima Ann.

It is an afternoon never to be forgotten, all the more enjoyable for the gloom, and terror, and hiding, that have gone before. Dolores enjoys it thoroughly ; the fleet horses, the rapid motion, the sparkling air, the gay equipages, the bright, sun-gilded park, the crisp, cheery talk, the deep, mellow laugh of her friend.

For the next two days life takes in its brightest colors, fear departs, care is thrown off. Dolores lives in the present and enjoys it thoroughly. "M. Paul" comes daily, and the lost bloom of happiness seems to return at his bidding, as if by magic.

But on the third day he does not come. The forenoon, the afternoon, pass, and do not bring him. Dolores grows alarmed—so little startles her now—when, just at dusk, he presents himself, but with a slowness of step and a gravity of face all unusual.

"Something has happened !" she cries, in quick alarm. "Sir Vane has returned !"

"Sir Vane has returned—yes."

He stands holding both her hands, looking down at her with his grave, dark eyes.

"Dolores, dear child, there is nothing to wear that frightened face for. He has returned, but not to trouble you. I doubt if he will ever trouble you or any one more. An accident has happened to the yacht."

She stands silent, pale, looking at him, waiting for what is to come next.

"It was last night—it was very foggy, you may re- member. One of the great passenger steamers of the Sound ran her down and sunk her. Three of the seven on board were drowned—the others were picked up by the steamer's boats. Young Colbert, the owner of the yacht, is among the lost, and from what is said, I think his guest, Sir Vane."

She sits down, feeling suddenly sick and faint, un- able to speak a word.

"The bodies have just been recovered; they lie as yet at a water-side hotel, awaiting identification. I am on my way to see, and, it may be, to identify your hus- band. Try not to be overcome by this shock. I will keep you in suspense as short a time as I can. Once I have seen the bodies, I will return here."

He departs. It is a bright, starry twilight, the street lamps are twinkling in the April dusk, as he strides rapidly along. He hails a coupé presently, and is driven to his destination. He finds a crowd already congre- gated, and much excitement; the police on hand to pre- serve order. He makes his way through the throng to the ghastly room in which the three stark bodies as yet lie. The gas-light floods the dead, upturned faces; the drowned men lie side by side, awaiting removal. The first is a slender, fair-haired, fair-mustached young man —Lionel Colbert. The second is a seaman; the third— he draws back and holds his breath. There before him lies his enemy—the man who has hated him, who has worn his title and used his wealth, who has done his best to break little Snowball's heart—Vane Valentine, stark and dead!

CHAPTER XL.

"ERE I CEASE TO LOVE HER, MY QUEEN!"

T is a May day, cloudless, flawlesss, sunny, breezy. Isle Perdrix lies like an emerald in its sapphire setting, in the dancing waves of Bay Chalette.

It is yet early morning—not quite nine o'clock, but, even at this matutinal hour, the shrill-pitched French-Canadian voice of old Ma'am Weesy rises on the sunny air in accents of keen reproach. The yellow-painted kitchen is one flood of eastern sunshine; the rows of burnished tin and copper make the beholder wink again; two huge family cats bask in front of the polished cooking-stove; pots of geraniums and pink roses on the window-sills scent the air; a fragrance as of tea and toast is in the atmosphere.

Unsoftened by all these mellowing influences, Ma'am Weesy stands, with hands on hips, and pours forth a torrent of reproach in mingled French and English. Jemima Ann stands near, and listens and laughs. The culprit, out in the hop-wreathed porch, tries—also in foreign accents—to make himself heard.

"Sure, thin, 'twasn't my fault—that I may nivir av it was, ould Wasy! It was all the doin' an' the divilment av Masther Johnny. Ax himself, av ye don't b'lave me. There he is now, foreninst ye, an' divil another word av ye're abuse I'll take this blissid day, av ye wor twice the ould catamoran ye are!"

With which Tim stamps away indignantly, and another manly form takes his place.

"What's the row?" demands this new-comer; "what the duse, Ma'am Weesy, are you and old Tim kicking up such a clatter about at this time of morning?"

"Ah ! bon jour, M'sieur Jean !"

Instantly all trace of wrath vanishes as if by magic from the face of Ma'am Weesy ; her coffee-colored visage beams with pride and joy. Tim has only forgotten madam's bouquet after all, but M. Jean has it, she fails not to perceive.

"Madam nearly ready, Miss Hopkins?" he says.

"Nearly ready, Captain John ; dressing. I will tell her you have come, and give her her bouquet."

"And *I* will give you some breakfast, M. Jean," suggests radiant Ma'am Weesy.

No, M. Jean says, he doesn't want anything. His appetite has deserted him this morning, it appears ; he looks and feels nervous and fidgety, and keeps pulling out his watch every few minutes and glancing at it with impatient eyes.

"I wish it was this time to-morrow," he growls inwardly, "all the to-do over, and Inno and I—dear little soul ! fairly out on blue water, with all the staring eyes and gaping tongues left behind. It's a capital thing to marry the girl of one's heart, no doubt, but it's a very considerable bore getting the preliminaries safely over. I'll go down to the beach and smoke a cigar, Weesy," he says aloud. "When madam is ready call me, will you?"

For Dolores—once Lady Valentine—is "madam" here, and for the last fourteen months has hidden herself and her sorrows and her widowhood in the sea-girt seclusion, so often sighed for, of Isle Perdrix. George Valentine brought and left her here when he departed to assert his rights, and proclaim his identity as the next in succession to Valentine.

And now, standing before the dressing-glass in her little room, she is robing for a bridal, and feeling as if the past years had dropped away from her life like a bad dream, and that it is the jubilant girl, Snowball, who sings softly to herself and smiles back at her own fair image in the mirror. It is John Macdonald's wedding-day, and Innocente Desereaux is the bride. It is a very fair and girlish Snowball who comes down stairs, pink roses in her cheeks and starry brilliance in her eyes— a rose and a star herself, as so it seems to Captain John Macdonald, who catches a glimpse of this sunny vision and comes in.

" By Jove !" he says, and stands and looks at her, "if Inno had not done for me before *you* came—well, it's of no use talking now of the might-have-been's. You look like a rosebud yourself, Snowball—queen lily and rose in one—and will outshine my Inno herself, it you don't take care. Nothing else in St. Gildas, of course, will have a ghost of a chance near *you*."

" What a charming courtier you are, Johnny," retorts " madam " derisively. "Such delicate flattery, such subtle compliment ! 'If you cannot acquit yourself more creditably than this, sir, you had better leave it to those who understand the business. Outshine your Inno, in- deed ! You know very well if the Venus Aphrodite rose from the surf there this moment, you would consider the goddess rather a plain-looking young woman compared to your Inno. Stand off a little and let me look at *you*."

John Macdonald does as he is bid, and laughingly " stands at ease," and folds his arms and holds himself erect for inspection.

" I really do not think Inno need be ashamed of you much this morning," she says, "only I hope you won't flounder about and be awkward, Johnny, and drop the ring and turn a bright crimson at the wrong time, and make a guy of yourself generally when we get to church. Père Louis will be sure to laugh at you if you do—you know his dreadfully keen sense of the ridiculous always ; and with the sisterly-motherly regard I have for you, my dear boy, it would pain me to see the finger of risibility pointed at you on your wedding-day. You will try and conduct yourself rationally ?" implores Dolores.

" Yes, I'll try," says Captain Macdonald, and laughs ;

"with your maternal eye upon me, how can I fail ? Ten o'clock, Snowball," pulling out the perpetual watch ; "look sharp, will you. like a dear girl ? Have you had anything in the way of breakfast, or will you wait for *the* breakfast ? It takes place, you know, at eleven."

"I know. I will not be late. I will take a cup of tea, please, Ma'am Weesy—nothing more. Did you " —she asks this carelessly, her face averted while sipping her tea—" did you receive the letters you looked for last night after I left—from M. Paul, I mean ?"

"One from M. Paul—Sir George Valentine rather— none from Rene. Sir George's letter is all right—what might be expected from such a thorough good fellow. *He* will come—will be here by the afternoon train (D. V.) to wish us felicity and all that. But it will be no end of a bore if Rene fails to put in an appearance."

"You still hope then, that he may come?"

"Well, you see, while there's life there's hope, as they say, and the very fact of his *not* having written encour- ages me in the belief that he may be on his way. I haven't seen the dear old boy for years; it will spoil even my wedding-day if he fails me now. Ready ? Come on then."

They go. As they enter the boat, Captain Macdonald takes from his pocket a letter, and hands it to her.

"Valentine's," he says, "read it as we cross. It is a capital letter, from the prince of good fellows, and there is a message for you."

For M. Paul Farrar is Sir George Valentine at last, in sight of all the world, and reigning Seigneur of Manor Valentine. The great fortune, the old name, lost once for a woman, have been regained. His claim was suf- ficiently easy to prove ; many still remained in Toronto who remembered George Valentine perfectly. And so it comes to pass that among the prim old Queen Anne gar- dens, up and down the leafy, lofty avenues, through the empty echoing galleries of Manor Valentine, Sir George walks and smokes and muses, alone. He is far more of a favorite with the resident gentry than the late baronet ever was; people—women particularly—think it a pity, a man still in the prime of life, still unusually handsome and attractive, should appear to think so little of marry-ing and giving the Manor a mistress. But George Val-entine, smoking his solitary pipe, and dreaming his own dreams of future and past, knows he will never marry—his one brief, disastrous experience has put an end for-ever to all thought of that.

And yet through these dreams he dreams—through these visions he sees arising in the clouds of Cavendish —there are the faces of little children brightening the dusky Manor rooms; he hears their gleeful shouts up and down these deserted garden walks, where no childish footsteps have trodden for more than half a century. Sometimes these babies of his fancy look at him with the dark, solemn, handsome eyes of Rene Macdonald, some-times the long tresses that wave in the wind have the pale gold sheen of little Snowball Trillon. But of these idle pictures he says nothing, "patient waiters are no losers." He bides his time and hopes.

*   *   *   *   *   *   *

And now it is eleven, and the bells—wedding-bells—are ringing out their jubilant peal. Père Louis, in sur-plice and stole, stands within the altar rails, and Captain John Macdonald, and pretty Innocente Desereaux, in her glistening bride's robe and vail, kneel to receive their nuptial benediction. It is all over, a bride has been given away, and even under the severe matrimonial inspection of "madame"—whose blue eyes are a trifle dim, to be sure—the bridegroom has not distinguished himself by any notable *gaucherie*. It is all well over, to Captain John's unutterable relief, for even to a "tar who plows the wa-ter" to be the center and focus of some fifty pairs of fem-inine eyes must be rather a trying ordeal. The break-fast is over, too, healths have been drunk, and toasts re-sponded to, and speeches made, and blushes blushed, and tears wiped away, with smiles to chase them, and it is afternoon, and nearly train time, and one heart there is beating, beating—ah! as hearts have beaten for all time —will beat still in that day when all time shall end. Others discuss the coming arrival, or arrivals it may be, only "madame" says nothing. A deep permanent flush burns on her cheeks, a brilliant feverish light is in her eyes, her pulses are throbbing with sickening rapidity at times, and then again seeming to stand still.

Will he come—will he come? Every feverish beat of her heart seems beating out that question. She has not seen him since that day, so long ago—oh! so long, long ago—under the trees of Valentine. By which it will be seen, by all whom it may concern, that it is not Sir George whose coming, or non-coming, is setting her nerves and pulses in this quiver.

She breaks away from it all, presently—the guests, the laughter, the music—and goes out. It is a little out of the ordinary routine, this wedding—the day—the last day for so long, is spent by the happy pair here among their relatives and friends. This evening they go on board the big ship waiting out there in the stream, ready to spread her white wings for South America, the first thing to-morrow morning. The shriek of the incoming train reaches Dolores as she steps out into the garden. That shriek, listened for all day, comes to her like a shock at last. She turns white in the May sunshine, and cold—what if it has not brought him after all! If it is so she feels she must bear it, just at first, alone, not under all those eyes in there, and so she hurries on, and down, aimlessly, to the water's edge. As she stands she can see Isle Perdrix, its tall light-house piercing the hazy blue, its long white strip of hard beach, the smoke curling up from the little peaceful cottage. And as she stands, some one comes up the path, and it is Sir George Valentine, and alone!

She sinks down on the low garden wall, and covers

her face with her hands.   He has not come !   At
last she is alone with her pain.   But, oh! she has so
hoped, so longed for his coming, so hungered for the
sight of his face, the sound of his voice.   All her life
she has loved him and known it not—it seems to her
she has never known *how* she has loved him until this
bitter hour.   "Rene—my love—Rene !" she says, and
stretches out her arms passionately ; "why have you not
come ?"

Have her words evoked him?   A hurried step, a
voice, a call, "Snowball !" a voice that would call her
back from the dead almost it seems to her, in the wild,
incredulous joy of that moment.   "Dolores—my
darling !" the voice says.   And it is Rene who stands
before her.   "Dolores ! my own, my dearest ! *Carissima
mia !* we meet at last !" he cries.

She slips from him, and sits down again on the
garden wall, dizzily.   Joy, rapture, amaze fill her.
What she *says* is in a weak voice :

"I thought you were not going to come."

He laughs, and seats himself beside her, possessing
himself of the two small, fluttering hands in a strong,
close clasp.

"Because Valentine came in first alone?   I met old
Tim at the gate, and of course had to stop a minute and
shake hands with the dear old fellow.   I just glanced in
the parlor, kissed the bride, congratulated the bridegroom, inquired for *you*, and was directed here.   I came
—I saw—I—*have* I conquered ?   Snowball, my little
love, my life's darling, *how* good it seems to sit here
beside you, to look at you, to listen to you once more !'

"I really thought you were not coming !"   In this
supreme hour it is all Dolores, ever fluent and ready, can
find to say.   But, oh ! the rapture, the unspeakable gladness that fills her heart as she sits.

"Thought I was not coming," laughs Rene again,
"*anima mia*, it has been all I could do to keep from com-

ing any time the past year. I held myself by force—
sheer force of will—away. It was too soon, out of con-
sideration for you, but you do not know, you never can
know, what the effort cost me. And those letters, few
and far between, formal and friendly, I used to tear up a
dozen drafts of each, in which my heart *would* creep out
at the point of my pen. Thought I was not coming!
Oh! you might have known me better than that. And
now I have come, and for you, my long lost love, never
to leave you again—to take you with me, my own forever, when I go."

What is Dolores, is any one, to say to such impetuous
wooing as his? It sweeps away all before it.

Rene, silent habitually, can talk, it seems, when he
likes.

"I have the programme all arranged. Our wedding
takes place—well, you shall name the day, of course—but
in June sometime, and there is to be no talk of elaborate
trousseau or delay, because I have neither the time nor
inclination to listen. We will be married in the little
church over there, and Père Louis shall perform the
ceremony. Then we go to Valentine for July and
August, to Paris for September and the autumn, and
back to Rome, our home, *Carina*, in the early winter. I
have it all arranged, you understand, and if you know
any just or lawful reason why it may not be carried out,
you will be kind enough to state it now, or forever after
hold your peace."

"Some one is singing. Listen——" is Dolores' still
inconsequent reply; "it is Inno—has she not a charming voice?"

Through the open windows the tender refrain of the
much sung love-song. "My Queen," comes to the
happy lovers sitting here.

" When and how shall I earliest meet her?
What are the words that she first will say?

By what name shall I learn to greet her ?
I know not now : it will come some day.
With this self-same sunlight shining upon her,
Shining down on her ringlets sheen,
She is standing somewhere—she I will honor,
She that I wait for—my queen, my queen !

"She must be courteous, she must be holy,
Pure, sweet, and tender, the girl I love ;
Whether her birth be humble or lowly,
I care no more than the angels above.
And I'll give my heart to my lady's keeping,
And ever her strength on mine shall lean,
And the stars shall fall and the saints be weeping,
Ere I cease to love her—my queen, my queen !"

"And all this time," says Rene, "I have not asked you once, if you love *me*, my queen ?"

Who is it talks of brilliant flashes of silence? Dolores does not answer—in words—and Rene does not repeat his question. They rise as the sweet song ends, and turn to go back to the house ; and who needs words when hearts are filled with bliss? ·For love is strong, and youth is sweet, and both are theirs, and they are together to part no more.

THE END.